- the -
Afterlife
of Mal
Caldera

NADI REED PEREZ

TITAN BOOKS

The Afterlife of Mal Caldera
Print edition ISBN: 9781803367767
E-book edition ISBN: 9781803367774

Published by Titan Books
A division of Titan Publishing Group Ltd
144 Southwark Street, London SE1 0UP
www.titanbooks.com

First edition: June 2024
10 9 8 7 6 5 4 3 2 1

Gregory Orr, "To be alive: not just the carcass" from *Concerning the Book That Is The Body of The Beloved*. Copyright © 2005 by Gregory Orr. Reprinted with the permission of The Permissions Company, LLC on behalf of Copper Canyon Press, coppercanyonpress.org.

Grateful acknowledgement is made to Doc Luben for their permission to reprint an excerpt of "14 Lines from Love Letters or Suicide Notes", from *The Diesel Powered Rag Doll*.

This is a work of fiction. All of the characters, organizations, and events portrayed in this novel are either products of the author's imagination or are used fictitiously. Any resemblance to actual persons, living or dead (except for satirical purposes), is entirely coincidental.

A CIP catalogue record for this title is available from the British Library.

Printed and bound by CPI Group (UK) Ltd, Croydon, CR0 4YY

"Oh, this book *aches*. Beautiful, messy, and incredibly human, *The Afterlife of Mal Caldera* will unstitch you and pull you back together again. This breathtaking debut comes at the tangled-up pain of loss from both sides of living, but it's also a celebration of life, love, healing, and friendship. I can't recommend this one highly enough!"

JULES ARBEAUX, AUTHOR OF *LORD OF THE EMPTY ISLES*

———

"A wholly original imagining of an afterlife full of sex, ghosts, and rock and roll, at once shatteringly personal and sweepingly profound. Reed Perez's debut tenderly conjures to life the messy, hilarious, heartbreaking Mal and a host of characters living and dead, all of them indelible. The ultimate afterparty readers won't want to miss."

LEANNE SCHWARTZ, AUTHOR OF *A PRAYER FOR VENGEANCE*

———

"*The Afterlife of Mal Caldera* is a warm, cozy burial shroud of a book, full of haunting atmosphere and a phantom found family that is simply to die for. Mal is addictively charming, the perfect companion on this hopeful, heartbreaking journey through a richly imagined afterlife."

CODIE CROWLEY, AUTHOR OF *HERE LIES A VENGEFUL BITCH*

To my younger self—
you didn't miss out; we've only just begun.

*How can something be there
and then not be there?
How do we forgive ourselves
for all the things we did not become?*
DOC LUBEN

*To be alive: not just the carcass
But the spark.
That's crudely put, but…
If we're not supposed to dance,
Why all this music?*
GREGORY ORR

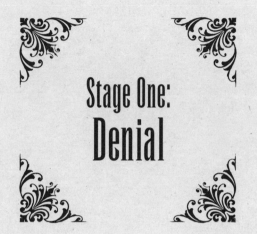

Stage One:
Denial

ONE

❋»» «« ❋

It didn't bother me much, being dead. I hadn't really been living anyway. At least now I'd never have to do the dishes in the sink, or worry about the bills piled on the table, or nurse any guilt about staying in every night. Nothing urged me to get out of bed anymore. It felt like I'd been rehearsing for this a long time—how to be a ghost.

But I couldn't haunt my apartment forever. No doubt it would be back on the market soon, despite being cramped and badly lit, the walls always thumping with aggressive bass, often accompanied by the banshee wail of sirens. My presence would be easy to clear out: just secondhand furniture, piles of laundry both dirty and clean, empty bottles of whiskey and packs of cigs. No decorations, like I'd barely moved in. I hadn't gotten around to buying plants, or finding art that spoke to me, or making enough friends to showcase on the fridge.

I could linger for however long the place remained unoccupied. But after that, I didn't really want company. If the next tenant walked around naked, or hosted lots of overnight guests, or brought a bedmate along with them, I didn't want to see it—well, unless they were hot. I had to wonder how many ghosts had once ogled me in the shower, or on the toilet, or getting busy. I liked to think they'd paid me the same respect I'd give anybody now, not looking.

If I'd been successful enough to afford a house in life, I could've stayed longer. Maybe forever, if I didn't mind someone moving in eventually. There would've been way more room, enough for me and them. I could've kept to an attic or basement if I wanted privacy, coming out to wander the halls at night. Then again, if I'd been better off, I might not have died so young.

It might've been days since it happened. I had no way to keep track, and nothing to do to pass the time, since I couldn't touch anything. I failed to make the curtains float, or knock the unopened mail off the coffee table, or force the lights to flicker. It felt like weeks already, but it couldn't have been that long, because someone ought to have shown up for my things by now.

The cops had probably found my purse on the scene, used my driver's license to identify the body. From there, they could look up my birth certificate to find my next of kin. They'd have no way of knowing my mother and I hadn't spoken in years, that she shouldn't have been the first to find out.

I wondered how it went down. If they'd woken her in the middle of the night and, once again inconvenienced by my existence, she'd asked what I'd gone and done this time. It didn't hurt much. Just a quick sting, like a muscle twinge, an accidental regression to my young and tender self, before I remembered and calloused up again. I'd been dead to her for years, anyway.

But I tried my best not to think about my sister. I would rather have nobody in the whole world give a shit than remember I had just one person who'd care.

Well, probably. We used to fight a lot.

The sound of the lock turning in the door made me jump. After leaving my body, my mind hadn't gotten the memo, supplying phantom limbs in its place. Hopefully it would just be the cops again, or my landlord.

I hauled myself up from bed, as heavy as if I still had bones. My chest thumped with the figment of a heartbeat.

Cris hovered in the doorway, reluctant to come in uninvited. Her eyes stared right through me.

I swallowed the lump in my throat and shot her some finger guns. "Hey, sis."

She didn't reply, of course. I barely dodged in time to avoid her walking through my incorporeal form.

I threw up my hands. "Make yourself at home."

It didn't feel like I'd gone anywhere. More like I'd said something to piss her off, make her slam the door on her way in, give me the silent treatment. And yet, my stomach twisted with a chilly sense of dread, like the feeling of being watched. As if she were the otherworldly presence, not me.

Or maybe I couldn't accept the reality of being separated by so much more than a couple of feet.

Cris's makeup looked a little smudgy, hastily done, or redone. We looked only somewhat alike, with the same deep, dark eyes, and admittedly good cheekbones and chin, but not much else. She had a flatter nose, way more lip, not to mention actual curves. Lately, she'd gotten more sun than me, tanning almost as brown as our mother, while I'd only gotten paler, like my late dad. She bleached our near-black hair blonde, though she'd skipped straightening it today.

It made my chest tight with nostalgia to see those waves bouncing as she drifted around. I used to tug them to hear her indignant squeak. Later on, I'd braid them.

When we met again as adults, I'd told her outright that I hated her new hair.

"You look like hell," I said, as if I looked any better. But I didn't have a reflection to check anymore. Not to mention, the state of the entire apartment made me cringe. Even without any acknowledgment from her, I went through our usual motions and deflected attention from myself. "Late night?"

If she could hear me and see my wink, that would've gotten a scoff. She'd always been such a prig, easy to provoke. But her face was unmoved, stone cold as a porcelain saint. The same old family mask our mother and I used to wear just to get through a conversation without yelling. I'd never seen my little sister try it, but she must've been a natural.

"Tough crowd."

It wasn't so fun trying to tease her without any reaction. But I couldn't help it. I had to fill the silence.

She kept circling the apartment. At first, I thought she must've been appraising the mess, taking inventory of all the stuff she'd have to pack up and give away. But then she started a second round, turning on the lights, rifling through the junk on the counters and coffee table, going through drawers.

"Whatcha looking for?" I asked. I couldn't touch the kitchen counter, but I propped my elbows over it anyway, suspended in the air, pretending to lean. "If you want drugs, all you have to do is ask."

Actually, I didn't have any. I'd gotten pretty boring in the last couple of years. No prescriptions, either, though I probably could've used some.

Cris picked up my trash can and dumped it on the floor.

"What the hell?"

She unfolded every crumpled-up piece of paper, squinting to read, before balling up the old résumés and overdue notices again and tossing them across the room. Through her teeth a strangled noise escaped, like the tea kettle shriek she used to make when we fought as kids. It made me cringe in instinctive terror, as if she were about to scream, bring our mother's wrath down upon me.

The ceiling lamp flickered.

Somehow, she reined it in, shaking but stony-faced. Apparently, she had an idea. She grabbed the notepad left on my kitchen table, scrawled with the half-hearted notes I took to look attentive at job interviews. After flipping through older scribbles, she turned to the next blank page. Then, she used a pencil to fill up the whole thing. There were no pale indentations revealing words I'd drafted, only to change my mind and tear out the page.

The notepad and pencil ended up across the room as well. She buried her face in her hands. Good, because I couldn't bear to see the look on it.

Last time she dragged me out to dinner, I told her I'd been doing better. That I'd gotten hired at another call center, and I'd text that guy at her church for a date, and I'd even drop by one of the charity bingo nights or cake walks or whatever else she helped organize, in lieu of going to Mass with her.

She must not have believed me. Not if she was looking for a suicide note.

My eyes stung. I never thought I'd feel *that* again.

It had been bad, for a while. I couldn't deny that. But I'd gotten so close to turning my life around.

"I didn't—" I dug my nails into my palms, clearing my throat like I couldn't let her hear me choke up. "You don't think I'd actually—?"

Both of us flinched as the light flickered again—once, twice—and then blew out.

All this time, I'd been working so hard to get a reaction out of my surroundings, interact with the world like I used to do. I hadn't been trying that time.

"My bad?"

Cris didn't read into it. She just opened the blinds for what little sun the room could get.

She finally got with the present and headed for my bedroom, grabbing my old laptop from the nightstand and perching on the bed. I climbed up behind her, looking over her shoulder as she set it up on her lap. She twisted her hair as she frowned at the password screen. I would've bet the cops hadn't tried all that hard to get in.

After warming up with the obvious, my birthday, "qwerty" and "password123," she guessed her own birthday. Damn it. Then she checked all my folders, opening every document she found, no matter the name. It mostly consisted of old job stuff, renter's insurance, nothing personal.

"What are you hoping you'll find?" I asked.

It didn't take long before she'd opened literally everything. She gave up, and went to my browser history.

"Oh, come on," I said. "I'm not an amateur."

Whenever I browsed for porn, or researched whether certain below-the-belt medical symptoms could flare up during a dry spell, or looked into the prognosis of various mental illnesses I might've inherited, I always did it incognito.

Finally, she slammed the laptop shut. I bristled, like she'd snapped at me.

"I didn't plan anything," I said. "It was an accident."

Cris shot up and went to rifle through the clothes hanging in my closet and even more still piled in a laundry basket. It didn't take her long to sift through all my boring old work blouses and skirts, none of which were fit to wear for my trip six feet under.

She picked nearly at random, then swept back out of the apartment as quickly as she'd come. I returned to my bed, and the silence, with a sigh—only to scramble up again as the lock clicked. She threw the door open without closing it this time.

"Did you forget something?"

She went back to my room, opening my underwear drawer, the only one she'd just eyed rather than raiding earlier. But they couldn't bury me without underwear. So she gave in and rooted around. I couldn't watch.

"You're not gonna like what you find," I said through my fingers.

Sure enough, once she'd figured out the purpose of the toy she'd found among the fabric, she shrieked. I almost laughed, but it didn't quite have enough momentum to leave my throat.

"It's not real. Your purity pledge is still intact."

She went to wash her hands, as if I wouldn't have kept it clean. After that, she gingerly peeled off the first bit of faux satin her fingers touched and a bra from the top of the drawer, hid them between the blouse and skirt she'd picked, and hurried off again.

I considered following, just to see the look on her face when she handed my clothes to the funeral home and found she'd grabbed a thong. I hadn't worn one in about three years. Now, I'd be wearing it forever. Too bad she wouldn't find it funny.

While I'd been floating around the apartment in a daze, she'd been busy. I'd left her a body to bury. She wouldn't be shoveling the dirt herself, but she still had a lot of work ahead of her. People to call, paperwork to fill out, arrangements to make. All the while believing I'd put her in this position on purpose.

I'd barely come back into her life, and already, I'd disappeared again. For good this time. But I hadn't meant to leave her alone, especially not with our mother.

I needed her to know that.

Stage Two:
Guilt

TWO

❋》》 《《❋

When I stepped out of my apartment building, the lack of air rushing past me felt odd. The gray sky and damp leaves caught in the crook of the curb made me rub my arms on instinct. The autumnal chill of my last moments still seemed to linger, freezing my bare feet.

I wasn't sure what to do when I got to the back entrance of the nearest hospital, since I couldn't touch anything. But I had to try looking, at least. There'd be paperwork about my death, perhaps a physical certificate. I just wanted to know how the coroner had ruled the cause, why my sister had literally gotten her hands dirty digging through my trash. Had she been looking for evidence I hadn't offed myself—or confirmation?

As I passed through the closed doors and wandered through the eerily bare, almost unlit hallways, I still had it in me to shiver. I didn't like hospitals. Especially not this lower floor, underground, practically a basement. If the frantic rushing to and fro on higher levels stressed me out, I didn't expect the lack of it to be even more harrowing. No patients, no hurrying nurses and doctors. There weren't any emergencies down here. The morgue attendant pushing a gurney in front of me had no cause to rush.

There probably shouldn't have been two people sitting by the side of the hallway—on the floor, since there were no waiting room chairs on this level. One of them held a notebook and pen, with a messenger bag slouched by her side.

They were talking without looking at each other, the writer scribbling away while the speaker droned on. What had sounded like a conversation from a distance now struck me as more of a litany, with occasional commentary.

"Thomas… Thirty-six… Episcopalian…" he said.

"You'd think I'd be able to spell that by now," she replied.

They looked pretty normal, even comfortable, sitting on the floor—the stout strawberry-blonde girl tucked into herself, and the lanky brown guy, still tall even hunched over. She wore a faded sweatshirt with pajama bottoms, her short hair pinned into a stub of a bun. He had on a jacket and jeans covered all over with patches and pins, curly hair bleached and dyed orange. I could've sat beside her in my college library during finals, bumped into him at a show back when I still ran in the scene.

The gurney took a turn, pirouetting on a stuck wheel, and passed right through both of them. They didn't even stop talking.

"This isn't happening," he recited. "I'm dreaming."

She sighed, or it might've been a yawn, if we could still do that. "If only."

The writer must have died with that notebook and pen, taking her bag along with her clothes to the other side.

Once the morgue attendant righted the gurney and moved on, at last, the two of them looked up at me.

The speaker interrupted his own recounting. "We've got a live one."

"So to speak," said the writer, with barely suppressed excitement. "Can you see us?"

I shrugged. "You really need to ask?"

They turned to exchange eager glances, before she shoved her notebook at him, and they scrambled to their feet. I backed up as she drew closer.

"Hi there," she said, her eyes alert, but voice a little flat, over-rehearsed. "We're conducting a survey regarding your experience on this extranatural plane of existence. If you wouldn't mind, we'd like to ask a few questions."

My chest swelled up with a laugh. I swallowed it back down in surprise. "What the fuck?"

The speaker elbowed her. "Don't just jump in."

"Sorry," she said irritably. "I forgot."

He apparently had to demonstrate how to talk to a stranger. "I'm Carlos," he said. "This is Danny."

"It's nice to meet you," Danny tried.

"Or, well, not so nice," admitted Carlos. "I'm sorry for your loss."

I would rather he didn't remind me. "Why sorry? Did you push me?"

He just laughed, like he hadn't caught the edge in my tone.

Danny couldn't wait any longer. "Now could you answer our questions?"

I crossed my arms. "So… you guys aren't waiting on your own autopsies? This is like ambulance chasing, but way worse."

Carlos muttered something in her ear. It sounded like, "Told you so." He turned to me. "I know, we're a little short of the welcome party you might've expected."

"Where else are we supposed to find an adequate sample size?" asked Danny. "There's no better place to meet people than the morgue."

"You're lucky I didn't just get here," I said. Not to mention that I hadn't been all that bothered, at least not as much as someone following their body down here out of separation anxiety. "What kind of answers are you even getting out of baby ghosts?"

"More than you might think," said Danny. "If all our experiences are consistent, that's worth documenting. With enough data, we might be able to draw some reliable conclusions regarding the nature of our new state of being."

She sounded practically academic. Like I was back in college, taking part in a psych department study.

"Are you sure you're not on the clock, professor?"

Her face went a touch pink. "Actually, I'm still working on my master's."

"Still?"

"Well, no one's going to hand it to me on a piece of paper, but I'd like to think I'll earn it, anyway."

So she'd found something to do with herself on this side. I couldn't begrudge her that. Some other wandering souls might appreciate this sorry little welcoming committee. Better than thinking they were all alone.

"What about you?" I asked.

"I have zero qualifications," said Carlos, holding up his hands to surrender any possible responsibility. "I'm only here to look pretty."

I couldn't help but smile at that. He did, in fact, look pretty.

And maybe they could help me out.

"Fuck it," I said. "Let's make it quick."

Danny grinned, then smoothed out her face and voice professionally. "So, ideally, I would have gotten to perfect this questionnaire with some more resources before field-testing it, but, well, these aren't ideal circumstances, so bear with me. These are all open-ended questions, by the way, so feel free to elaborate, all right? Are you ready?"

"As I'll ever be."

Taking her notebook back, she cleared her throat. "Tell me what you think is happening to you right now."

"I'm dead."

Her lips pursed, like that hadn't been as elaborate an answer as she'd hoped. "Did you witness your separation from your body?"

What a nice way to ask if I'd watched myself die. And I had, my soul splitting off early enough for me to see the whole thing.

"Uh-huh."

At least she didn't want any more details on that. "Let's talk about where we are in terms of metaphysical location."

That gave me more to chew on. It felt like I'd been called on during a lecture and had to bullshit an answer on the spot. "I guess we're on another plane of existence. Souls wandering around like—what's it called in the Bible? I think it's 'heavenly bodies'?"

After eighteen years of Mass every Sunday morning and Wednesday evening, not to mention Catholic school, I still remembered perfectly, right down to the verse: 2 Corinthians 5. I wished I didn't.

"Though we're not in heaven," I added. "Obviously."

Danny couldn't hide a slight smile, so that must've been a meaty enough response for her. "Any thoughts on our apparent bodies?"

"That's it, exactly." I found myself waving my hands to demonstrate. "They must be apparent. Apparitions. Based on our memories, or something. You ever heard of phantom limbs?"

"Isn't that how you explained it?" asked Carlos.

She elbowed him. "Shh, shh, she doesn't need my theories, we need hers." Then she moved on. "Is it possible to 'cross over,' and if so, how is it done?"

"I hope we're not going anywhere," I said. I really didn't want to follow that line of questioning to its conclusion.

"But do you think there is another destination for us?"

My fists bunched up involuntarily, but I slowed my exasperated hiss down to an innocent exhale. "Well, otherwise, we're stuck here, right? Only, it's not jam-packed, from what I've seen. All the other billions of people who have died over human history had to go somewhere. If it splits into the usual above and below, I know which direction I'm going—not up."

That got a smirk from Carlos.

Danny took a while to catch up writing. I envied her having something to touch, the scratching such a satisfying noise. After her pen went still, she stalled the next question, clearing her throat nervously. "Would you describe any people you may have met on this plane as… disturbed?"

"Come again?"

"We're still workshopping that question," said Carlos.

"What do you mean 'disturbed'?"

His eyebrows flickered up. "You'd know."

Danny tapped the end of the pen against her lips. "Now, would you mind giving us some, you know, statistical information? Name, age, religious affiliation."

"Mal," I said. "Twenty-seven. I used to be your typical bitter, agnostic ex-Catholic."

I used the past tense on account of not feeling so agnostic anymore, post-mortem.

She didn't ask me to elaborate any further, turning toward her companion. "Did you get all that?"

Carlos cleared his throat. "I'm dead, uh-huh, I guess we're on another plane…"

"Didn't you just write that down?" I asked.

Danny gave her notebook a shake. "We have to rewrite all the data we've collected."

"Why?"

"It goes back to blank pages every day. Nothing here lasts. If you die with, I dunno, some gum in your bag, and you try to chew it, eventually it'll disappear and turn up back in its wrapper. It all goes back to the time of death."

Carlos echoed my words again to himself, looping until they could get the chance to write it down. "I know which direction I'm going…"

I shivered. "Well, good luck with your research."

"Thank you so much for participating," said Danny.

Carlos smiled and waved, still muttering to himself. "Mal, twenty-seven…"

That was quite enough socializing for me. But I had a question for them. "How do I touch?"

"Hmm?" Danny barely looked up, already sucked back into her writing.

"I mean, are we able to touch anything? On the other side?"

I remembered the way she'd elbowed him. For a moment, I'd forgotten what we were, how significant it was that they could still touch each other, if nothing else.

Carlos held out his palms apologetically. "We can't."

"Not as far as we know," said Danny.

"Oh, I tried," he added. "I didn't get anywhere."

Well, shit.

"And you haven't met anybody who can do it?" I asked. "Never thought to put that in as a question?"

Carlos turned to her with a thoughtful shrug. Danny nibbled her pen. Even if they took my advice, though, that wouldn't exactly help me right now. And I'd been patient enough.

I couldn't keep from rolling my eyes. "Thanks for nothing."

Before they could react, I turned and walked through the wall—straight into the autopsy suite. After a brief eyeful of naked corpse and shiny surgical buzz saw, I put my head down and kept walking.

On the other side, I found a small, cluttered office. There were tons of filing cabinets, full of potentially relevant documents and a computer. But sheer need didn't make my fingers any more solid. My hands disappeared through the manila folders as if I'd dipped them in murky water. I couldn't get the computer to spark to life, either, like a TV in a horror movie.

At this point, I could safely assume I had about a fifty-fifty chance of my death being either correctly ruled as accidental, or lazily written off as a suicide. If they did a toxicology report, the tiny bit of alcohol in my system could've pointed to either. It might come down to how much paperwork the cops had bothered to do.

So I couldn't rely on any authorities to comfort Cris. For all I knew, she didn't believe the official cause, anyway, looking for her own answers. Nobody could convince her but me. I had no clue how to go about piercing the veil when I couldn't so much as lift a pen to try and communicate, but I couldn't just stand by and do nothing.

As a good Catholic, she still believed in hell. And suicide was supposed to be a mortal sin—first-class boarding.

All things considered, I didn't mind being stuck in the terminal for now.

THREE

Nightfall looked different when I headed back to my place. I couldn't see shadows anymore. The world simply lost its color, the gray broken up here and there by halogen light. I could see in the dark just as well as daylight.

As I walked through my door, my skin prickled, hairs standing on end. I never thought I'd get to feel goosebumps again.

The silhouette of a man wandered my living room in the dark. His pale skin flashed bright as he drifted in and out of the moonlight slicing through the window blinds. He hadn't turned on any lights.

It didn't surprise me when our eyes met.

"Malena Caldera," he said, with surprisingly good Spanish inflection. It startled me when he continued, speaking too fast for my already slippery grasp of my mother's language.

I cut him off. "I don't fucking speak Spanish."

That wasn't wholly true, but he'd caught me off guard, reminding me just how far the apple had fallen from the family tree.

"My mistake," he said in English. Now his voice lilted with the echoes of a fading British accent. "I said I've been looking for you."

I hoped he couldn't see my gulp. "How the fuck do you know who I am?"

He looked like he could be Death. Between his timeless double-breasted vest and trousers, old eyes in a young, symmetrical face, and wide grin like a scythe. Not to mention his multilingual fluency. Perhaps he'd run late to our appointment.

"I always read the obits," he said. "You never know who's just arrived."

"So you're not here to drag me to hell?"

His teeth flashed bright as he laughed. "I'm flattered, but you have me mistaken for someone else." He kept circling around me, rhythmically, restlessly, casting a sweeping glance over my apartment. Then he looked back to me, over his shoulder. "You live like this?"

"Not exactly." I shrugged in affront. "I'm dead."

"So am I. That's no excuse."

"I didn't think I'd have company."

"You sound disappointed." He turned and tilted his head at me with a sympathetic pout. "Not so happy to find you're not alone on the other side?"

"I've been enjoying the peace and quiet."

"Or you're resigned to it."

I crossed my arms. "Look, you can skip to the part where you tell me what you want."

It wasn't like I had much to offer. He and I couldn't possibly have use for money anymore, not that I'd had much in life. And I hadn't died with anything on me to give. Though apparently, we could still touch each other. I had to hold myself back from wandering too far down that line of thought. It had been nearly a year since I'd last gotten laid.

"Just delivering some good news," he said. "If you haven't noticed, our eternal judgment appears to have been postponed. So why not celebrate?"

He slowly turned up his palm in offering.

I didn't know who or what he might be, where on Earth or elsewhere he might mean to take me. Even if he weren't an angel or devil or intermediary, only another ghost, something about him felt off—uncanny. At the very least, he had to have been here a lot longer than me. Too long.

But I hadn't touched anything for what already felt like forever. There were so many little things I'd never given a second thought in life, not realizing how much I'd miss them. No more alarm clock, toothbrush, shower, towel, clothes, coffee, cigarette, keys, doorknob, rinse and repeat. Let alone a hand, something warm and alive—or lifelike, anyway.

Even if I didn't care for this guy's evangelical tone, I did like the way he'd undone a few shirt buttons, no tie, and rolled up his sleeves, showing off his forearms.

So I took his hand. I reeled back at the feeling, not just skin, but something more. Like I'd touched an electric fence, some force pushing or pulling against me.

He winked. In a blink, we weren't in my apartment anymore.

Something pulsed. It started as if from inside me, from my phantom heart pounding in my ears. It branched through my veins, my body shivering rhythmically.

"What the hell?" I asked.

"Close, but not there yet," said the stranger.

Above us glowered a dark mansion. I didn't have to look twice at the broken windows and creeping vines to recognize it as haunted, and not only by the two of us. The pulse tugged like a tide, growing louder and louder.

"Are you ready to join the afterparty?"

He didn't wait for my reply. I couldn't tell if he pulled me after him, or if the pulse itself strung me along. My feet fell in time to the beat.

Before us stood boarded double doors, stained with an orange watermarked sign reading:

CONDEMNED
DO NOT ENTER

We passed straight through it.

Moonlight flooded through the glassless windows, glinting on the shards among the dirt and dead leaves beneath our feet. Glowing marble flowered into the columns and arches of a foyer, framed on each side by a grand staircase. All the crumbling plaster of the walls went from gray to blue where they weren't covered with vines, their leaves quivering in time to the music.

That pulse lapped at my skin like a heartbeat. Wave upon wave of an undulation not quite in the air, not quite in my blood, but somewhere between.

"What is this place?"

He swept out a hand with pride. "Welcome to the Haunt."

Across the foyer, we reached doors thrown open to let out a column of light. I lifted my hand, trying to shield my eyes as we swept inside. My fingers glowed. So did all of the ghosts.

Around us bloomed the remains of a ballroom, full of dancers. They flickered through the silver light like phantasms, all different eras of the dead. Skirts flowed through the floor and slowly rose up and up, past the ankles, past the knees. Suits loosened up and slimmed down again, finally losing the jacket and becoming slacks, turning into jeans. There were top hats, bowler hats, newsy caps.

Bare heads with pompadours and mullets, bobs and beehives. Some of them looked modern, like me.

None of them clashed, despite their different eras and styles of dancing. Some danced with their feet, their arms, others their hips and shoulders. Arm's length from their partners, or arms entwined. Everyone mingled and blended perfectly, as if rehearsed. It must have been the band.

They were floating at stage height. In each of their hands, they held something even more intangible than they were, appearing with every pluck of a harp string, throb of a violin, strike of a drum, like a flash of gossamer and shadow. Even the pipes of a church organ flickered along the wall, as if illuminated by lightning. They played on the ghosts of instruments.

At last, I turned to the stranger, who watched me and waited as I took it all in.

"Who are you?" I asked.

"I'm the host," he said, like I ought to have figured that out already. "They call me Alastair."

Somehow, I got the feeling that he hadn't given me his real name.

He held out his palm again. "Come and dance."

I wanted it. Of course I did. My feet were already tapping, my shoulders shaking almost involuntarily with the slightest echo of a shimmy. Not to mention the sight of my potential partner, with that ethereal face and infernal smile, went down like wine.

But I'd just died. It bothered me more than I cared to admit, now that I'd seen how it affected Cris. I couldn't just shake that off with a little boogie.

Besides, this guy knew my name. No way he'd brought me here out of the kindness of his dead heart. I dreaded in the pit of my stomach what else he knew about me.

His grin made me shiver. "Or you could play."

It felt like I'd just been shoved on stage. Lights in my eyes, making shadows of all the faces surrounding me, my bandmates waiting at my side for me to tap the cymbals. Once, I never felt more alive than in the breath of silence before an opening riff, sticks poised to strike.

My bandmates were gone now. I wasn't supposed to be alone, standing there with no kit. I'd never had stage fright before, but my hands were shaking, eerily empty with nothing to clutch.

"We're in need of a drummer," said Alastair.

No fucking way. I couldn't go back up there. It hurt my dry mouth to even speak, still tongue-tied just from imagining it.

"You already have one," I said, gesturing toward the stage, or lack thereof. The moonlight wasn't any more inviting, nor all the spectral faces.

"All the players take shifts, for a turn to dance."

Well, this explained a lot. Contrary to what he said, I'd apparently already crossed over, straight to hell.

"I have to admit…" He looked me up and down, measuring the length of my gray chiffon skirt, counting the buttons done all the way up on my gauzy white blouse. I'd put it on for an interview, the morning of my last day. My final and forever outfit, delicate and prim, nothing like me at all. "You don't look like a drummer."

I nearly choked up. "Because I'm not."

At last, I forced my feet to shuffle in the other direction, toward the doorway. He appeared before me so abruptly, I couldn't help but flinch back. Even if he was only another ghost—who'd happened to die in an impeccable suit—he still gave me the screaming mimis.

His face twisted up in injury, suddenly not so pretty. "How on earth can you turn down this chance? As if you could possibly have anything better to occupy your time on this side?"

"You don't know my"—I almost spat the wrong word—"afterlife."

But I really did have something more important to do, and he seemed like the knowledgeable type. So I chanced the truth. "I need to get a message to the other side."

His laugh made me tense up. "Why bother?"

I barely kept my mouth from falling open in indignation.

"No need to occupy yourself with the past," he said. "It's as dead to you as you are to it."

"I can't just stand aside and watch my sister fall apart."

Admittedly, she'd been keeping it together so far, but I didn't want to find out just how much she could bottle up before she finally popped.

He pursed his lips, shaking his head. "Then don't watch."

I opened and closed my fists, tempted to slap him, find out whether either of us would feel it. I'd been trying to curb my impulsive, destructive tendencies these past few years. And I didn't want to burn this bridge just yet. So I just said, "I don't dance."

That worked even better than striking him, from the disbelief he struggled to conceal on his face. I permitted myself a moment to enjoy watching his cool facade fall apart.

Then, smoothing out his face save for the twitch of a smirk, he said, "Your mother didn't teach you that, either?"

Luckily for him, I didn't care to defend her honor. If I kept trying to have the last word, I'd be here all night. Instead, I laughed.

In the brief beat between songs, I managed to tear myself away.

"You shouldn't wander alone," he insisted. "No one will be around to help you if you start to go geist."

I slowed, not turning around. "Geist—you mean poltergeist?"

"Have you seen any yet? That's what happens if you spiral too far into your grief. It eats you from the inside."

That must've been what the guys from the morgue had been talking about when they asked if I'd ever met anyone "disturbed".

"I'll take my chances."

He called after me, just a hint desperate. "You're going to regret it."

Without looking back, I said, "That's never stopped me from doing anything."

I kept walking toward the front entrance. When I peeked to see if he was still watching, he'd disappeared. I grinned. I'd gotten the last word, after all.

There were plenty of other spirits here. I just had to wait until they weren't so occupied. Surely I wasn't the first to try piercing the veil.

I doubled back through the foyer and rushed up the left side of the grand staircase, my feet floating above the marble. Down the hallway on the second floor, I ducked through the nearest open door. I found myself in what looked like a bedroom, judging from the grand four-poster bed. It might've been the only bit of furniture in the room original to the mansion. Everything else looked modern, or at least, made in the last half century, mismatched and secondhand. As if some squatters had tried to get comfortable in the decay, covering the crumbling walls with posters, piling stacks of records and cassettes and CDs among the dust.

I lay down on the bed, the sheets beneath me forever made from lack of real use. Even if I could still sleep, I wouldn't have been able to drift off with the noise reverberating through the walls. At least a lifetime of insomnia had given me plenty of practice staring at the ceiling, waiting for dawn.

But I struggled to keep my hands quiet. I still caught myself drumming sometimes, my fingers dancing with imaginary sticks, haunted by songs that could have been. Except on this side, they didn't stay imaginary. Coalescing like plumes of smoke, my beloved old sticks became solid in my palms. The wood caressed smooth against callouses I'd lost years ago.

In my surprise, I dropped them. Rather than fall, they faded away to nothing.

If only I could do the same.

FOUR

❋»» «« ❋

By morning, it had fallen nearly silent in the Haunt. The pulse still whispered from a distance, but much more faintly, like a resting heartbeat. Piano notes lilted somewhere nearby, but they didn't pull at me like the pulse did. Through the wall beside me burst laughter I could nearly feel, like the rhythm of the dancers, making my stomach flutter.

My left slipper had come back, appearing on my foot as it had every day of my afterlife so far, no matter how many times I kicked it off. Going back to the time of death. I kept forgetting to pay attention to whether or not it faded into the ether, or sat around like an echo in the immaterial plane. I'd lost the other one right before dying, so I hadn't taken it with me like the rest of my clothes.

I lobbed the slipper under a chair. Then, just to see if I could do it, I shut my eyes and imagined the cool ceramic of a mug handle gripped in my palm, the aroma of steaming hot coffee. In my other hand I positioned my fingers as if I were holding a cigarette, recalling the taste of smoke, the rush of nicotine.

Nothing happened. No phantom from my memory manifested. Maybe it would've been different if I'd had a particular mug I'd loved, or an old-fashioned tobacco pipe whose feel I could recall better than any single disposable cigarette.

My drumsticks had felt like a part of me, once. Digging into my very skin, marking me with callouses, like an extension of my soul. I might as well have died holding them.

I gave up on my old morning ritual and headed out. Someone around here had to have some answers.

In the hallway, I jumped when a door slammed. Through the walls, voices mingled as shadows moved behind the slits of not-quite-closed doors. Under one came a dappled blue glow like a TV, along with the swell of a soundtrack. As the hallway widened into a landing, I stared up to find the skeleton of a skylight, nothing but a web of metal now, letting in a column of sunlight that illuminated the spiraling dust motes. As I floated down the grand staircase, I couldn't help but time my steps to the plink of the piano, drawn to it as if I'd heard a brook somewhere in a forest.

I never would've imagined that a haunted mansion could be so welcoming. Though I couldn't feel it, I could tell from the shivering leaves and free-falling light that the air wasn't stuffy and musty and full of cobwebs, flowing easily in and out through the broken windows and gaps in the walls. Though none of that sun could warm my skin, it still glowed golden through my hair, the same as all the dancing dust.

Not far from the foyer below, down one of the hallways near the ballroom, I followed some laughing voices. Aside from the vines, there were grasses growing here and there in patches of dirt accumulated on the floor, moss replacing the old carpets. Somebody had been keeping potted plants alive near every broken window.

I peeked into a parlor room, still furnished with faded velvet and embellished wood, covered in dust. Pretending to sit on those old chairs, surrounding a much newer cheap plastic table, a gathering of ghosts laughed. They were playing a card game. By the look of it, nobody had died with a deck on their person. Those were physical cards they were manipulating on the other side.

So, we could still touch things, after all.

One of them took notice of me, a lady in a bustle dress with a parasol lying across her lap. "Hello there," she called out. "Care to join us?"

They were all staring at me as I trod closer. Something in their glances gave me a chill. They looked more like proper ghosts than I did. Or it might've been something about their eyes.

A silver-haired, mustachioed man tipped his bowler hat to me. "You look fresh."

"A graveflower?" asked a girl with flowing hair and a long white dress. I'd thought she must've been about as old as the other two, or someone who'd died in a nightgown, but under the table, her swinging feet were clad in go-go boots. Just a hippie, then.

"Uh, I had some questions." I pointed to their playing cards. "How are you still touching anything?"

"You have to forget you're dead," said the bustled lady.

Well, that wouldn't be happening anytime soon. I couldn't just pretend to still have a body, that I hadn't been separated from the whole world—and from Cris.

I had to ask, just in case. "How do I do that?"

"Give it time," said the hippie girl.

The three of them had certainly lingered on Earth for a while. I shivered at the thought of sticking around that long.

"Sit down," said the man in the bowler hat. He gestured at the air beside him as if pointing to a chair. "Let us take your mind off it."

If it took having to settle in and unwind just to learn how to touch anything, I could be here for a long time.

"Maybe later," I said. "I'm in the middle of something."

Back to my original query. For some reason, even though I knew what I wanted to accomplish, I couldn't remember how to phrase it. I hadn't paid attention to the horror movies and bad TV dramas. Or *Hamlet*, though I had a feeling that this term hadn't been coined by Shakespeare.

"What's it called, when we have something left to do on the other side? From before we died, and we can't rest until it's done."

They barely looked at each other for answers, like they didn't expect to produce one for me. Perhaps they were too old to even attempt understanding.

"You'd do well to ask Alastair," the bustled lady said.

Bowler hat agreed. "If anyone would know, it's him."

"And he could show you around," said the hippie girl. "If he hasn't already."

Bustled lady gave a smile that I wouldn't have expected of someone from a supposedly genteel age. "He'll give you a *very* warm welcome."

"Or you could stay," said bowler hat. "And we'll welcome you."

They all laughed wickedly. What… the *fuck*.

"No thanks." I started walking backward, a little nervous to turn away. "Have fun with whatever weird shit you get up to around here. I'll pass."

I gathered up my skirt and gave them a wobbly farewell curtsey. At least I didn't have to go all the way to the door. Instead, I slipped straight through the wall.

Funny how much I'd changed. Back in the day, I would've at least given the weird shit a shot.

In the next room, I found what I think would have been called a conservatory, judging from the large empty frames that used to be windows and a dinosaur of a telescope, overgrown with vines. In the corner of the room played the pianist.

Her fingers were dark against the old, yellowed keys. Beneath a rosy pink headscarf, her coily hair rolled over her shoulders like dark clouds as she lost herself in the bittersweet melody. Under the stool, her sock-covered toes pointed as if in dance.

That was why the music didn't pluck my veins, like the otherworldly beat from the ballroom. She was playing an actual piano. Her lament couldn't reach my soul the way the pulse did, but it still moved me the old-fashioned way.

Then, her hands slipped on the keys. I cringed at the jarring cacophony of notes as she gaped up at me with a squeak of surprise.

She looked barely twenty, with a round face and big, sleepy-lidded eyes, her full curves smothered under her shapeless gown. It must've been a hospital gown, white with tiny blue flowers. Someone had covered up the open slit at the back with a long black tailcoat, too big for her.

I laughed as I stared back into her wide doe eyes. "My bad," I said, with a grin. "I didn't mean to spook you."

Her little smile was shy. "I shouldn't be so easy to spook."

She might've been a bit young for me, but my dead heart still stammered anyway. I liked the faint freckles dotting her brown skin.

"Are you newly dead?" she asked.

I couldn't help but raise my eyebrows at that expression. It sounded so glib. She noticed, shaking her head in apology.

"Sorry, I mean—um, how do they usually word it in the obits—recently passed?"

"Come on," I said, trying to hitch my lips up again. "It's not like you're breaking the news."

She gave a sheepish half-shrug. "I try to be sensitive, just in case. It's like nobody else here remembers how it felt."

I didn't want to admit that it hadn't broken me up all that much. Not at first. Then I remembered my sister, her stony face and shaking hands.

This girl looked more contemporary than any of the other ghosts so far. She'd probably watched all the same movies and shows as me. "What's it called?" I asked. "When you die, but... you're not done yet? There's something you have left to do?"

Her eyes widened in horror before I even got through the question. "You mean unfinished business?"

"There's no such thing," said Alastair.

She lit up as he approached. I groaned.

"Mal," he said. "Back already?"

I didn't dignify him with an answer, crossing my arms.

"Coming in," he said. She looked bashfully down while he gave her a quick kiss on top of her curls. His voice turned chiding. "Evie. There's no call for coddling."

She looked up at me with a rueful smile. "How am I supposed to break it to her?"

"If it's about crossing over, I don't care about that part," I said. "In fact, I think I'd rather not."

"Then why bother?" Alastair asked. "There's so much more we could offer you here."

I huffed an indignant laugh. "I don't know how long you've been dead, and all your loved ones—if you had any—but mine are still kicking."

Evie pressed her lips together in sympathy, but didn't say anything. Alastair, on the other hand, began ranting as he paced, feet moving like they were still compelled by the pulse.

"So what's your plan, then? At your grandmother's funeral, did she come back to give you a proper goodbye? Did she finally make up with your auntie-in-law about that thing that happened at the wedding? If everyone could do it, they would. We'd all put off our issues to resolve until we could have the last word as ghosts."

Once he finished, I unclenched my jaw, my cheek sore from catching in my teeth. "But since there are ghosts, and that's us, why don't we ever do that?"

"You know already. Don't ignore the dread creeping in your gut. It's there for a reason. You're a lot more attuned to the universe than you used to be, without a body between you and all the rest. Even if you don't know the reason, you know you shouldn't trespass any boundaries. There's a natural cycle of life and death you're not meant to disturb."

I cursed my guts for betraying me. They did gnaw.

"What about a medium?" Evie suggested.

"What's that?" Alastair demanded. Not like he hadn't heard—just giving her a chance to take it back.

Evie winced, but she still spoke up. "What about a medium to help her out? I mean, we haven't had any deliveries in a long while, anyway. I'd like to read something new, if it's not too much to ask."

Alastair tried to split a glare between the both of us. As he sighed, I gave him a big grin.

"So I can't talk to my family, because that's too risky, but you've contracted a psychic to bring you the latest paperbacks?"

He rolled his eyes. "It's not for nothing we haven't brought in any breathers lately. They're always more trouble than they're worth."

For a moment, they both went quiet, staring pensively as if into the same unfortunate memory. I might've thought they were giving an intentional moment of silence in honor of someone's passing, except that they didn't seem to have the same reverence for death on this side.

Alastair recovered with a shrug. "I'd tell you not to even think about it, but honestly, it's not as though you'd ever find a medium on your own."

"Watch me," I said.

"Why not stay here?" He canted his head playfully. "If you'd rather not dance, you'd be in good company."

Evie took his offered hand. He pulled her up, like in spite of what he'd just said, he intended to twirl her around. But he didn't.

"Do me a favor and show her around, would you?" he asked her. "I think you might have a bit in common."

With that, he disappeared like mist in the sun.

As soon as he'd gone, she reached for my sleeve, like she could see me tensing in concentration, trying to leave.

"I wouldn't follow him," she said. "It's best to keep a kind of bubble, anytime you spirit to somebody. It's like a courtesy here, you know, for privacy."

On second thought, he'd already proven to be impossible, anyway. But even if she was loyal to him, a sweet kid like her would be way easier to work over. And she already seemed to like me, for some reason. Bad judge of character.

"What happened to your last medium?" I asked.

She couldn't hide a guilty fidget, adjusting the sleeves of her strange coat. "I'd rather not say. I mean, nothing good. That's not to say it'll always end badly, though."

I tried not to think about it. "So, could I walk into a metaphysical shop and ask for business as usual?"

"I don't think everybody who claims to see us actually does," she said, a little cheeky. "But—"

She dropped whatever she'd been about to say, going quiet.

"What?" I asked.

"It's nothing," she said, shaking her head.

I'd always had trouble turning on the waterworks, so I tried the next best thing.

"Look." I didn't have to fake the lump in my throat, my voice going rough. I never spilled my guts if I could help it. "It's for my sister. I just need her to know, I didn't—"

My mouth went dry. The vines on the walls rustled. I thought there must be a breeze, but only the leaves beside us quivered. Something fell from the ceiling. We both jumped as a sliver of plaster fell between us, crumbling as it hit the floor in a cloud of powder.

"My bad?" I asked.

Those brown doe eyes of hers went heavy with sympathy. "There's someone I used to know…" She sighed. "I can't promise anything, but maybe…"

"Could you point me their way?"

She stood and held out her hand. "You'll wanna brace yourself. Since we don't have the physical barrier of bodies, we're kind of, well, just raw emotion and thought and memory walking around." Her nose wrinkled, like she'd grossed herself out with that phrasing. "Know what I mean?"

That must've been why the dancing last night had been so heady, like a collective drunkenness—we didn't have skin to hold back everything we felt from each other.

"So, um, don't peek in my head, and I'll do the same," she said.

I did as she instructed, trying to put up mental walls as I took her hand. She kept her thoughts to herself, but I did catch unfolding in my stomach a shy bloom of excitement, too tender to be my own.

FIVE

✳》》 《《✳

The bare walls of a dark, nearly empty studio apartment sprang up around us. At first, I figured the resident had barely moved in, but there weren't any boxes. Just a blanket tacked over the window, blocking out the light, and a mattress in the corner. Whoever lived here couldn't really have nothing. Perhaps there'd been a fire, or they'd left all their things behind in a hurry, running from something. Or they'd been robbed, because the handles of all the cabinets and the closet and even the fridge were bound with locks and chains.

We looked around, wondering where our medium could be, until we turned to the door as it clicked with the jingle of keys. It felt like we were waiting to surprise him with a much-needed housewarming party.

"Here we go," said Evie.

But when the door opened, the tall young Japanese man didn't even look at us, slipping his bony frame inside as quickly as he could and slamming the door shut with his back, as if he'd been followed. His height seemed whittled down by his hunch, shoulders caved to clutch too many groceries to his chest. He'd hidden most of his face under a gray hood and long dark tangles.

"Ren," said Evie.

At last, he flipped on the light beside him and looked up. My dead heart went hammering again. It didn't know any better, that we were on opposite planes of existence. It latched onto those cheekbones—pallor notwithstanding—and those full lips, even though they were chapped; and it definitely vibed with his dark, bleak eyes, with deep half-moons of exhaustion beneath them, matching mine.

He looked as dead as me. And I might've been dead, but I wasn't *dead*.

Then he switched the light back off, waiting a moment before turning it back on. When he saw we were still there, not just a trick of the eye, figments of the dark, he sighed.

His eyes flickered down to our feet. That's when I finally noticed—we didn't cast shadows anymore.

"Remember me?" asked Evie.

His jaw twitched as he glared, though he didn't meet her eyes so much as stare through her. "Fuck off, Brian."

Evie winced. "Nice to see you, too."

My chest cinched with a pang of recognition. "It's just a nickname for 'brain.'"

He edged around us and went to dump his groceries on what little counter his kitchen had to offer, unlocking the fridge and cabinets with keys on a chain around his neck.

"How'd you know?" asked Evie.

I didn't want to go into it, explain the coping mechanism for fighting intrusive thoughts. I'd learned from a shrink I'd seen briefly, though I'd never used the trick myself. And it wouldn't work on us. We weren't only voices in his head.

"He thinks we're not real."

"Oh," said Evie. "That explains… so much."

Ren let out a hiss of a laugh under his breath as he locked the cabinets back up. "They're talking to each other now. It's like I'm not even here."

Evie made sure I could see her approaching hand, giving me a chance to raise my walls before she touched my arm. Both trying to comfort me, and pressing me to go. "We should leave him alone."

I didn't protest. It wouldn't be a bad call to take a time-out before trying again. After all, I knew now where to find him. So I let her spirit us away.

After the dark of the apartment, we blinked in the sunlight streaming through the broken windows, swimming with dust. I'd forgotten the actual time, still morning. The pulse beckoned once more through the walls of the Haunt, low but steady. It wouldn't thunder until sundown.

"I'm sorry," said Evie. She looked so earnest with those doe eyes of hers. "I kind of forgot he's like that. I mean, not that I blame him, now I get it."

"How do you know him?"

"We went to high school together."

"Really?" I asked. "He looks older than you."

"I skipped a grade," she said. "So he's only a year older, but he kept growing, and I…"

She trailed off, like it still hurt, sometimes, being reminded of her state. I wondered how long she'd been on this side.

"He used to be known as the crazy kid," she said. "I don't think he ever said anything about seeing things, but we all put two and two together from the way he acted, the stuff he'd say while having an episode, or—you know—so we thought. No wonder he kept to himself."

I'd been a loner at that age, as well, by circumstance long before choice. "You mean he got bullied to hell and back?"

"Even by some of the teachers. They thought of him as a troublemaker, acting out for attention. I'm surprised he managed to graduate at all. I'm glad he did." She gave a bittersweet smile. "We were lab partners in chemistry. I used to take notes for him when he missed class, which was... a *lot*. He never showed up for labs. But he always brought me ramune from the Asian supermarket to apologize. Once you get past the broodiness, he's a real sweetheart."

As cute as her reminiscence sounded, I'd probably have a better chance of getting through to him alone, with none of these memories to distract him.

"Thanks for introducing me," I said.

Her voice wavered in concern. "You're still going to try?"

"Where else could I possibly find a medium?" Besides, I knew a little something about feeling crazy. "How do I do it? Spirit to him?"

"Just picture his place like you're there," she said. "Or think of him, but be careful—"

Whatever she'd meant to caution, I didn't catch it, the walls around me smoothing from cracked and worn to white and bare.

Ren's dark tangles peeked out from a nest of blankets. I rankled with envy, watching him sleep. He must've worked a night shift. Hence the makeshift blackout curtain over the window, and the big fuck-off headphones over his ears.

"You'll never have a future."

A voice out of nowhere made me shiver. I recognized its motherly chill.

An older white woman shuffled through the wall, wearing a black dress with shoulder pads. She almost seemed to be looking at me. But not quite. It gave me a sickly drop in my stomach.

"You want to burn in hell?" she asked.

I sighed, crossing my arms. "Mind your own death, will you?"

Ren didn't stir from his sleep. It seemed he didn't wear those headphones due to noisy neighbors.

"You have no life of your own anymore," said the woman.

I tried to back away as she bore down. When she reached out, I couldn't dodge in time. We didn't have skin to divide us, to protect my mind from hers. When she got a grip on my wrist, she took hold of way more than that, and didn't hold her flood of memories back.

Her daughter stood out clear in her recollections, even if the house where they'd lived looked indistinct, furniture moving around, the layout changing, like they'd moved often from place to place. Sometimes her daughter's age changed as well, getting younger and older, hair longer and shorter. I could barely keep up. Most of the time, she had blue braces and neat blonde hair, fresh and sweet.

I saw through the woman's eyes, storming into her daughter's room. My hand stung with the force of the slap, fingers wet with tears. Her words sounded more like thoughts than speech, as if she couldn't quite remember the exact conversation anymore.

You'll never have a future.

Her daughter's voice came through more clearly, her distinctive sob. *I could get rid of it.*

You want to burn in hell?

I could hardly understand the words through her crying. *What am I supposed to do?*

You have no life of your own anymore.

My throat strangled with the mother's scream, as her daughter went from crying on her bed to hanging in the closet.

Then it happened all over again. They were having breakfast in one of their old houses, her daughter's blue skin warming from death as she beamed about college applications. My hand stung again with that slap.

I wondered if my grandmother had slapped my mother like that, while I slept in her womb. Beginning our family tradition of disownment.

And then my mother's voice stung my ears, crackling through an old phone in my sweaty palm. I found myself not in the woman's house, but a familiar college dorm, my side of the room empty but for a packed suitcase. Seeing through my own eyes again.

You stay the hell put, said my mother. She might've yelled more often than speaking to me, but she never swore. It made my head swim, like I'd glanced down from a great height. *Or you can never come back.*

Back in my own head, I shook myself out of my memories and blinked in the present. I wrenched out of the woman's grip.

"You can never come back," she echoed. "You'll never have a future."

I ran, unsteady on feet that couldn't pound the ground beneath them. My phantom lungs burned, like I still needed breath, as I rushed through the walls and down the stairs.

At last, I couldn't go on. Looking up and seeing nothing peering over the railing, I nearly doubled over, shaking with cramps. I'd died so out of shape.

That must've been a poltergeist. She'd gotten trapped, somehow, in her memories, and tried to take me with her.

I couldn't quite bring myself to go see if any of that had woken Ren. I'd have to come back later—crossing my fingers that the geist wouldn't still be there.

Cris sat parked in front of a funeral home, lingering without getting out. When she folded her arms and cradled her head on top of the steering wheel, I got into the passenger's seat beside her.

I had to pipe up, because it felt too strange to see her and keep quiet. "This would've been a lot easier give or take, like, at least forty years, right? I could've made my own arrangements. You'd get to take it easy and enjoy a beach-themed sendoff in a tropical-print muumuu while drinking out of a coconut. Better yet, how about a destination funeral? I would've made up for dying first by sending you to scatter my ashes in Cancún."

I winced as a high-pitched noise escaped her mouth. As if she'd heard me, and I'd succeeded in making her giggle. She clasped her hand over her lips, eyes squeezing shut. It hadn't been a laugh.

My stomach went leaden. I braced myself. But, after clearing her throat, no further sound made it out. It would've been better for her not to bottle it up, but at least my limbs could loosen again.

I couldn't believe I used to make her cry all the time. Even at three years old, when they first brought her home from the hospital, I'd sensed which of us was actually welcome. When she got bigger, our mother brushed her hair without pulling, bought toys without her having to beg, kissed her bumps and scrapes instead of chewing her out for running in the house. So, naturally, I yanked her hair and stole her stuff and pushed her over. Then I resented her even more for waddling off to tattle, tears streaming down her red face.

Once I got old enough to babysit, though—while our parents went to church retreats to work on their marriage—for the first time, she and I could talk freely. Even being the golden child, she still had questions she couldn't ask anyone else, about sex and politics and the problem of evil. And as the black sheep, I had answers, awing her with my in-depth knowledge of fingerbanging, the queer community, and theological debate.

So we came to a truce. She'd play dumb whenever our mother asked about my latest mischief, and when she stole into my room after bedtime, I'd braid her hair and give her a secondhand dose of teenage rebellion.

But she didn't cry anymore. I used to think she just didn't have much going on, her churchy friends too stable and boring, and no dating allowed for a few more years. Up till I came home for summer after my first year of college, and she crawled into my bed and soaked my pajama shirt, blubbering about the divorce. I just lay there in shock, wondering why we'd never really hugged before that.

Now, if I had to watch her cry without being able to awkwardly put my arms around her, or at least brush her hair with my fingers, I didn't know what the fuck I'd do. I sighed in relief when she pulled it together and got out of the car.

Inside, she looked perfectly composed surrounded by caskets on display like new cars. But beneath her mask, her eyes were glazed as a man in a suit raved about the pros and cons of each model.

No wonder I couldn't help but slip back into old habits. Real old. I'd tried showing her my good side these last two and change years, but maybe she secretly missed the real me, who would never allow her to suffer any boredom. Even—or especially—at the cost of disturbing her peace.

"How about a test drive?" I asked, lying back in midair and rolling through the nearest coffin, pretending to lie in the cushioned interior with my hands behind my head and legs casually crossed.

She stared down into the casket. My heart stuttered for a moment, almost expecting her to notice me and freak out. Like I'd ever let her catch any blame for my antics.

I always suspected she needed that release, some vicarious mischief, so she'd never slip up herself.

"Live a little," I said.

She snapped out of it, turning to the staff member and interrupting his commentary.

"I like this one," she said, pointing at a minimalist white number.

"Really?" I climbed back out of the coffin. "Ugh, gross."

I would've preferred to be cremated, anyway. This whole business would probably be to her taste, not mine.

Then it occurred to me. "Where's Gloria?"

If our mother were involved in my death rites at all, she'd be here, making all the demands and decisions.

But she never appeared, not coming back from the bathroom or showing up late from important business. She must've extended my disownment post-mortem.

If she didn't care that I'd passed, that didn't surprise me. After all, my existence had never been planned, anyway. But did she really hate me enough to leave her preferred daughter to do all this on her own?

My hands curled into fists. "That bitch."

I bit my tongue, like I used to do to keep from talking back to Gloria. It worked about half the time; the rest, she had me filling up notebook after notebook with scripture relevant to my latest sins.

Cris picked out a temporary grave marker, thankfully not one of the crosses. Afterwards, she went into a small conference room with another staff member to work out the schedule for all my rites. My wake would be held on the eleventh. I didn't know today's date, but looking over their shoulders, and listening for context clues, it appeared to be the sixth.

So I had under a week. Judging from all the calls she made on the way back to her place, and all the messages I tried to read over her shoulder as she worked at her laptop, there'd be plenty of unfamiliar faces there accosting her on my behalf.

Ren would blend right in. I just had to convince him that I existed.

SIX

❋⟩⟩⟩ ⟨⟨⟨❋

Alastair had been right about the poltergeists. I didn't particularly want to find out what else he might've been right about, but I needed to know more.

I closed my eyes and pictured that annoyingly lovely face. As I spirited, I braced myself for the pulse, chanced being pulled under the tide if the dancing started at sundown. But I found myself amidst a much smaller crowd, in a far closer space. They gathered in the sultry red and smoky blue of neon, better than a drunken haze for its glow of deceitful appeal.

That must have been why, even with twangy old country blues on the jukebox rather than the pulse, I figured I must've been back at the mansion. All the walls flashed naked brick under the plaster, and the floor made you look twice, with a different pattern of black and white tile snaking through the brown. Coiling along the ceiling were cheap Christmas lights that failed to illuminate the smoky din.

Yet most of the partygoers were holding what looked like beer. As I peered closer, their clothes gave them away, mostly jeans, all more or less modern, though some of the outfits had perhaps seen better days. Just like this bar. In the window, a neon sign proclaimed the name backward: Clementine's.

For such a dive, there were so many people, wide-eyed tourists and trendy kids right alongside older locals and a couple of barflies paying no mind to the rabble. And on top of that were all the ghosts. If I couldn't tell from their clothes, passing right through people gave them away.

One of the living backed into me, literally. We stood in the same space, our bodies overlapping, my soul exposed to his. For such a big guy, he couldn't hold his drink. I laughed, because I couldn't hold his drink, either. It made me stumble, my stomach suspended with panic, as I tried to plant my feet with no ground beneath them.

That must've been how the other spirits were getting drunk, picking up on the spins and giggles, bellowing and bravado. Yet despite all the rubbing elbows waiting for drinks and clusters looking to snatch seats, the ghosts stood untouched in the middle of what might become a dance floor after a couple more rounds. It was as if they were haunting each spot, giving every passing drinker enough of a sober chill to urge them elsewhere.

Alastair had his arm around a girl. She definitely looked modern, in her loose tank and yoga pants, not pretty, but thin and blonde. They made such an odd pair, but perhaps he liked them young. I wondered how long ago she had died, whether she'd gone to her wake and funeral and everything, mourning along with the family and friends she'd left behind—or if she'd come straight here.

As soon as he saw me, he let go of her, rushing over—then slowed down, like he could still play it cool. "Well, well," he said, slightly louder than usual, possibly tipsy. "Looking for me?"

I tried my best to sound sober. "Don't get too excited."

"What are you having?"

"I'm not."

I wouldn't be able to stop at one more drink.

"It looks like I'll need another, then."

Blondie caught up to him, throwing her arms over his shoulders and letting her mouth brush his ear as she whined, "I wanna go dance."

"So go," he said, casual but firm. "I'll catch you in the ballroom."

She kept it classy and made sure to glare at me before sulking off.

"Why are there so many of us here?" I asked.

"Haven't you heard?" He leaned in, his voice low, reveling in the showmanship. "It's haunted."

"I thought we weren't supposed to trespass any boundaries."

"Do you see any of us breaking glasses, stacking chairs, harassing the staff? I've long taken care of the old geists that inspired the stories. It's come back around as a cover for us." He leaned just far back enough for me to see his conspiratorial grin. "Watch this."

He put up his hand, and with an unnecessarily showy flick of his wrist, all the lights began to flicker. In the crowd, there were a few whoops and hollers, but other than that, nobody paid much mind, especially not any of the servers and cooks hard at work behind the counter.

"I told you there's ghosts," said one of the drinkers beside us.

"It's an excuse not to renovate the wiring," said her killjoy friend. "It's not haunted, it's falling apart."

I squinted up at Alastair. "How come you get to spook the tourists, but I'm not supposed to reach out to my grieving family?"

"I'm not affecting anyone's beliefs. This place is a stop on ghost tours. It's hokey enough that nobody's going to be swayed by anything they see, whether skeptic or believer, tourist or regular."

"What about the staff?"

"They're usually soused."

I wouldn't want to deal with both customers and ghosts while sober, either.

"And what if you did get someone's attention?"

He beckoned me to follow him, toward the entrance, and then to the left, through a locked door. On the other side, up stairs that creaked without any weight on them, stretched a long hallway with peeling wallpaper and wooden planks exposed beneath like ribs. All the doors on either end, not to mention the red light, put me in mind of a real specific kind of shady hotel.

"Is this what I think it is?" I asked.

"These rooms were indeed once rented for that use."

They still could have been, from the moans behind one of the doors. I had a vision like something out of my younger and wilder days of pushing him into the nearest bathroom, bending over the sink, getting him out of my system before drinking enough to forget him.

We were met by voices from the next room. It must've been used as an attic by the staff, who probably meant nothing by stashing that busted-up pool table and pinball machine and ancient jukebox up here and forgetting about them. All the drunken, shouting ghosts sure appreciated it, as if these were offerings to appease us.

As we ascended, all the ghosts we passed, peeking heads out of doors and bumping elbows in the hallway, cried out to him in greeting. Alastair hailed them, stopping for back slaps and fist bumps, even a couple of kisses of varying modesty. But he didn't hog all their attention.

"Is that a fresh face?" asked a lady with a beehive hairdo.

"Who's the rotter?" said a blonde girl with a mullet.

A man in a zoot suit grinned. "Got yourself a graveflower?"

I tried my best to nod and smile, acknowledge every potential start of conversation, even though I didn't follow through on any of them. It had been so long since I'd been the center of attention, I'd forgotten what to do with it. I couldn't have been any further from cool.

"Why don't any of the living come up here?" I asked.

"Once they stopped renting out to ladies of the night, one of the original owners lived up here for the rest of her life, until she died. The new owner and staff believe she's still here—and they're right."

We reached the end of the hallway, which opened into a lounge. Not as big as the one downstairs, but it had another small bar, still decked out with yellowing photos on the back wall and various vintage advertisements for alcohol no longer being served. In the corner, a tiny, wizened Black woman jangled away on a dusty, slightly out of tune old piano. Even with the jukebox downstairs, I doubted it would go unheard through the ceiling.

"Hot stuff, Clem," said Alastair.

She looked up from her playing just long enough to wink.

"That's not asking for trouble?" I said.

"On the contrary," said Alastair. "The tourists love it."

We passed between clusters of ghosts, each vying for his attention, wondering who I was and how I'd earned the coveted place on his arm. The cliques were divided by age, with older ghosts in longer skirts and gentlemanly hats around the piano, and younger ones mostly in jeans of varying wash and width on the barstools. Once we'd passed by, though, none of them followed us, familiar enough with his habits to know he wanted to be alone with me. Some of them might have known him for actual decades. I wondered how many girls he'd paraded around like this through the years. If they were still here, asking about me.

He sat us by the window, right beneath the neon bar sign, casting us in green light and stark shadow. So that was why he'd brought me up here. Showoff.

I repeated the question. "So why the boundaries, and the bad feeling in my gut, and all that? Who cares if we show ourselves?"

"Ask anyone who's been here long enough, talked to enough people, corroborated stories. We all know of someone who's tried showing themselves to the other side. Those souls tend to disappear."

"What, like they finish their business and cross over?"

"They never get to finish relaying their message, or revealing themselves, or anything of the kind, before they vanish."

"Why?" I asked.

"There must be someone out there who doesn't want the world to know."

I laughed, because I'd believed a lot longer than I ever doubted, as much as I resented it. I'd grown up fearing that somebody watched me through my ceiling. "You mean like some higher fucking power?"

"Aside from the way our souls sever from our bodies, that's the best indication we have of somebody being in charge, after all. Who else could be cutting us off on account of free will?"

He leaned back, watching my face. I tried not to gulp.

I just hoped whoever watched over us wasn't the same God my mother believed in. It would kill me—again—if she'd been right all along. And that guy could be such an asshole.

"What do they even care?" I asked.

"If any of us were exposed to a whole crowd of people—strangers, skeptics and believers alike—and they all confirmed with each other what they saw, same time, same place... that's evidence. They can't choose whether or not to believe, because now they simply know. That knowledge precludes any possibility of faith."

"But only if it's a bunch of people?"

"Well, if one person sees us, they're crazy."

As I'd always expected, the powers that be didn't care too much for individual people. Like Ren.

"Even a few people, especially a household, could all be hysterical, or attention-seeking, or being slowly poisoned by carbon monoxide."

"What about poltergeists?" I asked. "Do they ever go after anyone in particular?"

"I don't believe so," he said. "They don't appear to notice their surroundings anymore, certainly not on the other side. Any havoc they wreak strikes me as accidental, just a manifestation of their grief."

"And that could happen to any of us?"

"I've seen it."

"How do you know any of this?" I asked.

"I don't," he said. "But I've been around for a while, and I've been paying attention."

"So where do we go?" I asked. "After we cross?"

He shrugged. "You tell me."

I'd spent my early years in constant, quiet terror of divine retribution. Even back when I tried to behave—fighting the impulse to fidget in itchy church dresses, keeping still, not jiggling my leg during Mass and classes, repressing the urge to throw paper and steal pencils to get my crush of the week to glance my way—I'd known, deep down, that wasn't the real me. No amount of good grades and keeping my room clean and wasting weekends babysitting ever seemed to appease my mother anyway. I could only take being tightly wound for so long before I'd finally snapped and started being myself, trying to wash down my existential dread with booze and older boys' hands down my jeans.

And then, when I moved out for college, I realized I didn't have to believe in hell or anything else. Especially after I finally gave in and started hooking up with girls, because I refused to give anyone the satisfaction of loathing myself for that when I had so many other so-called sins to choose from instead.

Now, I didn't have a choice about believing or not.

I coughed up a bitter laugh. "I'll be damned."

"Oh, don't flatter yourself," he said, rising. "I'm sure you're not *that* interesting. If I'm wrong, then as long as you're here, we may as well enjoy it."

He loomed over me, once again offering his upheld palm. I wanted nothing more than to take it. Not just to soothe the pins and needles in my numb skin with the warmth of his touch. If I danced with him, I could forget all about my death and potential damnation. I need only take his hand.

I flexed my fingers with a sigh. "Pass."

"Are you kidding me?" His accent disappeared for a moment, as if he'd gotten mad enough to forget where he'd come from. "Do you realize no one's ever resisted joining us this long? Not a *soul*."

"Really?" I gulped, not wanting him to hear the unexpected lump in my throat. "Does nobody give a shit about the ones they've left behind?"

I'd already ditched my sister once before. Well, I hadn't been allowed to see her, post-disownment. But I'd done a lot of partying on the road, while she grew up without me. I couldn't do it again— especially if she thought I was suffering eternal torment.

Alastair's voice went low, his eyes far more earnest than I would've expected. "They choose not to grieve alone."

I looked away, digging my nails into my palms, because no fucking way would I tear up in front of him. It hadn't occurred to me that I'd been grieving. I'd been trying my best not to stop and feel it, keeping myself busy with my own arrangements.

No need to reveal my plans. I shot him a glare instead. "I bet you'd like having me cry on your shoulder, wouldn't you?"

"If you need to cry, that's as far as I'd touch you," he said. Then, just as I'd expected, his sincerity gave way to a smirk. "After your tears are dry, I'd be glad to offer all kinds of comfort."

My skin flushed, hinting at just how much our apparent bodies were still capable of doing, the memory of hot blood rushing through my phantom limbs. But I tried my damnedest not to give him the satisfaction of showing it, fighting the urge to squirm. I couldn't believe I'd managed to resist joining the fun for this long. If I stayed any longer, my self-restraint might not hold out. It would be all too typical for me to give up and blow off what I owed to Cris.

I brandished some finger guns. "See you in hell."

SEVEN

❋⟫⟩ ⟨⟨❋

Ren wasn't in his apartment. I tried spiriting straight to him, but that only left me in the middle of a dark urban street, blinking in the rushing headlights of cars that roared right through me. He must've been driving.

I tried again in the morning, after sunrise. He looked even paler than before in darkness, lit only by the blue light of his laptop, curled up in a nest of sheets on his mattress.

He didn't look up as I approached. It felt so intrusive, kneeling across from him on the bed like I'd been invited. But he was my best shot at communicating across the veil. I had no choice but to pester him.

Then again, I didn't have to be a nuisance. This could be fun. I need only turn on the charm. Too bad I'd died in such a long skirt, and I hadn't thought to undo any buttons on my blouse.

I put my hands on my knees, leaned forward, and smiled. At the last second, I couldn't resist a joke. "Hey there, boo."

Nothing. Not even an eyeroll. He barely turned his head away from the screen. He didn't even flinch when I waved my hands in front of his eyes, though his jaw clenched.

"Ouch."

Evie and I might have gotten a rise out of him earlier, but now he was trying to take back some self-respect, refusing to talk back to his own supposed self. Striking a pose and a seductive grin in his bed might do the opposite of convincing him that I wasn't just a figment of his lonely imagination.

I sighed, imagining all the years of therapy and medication I'd have to break through. But he probably didn't need all that. Unlike me.

"I'm not Brian," I said.

His chest rose and fell with a silent sigh. I must've been hard to ignore. Unlike the raving geists, I talked right at him.

"I'm different from all your other so-called hallucinations, aren't I?" I said. "Way more coherent, right?"

He didn't answer, of course.

"Either you could choose to believe you've hit a new level of psychosis, or there's another explanation: I'm real."

His mouth curled with a strangled start of a laugh. That was something.

"We're all real, but the rest have been dead so long, something's gone wrong with them. I only just died."

I pressed closer, blocking the light with my legs as I dipped my head down, trying to look into his face. He shrank away, getting up.

As much as I didn't want to follow him to the bathroom, I had to confirm my suspicion. He blinked in the fluorescent light, fumbling in the medicine cabinet. Something clattered into the sink with a familiar clacking rattle, that warning shade of orange. I couldn't quite catch the multisyllabic medication listed on the label beneath *Takahashi, Renji.*

"I knew it."

He glared at his reflection as he popped the pills in his mouth, swallowing dry, with a tap-water chaser.

"I'm pretty sure that's not how you take those," I said. "They're maintenance, not at will; you can't pop 'em like candy and make me go away."

That won me a glance of a few seconds, his brow furrowed.

"Look, I've seen shit," I said. Normally, I'd rather die than open up, but between already being dead, and having my existence questioned, somehow it came easy. "I've never been diagnosed—well, not correctly. You know when you're seeing shit that it's not real. It doesn't make you question. Deep down, you know."

Most of the time, anyway. That's why I hadn't freaked out that much when I'd first left my body and couldn't touch anything. I'd figured it was an episode. I'd simply gone home and climbed into bed, like I could sleep it all off. In the morning, I'd finally get around to calling my old shrink, try sticking out some meds long enough for them to actually work.

I amended my assertion a tad. "Your brain usually recognizes its own self."

"Mine doesn't," he said.

"That's because I'm not Brian," I said. "I'm Mal."

He laughed again, but it sounded like a sob.

"You want me to prove it? Go look me up," I said. "You couldn't make up what you find when you search 'Mal Caldera.'"

"Why not?" he asked, still staring at his reflection, rather than me. "I'm so far gone that I'm talking to myself."

He picked up the pill bottle again, and from the way his eyes lingered on the warnings on the label, I could tell exactly what he must've been thinking. I'd done the same. It started off innocently, as if out of self-preservation: checking the recommended dosage, doing the math of exactly how many more pills it would take for a permanent cure.

I didn't know what to say.

At last, he put the pills back in the cabinet and took out his toothbrush. I waited in the doorway for him to finish, since he couldn't talk back with his mouth full. Once he'd spat and rinsed, he whipped his shirt off, and I barely turned in time as he dropped his jeans and boxers. My skin flushed just from imagining what I'd see if I turned around, so I sure as hell didn't need an actual glimpse. It had been way too long since I'd seen anybody naked in real life.

His showerhead whined, then roared. I wondered if he'd retreated to the shower on purpose, since I didn't want to follow him there. He might've been giving me some credit for sentience after all. I took a seat—so to speak—on the edge of the toilet, resting my head on my hands.

My heart swelled for a moment as he spoke, only to fall again, because he'd begun singing to himself. He had a good voice, low but soft with a bit of rasp, and utterly pissed, all but screaming except in volume. Maybe I'd been getting to him, making him feel witnessed, even if he wouldn't admit it aloud.

"You ever do music?" I asked. "I used to."

He went quiet.

I regretted it as soon as the words left my mouth. But if I really wanted, I could've shown him something he couldn't make up. I could sing him something I'd written, perhaps even conjure an instrument from my memory, like the band had in the ballroom. Even he'd have to admit his brain couldn't bullshit that.

Only I couldn't bring myself to sing a single note. My hands were too empty, sitting there without my kit. Even his fucking bathroom turned into a stage, the fluorescent light golden and glaring, faces I couldn't see staring up in the dark.

He threw the curtain back. I sprang up, somehow still not catching any more than a peripheral glimpse of skin. It felt like a test. After all, if I were nothing but his own subconscious running wild, I wouldn't be so embarrassed to look.

My own restraint surprised me. For once, I didn't do what I knew I'd regret. There were already so many other things in life I'd be missing out on. I didn't need to see all that skin I could never touch.

While he toweled himself off and covered up again, sans jeans, I waited on the mattress in lieu of anyplace else to sit. I didn't think about how I must've looked. But even he couldn't help but notice, sucking in a breath as he hovered over his own bed, as if contemplating whether he wanted to join me. I had half a mind to wink at him, but from the look on his face, it wouldn't go over well.

"Am I just lonely?" he asked.

His eyes were dark with hate, but not for me. I could relate.

At least I hadn't winked.

I got up, letting him have his bed back. He dove down, burrowing into a cave of piled sheets, like that could keep me and every other ghost out.

"I don't mean to piss you off," I said. "I know how annoying it is when someone barges in and tries to fix your life without your permission."

He pulled the covers over his head. "Then go away."

That sounded like he was talking to someone other than himself.

"I could help you," I said. I nearly added that I needed his help in return, but I thought twice. Not yet.

From under the blankets, his hand peeked out, flipping the bird. I laughed. That totally counted as acknowledging me.

Right then, something clamored in his kitchen. All the cabinets strained against their locks and chains as a shadow emerged straight through the wall, leaving the stove top burning red in its wake.

I didn't have to look twice at the trenchcoated businessman's blank face to recognize him as a geist.

"Good night," I said, as if it wasn't early morning.

He didn't say it back. I couldn't blame him.

EIGHT

※》》 《《※

Cris did most of the funeral planning at home, in the studio apartment our mother paid for instead of a dorm: tiny but upscale, the kind with exposed brick and a shiny kitchenette. I'd never warmed up to her minimalist style, all-white furniture and weirdly textured throw pillows, the only color in abstract art reproductions that didn't do much for me. It always looked so blank—like an empty canvas, undecided.

I'd moved out as soon as I could after crashing for three months, a little over two years ago. I'd felt like such an intruder in her neat, clean space. I couldn't take eating her food and using her expensive shampoo for long, even if she wasn't the one paying for it. Especially because of that.

She'd made a real mess of her desk and kitchen table lately, littered with pamphlets and samples from the funeral home, and old photo albums featuring way more baby pictures of her than of me. She'd found some old Polaroids I'd sent her, taped to gas station postcards from my tour days. I looked a lot happier in all of those than in any from my childhood, but I had a feeling she wouldn't dare use them. Gloria wouldn't approve.

Cris made frequent stops at our childhood home, a tall, severe white-and-black Victorian. Meaning our mother had to be involved after all. So, there would be no acknowledgment of my life post-disownment. It would be like I'd died on that day, still an obedient daughter, my future all planned out and tragically cut short.

I couldn't bring myself to go into that house. During their check-ins, I made do standing in the rose bushes, eavesdropping. Through the window, I'd catch glimpses of pink. Gloria's old dressing gown, which she hadn't broken out since divorcing my stepdad. I could almost smell the chamomile tea, which she went through like I used to go through whiskey, using my late abuela's good china. Maybe she wasn't quite as unaffected as I'd thought.

But I kept tagging along everywhere else with Cris. Out and about to go pick the funeral wreath, order the flowers, print out the programs and photos. All along, I tried to mess around again: peeking through the flowers, dragging the photos she'd picked, reading in obnoxious voices. Even if she didn't giggle—if she didn't even realize my presence—I didn't want her to be alone.

After that first night, I imposed a new routine on Ren. After each day shadowing my sister, by the time his phone alarm rang at five o'clock, and he emerged groaning from his blanket nest, I'd be there.

"Morning, sunshine! Or… moonlight?"

I might've been more aggressively cheerful than necessary; I envied his ability to sleep at all. He wouldn't dignify my presence with an answer. But he did give up trying to hit snooze.

I had to wait while he showered, trying not to think about him naked, how good it must feel to wash the passing of time right off his back. He wasn't so shy about singing anymore, as if to rub it in. He did look somewhat bashful when he came out in a towel to grab some clothes, retreating to the bathroom to change. He probably didn't think twice about getting to wear a different outfit every day. My own clothes had begun to feel like a second skin, not getting crusty, but ever the same, bordering on claustrophobic. And my left slipper still came back every morning. I started leaving it in the closet.

Once he got decent, he'd pull his shitty coffeemaker out of a locked cabinet and wait around while it percolated, watching carefully for any geists through heavy blinking eyes. Every time, I couldn't help but breathe in, imagining I could smell the coffee. When he took his cup out to the fire escape to pair with a cigarette, I'd chat to him, try to prove my sentience. Even if watching him drink and smoke made the white noise in my skin pitch.

I had plenty of stories I'm sure he'd never dream up himself. So much for not opening up anymore.

"It's not like I needed to steal it; I had friends with good fake IDs. I just did it for the blasphemy. Only the jugs turned out to be really heavy. Of course, I dropped them, and one of them exploded. The blood of Christ all over the rector's office. It looked like I crucified him myself. Anyway, never send your kids to Catholic school."

Sometimes, he nearly cracked, his mouth twitching in a smile that he tried to hide behind his coffee. But he couldn't hide his blush when I started sharing my dirtier exploits.

"So, I show up at the frat house where they're holding auditions, and I'm like, oh shit, I've been here before. Sure enough, the lead guitar comes to say hi, and I can see in his eyes that he recognizes me. Turns out, I gave him some generous head at their last party. I didn't even know him, but he totally thought I'd tried to casting-couch my way into their shitty ska band. And the worst part is that they didn't even choose me! After my moving performance! The head, not the drums. Joke's on them, 'cause I ended up joining an all-girl punk group and dating that lead guitar instead."

That was the only music-related anecdote I told. From before my career officially started, so it didn't count. I had way more stories from after my real band took off and started touring. Getting kicked out of a hotel for streaking. Gluing a few keys on a douchebag fellow opener's keyboard. Nearly brawling with a prominent emo singer after kissing his girlfriend.

But after what had happened—how it all ended—none of it seemed so funny anymore.

I left him alone when he went to work, graveyard shift. When he got home in the early morning, I'd be there again, my stomach gnawing with the memory of hunger while he made himself dinner. Since he always looked tired, I kept it low-key, partly because he usually watched something on his laptop while he ate. I missed TV almost as much as cigarettes and coffee, so I couldn't help but sit on the edge of the mattress, trying to catch a glimpse. Eventually, he'd let me, scooting over enough for me to see.

Sometimes we were interrupted by geists. Most of them simply hovered, barely even getting his blanket to billow up. Some announced their presence with noise, scaring both of us alert as they banged the walls and cabinets, or spurted water from all the faucets, or even made the laptop crash with a blue screen of death.

I'd make myself scarce whenever one showed up. Or when he got a call that he answered in a tone I recognized, even when he switched to speaking Japanese. That edge of exasperation could only come from familial intrusion. It made a fitting cue to go check on my own family.

Cris hesitated before ringing our mother's doorbell. Usually, she didn't stop to look at the rose bushes, and she definitely didn't reach out and press her forefinger to any thorns. But I got it. Drawing blood had always been easier than talking to that woman. I used to play with matches, prepping myself for hellfire.

Our mother answered the door in her now everyday robe, clutching one of my abuela's porcelain teacups.

I resigned myself to the foliage as usual, peeking through the curtains and listening.

Gloria clocked her right away, not that she usually bothered with niceties. "Did something come up?"

Her voice always shocked my back soldier-straight. It made me taste the word "ma'am," like biting too hard on a fork.

"We're going to have to change our plans for the wake and service," said Cris.

That garnered a breath too low to be a sigh, bordering on a hiss. It tensed me up, fight or flight. Cris wouldn't know what it meant. I doubted she'd ever been on the receiving end of it before, if she'd ever noticed it at all.

"Madre mía," muttered Gloria. "What did you say to Father Daniel?"

Cris pressed on, oblivious to any impending danger. "You think he didn't remember? We asked him to pray for her so many times."

I might not have been breathing, yet my lungs still seized up. Once upon a time, the sin of suicide earned an unmarked grave. But that was medieval. These days, the only thing that could deny me a Catholic burial would be renouncing my membership in the first place. And, of course, no amount of prayer had brought me back into the fold.

"We'll go to another parish," said Gloria.

"Wouldn't they tell us the same thing?" asked Cris.

Not necessarily. There were priests out there who valued kindness over tradition. One of them ran the AA meetings I'd attended a couple times.

Gloria would've hated him. She must've been really desperate.

"I already booked a room at the funeral home," said Cris. "And updated the obituary—"

I gulped. I'd rarely witnessed anyone, let alone my sister, contradicting our mother.

"No me digas," Gloria interrupted. "We'll talk to another priest."

I'd heard that pitch before, the octave just before snapping. Only I had ever riled her up enough to yell. Never her favorite, my baby sister.

"You want to lie that she died a Catholic?" Cris asked.

"Better than burying her like—"

I cringed, waiting for her volume to explode. But instead, she went silent. I peered closer through the window. What little I could make out of my mother's face looked worn, wrinkled eyes shut, mouth lined and trembling.

Her voice cracked, thin and strangled. "Like some godless—"

She didn't finish the thought, interrupted with a gulping, wet sob. I turned from the window, slumping against it, as if it could hold me up. Though I'd heard her through the walls, sometimes, she'd never cried in front of me. We weren't about to start now. It was a little late for her to suddenly give a damn. I didn't need her fucking crocodile tears.

My fists were shaking. Through the wall came a muffled crash and a gasp as something shattered. Abuela's teacup. Had she dropped it, or had I done that?

I spirited right the hell out of there.

~~~

"Shit," said Ren.

For once, he flinched at the sight of me, the spoon in his hand clattering to the floor.

He startled me right back. I hadn't meant to end up at his place, slouching through his kitchen cabinets, slowly sinking to the floor.

The kitchen light buzzed and dimmed.

"Sorry," I said.

He crouched to pick up the spoon, sugar glittering on the tiles. At least it hadn't been his coffee mug. I couldn't even help clean up the mess.

But he didn't seem to care. Once he'd stooped closer to me, he lingered, meeting my eyes for once. "You OK?"

He bit his lip, blinking hard, regretting ceding even this little bit of ground to my possible existence.

I laughed, preparing to deflect with a joke. Except he'd caught me so off guard by acknowledging me that somehow, I ended up matching his sincerity.

"Not really."

His lips twitched, so close to a smile, if a rueful one. "I hear that."

After pulling himself up, washing the spoon, and sweetening his coffee, he turned back to me, blinking thoughtfully. Then, he reached down, holding out his hand.

I stared at it, my phantom heart skipping a beat. But I must've waited too long, because he changed his mind, pulling away.

Maybe I didn't really want to know what would happen if we tried to touch. Nothing, probably. We wouldn't feel anything at all.

Once he got to the fire escape window, he turned back, waiting for me. "You still up for story time?"

I hoisted myself up on my own, laughing.

Ren and I must've gotten pretty used to geists by then. When we headed back in, neither of us flinched to see a wide, pale, baby-faced man with a wisp of a beard looming on the other side.

"You disgusting waste of breath," he said. "Don't you ever go outside?"

Ren slammed the window shut, quickly tacking up the blanket again. I hadn't realized before that it not only blocked out the light, but also cushioned the glass, which already had some spiderwebbing cracks. If he hadn't believed ghosts were real before now, did he think he'd broken it? That he'd been responsible for all the damage the geists left in their wake? Maybe he'd meant for all those locks and chains to protect his apartment from himself.

"No one will ever want you," said the geist. "Why don't you kill yourself already?"

Ren unlocked his closet, carefully creaking it open as little as possible while he fished out some jeans and his usual gray hoodie, trying not to expose any of his other possessions. Perhaps he intended to get away from the geist by walking, or going for a drive.

I wondered what he did for a living. Even if no one else could see his geists, their effect would be hard to miss. Then again, that would be too weird—too noticeable. They probably didn't act up around other people. Or there weren't many around except the ones following him—only catching up if he stayed in one place long enough, like home.

"Let me try something," I said.

For once, I had a plan before jumping in. As I approached the geist, I took a last look at Ren. If it went all wrong, that face wouldn't be a bad last sight. I grinned at him, then grabbed hold of the geist's wrinkled shirt.

This geist's memories unfolded more clearly than the last one's. We were always in the same apartment, but furnished differently, crammed with a bed and a desk with multiple computer screens. Every detail, down to the paint strokes of album cover art on the walls and dark soda rings on the desk, must've been long memorized, because aside from a slight flicker, like a film reel, his memories were crisp. He must not have left home much.

You disgusting waste of breath, said the pixels on his computer screen. *No one will ever want you. Why haven't you killed yourself already?*

He had one of my albums on his wall.

I let go of his shirt. We were in my family's old church, from back when I still went. I hadn't planned to bring him here, but it would do.

He tilted his head at me, and the knot in the pit of my stomach eased. In a reedy voice, he sang some familiar lyrics. "*I can't hate my guts when I'm nothing but bones.*"

I blinked, back at Ren's place. He rushed to me.

"What happened?" he asked. "Where'd you go?"

I still hadn't gotten used to meeting his eyes, especially not when they were so fixed on me.

"I left him in church," I said. "It seemed like someplace he could rest. I'm not sure if he'll try to get back to you, but it'll be a way to walk."

"What do you mean, can't he just… blink in and out, like you do?"

I shrugged. "We'll see. I've got a feeling he's not all that deliberate, in his state."

"So, um…" He ran a hand through his hair, down to his neck, rubbing distractedly. "Let's say, for a second, that maybe you and the rest aren't schizophrenic hallucinations, and I've been misdiagnosed, and… whatever's wrong with me, it's in my soul, not my brain, and there's no psychiatric manual for that. If that's the case, do you know why those things follow me?"

I could only shake my head. "Sorry to tell you I don't know that one. You might just have shit luck. But maybe it's turning around?"

He kept looking and looking at my face, making up for all the time he'd spent trying to ignore it. "Mal, right?"

"That's me."

"So… you're really dead?"

"I'll prove it," I said. "Read my obit already. Come on down to my wake. You don't think you're so far gone you could make that up, do you?"

"I hope not." His eyes went distant for a moment, but then he pulled back from the rabbit hole, looking back at me. "Though… I'm starting to think I didn't make you up."

"Why not?" I asked. "Would I have had a bigger rack?"

His laughter caught in his throat, nearly choking him. If only I could pat his back.

"Don't die on me, then we'll both be screwed."

That quieted him suddenly, making him blink. "Why are you helping me?"

I gaped, before turning it into a grin. "I'm helping?"

"You just vanished one of my demons right in front of me."

Time to shoot my shot. "Well… you're not the only one with demons. But mine are probably way easier to vanish. And, uh, I won't lie—it would be really cool if you could help me out with that."

He raised his eyebrows warily.

I rushed to clarify. "It might even be good for you. I mean, if you talked to my sister, that would prove I really exist. Or, you know, I did."

"Talk to her about what?" he asked.

"It's, um—" I didn't usually get tongue-tied like this. "The thing is, she—"

I'd only gotten as far as the urge to reach out. Now that I had the chance, I needed to figure out what the hell to say, then cough it up for someone else to pass on. Suddenly it felt weird having to involve a stranger in this.

"It's all right," said Ren. "I mean, sometimes I don't know what to say to my family, either. We've got time, right?"

"Uh… what day is it?"

"Friday."

I winced, shaking my head. "My wake's tomorrow."

His jaw dropped. "Aww, you're kidding."

"Well, you had to be so fucking stubborn."

I stopped, hoping he wouldn't take offense. He still hadn't agreed to anything.

"I'm sorry," he said. "It wasn't you. I even ignore other people, sometimes, until I'm sure they're not just in my head, either."

I didn't expect how heavily that weighed down the phantom heart in my chest. "That's rough."

His mouth twitched into a tentative smile. "Not anymore. You've changed my life. Even if the rest of the world still thinks I'm crazy, I'll know better."

I hated to bring it up and risk the hope in his eyes. "You might still be a little brain-sick, thanks to whatever's up with your soul. Take it from someone with her own bad Brian."

"No shit," he said, and then, for some reason, his pale skin flushed with color. It made him look less dead. "Uh… is it too late to go back to you not being a person? Because if you are, you've seen how I live." He gestured at his sad empty apartment. "And—me naked."

"I didn't look," I said, holding up my palms, Scout's honor. I had to bite my tongue to keep from mentioning how badly I'd wanted to. "Sorry, my creep factor must be off the charts."

He gave me the benefit of a shrug. "I mean, you're a ghost. It comes with the territory, right? Besides, you look so... normal. Like I could've bumped into you on the street."

I would've much preferred to meet him that way. Only I couldn't think about that. For a moment, I missed him not looking right at me.

Suddenly, his face fell. "Evie Green is really dead?"

"Sorry to say."

He looked away, his voice going rough as he stared at the wall. "I had no idea. It's been years since I brought her flowers at the hospital. She was in a coma for the longest time. I guess I just... I thought she'd still be there." His hands clenched in self-reproach. "Fuck, I missed her funeral."

I wondered if she knew how much he'd liked her, after all. "If it makes you feel any better, I could pass on your... uh, regards?"

"Yeah, my condolences, to both of you."

I didn't expect that to put such a lump in my throat. Usually, condolences went to the bereaved, not the deceased. Aside from the effect on my family, and the general inconvenience of being severed from the physical world, I hadn't really given much thought to my feelings about dying. They ran so deep, it felt like peering over a ledge to glimpse a long drop.

I could wait to make that descent, probably over someone else's glass of whiskey.

"Right," I said. Hopefully, he didn't notice how my voice rasped.

He gave a sympathetic nod. "I guess this is the least I could do."

My whole body unclenched, but not for long.

"Just talking, right?" he asked. "I don't have to solve a murder or anything?"

"I wish." If I'd been murdered, there'd be someone to blame. Way more cathartic than the explanation I'd be passing along.

His eyebrows shot up, but before he could voice his confusion, I went on. "I'll coach you through the whole thing. Let me go get the time and address and all that."

"I should do a few rides, then."

So that's what he did for a living. That would buy me some time to figure out what to say.

"I so hope you're real," he said.

This time, I couldn't help it. Before spiriting off, I winked.

Stage Three:
Bargaining

NINE

✴》》 《《✴

Evie sat outside, surrounded by moonlight, from above and reflected in the water below. She pretended to perch on the diving board of an outdoor pool, in what looked like someone's backyard. No need to worry about her socks getting wet as she let her feet swing through the water, unable to touch it. She stroked the tails of her headscarf, tied like a ribbon around a low, loose bun.

Once again, she yelped at the sight of me, clutching her chest.

"Come on," I said, with a laugh.

She gave a sheepish smile. "I know, I know."

Maybe she wasn't used to visitors, especially at this hour.

"I thought we weren't supposed to be alone," I said.

"Well, I don't dance."

"And everyone else does?"

I wanted to give her a nudge—tell her to live a little, so to speak. But then she might wonder what held me back, so I didn't mention it.

"Where are we?" I asked, settling down by her side with my legs hanging.

"It used to be my best friend's," she said. "Have you ever been reminiscing, thinking back on someplace, or someone, and found yourself accidentally there?"

Perhaps I had. It surprised me too much to admit it.

"Ren gives his condolences," I said.

She beamed. "See, he really is a sweetie."

"He mentioned you were in a coma."

That upended her smile. Her eyes widened with more alarm than I would've expected, like she didn't want me to know. It only stoked my curiosity.

"If you don't mind me asking... how'd that happen?"

Her voice remained steady, as if she were repeating a story she'd heard, rather than one she'd lived. Though she couldn't look at me. "My friends and I were drinking. We didn't, usually, we were—you know—good kids. But it would be our last chance for a high school party, sort of, after graduating, before we all split up and had to behave again in college. And I hoped my crush would be there, that it wouldn't be too late for me to get my first kiss."

She looked a couple of years older than a kid between high school and college. But I didn't want to interrupt. Not when she began wiping her eyes, struggling to keep her voice steady.

"None of us were good to drive. I should've said something, but... it's so stupid. I didn't want to spend our last night together being the lame, responsible one, you know? For just one night, I wanted to be cool."

Her voice collapsed with the vacuum of a coming sob. I looked away, feeling bad for cringing, but I'd never gotten much practice comforting anyone. If she were my little sister, I'd brush her hair behind her ear, but that would be totally out of line now.

As I considered putting a hand on her shoulder, she spoke again, her voice evening out until it went flat.

"Nobody made it out. Two went on impact. Another on the way to the hospital. And my best friend after three days in a coma. Mine... it lasted years."

Finally, she looked up at me. No wonder she seemed so shy for a young adult. She'd lost a few years, sleeping them away. At her real age, I'd long passed all teenage milestones, rushing through them as fast as I could.

I let out a sigh, trying to ease the weight on my chest. "You're just a baby."

That made her bristle. "I don't know about that. I had a lot of time to think in there."

I tried not to gape. "You were awake?"

Her eyes clouded, with what I could only imagine was the memory of darkness. "I've read some patients dream, but not me."

I definitely got it now, why she didn't want to party.

"How long's it been?" I asked.

"I'm not sure. It's hard to keep track, on this side. I think I've been on this side a year or so?"

If she was eighteen at the time of the accident, and had spent a few years in a coma, that put her in her early twenties, at least physically. Though she probably didn't feel that way when she hadn't been able to live those years.

After a moment, she asked, "How about you?"

"It's been a week or two."

"And how'd you die?"

She'd already opened up so much. I'd look like such an asshole if I refused to share in turn. But as I sat there in awkward silence, I couldn't even begin putting it into words, tongue-tied with shame. It had been such a stupid way to go.

I'd been perched exactly like this, smoking up on the roof of my apartment building. Too far for a good view of the skyline, much less the shore, but it felt good to let my legs swing in the cool air. Except instead of water, below me loomed a five-story drop.

Beneath us, something splashed.

"Whoa," said Evie.

I might've wobbled off the diving board in surprise if I were really balanced on it. Beneath us, the pool lapped like something had fallen in. But nothing floated in the clear water.

"It's all right if you can't talk about it yet," she said. I let out a pretend exhale. "I know, it's so much fresher for you. Plenty of us here act all nonchalant, but they've had a long, long time to get used to it."

"Thanks," I said.

But that memory would never get stale enough to casually share. I couldn't play it all the way through in my mind's eye before stopping. It was like I'd erased the rest of the tape. Nobody could find out what really happened.

"Wish me luck," I said. "My wake is coming up."

"You want some company? It's not safe alone."

"I won't be."

Cris slumped at her overflowing kitchen table, clutching a pen as she stared down at a notebook. I longed to poke her, spring her free of the tension in her shoulders. When I leaned over to glance at the page, it glared white and untouched, with a sliver of a fresh rip still clinging to the binding.

I didn't know what to say, either. Messages across the veil were just as hard to compose as eulogies. I tried practicing, ignoring the way her fancy light fixtures blinked in and out.

"I didn't kill myself."

No reaction. Not that I'd expected one. It sounded so strange, saying it aloud. But it wouldn't be me doing the talking.

I tried again. "She wouldn't have killed herself."

Cris closed her eyes, evened her breaths. That sounded worse, somehow. How would anyone else know how I'd felt, what I'd been thinking?

So, pacing back and forth in her kitchen, I bullshitted. Eventually, the lights quit flickering.

"We had concert tickets."

As if. I'd stopped even listening to the radio, let alone going to shows.

"She got a promotion at work."

At a job I'd just started a month ago, and also made up.

"I'm pregnant, it's hers."

Well, actually… it wouldn't be too surprising for her to find out that I'd failed to mention seeing somebody. Never mind that I hadn't been ready for a partner, but if she thought I had that going for me, it could make a compelling case that I hadn't meant to go anywhere.

Ren did look like boyfriend material. More wide-eyed than my usual type, but even that might go toward convincing her I'd turned over a new leaf. Of course, he'd have to be a good enough actor to pull off an entire pretend relationship. I could coach him, but he'd have to be quick on his feet.

The payoff would be worth the risk. She wouldn't feel so alone, thinking someone aside from our mother had lost me as well. I had a sudden sappy TV movie vision of her throwing her arms around him and bursting into relieved tears. I'd go into the badly green-screened heavenly light, and the credits would roll.

Cris took a long, deep breath, and started writing. After double-checking a program with my picture on it for the place and time, I left her to it.

Once again, spiriting to a moving target found me in the middle of a dark street. The car behind me slowed and pulled over. There were rideshare stickers on the windshield.

"Where to?" Ren asked, sticking his head out the window.

I shrugged. "I wish I knew."

That withered his smile. I hadn't meant to be such a bummer.

I slipped through the door into the front seat, sitting in midair by his side. He put the car in park and rested an arm on the steering wheel as he turned to face me.

"So," he said. "I went ahead and looked you up, like you told me."

Though I didn't move from my casual position, my whole body seemed to shudder with dread. I hadn't really thought that suggestion through.

"I got a lot of... weird results."

Of course, the first to come up wouldn't be my obit. My voice nearly cracked. "No shit?"

"Were you ever—uh—kind of famous?"

I shook my head, not trusting myself to lie out loud.

"You mentioned you used to play," he said, but without much conviction, like he still doubted his own perception. As if he might've hallucinated the conversation, if not my whole existence. "Am I right?"

"That's different," I said.

I shouldn't have lied. Not to him, with his grasp of reality still so fragile. But I couldn't stop myself.

Thankfully, he changed the subject. "Have you thought of what you need me to say?"

I gulped around the sudden lump in my throat. He had to know what we were trying to accomplish here. I closed my eyes and pretended to breathe in. "My sister thinks that I—"

We both startled as noise suddenly flooded the car. My hands flew up to cover my ears as the radio blasted an eerie tune, distorted with static. He tried to turn down the volume, but even with the dial at zero, the music didn't stop. Turning off the radio didn't work, either. Finally, he just killed the engine.

Even in the silence, my tensed limbs refused to ease up. "Sorry."

Ren shook with a silent laugh, briefly resting his head on the wheel before looking back up at me. "All good. It's not my first time dealing with horror-movie bullshit. I don't scare easy."

At last, I managed to uncoil a bit. I closed my eyes, pretending to draw a deep breath. I tried again.

"She's got to know I didn't kill myself."

His voice went low. "Damn."

I couldn't handle meeting his gentle gaze.

"I'm still working on the right words," I admitted. "This isn't exactly a conversation I ever thought I'd have in my life. Or, you know, afterwards."

He leaned over, reaching for my hand. I shrank back in surprise. He curled his fingers and pulled away again.

Instead, he said, "I'm sorry this happened to you."

I buried my nails in my palms. "Thanks."

He reached into the pocket of his hoodie, pulling out a pack of cigarettes and holding them up. "You mind?"

Like he hadn't already smoked around me. Only now he considered me a person, so he had to ask.

"I don't breathe."

"But your—um—chest still moves up and down."

My eyebrows shot up before I could stop them. I had to bite back asking why he'd been looking at my chest. I knew well enough. Even if we weren't on the same plane of existence, I still looked like a girl, and he still had eyes.

"Just going through the motions," I said.

I put my hands behind my head, stretching my legs out on the dashboard as I watched him roll down the window, his face glowing gold for a moment as he sparked up.

"Do you think we can pull this off?" I asked.

"Why not?"

"No offense, but it doesn't seem like you get out much."

He glowered at me. "What do you think I do for work? Do you have any idea how many people I talk to in a day? I might not be the picture of normal functioning, but I know how to bullshit. It's just the exact same conversation over and over."

He whipped out what must've been his customer service voice, low and laid-back—the carefree tone of someone who'd never seen a ghost in his life. I didn't expect it to go right to my spine, making me sit up with interest. "Hey, how's it going? Do you live here? Where do you work? Are you married? Got kids?"

I knew that conversation well. It went the same at every job, getting to know my coworkers, but not letting them know me. Same with the few dates I'd had the past two years, if you could call them that.

He dropped the voice abruptly. "On top of that, you know how many people I've had cry in my backseat? Lots flying home for funerals. Two people that got fired like five minutes before I showed up. This one poor girl leaving a vet's office with an empty carrier. So... I might not be that unqualified for this."

"Well, that's good to know." I shouldn't have underestimated him. Now it felt more like the cover story I had in mind for him could work. Especially if he used that voice at the wake. "If anyone asks how you knew me, let's say we were fucking."

He choked on his drag, coughing up smoke. I really ought to have put it more delicately. But I couldn't help but smirk at his rosy cheeks, even as I half expected him to reject me, set up some boundaries.

"I guess that works," he said. "I mean, aside from the part where I'm going to have to talk to your family about it."

"We could call it dating. Let's say I tried doing right by you, for a change. That's even better. If I show my sister I had something going for me, it might be easier to convince her... you know."

He sighed. "I'm gonna need a tie. And, well, the rest of the suit."

For once, I tried mentally dressing him, rather than the other way around. No doubt he'd clean up nicely.

"You're going so far out of your way for me," I said.

His quick little exhale might've been a laugh. "Where's my way? For all I know, I'm closer to it, thanks to you."

We grew quiet. I fidgeted, readying for another abrupt exit. While I was wondering where to go, he spoke up.

"You have any clue what'll happen, once I get your message across?"

I shrugged, throwing my palms out wide to indicate the enormity of my ignorance about the universe.

"If it's your last night—you know, on Earth—what are you gonna do?"

I shook my head in confusion. "Last night on Earth?"

"I mean, if this is your unfinished business, won't you cross over once it's done?"

I hadn't seriously considered that. My last night on Earth. Too bad I couldn't do much, in my state. Not to mention, my tour days were a hard act to follow. I'd already had a couple of nights that could've easily been my last.

"So how are you going to spend it?" asked Ren.

That sounded like an invitation. I couldn't help but smile.

I would've loved to spend my last night on Earth with him, except we wouldn't be able to do any of the things I really wanted to.

But I knew somebody else who could.

"See you tomorrow," I said, hoping it wouldn't be a lie.

TEN

※》》 《《※

I wouldn't dance. If I started, I might not be able to stop. But that didn't mean I couldn't scope out the scene, even carouse a bit. As long as I kept it to just the one night—my last night—and didn't get sucked in forever.

This time, I headed straight for Clementine's. It must've been a weekend, because it teemed with more cramped bodies than before in the neon dark. I looked around at the drinkers, hoping to find somebody holding straight whiskey or an old-fashioned. Once again, I didn't get to choose, jostled by somebody a few too many beers in. It made my skin flush hot.

"You there," said an accented woman's voice, exaggerated like an actress in an old black and white movie, one of the first talkies, rather than a real human soul. She came swishing toward me, her flapper dress champagne gold against her black skin. "There, she looked, one of us! She looks newly dead, but get a look at that skirt, hiding her knees!"

She knocked her own together for emphasis. I opened my mouth for a retort, but I couldn't untie my tongue in time, because she reached right down and lifted my skirt, brushing my skin. Her memories made me reel even harder than the drink. My tongue burned with bad bathtub gin, but I found respite in kisses stolen in a dark corner of a discreet club, where women in suits drank and smoked like men, sweeping dames off their feet.

And then my body and mind were mine again, and I couldn't tell if the touch had been too brief, or if the recollection itself was hazy, too tipsy to commit in the first place, because her lover's face had blurred, and the flashes of the club were like photographs, with only the awful burn of bootleg liquor strong enough to last the years and years of looking back.

I recoiled, slapping my skirt back down. "Buy me a drink first."

"Why so shy, little graveflower?" drawled a dark man in a slightly crumpled pinstriped suit, like a Southern gentleman whose Sunday best had seen better days, or just a bad last day. He had a guitar slung over his back like he'd died with it.

His hand on my waist showed me much the same picture. My nose filled with tobacco, sweat trickling down my spine in the smoky heat of a crowded juke joint, though he'd played so many, they all blurred together, too many counters and corners where there shouldn't have been, and the faces even worse, like an out-of-focus picture.

Even after I lurched away from him, my fingers itched to dance. I'd picked up guitar as well as drums and piano long ago, a little of everything, idle hands making the devil's music.

I might've come for a good time, but I hadn't expected to get this kind of friendly. They'd gotten under my skin without the courtesy of even taking my clothes off first.

"You're rather an antique, aren't you?" said a pale lady in nothing but a corset and bloomers. I had to wonder if she'd kicked the bucket looking like that, or if she'd left a phantom gown lying abandoned somewhere in the ether.

For a moment, I hoped she'd be more reserved, but even she had to go and try poking me. I leaned away from her finger as she went to tuck in a strand of my hair, but she got me in the cheek. Unlike the others, she had no parties of her own to show me. If she'd ever gone to balls, or concerts, or whatever they held in her time, she didn't have them in mind. Instead, I saw some flashes with no tastes or smells or touch, nothing but the swell of music and blur of dancing, swing and jive, twist and even disco. I couldn't tell if she'd been there, still dancing in death, or if those memories had been shared secondhand.

That must've been why they couldn't keep their damn hands to themselves. I wondered what I might've accidentally shared from all the bars and clubs and house parties where I'd danced, and worse, where I'd played. My memories would be fresher, like moving pictures compared to their stuck camera reels.

In any case, we had nothing to touch on this side but each other. I just wished it didn't come with so much baggage.

"When are you from?" the flapper asked.

I tried not to bristle at her having to ask, like I didn't blend into the crowd of living as well as I'd thought. "Now."

"I thought kids these days didn't know shame," she said, miming a phone, badly, with her thumb and pinky out, not how they made them anymore, and definitely not the kind that could take the pictures she imitated. "You just tweet tweet, tick-tock, all the livelong day!"

I'd never once done either of those things in my entire life. I hardly socialized in the real world, let alone online.

"You never once phoned a friend, sent a telegram, wrote a letter?" said a familiar voice. We all turned to meet it.

Alastair emerged straight through somebody, still cool and articulate even after taking our equivalent of a shot, though his grin was bigger and sillier than usual. As if the rolled-up sleeves weren't enough, even worse, he'd taken off his vest. Under the suspenders, his shirt buttons were half undone.

He threw his arms around the flapper and the guitar gent. "And you were boozing and sleazing the same, but nobody snapped any evidence."

The flapper girl held a finger to her lips. "Hush up, you old devil."

"Live fast, die young, leave a hot little corpse," said the guitar gent, like his own remains were anything but cold and dry by now, nothing but bones, soon to be dust.

"I sure didn't," said the corseted lady, with a haughty swell of her chest, her generous tits nearly spilling right out. I couldn't look anywhere else. It didn't help to think that she must've been twice the age of my late grandparents. That must've been why I didn't know how to talk to these old-timers.

"But you've more than made up for lost time, haven't you?" said Alastair.

He let go of the others and went to sweep her up, dipping her like on the cover of a bodice-ripping romance before going in for a shameless kiss. I had to look away, trying like hell not to openly cross my legs. The other two were looking, without much interest, like they'd seen it a hundred times but it still beat looking anywhere else.

For a moment there, I nearly thought he'd forgotten all about me. He pulled her back up, set her down glowing and giggling, and turned to catch my eye, licking his lips.

"Mal," he said. "I see you've met some of the band."

They turned back to me, looking me up and down like they were hungry—but not ravenous. Just peckish, lacking anything better to do but to polish me off.

Right when I thought to give up, like I didn't have it in me to party anymore, and I might as well be deader than dead, I jumped at the touch of yet another hand.

Alastair's fingers were warm in mine. He didn't force any memories on me, as if we were still alive. His walls were up, if a bit wobbly, like a carnival house. Mine were hopefully the same.

Did he hold back as a courtesy, or because he had something to hide?

He leaned in, and the memory of breath tickled my ear. "I won't ask," he said. "Just for tonight."

With that, he swung me around, through a young woman shrieking with vodka-driven delight as she approached her friends. I let out a yelp of my own, a roller-coaster thrill in my stomach, like when I used to gaze over the ledge of my apartment rooftop. As soon as he let go of my hand, I wished he hadn't. It felt so good, feeling again. I didn't want to stop.

We went upstairs, past the red-lit hallway and the rooms still in use, and joined the others in the lounge. This time, we mingled. Ghosts of all ages broke off from their clusters to surround us, and I found myself being introduced.

"For how long have you wandered?" asked the lady with a parasol.

"I just got here."

The man in the bowler hat clapped my shoulder in an ungentlemanly breach of personal space. If we could smell, he'd probably reek of brandy, or whatever they used to drink in his day. "Bully for you!"

"It's so much better on this side," said a middle-aged woman in a victory suit, with a smart hat and empty cigarette holder, which I didn't blame her for keeping to wave for emphasis.

"You're not gonna miss it," said a kid in such brightly colored polyester and denim, he had to be an eighties mall rat. "I don't even remember my life."

"It's a good thing you died young," added a man whose nipples showed uncomfortably through his tight sweater, in a shade of orange best left back in the seventies along with his bell bottoms.

Alastair put his arm around me. "Why so shy?"

"I'm not."

I hadn't realized that I wasn't saying anything in reply, letting everyone talk over me. It had been so long, I'd gotten rusty.

"Prove it," he said.

"I need another drink."

"Let me walk you," the seventies guy offered, taking my elbow.

"I'll do it," said the mall rat, taking my other arm.

So that's why they'd crowded around me, at least some of them. After however many decades they'd been here, they'd exhausted their pool of potential partners. If they hadn't paired off for good, they could only hook up with their own leftovers.

As for everyone else, they must've been bored, looking for someone new to talk to, if they could only remember to shut up and listen.

"Have some goddamn manners," snapped the flapper, shoving the seventies guy. On my other side, mall rat cowered away. "Go on, take a walk." She turned to me and offered her palm. "I'd be obliged to escort you, miss."

I flushed all over. Even with that lovely face of hers, those curves under the trembling tassels of her dress, I wasn't ready for another taste of terrible gin.

"Leave her be," Alastair said.

I left them behind and took off on my own, weaving through the milling bodies. On my way down the stairs, someone blocked me.

"Wait," said a young guy from the tens, judging from the man bun and skinny jeans, the narrowest in the room. I cringed, thinking he recognized me.

"What time do you come from?" he asked.

I threw up my hands. "What do you think?"

Rather than answer, he looked me up and down again. I raced past him, grateful that at least nobody downstairs could see me in my forever outfit. After another shot, I unbuttoned my blouse to reveal my tank beneath it, but that didn't do enough. So I took it off and left it on the floor, wondering if it would stay there.

My skirt couldn't be helped. At least, not until after my next drink.

"Ready?" asked Alastair.

His eyes were hazier than before, like he'd come downstairs for the same reason. They swept over my bare shoulders and slightly lower neckline slowly.

I looked him right in the eye and lied. "I died ready."

"That's the spirit."

When we got back, the crowd greeted me again with a cheer. This time, I took it like I deserved it. After all, I had earned it, back in the day. I held out my arms to gather up their attention.

"What's up, you dead fucks?"

This used to be easy. I just had to smile, and with loud and tipsy showmanship, own my mess.

"It's my last night on Earth," I said. "I'm having a dry wake in the morning, so let's get soaked enough to stay wet tomorrow!"

Another cheer, and more touching, less unwelcome this time around. Now that I expected the flashes, they weren't so disorienting. Or maybe they just matched the drunken spins.

"How did you die?" asked the tens guy.

That slowed my roll. If I'd had a better story, I wouldn't have minded the question so much.

"On this side, it's an icebreaker," said Alastair.

"I'll go first," the flapper interrupted. "I crashed and burned in a car race." She spoke so casually, as if relaying something she'd seen in a movie, not something that really happened, let alone to herself. "It happened so fast I thought I'd flown out of the car and landed on my feet somehow, right up until I saw the car smoking like blazes with my body still in it. They had to have a closed casket."

"I guess mine's not so interesting anymore," said the corseted lady, a bit miffed. "My horses got spooked and ran my carriage over a bridge. I surely broke my neck at the bottom, but I'm not sure. I watched from the railing."

That answered my question about the corset. She must've taken her dress off every morning.

"I dropped dead," the guitar gent cut in. "And I didn't even notice, so I kept walking, right on to the next town, leaving my own self behind in the dust. It weren't till none of the townsfolk would talk to me that I noticed anything funny. I'd got to thinking my reputation preceded me. Then I tried to open some saloon doors, and I went right through them."

After that, we went around in a circle. Most were similarly violent and mundane: thrown off a horse, crushed by an overturned buggy, hit by a bus. We didn't die young for nothing.

My turn came up. They all leaned in for a story they hadn't heard already. I knew now what to say, inspired by the last few narratives. I told the truth—only not the whole truth, or the chronological one, for that matter.

"I drank," I said. "Just drank, and drank, and didn't stop, so I could fly to the sun, crash and burn in a blaze of glory, and nobody would forget what a legendary night we had, or bring themselves to regret it."

But, as hard as I'd tried, it hadn't killed me. Somebody had called an ambulance, and I'd lived to have to detox, and after that, I hadn't had the heart to try again. Especially not once I ended up crashing in my sister's apartment. After coming back into her life, and trying so hard to put my own back together, I couldn't just leave again.

If I'd died a stranger to her, all this would've been so much easier. I might've been able to dance.

"Hear, hear!"

"Amen!"

"What a way to go!"

"I'll say," said Alastair.

From the way he tilted his head, staring with his lips pursed, he didn't believe me.

"There's no call to feel so guilty," Alastair said. We were downstairs after another round of drinks. Somehow, we'd lost our following, now alone in the neon shadows, probably around last call.

"Hmm?" I asked, playing dumb.

"It's too late to change however you came to be here," he said. "So you may as well settle in and enjoy yourself."

Long ago, in place of a pretty smile or curvy body, I'd learned to dust off a secret and flourish it. It would make strangers laugh, as if I'd palmed my honesty like a quarter from behind their ear. For a while there, my sleight of hand had gotten rusty. But now it felt good, flashing my old coin-trick smile.

"I'm the bastard child of a Catholic mother," I said. "Guilt is my birthright."

His teeth glinted in the red light as he laughed. "Let's send you off the way you came."

He leaned in, shadows chasing the light across his perfect distraction of a face. It wouldn't be a party if I didn't do something I'd regret—or someone. I couldn't help but glance down at his lips, biting my own. My mouth had gotten sick of its own taste, terribly empty for too long. It nearly watered, as if he were a meal, not a bad decision.

His eyes drifted shut as he kept leaning closer and closer. I wavered, thinking of how terribly smug he'd look in the morning, because I never settled for just a kiss. I need only make my usual escape, and after that, I wouldn't have to see him ever again.

Suddenly he pulled back, just enough to look at me.

"Wait," he said. "What makes you think this is your last night on earth?"

I fumbled drunkenly for a lie. Not fast enough.

He clapped his palm to his brow. "Your dry wake! I nearly forgot. Now, why the everliving fuck are you going?"

I shook my head in near disbelief. "It's been so long, you don't even remember how it feels, do you?"

"If you want to last as long as I have, you'll stay the hell away."

"I'm not sure I want to be here that long."

He blinked at me in disbelief. "You're not meant to stick so closely to the ones you leave behind. It's not pretty to watch."

"I'll be fine," I said. "It's not like there'll be much grieving, anyway."

"What about me?" His voice went nearly soft. "You don't think I'd grieve for you?"

I couldn't help but throw my hands up in a big shrug. "Umm… why?"

"I want to hear you play."

My blood ran hot and then cold, flushing and shuddering at once. "You said you wouldn't ask."

"Well, it wasn't a question," he said. "But I don't have musicians falling in my lap every day—let alone good ones."

So he hadn't just checked my obit. He'd listened.

I got to my feet. "I can't wait to never see you again."

With that, I spirited off.

ELEVEN

※》》《《※

Ren's place had a clock on the microwave. I only spirited there to check how many hours I had left to while away. If I'd known he'd be awake, sitting up in bed in the blue light of his laptop, no way I would've come. But we'd already made eye contact. Even worse, he raised his eyebrows, no doubt wondering where my button-up had gone. I'd never been so embarrassed to bare a little shoulder.

"You're still up?" I asked.

He shrugged under his sheets. "I can't sleep at night."

"Are you gonna be awake enough tomorrow?"

"It's fine, I hardly ever sleep."

"Sorry to bother you." I looked away, though there was nothing to distract me in the empty dark of his place. "I should go."

"Wait."

I did, mostly because I couldn't picture where else to be.

"Do you have anywhere—" He hesitated. "That is, I don't know if this is even a thing for you anymore, or if you'll take offense—"

"Fire away."

His brow furrowed in concern. "Do you need a place to sleep?"

My mouth fell in surprise, and a little indignation. He didn't even have a couch to offer. "You know how people say, 'I'll sleep when I'm dead'?"

"I've said it."

"Same, but turns out, it's a fucking lie. So don't worry about me. Rest while you can, I'll try not to hate you."

"Thanks, but I kind of can't," he said, guiltily. "But you could still stay here, if you want. We could—I dunno—watch something?"

I could've kissed him. Instead, I settled for sidling up on the mattress. He brought out the laptop again, which booted up with a heated sigh, taking its time lighting the cracked screen. Once it loaded up, he tried to give me first pick, but I insisted he return to whatever he'd been watching, because I didn't want to impose. I couldn't really focus, anyway. We had a big day tomorrow.

It must've been near dawn. With the blanket-curtain blown loose, blue light—or rather, an easing of the dark—crept into the apartment. He'd long given up trying to catch me up on the plot and characters of the dumb rom-com, letting me enjoy all the silly bits that didn't rely on context. I'd had to get up to take care of another geist, but after that, I'd gotten comfortable, lying down on my stomach with my head propped on my elbows. He lay down on his back, listening and resting his eyes occasionally, but never drifting all the way off.

At length, he opened his eyes, fixing them on me. "Goodbye Courage isn't what you consider famous, then?"

Even hearing the name made me taste bile. He must've been biding his time before bringing this subject back up, waiting for me to get comfortable. I closed my eyes to keep from seeing stage lights, but I could still recall their heat on the back of my neck, making me sweat.

"Maybe in the alt scene," I admitted. "We weren't mainstream or anything. And besides, it's over. Gone, done, scattered to the fucking wind."

"I'm sorry," he said.

"Don't be. It's not like I deserved fame and glory, or whatever. I just wasn't good for anything else. Especially not the nine-to-five life. But there's no way out of that except to cheat. That's why everyone wants to be a rock star."

He gave a curt little shake of the head. "I don't."

That took me aback, more than I would've thought. It shouldn't have felt so insulting. I'd long accepted how embarrassing it had been, believing for so long that I could actually make it.

"Haven't you daydreamed about it, at least? Or being an actor, or an athlete?" He made such an incredulous face that I had to backtrack even before finishing. "Even something small, practical, like opening a restaurant, or auto shop, or something?"

His voice didn't rise, despite the force behind it, as he stared ahead, looking no more passionate than if we were discussing weekend plans. "Before I met you, I had a hard enough time trying to imagine that I'd still be alive in a couple of years."

He snuck a glance at me for my reaction, only to be greeted with my mask. His tone was slightly brittle as he added, "So, you might want to lower the bar, and then tape it down, so we don't trip on it."

I knew exactly how he felt. But I couldn't admit it. I didn't want him to look at me and see his future.

Then the other part of what he'd said registered. "What do you mean, before you met me?"

"After you proved what's really going on with me—it's like, for the first time—" He gave up averting his eyes, searching my face to see if I was following his tentative realization. "I'm actually looking forward to being conscious, and wanting to stick around and see what happens next?"

I almost burst into laughter. "I can't remember how that feels."

His dark eyes were warm, both grateful that I understood, and sorry that I did.

"So you don't want to die?" I asked.

He waved a noncommittal hand. "I could wait. I did already, once. Too bad I can't remember it. I was literally born dead. Not breathing, no heartbeat, cold to the touch. It took twenty-eight minutes before they got me to take my first breath. I shouldn't have made it."

"Me neither," I said. "I nearly got aborted. Kind of wish I did, sometimes. But… I'm glad you're here."

"You, too." His eyes widened. "I mean…"

I waved him off. "Take it from me, you don't wanna rush into it."

He knitted his brow, studying my face. "You don't seem so bad off, though."

"It's not that bad." I didn't mean it as a lie, but it felt as heavy on my tongue. "It's not what I imagined, either."

"What were you picturing?"

"Nothing at all," I said. "No dreams, just void."

"You mean my life?"

We both laughed.

"After this, you really ought to get one of those," I said.

He nodded, with his eyes closed. "I'll try."

I'd hardly noticed that by this time, we were lying side by side, facing each other. It made it easier for me to bolt upright. Slants of orange glowed through the gaps around the curtain. My wake wouldn't be for another couple of hours, but I still needed to prepare. We both did.

"Is it time?" he asked. "It's still early."

"I wanted to scope the place out," I said.

It would be too early for that. I had another stop in mind first, something I wanted to try before possibly crossing over.

"I'll meet back up with you before it starts."

For once, I didn't want to take off without saying something. That's what I usually did, whenever I stayed the night with someone. After I'd done things with them that weren't possible between me and Ren.

At some point, my shirt had reappeared, as if I'd never taken it off. It would be the first time I'd left anyone's place more clothed than when I'd arrived.

"Thanks for having me," I said.

His smile made my stomach flutter. "Anytime."

I wondered if he really meant that.

TWELVE

✳»» ««✳

Something odd happened when I pictured my dad. Specifically, the face I remembered from the only photo one of my tías kept without my mother knowing. The only time I'd seen my parents together. He was a young, slightly goofy twenty-something white guy, his hair bleached bone white, tongue out, flashing devil horns. She had her eyes closed, head thrown back in laughter, resting against his shoulder.

If he'd stuck around, it might've been my last chance to see him. Apparently he'd crossed over, because trying to spirit to him only led me to his remains on Earth, leaving me standing at his grave.

As the sun rose, the headstones cast long blue shadows in the dewy grass. There were already a few other people here, but judging from their lack of eye contact, they were only visiting, not residents.

"Hey, Dad," I said, pretending to prop myself up against his headstone, the way I used to lean on it in life.

He didn't answer, as usual. I'd never really met the man, not in my waking years. But I'd listened to his music.

"I joined the club," I said.

He'd died at twenty-seven. I once wrote a song about it, leaving it open to interpretation whether I feared following in his footsteps, or planned on it. Assuming anyone cared that I'd gone, it might've gotten some clicks, even a little radio airtime. But not enough renewed fame to be worth the cost of admission.

"Your old lady would kill me, if it weren't too late for that."

I'd often wondered how my life would've gone if he hadn't up and died on her. She had to have been less of a zealot at some point. I couldn't imagine her making a baby with a drummer otherwise. Perhaps she would've loved me, instead of resenting the reminder of her wilder days, the mistake of choosing a man not long for this world. After his death, she'd repented her sin and returned to her family, who only welcomed her back on the condition that she brought me up in the church.

It should've been so easy to vilify him. He wasn't around to defend himself. Yet, somehow, I could never muster much anger toward the man. I had enough of that with the only parent I had left, too tired to drag him into it as well.

On second thought, if I would be meeting him soon, that might inspire me to give him a piece of my mind. Or return the broken one he'd passed down to me.

It wasn't a coincidence that we'd both died young.

I got up, reaching to brush my legs off thanks to muscle memory, though no grass clung to me. "See you soon?"

My wake would last several hours, guests trickling in and out. Ren didn't need to be there for the whole thing. While he went to go borrow a suit from his brother, I spirited ahead for a peek at the turnout.

From the outside, the funeral home looked nice enough, like a bed and breakfast. Inside, though, it couldn't shake the chill of a place of business, no matter how hard they tried with cozy grandma furniture, all warm mahogany and beige velvet.

I wandered down the hallways until I recoiled at the sight of my face, blown up on an easel, wreathed in flowers. They'd had to go all the way back to college to find a decent photo of me, right before I started dyeing my hair and wearing piercings. I'd long stopped, but there hadn't been any occasions for me to take pictures in the last two years or so. Not that I'd wanted to capture that time of my life, anyway. None of it had been worth remembering.

There ought to have been music for my arrival. I nearly hummed it to myself as I walked through the doors. *Here comes the dead.* Though I couldn't exactly make an entrance when nobody could see me.

Hardly anyone even showed. Mostly faces I didn't recognize. Those I did made me cringe with awkwardness, as if I'd have to greet them, try to remember their names. Extended family I'd only met once or twice; primly dressed older ladies who probably went to church with my mother; preppy, cornfed college kids who were no doubt friends of my sister. All unaffected aside from the emotional labor of looking respectfully sorry.

My old coworkers didn't look too devastated, either. I hadn't expected to see any of them when I'd only worked a few months at each position in the last two years, too restless to last long either boxed in a cubicle or chained behind a counter. It made sense to see some older, well-meaning office moms and dads here to shepherd, but I had no idea why some of the younger people I'd befriended and promptly abandoned bothered coming. Especially not the guy I'd banged and then tried my best to ignore despite working only two desks away. Or the girl I'd stopped flirting with after finding out she had a partner, trying to do better for a change but still offending her all the same.

Nobody from my past life showed, either. I might as well have been a stranger at my own wake. At least I wouldn't have to talk to anybody.

Just like in life, I headed for the snack table, wondering if there was booze. No such luck. Nothing but catered pastries and coffee, and comfort food brought in plastic and aluminum. I hoped someone had spiked the punch.

"You call this a wake?" I asked. "Where's the wailing and gnashing of teeth?"

The sunflowers were a nice touch. They peeked their ugly heads from every bouquet, including the one on my casket, bright and loud and totally inappropriate. I fucking loved them. Someone had remembered that.

That seemed to be the only concession made to my tastes. Everything else, from the Bible verses and images of Mary on the programs to the creepy altar music on an unseen stereo, even down to being buried versus cremated, didn't exactly put me to rest.

That's when I realized I'd gotten it all wrong. This party didn't belong to me.

"Thanks for coming," said Cris.

She lingered near the entrance, shaking hands, occasionally accepting hugs. Her mask had evolved, no longer still as she smiled with the right amount of effort, sad but brave. Ever the consummate hostess. She might not have been the life of the party, but she'd always been the perfect party planner, ready to quickly and quietly smooth over any unexpected interruptions.

"She was real nice," said an office dad whose name I couldn't remember, maybe Ted or Todd. I couldn't exactly blame him for not knowing any better.

He appeared to have started a craze, because that's what all the rest of my coworkers, as well as strangers who'd never met me, suddenly began to declare: I'd been nice.

My relatives knew better, so they stuck with an equally undeserved claim: "She was so beautiful."

They had the excuse of comparing my looks to my mother's, at least, though nobody would've agreed with them in life. But it made the loss more tragic to think so. Dead girls are always pretty.

"She's in a better place now."

I laughed out loud at that, the first time. After a couple of variations, even my sister's face started to twitch.

At last, she had to excuse herself. I followed, though I didn't particularly want to see under the mask.

Cris's destination looked like an office break room, with a kitchenette and tables. It didn't feel like a staff room, though. There were tissue boxes everywhere.

Gloria sat at one of the small tables, half hidden by a pocket mirror held in front of her face. Her other hand shook too hard for her to apply her eyeliner. There were tissues piled up beside her, smudged black. Were they from failed attempts, or crying? Had she begun getting arthritic, or had I shaken her up that much?

Then again, if she really did believe her daughter was going to hell—and so did all her church friends—that might've been enough to rattle her.

Cris watched silently, maybe considering leaving and pretending she hadn't seen anything. At last, she sat down across from her, waiting for acknowledgment, perhaps dismissal. Finally, she said, "I could get that for you."

Gloria responded by putting down her mirror. She handed over the eyeliner without a word and wiped off her last attempt before leaning closer. After only one or two deft strokes to each eye, she blinked, leaned back, and picked up her mirror again to examine the results.

"You do fine work," Gloria said. She didn't quite smile, but her voice loosened like it never did with anyone else. Of course, she had to occupy herself rather than look at her as she spoke, curling her eyelashes, risking some mascara. "You did so well making all the arrangements, with few mistakes. It's good I can trust you."

Cris skipped straight past the praise. "What mistakes?"

"Small, more or less forgivable mistakes—aside from the change of venue." Gloria raised her eyebrows, letting her lips pucker in distaste. "And those ugly sunflowers."

After packing up the makeup and tossing out the tissues, they looked at each other, like they were checking a mirror for any last flaws to fix.

Gloria reached out to brush her hair, as subtle as if merely straightening it. I recognized the gesture. She'd never been that gentle, fixing my own locks. No wonder I always kept mine short. She wouldn't give me permission, so I forced her hand by doing my own hack job with craft scissors, necessitating an emergency salon correction.

And yet, in spite of trying to cut that part of me away, I still took after my mother. Instead of hugging, I always reached to stroke hair.

"You've become a fine woman," she said. "So brave and dutiful."

Cris didn't look proud, or even grateful. Not only because of where they were, what they were doing. She'd always taken our mother's praise like that. I used to think of it as simple humility. Now, for the first time, I wondered if she heard those words as I had always heard them: Everything she is, I am not.

Was not.

THIRTEEN

※》》 《《※

Ren parked way down the street so we could walk and talk without being seen before going in. When he stepped out of the car in his suit—though it didn't quite fit, the sleeves and pants stretched too short on his tall, lithe frame—it stole the breath I didn't have anymore. He ran an anxious hand through his carefully combed hair, mussing it up perfectly. I bit my lip to keep from smiling too wide.

"Lookin' good," I said.

"Really?" He rubbed the back of his neck and looked down at himself. "It's not too formal?"

I craned my head this way and that, like a new angle would change the answer. "It is, but who doesn't want a mysterious hot stranger showing up to their wake?"

He laughed. "Gotta have goals, right?"

I'd really gotten to like making him blush.

We fell in step, heading toward the funeral home. It must've been one of the last bright days of autumn, before the chill crept in. I had half a mind to ask how the weather felt. That unearthly kind of blue sky always made me shiver. As a kid, I used to look for a cloud that might be big enough to hold the kingdom of heaven.

"We're really doing this," he said.

My stomach dropped, like I'd forgotten why we were here, that I hadn't brought a date to a party just for fun. I might have a shot at crossing over. I'd really gone out of my way, getting an actual medium to deliver my last words. I couldn't imagine many ghosts ever accomplished that. Otherwise, they wouldn't go geist.

Wherever I headed next might be a lot worse. But after dragging this poor guy all the way out here to help me, I couldn't just change my mind on a panicked whim. And my sister deserved an explanation. I owed her that, if nothing else.

So I asked, "You ever pray?"

"Um." He winced with a look I'd worn myself, an agnostic anticipation of judgment. "Sorry, no."

I hugged myself, trying to savor the feel of my own body, while I still could. "Never mind."

In a low voice, like a tentative touch, he asked, "You want me to pray for you?"

"Only 'cause I can't do it myself."

"Why?"

"Every time I used to try, it felt wrong."

Praying felt like trying to ask my mother for anything. I'd never behaved well enough to earn the privilege of asking favors. As for giving praise, and thanks, and all that, it tasted so coppery on my tongue, like the word "ma'am." I just didn't have it in me to bow my head and mean it.

He shrugged, like it was no big deal. "I could try."

I wondered if his family had ever practiced anything. If they'd found a Buddhist or Shinto temple within a reasonable distance to commute. Perhaps his mother dragged him to a Unitarian church at Christmas and Easter.

We were getting closer to the funeral home. There were visitors in the parking lot, almost within earshot.

"You know what, don't bother."

He stilled, standing aside on the sidewalk, so we could still talk freely. "I don't mind, really."

I made as if drawing a long breath as I turned around, finally meeting his eyes.

"Look, I know my old religion's probably not the one true faith, if there is such a thing, but if the world really is that cruel, so cruel that most of the people that have ever lived are going to hell, just for being born on the other side of the world and never meeting a missionary—"

I got lost, for a moment, thinking of all the graves all around the earth, marked and unmarked, towering monuments and ashen pits and long-forgotten final beds fossilized beneath rock and paved over with roads. Then I remembered myself and flashed a brittle grin. "I'll be damned."

He didn't look all that impressed by my speech, squinting skeptically at me. "What if yours isn't the one true faith?"

I threw up my palms. "I'm fucked anyway, for following the wrong one! I'll probably reincarnate as a dung beetle."

"No way," he said, dismissive, but not unkind. "You can't be that bad."

"I'm not that good, either."

"Bullshit." He gave me a soft smile. "I don't think you helped me just so I could help you, am I right?"

I gave him a mild glare. "What if I'm only using you for your body?"

He tried not to dignify that with a laugh; it came out strangled. "I wouldn't be surprised if you end up flirting your way past the pearly gates. I'll still pray for you, if it makes you feel any better."

I gave a vague, slightly embarrassed wave of approval. He closed his eyes, only to open them again.

"Um, who should I address? Just God, whoever that might be?"

"Whoever you want," I said. "I'll take whatever help I can get."

"I can't even remember who my baba used to address, spirits or the universe or something." His brow furrowed as he shut his eyes again, searching within.

"Wait," he said, eyes snapping open again, wide with realization. "If you're still here, then there might really be something out there."

I cracked up, pitchy with nerves. "I know, right? Why do you think I'm freaking out?"

"Don't do that," he said, gently. "If you're here, that's a good sign, isn't it? If there were some kind of punishment waiting for you, what's the holdup? Why didn't you go straight to it? There must be a reason."

As much I wanted to contradict him, against my every god-fearing instinct, I let myself sink into the warmth of his voice. He closed his eyes again, and I did the same. For once, unlike in church, I didn't feel pressured to feel a connection. I already felt one this time.

We both opened our eyes at the same time, exchanging smiles that didn't quite reach our lips, before we continued toward the entrance and through the doors to meet my fate.

There weren't any other visitors left in the entrance. We found the room number on a sign and wandered alone down the hallways looking for it.

"You ready?" he asked.

I lifted my fingers to my lips, in case he needed reminding. He rolled his eyes and gave me one last open acknowledgment by opening the door for me. If only he'd gone in first. I could've snuck in one last private moment of panic with his back turned.

It had gotten even emptier since I'd gone. Some of the guests must've stopped by just to leave food. Touch and go.

Ren didn't move, as if trying not to draw any attention to himself, while waiting for my direction.

"Wanna turn back?" I asked. "Forget about this whole thing?"

He shook his head ever so slightly.

While he busied himself signing the guestbook, I looked around for anyone that would be easy for him to try and mingle with, warming up before finding my sister. I half-wished there were some of my old bandmates here, friends from college and on the road, somebody for him to talk to who really knew me.

Before I could find anyone better, somebody broke out of her cluster to approach. One of my former coworkers, wearing what looked like a fucking summer dress to my wake.

Ren didn't seem to notice how she eyed him up and down. She introduced herself like they were at a barbecue, all but giggly.

"So how did you know Mallory?" she asked.

My mouth fell open in a laughing gasp. She didn't even know my first name.

"Malena and I were dating," said Ren.

I grinned. I hadn't told him my full name. He'd been paying fucking attention.

"Oh," she replied. She didn't catch on to his correction, clearly preoccupied. "I didn't know she had a boyfriend."

He didn't answer that, perhaps catching on now to her original intent. His silence must've intimidated her, because she gave a nearly submissive little tilt of her head, and in a practiced tone, almost singsong, she said, "I'm sorry for your loss."

"So am I."

As he moved past her, as if with a purpose rather than as an escape, I tried to guide him, like we were at a party where he didn't know anybody else but me.

"You should go take a look," I said, tossing my head toward the casket. "Try to choke up, make it look legit."

We approached, slowly, like we didn't already know what we'd find in there. His lips parted as he stared, looking from the casket, to me, and back. Meanwhile, my mind instinctively protested at glimpsing my own body as I never should've witnessed it, from the outside.

My face didn't look much like the one I knew from reflections and photographs. I blinked, shaking my head to clear my vision. All my proportions were ever so slightly off from what I'd expected. I wondered if the mortician had done some reconstruction.

The makeup didn't complement me in the slightest. They'd chosen rosy shades of lipstick and blush, trying to make me look wholesome, cover up my pallor and the dark circles under my eyes. Combined with the boring work outfit my sister had picked out for me, it worked. She looked like someone else: a young woman who could've been going places.

Ren's eyes filled. At first, I thought he was acting, damn well. He sniffed, turning away from me as he wiped a hand over his face. I wondered if it was the validation of his sanity again. Or he hadn't processed the reality of my situation, since I appeared before him talking and joking like a normal person. I might've been there, but at the same time, I'd gone, and I was never coming back.

He cleared his throat, trying to smile at me, though his eyes were red. I couldn't think of what to say, what he should do next.

And then I heard it. I knew the sound so well, it seemed to come from inside my own head. Except all the guests were turning toward it. Guitar riffs. I'd helped write them. And, even after all this time, I both loved and hated the result. Mostly hated.

Weren't you going to wait till you're twenty-seven?

I blinked against a sudden glare above me, harsh white light bouncing off close white walls, no windows. My wrists and ankles chafed with an odd tightness, like I'd been bound.

My stomach cinched with worry, too warm to be my own. The light dimmed. My limbs were free again. I jerked, looking around, wondering where I'd gone and come back from.

"Mal?"

I knew this man. How did I know him? His hand withdrew, like he'd been touching me, but I hadn't felt anything. Well, nothing physical. That's what had warmed me.

Ren was speaking aloud to me in his concern, if only under his breath. "What happened? Your eyes went all blank, and you just took off, like you were sleepwalking, or—"

I managed to raise a finger to my lips.

"I'm sorry," I said, as he stared, begging an explanation I couldn't give him for what had just happened—losing myself so deep in a memory, I'd almost gone there, soul and all.

He shook his head, whispering one last time. "You looked like one of the others. You know—the not-so-nice ghosts."

Someone had turned the music off. Another familiar voice jolted me out of my haze.

Gloria glared, her face indignantly stiff. "Who put that on?"

For once, her mask didn't look so unnatural. It would look to any guest like she was putting on a brave face. How courageous, they'd think. What a strong woman, putting aside her grief to be a good host. And how righteous her anger toward whoever had put on that inappropriate racket. Not many people here could've put two and two together. They didn't know me.

Behind her, fold-up chairs were being brought in. A stand-in for the priest my family had wanted, the funeral director or someone, stood at the front of the room and announced, "Everyone, thank you all for being here. If I could have you finish up your drinks and please start taking your seats, we're going to have a service starting soon."

Ren and I exchanged charged glances.

"Let's wait—" I started.

"Hey there," Cris said.

We both froze. She didn't even search for any kind of familiarity in his face before extending her hand. Her eyes looked dull behind her fixed expression.

"Thanks for coming," she said.

Before I even had a chance to mention it, he asked, "You're her sister?"

"That's right."

He smiled, too big, as if this were a happy occasion. "I, uh, this is a little weird, because she never introduced me or anything…"

She barely raised her eyebrows. I cringed, trying to keep from shaking, my stomach knotting up. He caught on, coughing as he sobered his face and gave his name.

"Um, I guess, she might not have mentioned me. We'd been dating a while. Me and Mal."

Cris hardly reacted, except perhaps with an instinctive glimmer of pity. She probably suspected he thought we were more serious than I intended. I'd always been an escape artist.

"Nice to meet you," she said.

"I mean, it would've been nicer under any other circumstances." She nodded vaguely. "Right."

We ought to have workshopped this more. Come up with a more natural approach.

"Listen," he said. "I don't mean to be like, forward or anything, but I have to tell you."

Ren looked at me expectantly, while she stared at him with the same look. I'd been putting off trying to find the words, hoping that any moment, my instinct for bullshit would kick in like usual, right when we needed it most.

Except he wasn't me. He couldn't flash her my coin-trick smile and dazzle her with the truth.

"Yes?" asked Cris. She looked relieved for the brief rest of waiting, like she'd fallen asleep with her eyes open, forgetting to care what yet another stranger had to say about me.

"So, uh—here's the thing about Mal—"

I gave in to the restlessness in my feet and started to pace. Better than bolting and leaving him there, like my instincts screamed at me to do. I'd gotten him into this. We had to finish it.

But the words still didn't come. My tongue went numb.

He gave up waiting for me, skimming his hands through his hair on his way to clutch the back of his neck. "She's—I mean, she'd been doing way better."

Cris narrowed her gaze, wide awake now. I pressed my hands together, as if in prayer.

"We were good," he said. "Like, really good. Deep in it, you know what I mean? It happened so fast, maybe that's why she didn't mention—"

He'd almost had it. I trembled on his behalf.

"Anyway, it doesn't make sense," he said. "She never would have—"

"What are you saying?" asked Cris, keeping her tone even.

It hadn't been "never." That's what made this so fucking difficult.

Ren gave me one last glance, looking for an out. I shrugged at him. We didn't really have a choice but for him to just say it.

He kept his voice low, so nobody else would hear. "She couldn't have done it."

She let out a clipped breath. "What?"

"Killed herself."

The curtains next to us billowed, but none of the windows were open. It would be too cool outside for air conditioning.

Her jaw clenched, but her voice still fell flat. "Thanks so much for your input. Really, I appreciate it."

"Hold on." He swallowed, voice hoarse. "You believe me, right?"

She didn't quite laugh. It came out more like a sharp exhale, but she grinned, all the same, even as her eyes glinted with tears. It made me shiver.

That wasn't like her at all. More like me, really.

"You know, plenty of strangers have lied to my face about her today," she said. "But yours has got to be the hardest to swallow."

So she'd made up her mind about how I died. I waved my wrists, shuffled my feet, fighting off the strange, encircling ache. At least I didn't have to wonder anymore.

"I'm not lying," he said. "I know her, she wouldn't—"

"Did you?" she asked. "Look, just because she made special friends with you doesn't mean this is any of your business. You don't just talk to people like this! What kind of a psycho are you?"

His whole body tensed, like she'd just slapped him.

The funeral director got up to speak at the pulpit. He tested a mic, though there weren't quite enough people to justify using one.

Cris glanced up, on the verge of turning away.

"Wait—" Ren shot his hand out onto her shoulder.

She jerked away. "Don't touch me."

The office dad, Ted or Todd, sidled up to them. "Is everything OK here?"

Ren put his hands up. "I'm sorry."

"It's fine," said Cris. She shot him a warning glare, like she wouldn't hesitate to ask for help getting him kicked out. "He's having a rough time."

Ted or Todd put his hand on Ren's arm. It could've been either a comfort, or a warning. Ren went rigid, his eyes glazing, but he endured it for a peacekeeping moment before the other man withdrew.

Cris turned and started herding some of our family to their seats, busying herself to the last. Ren and I stared after her.

"Well, fuck," I said.

Deep down, I hadn't really expected this to work, anyway.

But the knots in my stomach eased. I wouldn't be going to hell today. Just enduring the hell on earth of my continued existence, however long that lasted.

FOURTEEN

✦》》 《《✦

I gestured at Ren as best I could without being able to grab his arm. He caught on, following me into a curtained-off little room toward the back of the reception area. This would normally be someplace visitors could go to blow their noses in peace, but it would do for us.

Once we were as alone as we could get, he sighed, burying his brow in his hand. "I fucking croaked back there."

I shrugged, trying my best to hitch up a smile, perhaps lift some of his guilt along with it. "You did good. I didn't."

That did nothing to ease the burden on his brow. "You didn't cross over or anything—does that mean it didn't work?"

"That's not why I wanted to do this."

I could nearly feel the weight of his heavy sigh. "I'm so sorry."

My hands itched. If my words couldn't reach him, perhaps I had nothing left but to try the warmth of touch. Only, I couldn't, of course. I couldn't even attempt to straighten his tie.

"You've done more than you know," I said. "If you want, you don't have to sit through the rest."

"Seriously?" he asked, his face all sober. "I wouldn't miss it."

Finally, he returned my attempt at a smile. I followed as he pushed back the curtain. There were more than enough open seats left.

Everyone around us was whispering as we took our places in the back. The service hadn't started yet. I looked up, and gaped along with everybody else as the funeral director found himself joined at the pulpit. He stepped back in surprise, unintentionally making room for the buxom, bespectacled redhead.

I choked on a laugh. She'd always been good at cracking me up, even while I broke her heart.

Ren stared at me, his eyebrows questioning.

"That's my best friend from college, and, uh, ex."

Vicki wore exactly what she'd always joked she'd wear if I died, black satin with a plunging neckline, and a classic mourning hat, complete with the net. I wondered how she'd found out about this, because I couldn't imagine she'd been invited. Or why she'd even want to come. I didn't know if this meant she'd forgiven me, or she'd come to gloat.

"This is just sad," she said, in her tiny, sultry voice. "I know, it's a wake, it's supposed to be sad. But this is a goddamn tragedy."

Gloria was stony-faced as ever, not about to dignify this interruption with an acknowledgment. Cris, on the other hand, stood up, hovering in indecision. Not so quick to quietly smooth over any interruptions as I'd expected.

The funeral director cleared his throat. "Have some respect."

Vicki reeled on him. "Excuse me, but I have way more respect for her than anybody else here. You all even know who the hell it is you're sending off?"

Good fucking question. Around us, the guests murmured. After all, they clearly didn't know me.

The funeral director left the pulpit purposefully, on his way to find somebody to deal with the situation.

"You call this a wake?" asked Vicki. "There ought to be booze, and beautiful men and women tearing at their hair and clothes, and music, for God's sake!"

My whole body shuddered. I could feel my last meal, climbing up my throat.

"Please don't," I said.

"She was an artist," said Vicki. "That's her biggest legacy."

All the strangers around me were swiveling their heads, talking openly, looking around as if someone here might have an answer. My mother and sister did, of course, but they didn't say anything.

"Shut up," I said.

"You're not even gonna play any of her songs?"

Maybe now they'd start putting two and two together.

I got to my feet. "Would you shut the fuck up?"

They didn't know. I'd worked so hard so they wouldn't know. Better that they thought I'd always been a nobody than a failed somebody.

"She should've gone out in a bang, not this sad little whimper."

One of the lamps behind her blinked a few times.

"That's enough," said the funeral director, returning meekly. Behind him hovered a big guy in a suit, security. He looked apologetic, awkward about putting his hands on a lady, even a rowdy one.

"I'm not finished!"

Vicki complained all the way as security gingerly showed her out. Like she didn't love the dramatic exit.

Cris stepped up in her place. The mic picked up her throat-clearing.

"Well, that was awkward," she said.

That got some surprised laughter, nothing too loud, but enough to relieve the tension.

"She's right, though," said Cris. It went dead quiet. She flashed that brittle, teary-eyed grin again. "We've all been pretending, but isn't it a little late for that? I'm sick of acting like I'm not fucking furious."

My whole body shuddered in surprise. It might've been the first time I'd ever heard her curse. And it wasn't even funny, like I'd always hoped it would be.

Gloria stood, but didn't approach. I wondered if she was frightened, seeing her better daughter behaving this way, realizing it had never been so cut and dry as the golden child and the black sheep.

"Some people still say it's a mortal sin, what she did," said Cris. "I don't wanna believe that I'll have to pray for her the rest of my life to try and get her out of purgatory, not knowing if it's working, if it'll ever be safe to stop."

At last, her mask cracked, tears spilling freely down her cheeks. She struggled to speak past her sobs. I dug my nails into my palms, my own eyes stinging.

The two lamps on either side behind her went out, only the ones overhead keeping the room from darkness.

"But I'm already so tired of praying, and praying, and feeling like an idiot doing it, because I don't even know if there's anybody on the other line. Because what if there's not? What if she's just—" Her voice broke. "*Gone?*"

In the dim light, she crumpled in on herself, our mother rushing and taking her in her arms as if she were about to collapse. I got the wailing I'd hoped for after all.

Something shattered, glass breaking, sunflowers spilling.

"Mal?" Ren said. Out loud, in front of everyone.

The remaining lights went out. But it didn't go dark, not for me. I shut my eyes against the glaring white.

FIFTEEN

❊»» ««❊

I woke up, choking, as if on my own breath. My eyes burned with tears as my body realized ahead of my mind what must've happened. Above me glared the white of a ceiling. My hands shook as they curled into fists, chafing against their restraints.

I'd lived.

Someone must've called the paramedics. I wanted to scream, but I had a tube down my throat, forcing air into my lungs. Thrashing around would've been the next best thing, but they'd tied my wrists and ankles down to the bars of the hospital bed.

Above me floated a familiar face. I'd once known it so well, sneaking glances across the room, picturing it while bent over by my boyfriend, later waking up and staring at him beside me in bed with mingled wonder and guilt. Yet somehow, he looked blurry. His pale, boyish features floated in and out of clarity, like a camera trying to focus. But his green eyes were clear through the haze, normally so bright, turned dull and red.

Just like when we broke up.

You're going to be OK, Liam said. His voice echoed strangely, the movement of his lips not quite lining up with his words.

My ventilator sounded a brief alarm as I laughed without sound. Everything hurt, all tubes and needles and restraints.

He leaned over my bed from a chair pulled up beside it and explained I'd gone into a brief coma after they'd brought me in with five times the safe blood alcohol limit. I'd blacked out whatever I'd done for my intended last night on Earth. I probably couldn't top it if I were to try again. It must've been one hell of a party.

I had to wait hours before I could reply, after proving I could breathe on my own. My voice grated from my aching throat. Where is everybody?

He jerked awake in his chair. It was the first thing I'd managed to say.

I'd just tried drinking myself to death. I would've thought my best friends might notice. Then again, there'd been a reason I hadn't opened up to any of them, other than in song. Perhaps they thought my morbid lyrics were only poetry, that I didn't fucking mean what I wrote. Or they were just happy to profit off my existential despair. Until it got too inconvenient.

You need to rest, *he said, leaning over to tuck in my thin blanket, but not looking at me.*

I shifted, though I didn't have room to flinch from his touch. What does it look like I'm doing?

You shouldn't get too worked up, in your state.

Then tell me, *I said.* Where is everybody?

But I'd known this would happen all along. It hardly came as a surprise when he admitted, They're on the road.

Without us?

He got up from his chair so fast it screeched on the tile floor, so he could pace, as far as possible in the cramped hospital room. We're not stopping the tour.

My throat hurt too much to push up another laugh. So I've got to get better quick.

The room didn't have a window, which would've been better for the glowering he had to do. I'm going to fly to catch up with them. I've got a couple days to stay.

I phrased it more shocked than I really felt. And what about me?

I'll be here with you, *he said, deflecting again.*

I mean, what about your drummer?

He didn't answer, staring at the wall. They'd left my goddamn ex to give me the news, and now, he couldn't even bear to look at me, go for the kill.

My voice croaked, too hoarse to raise it as much as I wanted. Just fucking say it.

I'd replaced their last drummer, and now, they were replacing me. I wondered if they'd left their last one in the hospital as well. If they'd taken off without a word of goodbye.

Maybe this had been my way of quitting before getting fired. That didn't make it hurt any less.

You can't handle the pressure of coming back right now, *he said to the wall, as if rehearsing it.* This lifestyle you're trying to push will be the death of you.

But I'd go out with a bang.

My silent laughter must've been contagious, because he let out a painful giggle of disbelief, finally turning toward me. Weren't you going to wait till you're twenty-seven? You've really taken the whole rock-and-roll martyr persona way too seriously.

I could only lift my hands so far in the restraints, but I still formed the shapes on instinct, echoing my usual finger guns. It's called a coping mechanism.

You mean like your drinking?

That caught me off guard. He'd never brought it up before. It might've been helpful to have this conversation before it became a problem.

Actually, that's called self-medicating, *I said.* All the greats drank. Not to mention, died young.

I cracked my chapped lips trying to flash my coin-trick smile. Now you're getting it.

You always do this, *he said.* Try to joke and charm everyone into thinking you don't mean the fucked-up things you say.

I couldn't tell if that was an excuse, his attempt to deflect the blame. Until he looked me right in the eyes and lied. We only want what's best for you.

So where's the intervention? *I asked.* Here I am, crying for help, and where is everybody?

I had nowhere to go. Good for nothing but this. I'd dropped out of college to go touring. When my mother found out, she'd told me to stay the hell put and finish the pre-law degree she'd funded, or never come back.

He obviously regretted looking straight at me, and yet, he couldn't look away. I must've been a real spectacle, like a pile-up on the highway, or a body falling from a building.

I didn't want this, *he said.*

My eyes ached in lieu of crying, my body too dehydrated to give up any tears. But you're running back to them, aren't you? You're gonna leave me behind, just like that.

I'm not, *he lied.*

You're on your way up, and you can't have me dragging you down.

He snapped, at last. Is that what you were trying to do? Save us the trouble?

The voice of self-loathing in my head couldn't have put it any better than that. His face softened in apology, but he let it hang in the air, unspoken.

Once again, he couldn't bear to face me. You're not dead. Neither is your career. After you get better, you could find another group.

I didn't have the strength to shake my head. I'm not getting better.

What other choice do you have? *He approached the bed, his hand hovering over mine, but he didn't take it.* I don't know how to help you. But you're going to get help, whether you like it or not.

No shit. They wouldn't let me out without detoxing. I had a long way to go before getting out, and once I did, I'd have to start all over again. Only I couldn't repeat a legendary night like that, dying like so many rock stars before me. My wings had melted. I'd have to take some ordinary route, all alone in my bedroom and anonymous once again.

Leave.

He winced. I'm not going to leave you like this.

I pressed the emergency button on the side of my bed. That's exactly what you're going to do.

We kept arguing until the nurse came in. I tried calling after him as they escorted him out, but it came out barely a whimper.

Have a nice life.

All too soon, they moved me from my nice single to the psych ward slash drunk tank, bedded beside the mostly forty- and fifty-year-old alcoholic vets and transients, and one or two people in the middle of some real bad schizophrenic or bipolar episodes. Right in time for me to start having hallucinations. Possibly from withdrawal, or just my own bad brain.

There were angels and demons. I couldn't see them, not quite, manifesting as shadows in the corners, and lights like the passing of cars through the window blinds. They were speaking some language I didn't know, and wished I couldn't understand. But I did. They were arguing over my soul, half-heartedly, as if the angels were only there because they had to be, and the demons knew that.

I laughed, and that triggered one of the other patients into joining me, like they'd missed a joke and pretended to get it, anyway. Someone told us to be quiet, perhaps a nurse. I couldn't remember, all the faces nothing but blurs, because I was too scared to look at any of them dead on.

Only one face stood out in the blue dark.

"Mal," he said.

I knew him. He looked younger, somehow, strapped to one of the beds, like me.

"Ren?"

Then he was standing before me, looking almost like I knew him now, even down to the suit. He appeared translucent, as if he were the ghost. Around him glowed a faint halo, like the rings around the moon.

"I won't let you turn into one of them."

His eyes were so clear, watching from somewhere outside my memory. Unable to reach me. He could only stare, so tender, but useless.

"Stay with me."

For a moment, I thought his glow had lifted the darkness. But he'd disappeared.

And yet, I wasn't alone—though I wasn't in my own head anymore, either.

Once again, I lay strapped to a hospital bed, my wrists and ankles restrained. No, that wasn't right—they were free, but I still couldn't move.

We couldn't move.

The signals were there, synapses frantically firing, but none of our muscles responded, arms and legs offline. Not even a single finger or toe obeyed the command to twitch, let alone the burning urge to flail and thrash as panic built up inside us with no release.

Then our rational brain kicked in. This must've been sleep paralysis. We'd never had it before, but there was a first for everything. Lots of firsts today.

Except I didn't recall going to bed. Coming home from my first real party that night. Saying goodbye to my friends.

Last I remembered, we were driving. I'd almost piped up, said we should order a ride and split the cost, or call somebody's mom and try to act sober, we could always drink some water and hang out a while longer and get in trouble over curfew instead.

But I hadn't said anything. I didn't want their last memory of me to be ruining the coming-of-age movie moment. So we drove, with the skylight open and two of us standing up with hands in the air, all of us laughing and singing along to the radio, and then—

No, no, no no no—

I couldn't even cry, let alone scream. The darkness just went on and on. Voices came and went. None of them belonged to my friends.

Over time, I started recognizing the nurses and doctors. I could tell from each touch as they exercised my limbs, and whether they spoke to me, if they thought I was still in here at all.

Mom and Dad tried to talk as if everything were normal. They told me about their days like they were picking me up from school or sitting down to dinner. Never telling me to please wake up, not give up, come back. I wished they would. I needed the help.

Leah never said much. But it sounded like her crying, sometimes.

Of course, I tried to wake up. Every single day. It got harder and harder to tell the days apart from inside my head. After the first few months, or years, I stopped trying. And stopped caring. After so long, I started trying the opposite. Going to sleep. The even bigger one.

At long last, it happened. I couldn't breathe. My lungs pounded empty and dark, like the opposite of a birth cry. I welcomed the change of pace.

Someone lifted me up. Finally, I could open my eyes. And, instead of a blur of color, my vision turned out clear.

I found myself looking up in the arms of a beautiful man. He must've been an angel. My heart-rate monitor wailed behind us, flatlining as he grinned down at me.

I tried to speak, to ask if I were dreaming, but I couldn't remember how.

You're not dreaming, *the angel said.*

"Wake up," said Evie.

Stage Four:
Reinvesting

SIXTEEN

✻》》 《《✻

Evie and I both gasped. I looked down at both our crumpled bodies, my bony nothing and her soft plenty, trying to convince myself we were separate. I couldn't quite remember where I even met her. Her dress looked like a hospital gown. But she didn't look like one of the psych ward patients, as far as I could remember. Beneath us, grass glowed in the sun. Were we in rehab together or something?

No. I didn't go to rehab. And I'd never met this girl in my life.

"Am I dead?" I asked.

She nodded, looking as if she were struggling to speak. I squinted up to find us on the lawn outside the funeral home.

"You were going geist," she said, her voice hoarse like she hadn't used it in years. "Good thing I came to check on you. I almost left right away when things were getting awkward with that lady with the hat, but... well, I'm glad I stuck around. I barely managed to get in your head enough to pull us both out."

It seemed obvious, now, given how patchy my memories were, that I hadn't really gone back. Like in a dream, I couldn't recognize it while it was happening. If I'd kept looping back, like the geists I'd touched, I might never have gotten out.

"Did you see all that?" I asked.

She started to shrug, but turned it into a hesitant nod.

Well, fuck. That explained the pity in her eyes when she finally glanced up. I couldn't handle it. There'd be no taking back what I'd shared. Getting my clothes torn off by a stranger had nothing on the nakedness of a memory laid bare. I had no choice but to sit there and simmer in shame, too late to try and cover up.

"I don't understand," she said.

I shut my eyes. I could just recall where my memories had blurred into her own. That must've given her the chance to take over, pull me from my mind to hers. She'd only wished for death long after her will to live had burned out, like a signal flare unseen by passing ships. I couldn't imagine what she thought of me having once chased it, trying to drown myself.

Her voice trembled. "How could they do that to you?"

At last, I met her gaze.

"You loved them so much," she said.

The tears came hot and stinging, held back for too long. Years, in fact. At least my wrists didn't ache. Just aftershocks, not another disaster.

Since she'd already seen enough, I went ahead and filled in the gaps. At least I kept my voice steady.

"My sister and I could open up when we were alone, but… well, I always worried she secretly judged me, believing I was a sinner. So when I first met my bandmates, it clicked. Oh—so this is what I've been missing out on all my life, what family means. I got to be myself, judgment-free. We were going to take over the world together. And we got so close."

Just telling it made me nearly forget what happened next. Because even afterwards, I still missed them. Rather, who I thought they were.

"But then… I got down again. I kind of hoped I'd beaten my old existential despair, that it would never come back. When it did, it turned out they weren't really the family I'd thought. Not so interested in me sad and useless."

She wiped her face. I kind of felt bad for having pushed my feelings on her, literally, and again, out loud.

"I did some dumb shit to retaliate." I couldn't bear to elaborate how I'd started missing writing and recording sessions. Whenever I had shown up, I'd fought them on every single decision. Up until it escalated to taking Liam's favorite guitar and smashing it, before storming off and setting my lyric notebook on fire. "…You know, typical diva stuff."

And I didn't even touch on any of the love triangle bullshit.

"That only made them resent me more, gave them reason to cut me off. Just like my mother." I smiled, because I couldn't go on this long without making a joke. "You ever get the feeling you're not wanted?"

She didn't return the smile, not letting me off the hook yet. "That's not true."

On instinct, I opened my mouth to protest, only to let it hang for a moment. After all, I hadn't even cried for help, and yet, she'd answered. For some reason, she must've liked me.

"Why risk it?" I asked. "I mean, pulling me out."

Her big eyes were so earnest it made me ache. "I'm sure you would've helped me the same."

Whatever gave her that impression, I only hoped I could live up to her high esteem. It didn't sit right, how big I owed her, given how I tended to disappoint.

"Thanks," I said, though that didn't nearly cover it.

At last, I had to ask about what she'd shared in return.

"So… about Alastair."

Her cheeks darkened, like I'd found out a secret. Funny that we'd both confused him for something else. No wonder she'd taken him for an angel. The first face she'd seen in years, after so much darkness. And he'd delivered her from it.

"He killed you?"

"It sounds awful, when you put it like that," she said, looking down, tugging nervously at the grass. "I wanted to die. He could feel it. So, he helped me out."

I didn't blame her. I'd thought I felt trapped in this phantom body. At least I could still see and hear and move around. No wonder she hadn't even felt scared when she found herself lifted up in nice, solid arms. It had felt so good, that memory of touch. Better than needles and restraints, anyway—and yet, weirdly enough, my body felt so numb now, without even that. Even if it was painful, it had still been something to feel.

"How did he find you?" I asked.

"Don't tell him I said so, but he wanders a lot. All over, but especially hospitals and old folks' homes and such. He's more thoughtful than he lets on, always trying to find answers. Not to mention bringing home the newly dead. For all that he acts so cool and mysterious, he's secretly a softie."

She smiled, like she couldn't help it, her mouth curling irresistibly at the thought of him. I winced with an unwelcome pang as I realized she must feel more than gratitude toward him.

"But, like I said, don't tell."

"I won't," I promised.

At last, we both got up, brushing our clothes like we could've had any grass clinging on.

"I take it you're not joining the band anytime soon," she said.

I just shook my head, wrung out but lighter. At least she

understood. I couldn't even look at a drum set, any more than she could have a drink.

"So, what are you going to do now?" she asked.

"I don't know."

I couldn't go back to check on my family. Not yet. Now that Cris had finally let herself cry for me, I didn't know when it might stop. Whether it might trigger this reaction all over again.

"You could still come to the Haunt," she said.

My feet didn't exactly feel lively. Not with my sister's wails still echoing in my head, so much louder than the memory of the pulse.

She must've caught on to my hesitation. "You don't have to play, or even dance, if you're not ready."

"Are you sure about that?" I asked, unable to help but raise an eyebrow. "Alastair is a menace. Why doesn't he bother you about joining, anyway?"

She fiddled with her sleeves. "It's kind of complicated."

That must've been his tailcoat she wore. He probably had to give it to her every morning, so she wouldn't have to worry about the slit in the back of her hospital gown.

As much as I wanted to pester about how she'd gotten a pass, I couldn't hold it against her if she had more secrets. We'd already swapped so many.

Her eyes widened with panic, like she'd remembered something she shouldn't have forgotten. "Ren must be worried sick about you."

My chest caved in.

"He tried to get through to you, only he couldn't, with a body between his soul and yours. Not to mention, there were so many people around."

As badly as I wanted to go to him, I couldn't take off like I usually did. Not after what she'd done for me. I put up my walls and reached for her hand, giving it a squeeze.

"Don't be a stranger," she said.

"I won't," I promised.

I'd try my best to keep to it. Though my best had never been much.

Ren hunched on the hood of his car, burning furiously through a cigarette.

"That'll kill ya," I said. "If you live long enough."

He dropped it in surprise, gaping at me. I stepped back as he sprang up, holding out his arms, reaching for me. Before I could think to reach back, work out some kind of embrace, he let his arms drop, folding them around himself instead. I did the same.

"I heard you were looking for me."

"I didn't know if I'd ever see you again," he said. "At least, not as yourself."

His eyes were red. I couldn't imagine how he'd taken it, thinking he'd lost the only witness to his sanity.

He buried his face in his palm. "It's been a long time since I've looked this crazy."

I thought to try putting my hand on his shoulder. Instead, I said, "I think it helped, seeing you."

That drew him back out of hiding. "Really?"

"I don't know what it is about you, but your soul is real bright in the dark."

Maybe that's why geists followed him around, moths to light. Since he'd already died once, perhaps he hadn't shut the door all the way closed when his soul returned to his body, leaving it open just a crack.

His smile didn't last long. "So… what's the plan?"

I turned up my palms. "Well, uh, we need to regroup. My sister hates your guts now, and I almost lost my metaphysical mind. I think we need a breather—so to speak."

"Same here," he said. "What are you gonna do now?"

I didn't bother holding in my sigh. "Looks like I'm not going anywhere, huh? I mean, not that I really looked forward to facing my eternal judgment, but…"

I'd have to keep busy if I didn't want to dwell too hard and go geist again.

"You know…" He bit his lip. "If you ever want to hang out again, I'd be down."

That put a spot of color on my own cheeks, judging from the burn. I should've told him I'd interrupted his life enough. He deserved better company than mine.

But I could use the distraction. I almost forgot I didn't need to breathe, my voice close to cracking. "Cool."

He grinned. "Uh, are you doing anything later? I mean—not to rub it in, whether or not you're able to do things—but I know you like watching stuff, and going out might make you feel better after today, so…"

I blinked. That sounded awfully like he'd just asked me out.

"I'm not," I said. "I mean—doing anything."

I didn't know what to do with myself, period. I wasn't sure I could even risk going to my funeral anymore. Since I still couldn't touch anything, I couldn't even pick up a book to while the time away. Or join a poker game with the other ghosts, not that they'd be my first choice for company.

If I wouldn't be crossing over anytime soon, I had to occupy myself somehow. I wondered if boredom alone could tilt me toward going geist. But at least having just this one thing on my agenda would make it feel less like I didn't have any future at all.

My face flushed, for some reason, as I smiled up at him. "I mean, I'm free."

I guessed he thought I wouldn't notice the way he bunched his right hand at his side, in a quiet echo of a fist pump. "Well, you know where to find me. I'm gonna nap, but come by anytime."

He did look wrecked. I'd thoroughly destroyed his sleep schedule, and not in the way I usually preferred. Too bad that wouldn't be on the table.

Well, unless I could finally get touch figured out. I shouldn't have trusted the advice of the first ghosts I'd questioned, anyway. As much as I hated having to ask around for help again if I kept lingering on my own, I might just wither away.

I flexed my fingers, looking him up and down in that now rumpled suit, his hair mussed from stress ruffling. Maybe, after some practice, I'd have way more fun in store for me than books or poker.

"So, I'll see you?" he asked.

I resorted to my usual finger guns. "It's a date."

SEVENTEEN

❋》》 《《❋

The pulse greeted me with too much familiarity, wrapping around me like a lover trying to coax me back into bed. I closed my eyes and, with a sigh, let it in. It couldn't really tempt me, not in the late afternoon sun. My feet were rooted, hands static, hips dull. Perhaps that would change once the band went from warming up to full heat.

"Welcome back," said Evie. She sat at her piano, as usual, across the hall from the ballroom. "That didn't take long."

"I'm not here," I said. "Just stopping by."

She smiled up at me. It weighed down my chest, seeing her in the same spot yet again.

"Is this all you do every day?" I asked.

"That's how I play so well." I couldn't tell if she were showing off, talking and looking at me without missing a beat, until she dipped her head down as if to withdraw her words. "I mean, I'm no virtuoso or anything, I've only had lots of time to practice." She widened her eyes at me for emphasis. "Lots of time."

I watched her fingers dancing across the keys, sick with nostalgia.

"You play?" she asked.

"I don't," I said, on instinct. Then I remembered what she'd seen in my memory, so I shook my head and took it back. Besides, I had a different stage in mind than usual. "I mean, I haven't played in years."

It had been my first instrument. I'd taken private lessons from our church's organ player from seven years old until well into my teens. My mother once thought she could channel my passions toward God. As much as I'd hated playing nothing but hymns, I'd loved my first taste of an audience during recitals, even if my heavenly father never did show up.

I'd switched to guitar—and finally drums—as soon as I'd left home and started college. But it had been long enough now that I might not feel like I'd just stepped back into church.

"Wanna give it a try?" asked Evie.

She scooted over on her little bench, making room for me. My chest nearly buckled, but at least I had a good excuse to turn her down, and a segue to the reason I'd come.

"I don't know how to touch on this side."

"I'll show you."

I did need to learn. It might even make it easier to try it out on something so familiar. She must've read into the stillness of my mask.

"You don't have to," she said.

She sounded guilty. But I'd already thrown my weight into it, hard, just to get myself to budge, and now I couldn't stop the momentum. I drifted closer, standing and letting my fingers float over the keys. It felt like lifting a sheet in an attic, coughing up dust.

I pressed my forefinger down. It took a moment for me to hear the silence as it went straight through the key. That delayed my huff of frustration.

"You've got to try to forget you're dead," said Evie.

I still didn't know what that meant. Telling me to forget only reminded me of my condition. Looking at my hand, I wouldn't have been surprised to find it see-through, as intangible as I felt. Pretending to still be flesh and blood seemed so stupid when I knew the truth.

I let my hand drop, backing away. "As if."

Around us, the shadows were dragging long, the light turning golden as the sun began to set. Voices laughed in the hallway, ghosts holding hands and spinning and shimmying past the doorway, already warming up to dance, as the pulse pitched louder and louder. On instinct, my toes started to tap.

"Um," said Evie. She stood awkwardly. "I have to go, but... I'll catch you another time?"

She had to be more tempted than she let on. I wondered where she went to distract herself during the nights.

"Sure thing," I said.

She spirited off. After a moment, I did the same.

Alastair probably wouldn't be dancing yet, busy pregaming at Clementine's. As much as I didn't want him to know I hadn't crossed, if I wanted to last on this side, I really needed the use of my hands.

The Haunt looked different in the daytime, broken windows catching the late afternoon sun as if glowing from the inside. When I'd first seen it in darkness, I hadn't noticed the chain-link fence with barbed wire on top, let alone the lonely urban street. I'd assumed it stood miles outside of city limits, where it could be left undisturbed. Instead, it loomed on the corner of a quiet intersection, boarded on one side by younger, smaller houses; on the other, and across the street, there gaped empty lots of grass.

It looked out of place. Out of time. It must've watched its historical brother and sister buildings in the surrounding plots come down. The only one left of its kind, like a mammoth, or an ancient shipwreck.

Alastair worked in the yard, among the overgrown grass and towering weeds. He grunted, probably more from frustration than actual effort, as he tugged at something. I moved closer for a glance.

It looked like a sign. My dead heart skipped a beat as I skimmed, hoping it wouldn't say **FOR SALE**.

Even worse, it read:

VANCE PROPERTIES

The sign came crashing down, dented in half with a good kick.

"Don't fret," said Alastair. "We're always passing from owner to owner. But the damage is too extensive, both repairs and demolition too expensive, and, of course, I've gotten very good at making appraisers feel…" He paused, but then went for it with a slight bow. "…Apprehensive."

I rolled my eyes.

"Anyway, you're still here?" he asked, busying himself breaking apart the wooden supports, bit by bit. "Did you finish your business?"

I flung out my hands, gesturing to my continued person. "What do you think?"

He scoffed, punctuating his words with snapping wood. "Oh, the whole notion's balderdash. You really think most folk die with absolutely nothing left unsaid, no duties left unfilled, dreams unsatisfied? We'd be swimming in a sea of souls if that's why we linger. You're fortunate the whole effort didn't make you go geist."

I pouted, though he didn't look up to appreciate it. "Aren't you relieved to see me, then?"

"Not during the day. Did I forget to tell you? If you need me, it has to wait till after sundown."

How many other chores did he perform that he didn't want anyone to catch him doing? It certainly clashed with his carefree facade.

"Isn't it sundown somewhere?" I asked.

He gave back my eyeroll. "Why are you pestering me?"

"Just returning the favor," I said. "And, uh…" I nearly choked on the words. Half of them didn't come out. "I need to touch."

At last, he looked up with his usual grin. "Where's the romance? We may have had a few drinks, but we still haven't danced."

I didn't want to give him the satisfaction of a glare, but I couldn't help it. "I swear on my grave I am never going to dance with you."

He sucked in a hiss of a breath, his lips puckered. "Your poor grave."

"Are you going to help me or not?"

"I've been trying." His voice grated with weariness.

"Well, I'm ready now."

He picked up a piece of the post and tossed it in the air before catching it. Then he threw it toward me. It fell through my hands, disappearing into the long grass.

"There's a trick to it," he said. "You have to forget you're dead."

Evie must've been echoing him earlier. I wondered how many other people he'd tutored before me, making our afterlives easier to endure.

"Of course, it helps to have some distraction," he added. "Up for a drink?"

Clementine's must've barely opened for the evening, though it already had plenty of drinkers to choose from, lining up in the last light of sunset pouring through the windows. He paraded us straight through all of them, since they were only tipsy, nobody full-on drunk quite yet. But putting them all together gave me the spins. Like my first time, I stumbled, my feet looking for ground and finding nothing. I might've let out a yelp.

Alastair laughed, putting his hands on my shoulders. "Steady there."

He spirited us straight upstairs, letting go and pulling a pool cue off the wall rack. "Here's to a second chance."

The cue left his hand, flying toward me. I put out my hand, but just as my fingers began to curl around the wood, I flinched with doubt. The cue slipped straight through my arm and my body, clattering somewhere behind me.

The noise didn't stop. Suddenly, all the billiard balls scattered across the table, smacking into each pocket, leaving only the nine-ball. It was too deliberate a move to be a geist fit.

Alastair let his head loll in a weary tilt. "What's it going to take?"

He took up another cue, bowed deeply, and sank the last ball. Just for show, since, apparently, he didn't even need to use his hands to bend the world to his will.

"Were you forgetting about being dead just there?" I asked. "It looks like you're really enjoying it."

"I doubt you'd find that approach any more fruitful," he said. As he ranted, his accent swayed more and more British. I wondered if he reverted when he drank. "In all my years, I've never met such a killjoy. You won't play, you won't dance, you won't let yourself savor a single whim. If it weren't for your portrait in the papers, I would've thought I had the wrong girl. For fuck's sake, take a look at yourself."

He threw up his hands, his inflection swinging all the way back to American. "I'd take you for a wallflower, except if you were, I would've *rocked* your fucking *world* by now."

I spent too long spluttering for a response. "I'm not a killjoy."

"So prove it, would you?"

My lips pursed as I thought about it. Back in the day, I wouldn't have hesitated before crawling into his lap. I'd never let a dare go unanswered.

But he wouldn't be easy to escape in the morning. He could just spirit after me.

As he watched me and waited, he sighed. "I fucking beg of you."

"Is this all it takes?" asked the corseted lady, followed closely by the guitar gent and the flapper. "If I held out on you for a decade or so, would that be long enough for you to come pleading back to me?"

"You'd never last that long," scoffed the guitar gent.

"I would, as long as you'd be gracious enough to keep me company," she said, tucking herself under his arm, even guiding his hand down into her bust.

"What makes you think I'd be fool enough to believe you this time around?" he asked, even as he indulged in exploring, taking the obvious bait. I couldn't watch, my skin flushing hot.

The flapper sighed in boredom. I wondered how many decades it had taken them all to hook up, or whether it had happened right away. They were obviously close enough to be family, like my band, but with a way longer lifespan. This pseudo-incestuous tension felt exactly the same. Sometimes it took bringing in fresh meat to break it.

I wanted absolutely no part in that—not again. Maybe I couldn't have helped that sleeping with my band's lead guitar before joining had led to somewhat reluctantly dating him for real after he asked me to fill for their drummer. And maybe I couldn't help falling for our bassist, either. But we had to see each other every day, crammed in the same tour buses and hotel rooms and backstage hallways. Boyfriends and side guys should never be that close, let alone help write songs about each other.

And I *really* shouldn't have tried rubbing out our poor shy keyboardist so he wouldn't feel neglected. That one was definitely on me. Giving up and declaring myself the bad guy had felt so satisfying, like when I'd abandoned the notion of ever getting into heaven as a teen, reveling in causing as much trouble as I could on the path to hell.

"It must be the years and years of never learning," said the flapper. She'd gone from bored to restless, looking at me with slightly tipsy desperation. She turned to Alastair. "You ever consider that you're not her type?"

"You're always trying to poach," said the guitar gent, tearing himself away from a kiss long enough to speak. I wondered how long it would take to get her out of that corset.

"Go on and try," said Alastair.

"Why, don't mind if I do," the flapper retorted.

She smiled like a starlet, totally out of my league, yet still reaching for me with teasing fingers. I wavered, but at the last moment, shrank away from all of them. Even if my skin was numb, my mouth sick of its own taste, I'd already bared too many memories today. And if I did get all the way naked, I didn't know what I feared more: being pressured to play, or tossed aside.

"See what I mean?" said Alastair. "She's just a drag."

I'd probably be better off figuring out how to touch on my own.

EIGHTEEN

✹》》 《《✹

Ren woke, rousing from his blanket nest and yanking off his headphones, like he could sense my presence. He blinked, stifling a yawn before grinning. "Mal."

I dropped down beside him. "So, what are we watching?"

"I'm not sure yet," he said, getting up and heading for his closet. He kept talking as he pulled some jeans over his boxers and a flannel shirt over his tee, then donned his eternal hoodie. "There's this historic theatre that looks really cool. They play classics and artsy shit. I've been wanting to go forever. I drive by it all the time. You know, like, dropping people off for date nights. They usually only play one or two movies a night, so we'll see what it is." He turned to me, biting his lip. "How does that sound?"

Back in the day, catching a movie meant my date and I weren't really going to watch anything. But he couldn't exactly take me to dinner instead.

"What are we waiting for?"

He got the door for me, even if I didn't need it.

I tried not to think too hard about what the hell we were even doing. We took the subway uptown, so we wouldn't have to worry about parking, but probably more because he could use the break from driving. There were too many other passengers around for us to talk, but that suited me fine.

Once we got off the train, we walked for a while, down a rain-slick street lined with young trees and glowing shops. Leaves hovered thick over our heads, like a party pavilion, while the moon swung like a lantern between the branches. From a distant coffee shop spilled the hum and trill of live jazz. I bet the air smelled sweet with wet green and rich coffee.

"How's the weather?" I asked.

"Hmm?" he said, seemingly distracted, though I couldn't tell by what.

"Never mind."

His lips parted in protest, but before he could speak, we were split up by a passing couple. I barely moved through a chalkboard café sign in time to avoid picking up any emotional broadcast. By the time we'd let them move out of earshot, the moment had passed, and he didn't bring it up again.

Across the street, as we approached, the theatre greeted us with old-fashioned rows of lightbulbs all around the matinee. Neither of us had heard of the French film displayed most prominently, but we agreed it might not have drawn too much of a crowd tonight.

He couldn't pronounce the title at the ticket window. It made the pretty brunette behind the glass smile.

"All alone?" she asked.

"No," he said, blinking in puzzlement, before shaking his head and saying, "Yes, maybe, I don't know."

She laughed. "I hope she shows up."

It didn't sound like she did. I should've tried giving him a nudge or something, but I didn't think of it until after he took the tickets. The tips of their fingers brushed.

Such a tiny touch. I wouldn't have thought twice about it in life. Now, my skin itched with heat. Not in a good way.

He gave a nearly surly "Thanks!"

As soon as we had some space to ourselves, he said, "She thinks I'm getting stood up tonight."

"So she hopes."

He gave a shrug of disbelief. "Why?"

I bit my lip to keep from laughing too hard. He shrugged harder at me for an explanation, but I didn't want to tell him. I tried not to think about why my tight chest eased in relief.

Once again, he held the door open for me. Inside, there were too many people, lined up for snacks and browsing the posters and holding hands as they made their exit. I fell behind, trying to avoid touching any of them.

Ren waited as best he could without looking like it. He didn't get the chance to hold the door for me again, swept up by the herd entering the theatre all at once. As I tried to keep up, the door shut through me.

The silver light from the screen fell on far too many filled seats. He met me in front of the stairs, eyes flicking between me and the illuminated faces. I brushed past him, leading the way up the stairs to sit in the last row. He sank down beside me. I held up my hands in defeat, and he nodded silently, lips tight, as commercials played out in light across his face.

We were surrounded. There were singles and groups and couples. Too many couples. Teenage, middle age, even some elderly couples, sitting with nothing to divide them, arms over shoulders, heads on chests. In front of us, a hand appeared and disappeared. Under long hair, over skin. Now you see it, now you don't. Where did it go? Down a blouse, between legs?

Ren kept his hands in his lap, forced into fists. I clasped mine, leaning forward to trap them between my knees. Once the movie started rolling, we relaxed a little, but not all the way. There were a lot of romantic scenes.

Afterwards, we waited for the crowd to disperse before sneaking out through the emergency exit. We fell in step under the neon light outside. A breeze carried the lilt of a piano, probably the smell of popcorn as well. It whirled the dead leaves around our feet and tugged like a flirt at his hair and clothes. I shivered, though my clothes hung limp around me, my skin unpinched by cool air. Aside from my feet. Those were still chilled from dangling over the edge of the rooftop. I bent and touched them, like I could gather the cold and rub it over the rest of me.

"What are you doing?" asked Ren, with a laugh in his voice.

I stood, smoothing my hands over my arms. "How's the weather?"

"What do you mean?"

"I can't feel it. Please, tell me. How does it feel?"

He stared, dark eyes brimming, though I couldn't tell with what, under his gently furrowed brow. His open mouth finally settled on the shadow of a smile.

"It's cool. Just enough to bite, but kind of playful, you know, like in a Christmas carol. It smells like rain and leaves and popcorn. There's a breeze that goes right through your clothes. You'd be freezing in that outfit. I'd have to give you my hoodie."

My knees shook, as if I really were cold. I shivered and wrapped my arms around myself. He laughed.

As we fell back in step, walking down the street, I froze at a sound from somewhere below us. I lifted my foot. We both looked down at the flattened leaf under my heel.

"Huh," said Ren.

I gaped at him. He happened to be the closest thing I could touch. I tried grasping at the strings of his hoodie. Though I couldn't feel them, they tightened. He stared down at my hands.

"You can touch?" he asked.

That cut off my laugh. Probably not. But we only had one way to find out.

I held up my hand. He did the same. We lined them up, slowly drawing closer, like we were about to try one of those old, old ballroom dances, before the waltz, back when people got married having only ever circled each other palm to palm.

"Bottoms up," I said.

Our fingertips wisped together, overlapping in our respective planes. My whole body bloomed with sudden warmth. Those might've been his butterflies in my stomach. They sank all too soon, dead weight.

My hand tingled, but not from the thrill of skin on skin. There was no physical friction. His fingers hovered through mine, unable to hold.

"You feel anything?" I asked.

His voice rasped. "Yeah."

"I mean, like—"

He shrugged, his warmth slowly receding in the wake of his doubt. It made me shiver. "Well, not physically. Just your presence, which feels good, in a strange way, but—"

"Not as good as a warm body."

I wouldn't get to find out whether his lips were as soft as they looked. If they tasted sweet.

We dropped our hands. He stuck his in his pockets, gnawing his lip. I brushed mine over my hair, my skirt, feeling myself in lieu of him.

"Well, shit," he said.

"Never mind, I guess."

He looked me up and down, taking in everything he'd be missing out on, before fixing on my face. His shoulders heaved with a deep inhale. "So, um, just to be clear… you'd only be down if we could actually smash?"

I cracked up, not expecting him to say it out loud. The longer I laughed, the hollower it felt.

"You know me," I said. "Skin deep."

That ought to have broken the way he stared at me. But it didn't. He kept on gazing, taking me in the only way he could. I wanted to bury myself in the dark earth of those eyes. "I guess you'd be mad if I, like, fell in love with you?"

I choked on a weird noise, unable to keep it down. It might've passed for a scoff. So I grinned, playing as if I were still laughing, instead of tearing up.

"Fucking livid," I said. "Don't try any sappy shit."

He held up his palms in surrender, smiling back. "I won't."

As we fell quiet, we couldn't keep our mouths hitched up for long.

"This sucks," he said.

I shook my head. "You're better off. I would've ruined your life. Just like I did with mine."

He had no business looking at me so warmly. "At least you would've done something interesting with it."

"Go on and have some adventures for me."

"I'll try," he said. "Is this it, then? You'd rather not hang, until… whenever you want to try again with Cris?"

If I couldn't pull my usual one-nighter and had to spend actual time with him, I didn't know what would happen. We'd been stupid to try reaching my sister so soon, ambushing her when she'd barely even begun processing my death. We needed to wait until the wound wasn't so fresh, at least another month or so. If I could last that long on this side.

That would be way too much quality time together. No guarantee that it wouldn't get sappy.

But I couldn't put all that into words. So I just said, "Nah."

At least that got a laugh, if a broken one.

I never usually stuck around to say goodbye. Most of my dates ended with sneaking out in the morning. For once, I didn't want to leave, even if we were only dragging out the unfairness of the whole shitty situation.

I gave him my best effort. "Thanks for this."

"Anytime," he said. "I wanted you to have some fun, after what's happened to you. You deserve better."

I stared into his eyes, but they didn't mirror any of my usual tricks back at me. Those depths turned up nothing but sheer earnestness. "You really think so?"

He nodded, his voice dropping nearly to a whisper. "I'm glad we met."

At least it had happened, if a little too late.

Slowly and carefully, so I could move away if I wanted, he dipped his head down. I gasped as his lips alighted on mine. Though our mouths could only graze through each other, unable to taste, explore deeper, the warmth of his longing burned hot. It seared like thawing from numbing cold, tingling with the best kind of pain.

When he pulled away, I still ached with hunger.

His voice rasped breathless. "See you around?"

Unfortunately. I could only nod in response.

He took a few backward steps, still looking at me, before finally turning to leave. I watched him go, wondering if it was still his regret tightening my chest, or my own.

We really shouldn't have done that.

NINETEEN

❋》》 《《❋

My apartment loomed empty. No more dishes in the sink, junk piled on the counters, trash starting to stink. All my furniture had probably been donated. Someone else would be leaving half-finished beer on my coffee table and having sex on my old couch. I'd bet the girls who wore my clothes next would look nicer in them, with better jobs and brighter futures.

Too bad I couldn't use my laptop anymore. I'd come back hoping to catch up on some TV. But this would be for the best. I would have been all alone here, just like everyone warned me I shouldn't be.

Time for me to move on, find a new place to stay. I wondered how other ghosts kept from going geist, if they didn't reside at the Haunt.

Those kids back at the morgue seemed to be doing all right. But they were together. That must've been how they managed to last so long, even while doing nothing but talking to the newly dead. I didn't think they were a couple, but there had to have been some nights they'd at least huddled close, let some memories slip through the skin. For research, if nothing else.

I went to go check on them, hoping I wouldn't end up witnessing the worst kind of cautionary tale. Thankfully, I found them sitting side by side on the floor of another morgue. This one stored its cadavers in drawers.

"This isn't really happening," Carlos recited. "You people are a figment of my dying consciousness."

Danny sighed as she dragged her pen across the page. "So self-centered."

"Hey, there," I said.

They both jolted in surprise, staring up at me.

"Come on, guys, you know what we are?" I asked. "You shouldn't be spooked so easily."

Carlos peered up at me, somewhat warily. "Mal, right? I didn't think you'd come back."

"No one's ever come back," said Danny. She didn't stop scribbling.

I'd forgotten that my goodbye last time hadn't been the friendliest. But I could make up for it. I had some pretty valuable data for them.

"I've got something to show you."

Since I didn't particularly want to touch any autopsy instruments, I pulled on one of the drawers. It came out unoccupied, so I hopped onto it, posing with a bit of showmanship, grinning at my captive audience.

Danny dropped her pen, her hands flapping in excitement. Carlos whistled.

"How are you doing that?" asked Danny.

"It's easy, after the hard part, which is forgetting we shouldn't be able to touch."

Carlos tried it, going for another drawer. His hand went through it. He tried again, and again. "It's not working. Am I broken?"

"Let me try," said Danny. She passed the notebook to him and did the same thing, reaching right through the drawer.

Slowly and deliberately, I leaned in and opened the drawer. It came with the shape of a bag-covered head peeking out, so I quickly slammed it shut again.

"Give it time," I said. "Besides, that's not all."

I motioned for them to approach. Neither of them took my offered palms. Not yet.

"What is it?" asked Danny.

"Come with me."

Carlos reached for my hand first. Danny tucked her notebook and pen into her bag, slinging it over her shoulder before following suit. Though I tried keeping my walls up, their apprehension soaked through their shaky fingers.

As the sterile walls turned pocked and covered in vines, both grasped my hands tighter, the pulse rattling us to the bone. They turned to stare in awe through the doors of the ballroom at all the phantom dancers, blue as smoke in the moonlight.

"This is a good sample size, isn't it?"

Danny's gape turned into a giggle. She sniffled, drawing a sleeve over her face. Carlos put his arms around her, laughing into her hair.

"Would you like to dance?" I asked. Not that I'd join them, yet, but just to give them a nudge.

Her averted glance seemed a bit shy. Another wallflower. "We've got a lot of work to do."

"Come on, it could wait," he said, already bouncing to the beat. "We deserve to party."

"For real?" she asked, still sniffly. She tapped her fingers to her lips. "After all we've been through for this information, you want to drop it and risk forgetting, so you can go rave?"

He went still, bending down to look her in the eyes. "I would never forget any of it."

"What if you do, though?"

"I won't!"

She tapped even faster. I was about to offer to keep her company if he still wanted to go dance, but then he rolled his eyes, putting an arm around her. She busied her hand returning his embrace instead.

"Whatever, professor," he said. "No fun till homework's done, right?"

They shared a laugh into each other's shoulders before pulling apart, composing themselves, like they'd forgotten they had an audience.

"How'd you guys meet?" I asked.

They looked at each other, wondering who should tell the story.

"We met at a morgue," he said, with all the due morbidity of that locale.

"Where else?" she added cheerily.

"She surveyed me, of course."

"He kept coming back and asking me how it was going, even when I hadn't met any more people to survey."

"I felt bad for bothering her so much, so I said I'd help."

She gawked at him. "Is that why?"

He threw his hands up. "You were so obviously annoyed by me!"

Her bashful dithering owned up to it. "I mean, I wouldn't have minded, but I had so much data to remember, and you kept wanting to talk about music and stuff."

"That's why I volunteered, so we could keep talking."

She seemed torn between injury and gratitude. "What about the science?"

"I'm all for science!" he said, like it went without saying, something everyone could get behind, like chocolate. "But the company wasn't bad, either."

They might've forgotten all about me, from the way they were beaming at each other. It ached, seeing how little they had in common, and how much they still loved each other anyway. Even if it came out of necessity, of having no other choice for company. They'd thought they were alone, adrift at sea. Then they were sharing a life raft.

I wondered if it would last, now they'd reached land, and had other options to not be alone.

They turned back to me at last. "Have you got anything to write on?" he asked.

In the library, amongst the ancient tomes and yellowing paperbacks, I found an old but blank leather journal. They both managed to get a hold of it, but Carlos let Danny hold it to her chest.

She turned to me. "I can't tell you how much this means to us."

I didn't know what to say. I tried shrugging it off.

"I'd better get to writing," she said.

They curled up side by side. "You have a pen?"

We scoured the entire library, until we must've displaced every piled book, stirring up a storm of dust.

"We'll find one," I promised.

Evie would know where to look. But when I tried spiriting to her, it only brought me into the midst of the dancers. Just as I remembered she didn't dance, the sound and crowd and pound of the pulse swallowed me up, going to my head like wine. Someone took my hand.

I forgot why I'd come as I let myself be taken for the ride.

I couldn't help but answer the call spoken through skin, telling me to brace myself for a whirl. My stomach leaped with a roller-coaster thrill as the flapper girl spun me around, her dress bright as city lights against the warm dark night of her skin. She laughed—and for a moment, as our hands touched and she taught me dances long dead without speaking a word, I fell a little in love with her.

My heart broke when she let go and went shimmying away, until I fell into another's arms. His body barely let mine know ahead of time before he lifted me up high and suddenly dipped me back down, through the arch of his legs. When he put me back on my own feet and swung me out wide, he almost let go, but he felt my call to stay. He wasn't as pretty, pale and square in his plain brown suit, but he sure knew how to swing.

As I rode along, my starving skin woke to the touch of so many hands and arms and hips, as I met more and more dancers, each pulling me closer and closer as they felt their welcome from my first touch. I couldn't even remember when I'd been born, seeing so many ballrooms and dance halls and discos in their memories, whirling dresses real and remembered, sweethearts watched across the room and lovers taken to bed and tonight still up in the air, hunger all around. Even the singer's voice ran ragged with loneliness, so distant, trying to pull us all closer. I could hardly believe it when I looked up at the floating stage and recognized her.

"Evie?"

She hid her appetite so well. As if the pangs of longing came from us, not her. Why yearn, when she could join in?

The feel of a familiar hand made me falter. My partner and I went still as everyone moved around us.

"Come to dance?" said Alastair.

The spell had been broken—just long enough for me to remember myself. It all came back to me. Sunflowers spilling at my wake. Trash flung across my bedroom as my sister searched in vain for a suicide note. The wind in my hair up on my apartment rooftop.

I spirited right the hell out of there, taking him with me.

"Seriously?"

I wrenched my hand away before he could take us back. Through the walls of the piano parlor, the pulse kept beckoning. I couldn't bear to go much farther.

"I can't do this."

He dropped all his usual pretense, riled up enough for a modern inflection again. "You *were* doing this!"

"I forgot that I died."

"Exactly! Why do you think we dance?"

I closed my eyes, still fighting off the pounding of the pulse in my head. "My family is burying me tomorrow, and I've been out drinking, and dancing, and I even went on a date! I don't deserve to forget what I've done."

He stared at me, too still not to be roiling under the surface. At last he said, "What date?"

At least I still had it in me to smirk, for a moment.

His eyes went clear, cool and pale as moonlit snow. He slowly leaned in, trailing the tips of his fingers over mine. For once, he didn't hold back. He didn't share any memories, but he cracked the door just wide enough to let something slip through. His blood called to me, the same as mine to my dance partners, letting them know I didn't mind getting close.

"There's no taking back what you told me on the dance floor," he said.

I gave up a sigh. "I know. Why do you think I can't stay?"

The pulse drowned out the wailing in my head. It shouldn't have. The least I could do was feel it, even if it made my wrists chafe.

The geists were in hell, and I deserved to join them.

He reached up to touch my face. I wanted it, though it nearly hurt. My numb skin woke in shock the same as an icy wind, or cold shower, or pain. His thumb brushed my lip. I couldn't help it. I had to know. I stuck out the tip of my tongue to see if we could still taste.

His skin tasted like I remembered skin tasted. Even if it were only my memory, not new, not his own taste, I never thought I'd get to feel it again. So I didn't care. I sucked the rest of his finger into my mouth like I meant to fucking eat it. He watched with a knowing smile.

"So this is why you've been so uptight," he said. "If you let loose, there's no holding the real you back."

He hardly flinched as I chafed his skin with my teeth, before I pulled off with a last lick. I already missed the fleeting tang of salt and skin. My mouth was so stale, sick of being empty. I wanted more.

"I'll just have a bite before I go."

I grabbed him by the collar and muffled his gasp as I pulled his lips down to mine. He tasted as sweet as rain on a parched tongue. His arms closed tight around me. I couldn't help but moan. I'd so badly wanted a good, hard kiss tonight.

All too soon, he let go, pulling away. "Who's the boy?"

Oh, shit. I'd forgotten to keep my walls up. Even if that face had only slipped into my head for a fleeting moment, it had been long enough.

"Did you leave him behind?" he asked.

Correcting him would mean admitting I'd gone out with someone who still had a pulse, and I really didn't want to hear his take on that. I kept quiet, lying by acquiescence.

"So that's why you've been dragging your feet."

"What's the deal?" I asked, as casually as I could. "I thought you wanted me to move on."

"When you have me, I'd rather it be with joy, not grief."

"As if," I said. As if this hadn't just happened. I couldn't bear to look at him.

His voice went soft, even tender. "It will come as a relief, once they bury you. As it is, you're still a burden. Once they release you to the earth, and your eternal fate, they'll carry on. So will you."

I didn't reply. As much as I wanted to refute him, that sounded about right. They couldn't mourn me forever. And I couldn't keep mourning myself, even in strange ways like this.

He put a hand on my arm. I tried shrugging him off, but not too hard. Slowly and surely, I let him pull me closer, until he had me in his arms, burying my face in his shoulder. I couldn't decide what embarrassed me more—making out, or this. I put my fist on his chest, like I meant to pound it, push him away, only to let it rest there.

His laugh rumbled against my ear. "You were looking for a pen?"

TWENTY

»» ««

Danny and Carlos were still sitting where I'd left them in the library, dictating and writing for old times' sake, one last time. They didn't even look up. That gave me a moment to compose myself. It felt like I'd been through way too much to bring back this bounty. I worried they'd be able to tell, my skin still flushed, legs too far apart, trying to cool off. Through the walls, the pulse still called.

"Here you go," I said.

They weren't so spooked this time, all but tripping over each other trying to get up. I braced myself for yet more gratitude. Once they were on their feet, they looked at each other, as if I were handing over something much rarer than a pen, even the nice fountain kind, and they had to decide who would get the honor. But they knew their roles by now. He stepped aside, and she steadied herself.

I played along, adding a little ceremony with one hand folded behind me and the other presented with a near bow. She beamed as she accepted her prize.

"You're a lifesaver," Carlos said.

His phrasing stung more than I would've thought. "Don't mention it."

"How'd you find this place?" he asked. Like he was beating himself up for not coming here sooner, wondering what signs he might've missed, if he could've simply followed the pulse. It still called to me, making me shuffle my feet, rustle my skirt.

"I didn't. They found me."

"Wait, who, and like, how?"

"Their band manager follows deaths in the news."

That had been the wrong answer. He put two and two together, his face lighting up with surprise. "Did you join the band?"

I shut my eyes, wishing the dark behind my lids were the void. If I weren't still around, I wouldn't have to keep answering this fucking question.

"Stop asking me!"

Carlos blinked. "I only asked once, but fine, I won't do it again."

I nearly apologized. But I didn't. It felt good to snap. They didn't make me regret it, moving right on.

Danny set the pen down on some dusty tomes, freeing her hands to flap in excitement. "So did all these ghosts originally gather together as an audience?"

"I guess?"

"How many are there?"

"I dunno, you'll have to go count them."

She must've finally noticed my restless feet. "Sorry, I know you're not an expert, I'm just so hyped to start! It looks like a full-fledged community. Do you know what that means?"

"We've got some company?" Carlos grinned.

Her hands were fluttering like wings. "I mean, of course, but think of the word of mouth! All these ghosts comparing their experiences and views of what's happened to them. Once beliefs are shared, they start to become *folklore*."

She relished the word, with a reverence I wouldn't have expected of a scientist. As if it were holy.

"What is your field?" I asked.

"I'm an anthropologist."

I raised my eyebrows. "I'll bet these weren't the dead people you imagined studying."

"True, that," she said, laughing. "But I'll take it."

"What about you?" I asked Carlos.

He gave the slightest wince, welcoming the question as little as I used to. "I just worked here and there, you know, dishes, line cook, barista, scraping by."

"Same." I didn't want to get into my job history, either. It didn't matter anymore how we used to make a living, if you could call it that.

This had been enough bonding for now. They had work to do.

I gestured toward their new tools. "Are you going to get it all down, or what?"

Danny seized the pen once more, sending dust flying as she slapped the notebook open onto a desk. Carlos got comfortable, sprawling on an armchair as if he could feel the ancient leather. I took the opportunity to bow out before they could ask me where I was headed. I wouldn't be far.

As dawn bloomed gold through the leaves on the walls, the pulse began to fade, like the receding of the tide. It would be back, but for now, I was safe. Though I still didn't trust myself to peek out at the voices in the hallways as the dancers emptied from the ballroom. I wondered what the band did after the show if they didn't have to pack up their instruments, head to any afterparty, or back on the road.

Whatever they did, Evie clearly didn't join in. She sang for them, but she still never took her turn to dance. I had to know how the hell she managed that.

Rather than risk spiriting again, I waited for her to come to me in her piano parlor. When she finally showed, she was carrying an old teapot. At first, she beelined right for the potted plant by the window, growing alongside some vines coming in from outside. Then she noticed me and stiffened, like a startled rabbit. Her eyes were strangely cold.

"I thought you were with Ally," she said.

Her voice sounded so little like itself, now that I knew her range. It curled up in the vocal equivalent of a hunch.

It took me too long to realize what she was implying. She must've seen us on the dance floor together. I guessed, if I'd gone further with him, we wouldn't be done yet.

"As if," I said, like I hadn't tried to make it happen.

That helped her unfold somewhat. I had to go and ruin it. "Wait, have you and him ever…?"

Her blush answered for her, well before she got her mouth to work. "No!"

She nearly dropped her teapot. As she bent to set it down, the handle slipped through her fingers. It clattered, spilling, but settling upright.

I rushed right in, too impatient to try warming her up, getting her comfortable. Maybe I didn't want her comfortable. "All this time, you've been in the band?"

She went still, as if hoping to blend into the wall, like furniture or one of her plants.

"I thought you didn't partake."

Her curls fluttered as she shook her head. "It's not the same."

"There's no need to play coy. I mean, you can't exactly hide how you feel, with your voice in our veins."

That made her gulp, struggling to maintain eye contact. We both knew who I sounded like.

"Why haven't you joined us?" I asked. "I mean, them."

She braved a glance. "You really think I'd be welcome?"

"Why not? As long as you loosened up. I'm shocked nobody's offered to help you out with that."

Her eyes dropped again as she crossed her arms, rocking a bit. "You remember how old I am."

I'd totally forgotten. No wonder her voice drove all the dancers closer together, her prolonged teenage yearning wracking us with pangs like hunger. Only, unlike her, the rest of us could have our fill.

I couldn't imagine any of the other ghosts would take issue with her inexperience, especially coming from different times. They'd eat her right up. If I'd died that young, I would've joined the party in a pretend heartbeat.

Then again, I'd gone and sped through all my firsts. It hadn't gone particularly well, or particularly badly, because I'd been with other kids. I had to consider if I'd died younger than her—back when I still kept my abstinence pledge and only drank during communion—whether or not I would've succumbed to any of these old souls, given the gulf of experience between us, young and terrified meeting old and bored. I already found them intimidating enough, even in my seasoned years.

Still, I doubted I would've waited long enough to consider myself legal. There weren't any laws on this side, anyway. I should've known she wouldn't have any advice for me about self-control, how to abstain. That wasn't what held her back.

"You're mature for your age," I said.

She sighed, like she'd heard that before. I kept going, so she wouldn't get the wrong idea. "I mean, mature enough to know you're not nearly mature enough, compared to everyone here."

That got her to smile in relief, through the melancholy. She'd been on Earth longer than eighteen years, now, but she had good reason not to count age by years.

Alastair must've respected that. It was why he didn't pressure her. I couldn't help but think better of him for it.

"What about you?" she asked. "Why haven't you joined the band?"

I'd already snapped, earlier, so it felt like I'd gotten it out of my system. Besides, she'd been right there, in my head. "Didn't you see it all?"

"But it's been long enough, hasn't it?" she asked. "You weren't hurt by the music. Just people. It might heal instead of hurt, if you tried playing again."

For once, I didn't look away, shaking my head slowly. I didn't quite expect my voice to curl up so small. "It didn't save me from myself."

She pressed her lips together. "You can't expect that from just one thing. It takes lots of ropes to make a net."

I laughed. "And just one to hang yourself."

She didn't share my mirth, eyes wide and wistful. "Well, if you need a lifeline, you know where to find me."

She put her arms up, leaving it up to me whether I wanted to go in for the hug. I'd already exceeded my usual quota of "none" today, not being the touchy-feely type. But we didn't have much else to touch on this side, and I didn't know how often she got to be held. I tried to ease my usual instinctive stiffness and leaned in. Aside from having to keep my walls up, it didn't feel so bad; my limbs melted into her softness. I missed her warmth as soon as we parted.

TWENTY-ONE

❋》》》 《《《❋

The cemetery glowed green in the morning sunlight. It sprawled wide, pristine headstones clearly announcing new arrivals beside those struggling to whisper weather-beaten, moss-covered names. So I'd made the family plot. It gave me a bitter little chuckle to be buried next to the grandparents who thought of me as a bastard.

As I approached the gathering of black amongst the green, I hovered, keeping my distance. The crowd stood on fake grass, keeping the dirt off their good church shoes. My casket sank into the ground aided by what looked kind of like a mechanical altar, fringed with green cloth as if to hide the machinery. Behind them, a tractor waited to do the actual burying once everyone had gone.

My turnout looked even smaller this time. I didn't linger on my mother and sister's faces for long. Only enough to see their masks, not any cracks.

There weren't any new faces, save one near the back. Though nobody seemed to pay him any mind, I had to get closer, see which asshole had shown up to my funeral wearing jeans.

He didn't look bad, wearing a nice sweater and fitted denim over his dad bod, but it was nowhere near appropriate for the occasion. I resented his familiar attractiveness, blonde and clean and somewhat baby-faced under the beard. Once I recognized him, my insides frosted over.

Liam. I'd never seen his natural hair color under his black dye of old. He'd put on some weight, and carried it well, his old edges softened.

I looked at him. He looked back. Then he smiled, the painful overdue smile of *long time no see.*

"It's awful to see you," he said.

That stung for a moment, until I realized what he meant. "You too."

We fell in step, instinctively looking for a more private place to talk, although no one could see us.

"When did you bite it?" I asked.

"Fuck if I know, it's hard to keep track. It's been… months, at least."

My stomach sank like a stone. I hadn't gotten my hopes up for myself, but I would've thought he'd make some front pages, or second or third, at least. Then again, I hadn't been paying attention to the news.

"I hadn't heard," I admitted.

His eyebrows flickered up. "For real, nobody told you?"

"You think I kept in touch with anybody?"

He found it in him to smile, like we'd intended to meet like this, old friends catching up. "You did make yourself hard to find. I take it you never got my emails."

I had, but I'd left them all unread.

"Now I get why you didn't seem sad," he said. "At least, no more than usual."

I managed to keep the terror from widening my eyes too far, but I forgot about my voice. It cracked as I spoke. "You checked up on me?"

"I didn't mean to spy, but what else could I do? You were doing it just now. It's all we've got."

So he'd seen firsthand how pathetic I'd become. I really ought to have died sooner. Then, he wouldn't have had the chance to betray me, and we wouldn't be on the brink of the conversation we were about to have now.

His voice went rough. "I hate what we did to you."

I kept my gaze firmly ahead. "For once, could you give me some credit? I orchestrated most of my own destruction."

"But I gave it some finishing touches."

I couldn't help but laugh at his old refrain, usually applied to writing songs. He joined me with his unusually big guffaw. It suited him better now that he'd filled out.

"It looks like we both got what we deserved."

He gave me a look I recognized, meeting my casual cynicism with a stare that forced me to question whether it was warranted. "I don't think we did."

That might've been harsh. I shouldn't have lumped him in with me. "How did it happen?" I asked.

He let his breath out slowly, bracing the back of his neck with his hand. He must not have met any other ghosts, telling the story over and over until it came as naturally as any other ice-breaker.

"I had a heart attack."

"Really?" I asked. "At your age?"

"They think I had an undiagnosed condition."

That, or we'd partied way too hard back in the day. We'd tried some of the hard stuff. Come to think of it, as much as he'd tried, maybe he'd never quit for good.

"Did you hear how I went?"

"I did," he said.

So I didn't have to elaborate. Before he could go ahead and ask anyway, I changed the subject. "What have you been doing with yourself?"

It sounded so mundane. No wonder he mistook my meaning.

"You mean, what did I do for a living?"

"I meant after dying."

His head rolled on his shoulders. "I've been drifting around, peeking at people I used to know, people I don't know, keeping up with the scene. I get to see all the shows at our favorite spots without asking to be put on the list."

As if hardly any time had passed, no more than a day or so of misadventure separating us on the road, he asked me if I'd heard of this or that band, chided me for my ignorance, and promptly began whoring it up on their behalf. Same as ever. I found myself flushed with both annoyance and affection.

There'd been a reason I sort of cheated with him. Even if I'd had an open relationship with my boyfriend at the time, that only meant he could fuck groupies and I could sometimes settle for a roadie, not that I could fall for our bandmate.

"It's nice to see you haven't changed, you fucking snob."

"I've changed some."

As we wove around the headstones, it surprised me how different he looked. Rather, how different it felt to look at him. I could meet his gaze now without that old tug in my chest, the pull of the tide toward the moon. I'd never felt so firm on my feet in his presence.

It wasn't just the beard and the dad bod. I'd gotten far past caring about appearance with him. I wondered how I looked to him now, bonier than ever, tattoos covered, piercings closed up, hair back to its natural color. We sort of matched. If anyone could see us, we might've passed for a suburban couple.

It still hurt, what he'd done. Even though he'd been the one to stay behind with me for a while, and he'd tried to reach out, make amends. But he no longer resembled the man who'd hurt me. He felt like a stranger, someone whose potential for regret lay ahead, not behind.

We drifted to a halt under the dappled shade of a tree. I guessed we were done pretending not to stare at each other. As I finally got a good look into those eyes again, I sighed. The old hollow in my chest where he used to be had closed up. The love no longer ran through me, any more than old blood on a bandage could flow back into the wound.

But it had been too damn long. After last night's teasing, I couldn't wait any longer, even if it was a terrible idea. At least his memories might not be so disorienting, since I'd share some of them.

Besides, we were at a funeral.

I put my hand on his arm, so he wouldn't be too startled if he didn't know we could touch. He didn't look too surprised. I stood on tiptoe like old times, threw my arms around his shoulders, and laid it on him hard and fast.

Our mouths burned, and so did the rest of our bodies, tingling painfully from numb to overstimulated as we went down weightlessly onto the grass. I landed on top. Neither of us took any clothes off. We didn't even need to voice our uncertainty over whether we could put them back on again. We simply pushed them aside as best we could and got busy.

It felt the same as the dancing, memories that weren't mine swimming before my eyes. I dug my nails into his shoulders, like that could keep my head from spinning. Somewhere far away, my body keened and sang, and so did his, more like a sex dream than the real thing. Sometimes I saw him, with black hair and a thinner frame, and myself, a kaleidoscope of hair colors and slightly fuller curves and endless miles of skin. Other times, our faces changed, as different lovers came and went in our thoughts, unbidden and mostly unheeded.

Only one of them kept coming back—his wife.

"Shit," I said.

I stared at him, back in the cemetery, blinking in the sun. He must've thought I'd cried out in a good way, because he didn't even open his eyes. We'd already gotten this far, anyway. I'd learned a long time ago that I couldn't un-fuck this guy. And I'd been alone so long, it felt like if I didn't get off, I'd die again.

So I closed my eyes and tried my best to ignore his memories, riding him till we both finished at once. We'd never done that in life, but it helped to be in each other's heads.

The afterglow didn't last long. I got off him, not just because I didn't go in for cuddling.

"Thanks, buddy." Somehow, my voice didn't feel the same in my throat. It pitched lower, with more growl and crackle. I wouldn't have been surprised if my hair had changed color. "So, just out of curiosity, were you still with Haley?"

His eyes snapped open, startled out of post-coital drowsiness. Then he laughed, much quieter than usual. "Till death."

We both stood and fixed our clothes back in place.

"Is that a problem for you now?" he asked. "You never used to care."

He had a point. I hadn't even thought to check for a ring. Once we'd broken up, I'd been too bitter to try putting any moves on him again, especially after he'd tied the knot. I'd gotten drunk and slept through his wedding, and not because I hadn't gotten over him. The band had been too busy for him to commit to anything—or anyone—aside from us.

But between his failed attempt to go straight edge and my

commitment to spiraling, we'd pulled the band apart. Even kicking me out couldn't keep the rest of them together.

That must've been what turned me off, more than infidelity. Now that I'd gotten off, I couldn't keep that closet full of skeletons shut.

"She's moving on," he said. "Why shouldn't I?"

That seemed awfully soon. "This is why I never bought you as the marrying type."

"Well, neither were you."

"Damn right. You and I were supposed to get famous enough to keep getting laid even in our saggy old age. Wait, no. We were supposed to get famous, then die young, because fuck marriage and old age, right? Better to be immortalized young and dead than forgotten old and kicking."

He hadn't forgotten himself like I had, looking at me like he was so much older and wiser. "That didn't exactly work out, did it?"

"Neither did your marriage."

"Oh, fuck off," he said. "It didn't fail. I died."

"You could've spared her the pain."

"And then my daughter wouldn't exist."

My mouth fell. I choked on the words. "You've got a kid?"

He smiled, like he couldn't help it, thinking of the little one. Even if he'd lost her, or rather, the other way around.

The smile turned into a grimace. "You're not jealous, are you?"

I tried not to shake my head too emphatically. "I'm not."

I'd always dreaded this part. We used to be quiet, muffled by our unspoken guilt, as I'd get dressed and leave the hotel room. Even after I'd broken up with my boyfriend—our lead guitar—Liam and I never spoke after sex. I'd face the other way in bed, his arm on top of me like an anchor. He never could hold me down.

No wonder he'd dumped me for someone more tangible.

Somehow, even after all this, he found it in him to reach for me. A tentative touch on the arm, an unspoken question.

"Do we have to do this?" I asked. "Were you thinking we could pick up where we left off?"

"If we're ever going to work out our issues, it's now."

"I know you've had some time to think about your life, post-mortem, but if you haven't noticed, I'm barely getting buried. It's not the best time for me, right now."

He gave a huff of a laugh, spreading his arms. "What else are we going to do? There's nobody else left in the world."

"That's not truc."

"What do you mean?"

I held out my hand. "Let me show you something."

He'd have plenty of other company where we were headed.

Liam looked around the ballroom in wonder. Sunlight streamed through the broken windows in golden columns, leaves glowing transparent on the vines pouring inside.

"What is this place?"

I shrugged, trying to be cool about it, not revel too much. "Welcome to the Haunt."

The lady with the parasol waved as she approached us, arm in arm with the hippie girl, taking a turn about the room.

"It's not just us?" he asked.

He might've been regretting the hookup, realizing there were other ghosts to choose from instead. That's exactly why I'd brought him here.

"You're in for a ride."

I couldn't stay long. It would be too weird to introduce him to Alastair.

"Make yourself at home," I said. "I've still got some stuff to wrap up."

For once, I went ahead and showed how bummed I felt, letting my shoulders slump and brow furrow, trying to remind him we'd just come from my funeral.

"Of course," he said, reaching out to rub my arm. I barely got my walls up in time.

"Hello there," said parasol lady.

"I haven't seen you around before," the hippie girl added.

Their voices were giggly, eyes roving shamelessly over him.

Liam cleared his throat, blushing. "Uh… ladies?"

I patted his back in approval.

"Catch you later," I lied.

By the time evening rolled around, and the band began to play, hopefully he'd forget all about me.

TWENTY-TWO

✹))) (((✹

Gloria's house hadn't changed much inside, still as opulently furnished as a small cathedral. Though I'd never seen it host so many people, bustling with remaining family and friends after the post-burial lunch. Most of them wore dark hues, if not black, just as traditional as her. They looked right at home amongst her crosses and saints.

I didn't see Cris.

"This explains a lot," said Alastair.

I nearly hushed him, like an unwelcome guest I had to get out of sight. As soon as our eyes met, my skin caught fire, remembering the last time we'd seen each other. He shouldn't have been able to step into my mother's house. It felt like this was consecrated ground, and he was a malevolent spirit.

He reached out and caught something, all nonchalant, like the porcelain saint had fallen on its own. I wanted to knock it over, with my hand this time. But I'd always felt a rapport with St. Anthony.

"Sorry, Tony," I said, then crossed my arms, looking up at Alastair. "What are you doing here?"

"Is this not the kind of event where you bring a date?"

I shoved him. His eyes lit with anticipation for a moment, before going out again. He'd thought I'd pull him closer, not push him away.

"Why can't you just leave me alone?"

"What have I told you? You shouldn't be."

I could only hope he was still desperate for a drummer. Not that he'd read into our regrettable makeout.

I didn't even feel like making the effort of rolling my eyes anymore. "Are you bored yet?"

"You don't know boredom."

I raised my eyebrows, but before I could try and turn it around on him—didn't he make enough entertainment for himself on this side?—he turned away from me, beginning to pace.

I wondered if he were only feigning interest in the family photos on the walls, or if they really did distract him. I sidled up to him, like we were strangers at an oddly intimate little museum.

"You're not in any of these," he said.

I raised a finger to point out one of the smaller pictures. In the yellow phosphorescent light of an old camera, a bunch of costumed kids stood on stage, putting on a nativity pageant. My sister had been well-behaved enough as a baby to play her namesake, replacing the usual plastic doll at my mother's insistence. She took up the center of the photo, as usual. Off in the corner, far from my flock, I stole the show as a wandering sheep.

He stared for a long while, his fingers pressed to his mouth. I'd wanted him to see me as a kid. As if that might make him more sympathetic, learning not only that I'd had a family, but that I'd been a child once, with so much potential, so much life supposedly ahead of her. I dug my nails into my palms, trying not to think too hard about it, myself.

At last, he cleared his throat. "You know, it's a myth about hair and fingernails."

"What about them?" I asked, trying not to let my voice sink.

"They don't keep growing post-mortem. The skin simply shrinks back as it decays, creating an illusion of change. We don't keep growing after death."

I got it, then. He saw what I'd been, what I'd become, and now, what I'd always be, until the trumpets rang.

"How about the soul?" I asked. "It grows all the time, doesn't it?"

"On the other side, it might, sometimes. But here? With no world around it, nothing to nourish or challenge it?"

I hadn't expected the melancholy weighing down his eyes, his face unmasked as he searched mine.

"That can't be true," I said, allowing some gravity in, before I grinned. "We could always get worse."

His laugh was labored, but I got it out of him all the same. "We might not grow, but we sure do rot."

He lifted his fingers up to my face, casually, not questioning whether I'd welcome it. I might've already gotten my fill of touch earlier, but I still had to keep from letting my eyes flutter closed.

"Don't even think about it," I said, as he leaned in. I pushed his face away. If I gave an inch, I'd end up taking a lot more, judging from the way he filled out his pants. Maybe then, he'd quit pestering me. Or he'd become even more insufferable. I could wait to find out.

"What's the deal?" he asked.

"Did you forget where we are?"

"We should get out of here, anyway," he said, now more sober. "There's nothing left to see. It's all over."

He brushed my shoulder, like he thought I might be slipping. Some of the china in the cabinet trembled with a nerve-wracking ting. I was still convinced my mother had collected all those breakables just to punish me when the inevitable happened.

"It's not," I said. "Not yet."

I hadn't seen Cris.

"When will you be satisfied?" he asked. "You're really determined to go geist, aren't you?"

I shrugged off his hand. "What's my alternative? Forget who I left behind? You want me to fucking rejoice in that?"

"Not forever," he said. "But you'll never make it to forever if you don't start—"

Thankfully, he didn't follow me when I disappeared, though I'd only spirited upstairs.

Cris lay curled up in bed in her old room, full of technicolor musical posters and high school softball trophies, left behind when she moved into her apartment. The rest of the room had been picked over. On the wall above her head a white space glared, the opposite of a shadow, where a cross used to be.

"There you are," said Gloria.

I moved aside so she wouldn't pass through me. But she remained in the doorway, staring with her arms crossed.

My sister didn't reply, or even move, just lay there wrinkling her dress suit.

I wondered how it went down after I left the wake. Perhaps she'd anticipated what our mother would want, as usual, and apologized without being asked. Or she'd been berated, exactly like I would've been.

Most likely, neither of them had acknowledged it at all.

"Are you praying?" asked Gloria.

Cris rolled over on the bed, pulling herself up and hugging her knees as best she could in her stiff clothes. "No."

"You should write to your professors," said Gloria. "They'll understand you need time off."

"I don't want to get behind."

"You can stay here," said Gloria. Only my sister and I would be able to hear the plea hanging off the edge of her words.

Cris shook her head, slightly, not in protest, but as if to settle the words in her ears. "I thought you'd want me to go back."

There she went contradicting our mother again, like it was nothing. I hadn't even realized I'd tensed up, my shoulders practically aching.

Gloria's breath pitched as her mask finally gave, just a little. Brows raised, her mouth tighter. She drew herself up and gave a taut nod. "It would be best to try returning to normal."

She always stated, never asked.

"It's not just that," said Cris.

I didn't think my mother could draw up any straighter, yet somehow, she managed it. "What is it?"

Cris still couldn't muster the courage to look at her. I never could, either. It took enough nerve to talk back without seeing its lack of effect, like standing in the eye of a storm. Back when I used to believe, it felt the same as blaspheming. You never knew when lightning might strike.

No wonder she and I had both developed the habit of clenching our fists like that, digging nails into our palms.

Finally, she spat it out. "I can't stay here with you."

"Why not?" asked Gloria.

Cris couldn't hold up her mask anymore. When it crumbled at last, her eyes were hard. "You cast her out."

Gloria snapped. "¡Cómo te atreves!" I'd heard that often enough not to forget it: *How dare you*. In English, she said, "I did not! She refused to come back."

Cris didn't flinch. I'd never seen her eyes blaze like that, the same cold fury I'd grown up fearing turned back on our mother.

"What did you expect? That you could shut her out and wait for her to change on her own, return the prodigal son? You just made it that much harder for her to live, fending for herself, when you *knew*—" Her voice cracked. "Suicide runs in the family."

My dad had drunk himself to death. Maybe on purpose. I had to find out reading old newspapers online at the school library, because if I ever dared bring him up, I'd be sent to bed without dinner.

Gloria raised her chin, too late to knock back the tears. She ignored them, her mouth twitching and voice shaking with rage. "You weren't there for her, either!"

I wished I could be surprised that she would try to deflect the blame, deny any wrongdoing. For a Catholic, she didn't handle guilt well.

"I took her back," Cris snapped. "Just because she didn't believe, that didn't make her a bad person. You were just too prideful to admit you didn't know how to help her."

Gloria's volume made me tremble like a scolded child. "How can you talk to your mother this way? I raised you better than that."

Cris got up, approaching her. For a moment, I thought she'd take it back, revert to the golden child. Go for a hug, nothing like the stiff embraces I used to get. It stung. Instead, she tried to edge past her in the doorway.

"I'm sorry," said Cris. "I can't do this."

The curtains billowed, though the window wasn't open.

Gloria didn't budge. The tears had dried on her face. Her voice was flat, if slightly husky. "You're not going anywhere."

Cris stared, as though struggling to put the apology in her eyes into words.

Then she turned around and dove for my old escape—out

the window, down the trellis. I almost laughed in sheer surprise.

Gloria stumbled after her, sticking her head out the window and screaming, "Cristina!"

But my sister had already taken off running across the lawn. "You stay the hell put, or—"

She didn't say the rest, not out loud. It hung in the air unspoken. *You can never come back.*

Last time she'd said it, it had come true. Now she only had one child left.

Something crashed. One of the old trophies fell off the dresser and into the lamp, shattering the bulb.

This time, I knew not to linger. Not alone.

And aside from the Haunt, I still had one other option for company.

Ren slept on his usual schedule this time, all covered up but for his hair. I didn't expect the mere suggestion of him under his blankets to make my dead heart skip a beat. Just as I considered spiriting straight off again, he stirred.

Somehow, he always seemed to wake right when I showed up. As if he could sense my presence. I wondered how he managed to get any sleep at all with geists around.

He sat up and pried down his headphones, rubbing his eyes as though he half-expected I'd vanish like a dream. "Mal."

"So, here's the thing." I couldn't help but pace, my feet not ready to take root anywhere. "If I don't want to end up a poltergeist, I can't be alone. So, uh, I've changed my mind about hanging out. That is, if you're still down?"

He smiled, before a yawn interrupted him. It lingered in his voice. "I wasn't sure if I'd see you again."

My chest ached suddenly. "Actually, that's probably for the best. I wasn't thinking. I should just—"

"Stay," he said, quick, before I could disappear on him. "Seriously, you can crash as long as you want."

I hadn't planned to hang around long enough to call it crashing. "Are you sure?"

He just shook his head at me, pulling his laptop out from under the mattress. "What do you wanna watch?"

I sank beside him on the mattress, folding myself up, head on my knees. It had been years since I'd been so nervous on someone else's bed. I'd never had a roommate who didn't eventually become my bedmate, as well. If I couldn't push him back down on the mattress, I didn't know what exactly to do with him, or myself.

It took way too much concentration to simply sit quietly and watch the show he'd put on while the ones I used to watch in life were downloading. He eventually lay back, falling asleep again. His head rested awfully close to my lap.

He'd only be around half the time, and mostly unconscious, anyway. I'd have the place to myself, not much different from my own. At least here, it would be quiet. I wouldn't have to forget.

"One more thing," I said.

"Hmm?"

"You remember how we, um…" I didn't want to bring up the kiss-that-wasn't. "I mean, that time we went to the movies?"

His lips curved up. "Yeah?"

I gulped, my throat going painfully dry. "Could we just agree none of that happened?"

He sighed, but still went ahead and asked, "What movie?"

My voice cracked. "Exactly."

That made it easier to settle down beside him, resting my chin on my hands. It didn't count as sharing a bed if we couldn't touch each other.

Liam scared me. I took him for a geist as he spirited in, springing to my feet with all my muscles tensed. Ren had gone to work, and I didn't particularly want to tangle with one of those things alone. Then he laughed. I uncoiled a little.

"What are you still doing here?" he asked, glancing down at the chattering laptop. "Were you planning on hanging out till somebody else moves in? Or did you want to stay and haunt the poor bastards?"

He must've mistaken this sad, empty apartment for my old one, thinking it had been mostly packed up already. No need to correct him. If I did, I'd have to explain my weird new rooming situation.

I wrapped my arms around myself. "I'll be fine."

"Why settle for that, when you could be better off?"

My stomach dropped with dread.

"You know what you're missing, right?" he asked. "You're the one who showed me the Haunt."

I couldn't look at him, my feet already bearing me away, seeking an escape. I settled for prying back the tacked-up blanket and looking out the window, as if there were much of a view. No reflection peered back at me, so I couldn't see how well my mask held.

"Why aren't you in the band already?" he asked. "We should be doing this together. It's like a second chance."

I closed my eyes. "Please, just… shut the fuck up."

"We don't even have to play together, if you want. I could take a different shift."

"I mean it, you goddamn traitorous asshole." I whirled on him, letting him see as well as hear me snap. "Thanks for the quickie, but there's no need to get clingy. I'm not really looking to make up."

He stepped back like I'd struck him. "Well, shit. I mean, I didn't think we were getting back together. But you don't have to stay away on my account."

"It's not all about you."

"Then what is it?"

I shook my head in disbelief. "If you wanted to keep up to date on my deepest, darkest thoughts, you shouldn't have left me on an IV."

"I'm just trying to make it up to you."

"If you mean that, you'll give me some space."

"You don't need space," he said. "We're not supposed to be alone."

Someone had given him the 101. Damn it.

He reached out to put a hand on my shoulder, but I jerked away. "How can I keep partying knowing you're here on your own?"

"I dunno, how'd you manage last time?"

His jaw clenched. "I didn't."

I curled my hands into fists, recalling the satisfying splinter of his guitar against the floor, how it went from being so heavy to much lighter broken in half.

"Look," I said. "If you can't handle the guilt of the lurch you left me in, that's your problem, not mine. I don't have to fucking forgive you. Just leave me to rot." I couldn't help but add, "Again."

His eyes glistened as he shook his head, looking just like he had the last time I'd driven him off, right before a nurse escorted him out. "How can I make this right?"

"I already told you, get the fuck out of my face."

"You know I can't do that," he said. "If you go geist—"

Somehow, whether I meant it or not, I always knew the worst thing to say. "I almost did already. It made me relive the worst moment of my life, over and over. And you know who I saw? You. So if it happens again, think of it this way: You'll still be here. I'll never be rid of you."

This time he turned away, resorting to pacing, just like in my hospital room and so many hotel rooms before that. He never had enough room to walk off my words.

"I forgot how fucking hopeless you are," he said. "You'd take a fate worse than death over letting anyone help you out?"

"Not anyone," I said. "But you, for sure."

"Well, I hope someone gets through to you," he said. "I tried."

I blinked, and he'd disappeared, so much faster than last time. I'd missed the opportunity to watch him leave, to hurl one last insult with his back turned.

Instead, I muttered it to myself. "Have a nice afterlife."

Stage Five:
More Denial

TWENTY-THREE

✳»» ««✳

Ren haunted his own apartment the same way I once did, even before I died. Aside from flipping day and night, it went exactly the same: sleep, work, eat while watching TV, rinse and repeat. Days off were for visiting sisters (and brother and mother in his case) and doing laundry. As far as I knew, he never went out, and he didn't exactly have friends over, either.

I'd meant to stay just long enough to finish catching up on the shows I used to watch. But since I didn't need to eat or sleep or hit the toilet, that only took about a week. Afterwards, I didn't have anywhere better to be. And he clearly needed the company.

Now, when he smoked his first cigarette of the day out on the fire escape, he let me share each drag secondhand. I usually put my hand on his shoulder, trying to keep it friendly. This time, we took turns swapping the stories.

He mumbled, unable to look me in the eye. "So, I pick up this girl from an apartment complex, even though she has that same address listed as the destination, which… weird. She asks if I can just drive around for a while because she wants to clear her head. I do, and we start talking and laughing, then she asks if I want to park, and…"

He trailed off, blushing terribly.

"Aww, come on," I said. "You can't leave me hanging."

I wanted to share his next drag, but I worried what other sensations I'd pick up.

At last, he looked me in the eye. "I lost it in my back seat, all right? The one teenage rite of passage I got to have, since there weren't any geists in the sketchy alley, though there were a couple of drunks who knocked on the window and gave us some thumbs up. Satisfied?"

Far from it. I never usually got jealous over past lovers. For once, I hadn't gotten a turn myself.

"That's all I've got," he said.

"Don't you hold out on me." I didn't mean to reach out and give him a slight shove, but I couldn't stop myself. "I've dumped my whole dirty laundry bin over your head."

His lips flickered up, but the heat flowing from his shoulder down my arm didn't sit so well—the prickling discomfort of shame.

"I haven't been with anyone else. Just a couple of awkward dates set up by my sister that didn't go anywhere, and… well, the high school crush I never ended up asking out, 'cause I didn't think she'd want to be seen with the class freak."

His words weren't bitter. If anything, his eyes were weary, just resigned. I wanted to take his face in my hands.

Instead, I said, "Well, you could give it another go, now that I'm taking care of your geists."

It didn't get any less terrifying, every time I tried spiriting one elsewhere. But I didn't mind. I had no other way to thank him for letting me stay. Not to mention, he looked so much better now that he'd been getting a good bit of sleep. His eyes were brighter, without any shadows beneath them, and his skin flushed with color, not so dead anymore.

At this rate, it wouldn't be long before he caught somebody's eye. Rather, before he'd let one of those many somebodies in at last.

He looked down at me thoughtfully as he exhaled a drag. "Maybe I will."

Before I could reach up, he rested his hand beside mine on the balcony rail, letting our fingers overlap slightly.

"You'd better," I said. "Remember that time you promised to get a life?"

He rolled his eyes. "I didn't expect you to stick around and hold me to it."

I turned around, leaning back on the railing for a better look at him. "Have you thought any more about what you wanna do? I mean, with your continued existence?"

"Not really," he said, tapping ash into an old soda can. "I'm still just trying to last the week. You know how it goes. Although..." He flicked his gaze back up to me. "It's gotten a lot easier, coming home to you."

My mouth went dry. I could imagine how much easier it might've been enduring any of my shitty old jobs if at the end of the day, I had someone waiting for me at home. Eating dinner and watching TV every night went from lonely to cozy with two. Not to mention, instead of having to make the effort of getting dressed up and going out whenever I wanted to get lucky, I would've been able to just reach over and undo his belt.

Too bad that wouldn't work now. I thought about it every time we curled up around the laptop together. Whenever he left for work, after waiting to make sure he didn't come back for any reason, I'd look up a little porn for some me time. And I couldn't help but notice that sometimes his showers ran long.

He waved his fingers in front of my eyes. "You there?"

I shook my head. "Sorry, it's just… no, I'm literally not here." Aside from the fact I couldn't jump his bones, I wasn't exactly helping with rent, or doing the dishes. "I'm an actual deadbeat."

"It's not like you're emptying my fridge and trashing the place. Even if you weren't on top of pest control, I'm just glad to have your company."

That wasn't much. I wished I had more to give.

He drained his coffee and headed back inside. I lingered, looking back around over the side of the balcony down at the street below, not unlike the view from my apartment rooftop.

The next morning, while he showered and got dressed, I made the coffee. When he got out of the bathroom, combing his fingers through his damp hair, his grin barely outpaced his guilt.

"You shouldn't have," he said, like he meant it.

"It's not for you," I said, as I poured him a cup. "I just want the secondhand caffeine."

He nodded. "Sure, of course."

At least I stopped short of adding the sugar, even though I knew he liked two spoons. When I handed it over, our fingers brushed. For a second, I thought the heat came from the coffee, nearly dropping it in surprise.

His eyes were unbearably soft, nearly golden in the late afternoon sun. "Thanks, boo."

Before I could so much as stutter, he reached up and brushed my jaw with the back of his fingers, igniting my skin. Then, as casually as if we did this every morning, he turned and headed for the fire escape.

Once he'd stepped out, I went ahead and sank to the kitchen floor. Even if I couldn't feel the hard press of the cabinets at my back, the coolness of the tile beneath my legs, it still grounded me somewhat, a comforting place to have a quick crisis.

I got up and followed him outside, so he wouldn't get suspicious, and I told him about the time I ruined a church piano recital by swapping out "How Great Thou Art" for "Wonderwall." If he noticed the way my hands trembled as we tangled our fingers together, hopefully he chalked it up to coffee jitters, not the recent realization that I didn't just want to jump his bones. I longed to feel his hand in mine.

Cris hadn't moved out from her apartment yet. Gloria might've paid the rent in advance, or my ex-stepdad could have helped out this month. But she'd begun to pack, boxes piling up in her living room and kitchen.

Aside from that, I couldn't really tell how she was doing. Usually, I found her in class, or studying at her school library. Not the most thrilling eavesdropping experience, but at least it made me worry less. Her reverse disownment wasn't as dramatic as mine had been.

Then again, our mother could have humbled herself for a change, begging for forgiveness. I doubted it. For once, I went to see her.

My childhood church hadn't changed much, one of those historic cathedrals with high ceilings and marble saints, the last rays of sunset falling red and blue across the stone floors through the stained glass. My skin pinched with goosebumps as I walked down the aisles, my footsteps eerily silent. They used to echo when we came to confession on Saturday evenings instead of Sunday mornings, since there'd be less of a wait. Or maybe for privacy, so no one would clock our time, try to estimate our number of sins.

Gloria kneeled in the booth, resting her forearms before the wooden lattice window. I sat in midair behind her, keeping my eyes on her conservative black pumps sticking out under her long skirt.

"Forgive me, Father, for I have sinned. It has been seventy-one days since my last confession."

My jaw dropped. I'd never known her to skip confession for so long. Doing the math, she'd stopped right around the time of my death. What did she have to hide? Not from her omniscient Lord, but the priest's judgment. Or her own conscience.

"I lost my daughters."

I clasped a hand over my mouth. Here, it wasn't just a statement of fact, but an admission of guilt. The first I'd ever heard out of her lips.

"You remember my oldest, Malena. Born outside of marriage. I worried my sin would haunt her the rest of her life. So I had to be hard on her. She needed it, always getting into trouble. I used to say she had the devil in her..." She sighed, muttering under her breath. "Dios mío, ayúdame—she had too much of *me*."

All these years, I thought I'd taken after Dad. That whenever she looked at me, she saw a ghost. Well, perhaps she did, just not the one I had in mind. Like her old self had died and come back to haunt her.

No wonder she'd never seen me.

"When she quit school so she could run off and repeat her father's mistakes, I lost it. I found myself screaming the same words my mother said to me, because I finally understood how it felt, being so helpless to keep my lamb from putting on a fur coat and running with the wolves. But when I said she could never come home—I didn't mean it."

The shock made my hairs stand on end, as if she were the otherworldly intruder, not the other way around.

"I always thought she'd return, like I did. I regretted ever turning from my parents, and from God. Perdóname, por favor." Her shoulders were shaking. So were my hands, too weak to curl into fists. "She never came back."

How could I have known she would have welcomed me home? Except, of course, she would've expected repentance. For me to come back a different person. Devout, obedient, straight.

Her voice pitched, swollen and broken. I couldn't help but wince. "Cristina me echa la culpa. She's cut me off."

I couldn't blame Cris. As much as I worried about her living situation, suddenly being on her own, at least she'd sided with me, if a little late.

The priest's voice jostled me. I'd forgotten he'd been here with us the whole time, on the other side of the booth.

"You are not to blame," he said. "Your daughter's sin is her own."

I bristled in indignation. "Fuck off, Father."

Never in my life had my mother admitted any wrongdoing. I'd be damned if he ruined it. Maybe literally, because I whirled out of the confessional and knocked over the first object my fist met. The crucifix fell off the altar and clanged to the floor, echoing loud enough to bounce off the high ceiling the same as voices singing praise. All the candles blew out.

Gloria's voice rang shrill. "What was that?"

I spirited off as fast as I could, before I could risk angering any higher powers further by boiling the holy water, shattering the stained-glass saints.

I expected to find the usual blank white walls of the apartment, not friendly floral wallpaper, covered in framed photos and traditional Japanese art. Ren sat surrounded by people at a dinner table, speaking in a language I didn't understand. Their laughter fell silent as the warm yellow light hanging from above dimmed and then brightened, the curtains of the nearby window shuddering. My stomach cinched with guilt for interrupting.

"I'll be right back," said Ren.

He sprang out of his chair and made his way around the table toward me, lifting his hand just enough to brush my fingers. It couldn't ground me the same as another ghost, but at least it gave me something to feel other than the chafing on my wrists.

The elegantly dressed woman with a touch of gray in her hair sitting at the head of the table must be his mom. She brought her hand to her collarbone, saying something in Japanese.

Though I didn't know the words, I recognized the tone of concern. He answered in the same language. The other two people at the table, probably his brother and sister, exchanged wary looks.

I followed him down the hallway into a dark room. He didn't even bother hitting the lights, shutting the door quickly. For once, he didn't hesitate to throw his arms around me. I swallowed a gasp. Though I couldn't feel the shape of his body, the warmth of him still wrapped around me like a beloved old blanket.

"Hang on," he said. "Don't go anywhere."

I tried my best to bury my face into his neck, wishing I could breathe in his scent, whatever that might be. Then I remembered the look of worry on his mother's face.

"Sorry to interrupt," I said. "I don't mean to keep you from your family."

I choked on the last word, my eyes stinging with tears. At least he couldn't see them with my face tucked into his shoulder, his chin on my brow.

"You're fine," he said, stroking his hand over my hair. "They probably think I'm having an episode. I'll be here as long as you need."

He had even more literal demons than I ever had, and yet, his mother still invited him back home for dinner, fed him and laughed with him and let him have his space if he needed it.

I wanted to shove him away, curse at him, make myself even harder to hold.

But now I knew where I got that urge to push people away. From the same person who taught me how to make myself scarce afterwards. So, just to spite her, I resisted. Taking a pretend breath, I went slack, letting my limbs go soft.

"Are you all right?" he asked, pulling back just enough to look into my face.

I nodded, tongue-tied.

"Did something happen?"

Shaking my head didn't quite cover it. "I keep going off alone when I'm not supposed to be."

"Well, don't do that," he said. "I can't lose you."

I wanted to warn him that he already had. Instead, I tried my best to sink deeper into his arms, just short of curling up under his skin. His face pressed into my hair felt like a patch of sunlight.

When I eventually opened my eyes, I finally took notice of the room around us. It was almost as sparsely furnished as his own place, nothing but a twin-sized bed and a trunk, too heavy for any geists to knock over. The walls were covered in heavy metal posters, some pretty angsty charcoal drawings, and a handful of bright, smiling family photos. There probably weren't many geists hanging out at beaches and theme parks.

I couldn't keep my voice from swelling, not just with laughter, but fondness. "Is this your room?"

"Look, considering I had a literal horror story of a childhood, I regret nothing."

It nearly hurt to pull away, lose his warmth. But I wanted a better look, grinning as I circled around.

"It's too bad I can't meet your mom," I said. "I would've loved to see some baby pictures."

I found myself blinking in disbelief at the words coming out of my mouth. I'd never even met any of my exes' parents, not exactly the bring-home type.

"You're missing out." He smiled, just teasing, but the truth of it stung. I wondered who the lucky girl he'd end up introducing to his family would be. The longer I stayed with him, the less time he'd have to look for her.

"Are you good?" he asked.

Far from it. But taking in that face of his, I found it in me to smile anyway. "Go spend time with your folks."

"I'll see you at home."

As soon as he left, I lay back on his old bed, wondering if there were any chance in hell his mom would've liked me. At least mine would never have met him, anyway.

TWENTY-FOUR

))) (((

Alastair couldn't leave me alone for long. I expected the interruption, resigned to his pursuit, like the devil my mother used to blame for my misdeeds. Though I'd half-hoped that leaving a bassist on his doorstep would appease him.

He spirited into the apartment right after I'd just finished brewing some evening coffee. By now, I'd learned not to jump when I heard his voice. "I cannot believe you."

Ren had just gotten into the shower. Hopefully he wouldn't hear anything over the water. Or he'd hear everything, so I had to watch my words.

Alastair did his best to pace with the little room he had, circling the kitchen. "You've sent me your ex—who's in the band now, by the way—and you've steered over a pair of foundlings you met at the morgue, but you yourself are still too good for us?"

Not too good. More like the opposite. But I kept that to myself. He'd already gone ahead and said a whole lot I didn't really care to explain to Ren.

"What on earth are you doing here?" asked Alastair.

I shrugged. "It's quiet."

"You're no better than how I found you."

That wasn't quite true. I just couldn't tell him why.

We both turned at the sound of the bathroom door swinging open. Ren stepped out in just a towel, but he didn't rush to the closet, heading toward us instead.

Alastair's eyes widened ever so slightly. I'd almost forgotten. It made me flush, remembering why our kiss hadn't gone farther, who he'd seen in my head. I should've spirited us out of here when I had the chance.

"Is this guy bothering you?" asked Ren. I might've smiled if I weren't mortified.

Alastair ignored him, instead leaning right in and extending a finger.

"Watch it," said Ren. Not that he could do anything about the digit reaching for him from another plane. The finger poked through his bare chest.

"So, you found a medium after all," said Alastair. "I shouldn't have underestimated you. But I didn't think you'd be rubbing elbows—or more."

That did it. I grabbed him by the collar and spirited to the Haunt. I would've spirited right back, but then he'd follow me back and forth, so we might as well just have it out.

"What do you want?" I asked.

He went back to business-like. "Your foundling is bothering everybody with theological speculation."

Danny and Carlos must've been surveying all the ghosts. Good to know they'd kept at it.

"I'd say it's more like metaphysics," I said.

"Whatever it is, it's asking for trouble."

I rolled my eyes and made some traditional ghost sounds at him. "God forbid they get all these souls to question the nature of their existence."

"You're getting ahead of me. That's exactly right."

"God forbid?" I asked, squinting at him. "Are you saying they'll be smited?"

"You mean 'smote.'"

I threw up my hands. "You can't expect them to believe that."

"They should. Why else do you think no one's let out the big secret?"

He had a point. I tried not to let it show on my face.

"It's not like they're going to publish it," I said, mirroring his usual head tilt. "Besides, aren't you curious?"

"What about?" he asked, indignant. As if it hadn't taken decades of observation and reasoning for him to act like he knew everything.

"Wouldn't you like to see if they uncover any patterns, reach some reliable conclusions?"

His eyes glimmered, briefly, before he turned it into a glower. I had him, and he knew it.

"I've been around long enough to come up with my own," he said. "If you don't caution her out of her fool's errand, I will."

I dropped my shoulders, letting my head loll from the blow of defeat. At least he'd given me the chance to talk to them, gentler than he would himself.

"I'll chat with them."

"Just the young lady," he said. "I've got the boy in hand."

I didn't like the sound of that. But I might be reading into it too much, my mind wandering where it shouldn't. It felt like way too long since my last lay at the funeral. I wondered how much time it had been since I'd come to stay at Ren's apartment.

Alastair's voice lowered, like he wasn't just trying to get a rise out of me. "Whatever you're doing with the medium, it can't be good for him."

He left me at that, with my hands fisted, nearly shaking.

~~~

Danny had really made herself at home, taking a corner of one of the parlors and turning it into an office. There had already been a desk with a boxy antique computer, the kind found in underfunded school labs. She'd set up there, pulling up an old coffee table for more surface area. She'd even cleaned, dusting and sweeping, though she hadn't tidied, leaving the clutter and making chaos of her own, papers scattered and books splayed open.

"How goes the research?" I asked.

She must've been really focused, her fingers flying on the keys, because she gave a slightly delayed yelp.

"It's you," she said, not entirely displeased, even taking her eyes off the screen a few times to peek at me. "Long time no see. I've got all my previous research written in longhand as well as typed, and I've conducted several new surveys as well. Now I'm trying to reference my current findings with any existing research."

I came up and pretended to lean on her chair, looking over her shoulder. "How are you powering the computer? Let alone getting Wi-Fi?"

"They showed me how to do it. You know how in horror movies, the poltergeist makes the radio turn on to a spooky old-timey song, or talks to the kid through the TV? I actually never watched that kind of stuff, it made me too anxious, even if it's not real—or, well, I didn't think so at the time. Anyway, it's like that, but instead of terrorizing mortals, I'm psychically accessing the internet. I hardly even have to think about it, I just have to act like I have electricity and Wi-Fi and corporeal fingers for typing. My only real challenge is finding reputable sources for some approximation of peer review."

Listening to her made me feel out of breath. I exhaled, then dived in. "Do they have to be reputable? Given your state of being and all. I mean, you believe in… yourself, right?"

Her shoulders drooped. "Fair point. Scholarly journals won't touch the subject of anything paranormal, naturally. General searches are all clickbait and ads for Halloween décor. There are some interesting archived sites from the old web that might be useful, but… well, just look."

She leaned back to show me one of the relics of the bygone internet, which managed to hurt my incorporeal eyes with a bloody red font over a black background. The flashing animations of dancing sheet ghosts made me laugh.

"Cute." Speaking of which. "Where's your assistant?"

Her face darkened. "I, uh, haven't seen him, for a while."

"How long is a while?"

"It may have been a week or so," she said, in a tone that implied she'd definitely been keeping track of time, and it had been at least a week since he'd come around, maybe more.

I groaned. "Let me guess, he's been partying?"

She took her old phantom pen out from where she'd tucked it behind her ear, no longer for writing, just for gnawing the cap nervously.

"He's just on a bender," I said. "Probably too embarrassed to show his face. I've been there."

Her voice slowed down, going quiet. "Or he doesn't care about me anymore."

"No way," I said, because I meant it. I'd been there. He couldn't really mean to hurt her. I never had, even if I couldn't help myself. "I'll go pull him out of whatever gutter he's in."

She peered up at me with tentative hope. "Are you sure?"

"You want me to leave him there?"

"I guess it wouldn't hurt to check," she admitted. "I owe you one, or, well, another one."

"Don't mention it."

Carlos had made himself just as at home as Danny, in his own way—at Clementine's. I only recognized him by his punk threads; he had his back to me, draped across another man's lap with his head bent down for one hell of a kiss. They literally didn't need to come up for air, so it could be a while. I nearly thought to nip downstairs for a quick sip.

When they parted at last, my eyebrows shot up. He'd been making out with Alastair.

"I told you I had him in hand," he said, all rosy-lipped and self-satisfied.

Carlos gave me a dazed smile. "Oh, hey, long time no see!"

I didn't particularly want to carry on this conversation. I finger-gunned in goodbye, as if it were usual for me to be here, making the rounds. Only by then, I'd been noticed.

"Welcome back, foundling," said the flapper. "We all thought you'd gone geist, for sure!"

"I guess you didn't part those covered knees of yours," said the corseted lady, like she was making a much coyer observation. "He already passed you up for lower-hanging fruit."

Carlos stumbled slightly as he got on his feet. "What did you call me?"

"Don't pay her any mind," said Alastair, though he rose himself.

"If you weren't a lady"—Carlos bunched his hands into fists—"I'd tell you to step outside."

"Why would I do that?" she asked, blinking cluelessly. Not sarcastic, just ignorant.

By now, a bunch of other ghosts had quieted in their clusters, watching, but not with as much interest as I would've thought.

Alastair took the lady by the arm somewhat roughly; judging by the glint in her eye, that had been exactly what she wanted. They disappeared into one of the rooms down the hall, but the walls gave them no privacy.

"I've grown weary of having this conversation with you," he said.

Her voice whined. "It's only taken us a century to try finishing it."

"You know I've never pledged myself to you, or anyone."

"But you've never been with anyone else as long as me."

You'd think, given however many decades or centuries or whatever they must've been fucking, that she would've figured out by now he wanted to see other people. Perhaps she liked having an adversary, an excuse to fight. It's not as if he could leave the toilet seat up.

Whatever they were doing, after a few moments, it went quiet, like they'd spirited off for more privacy.

"I don't want to be her fallback, anyway," said the guitar gentleman.

That made the flapper laugh. "You always say that, but you've never passed up the chance. Some of us are still waiting for their shot, you know."

Carlos didn't seem so amused. I got up the courage to reach out, putting my walls up. But once I got there, my hand on his shoulder, it felt awkward.

I spirited us straight downstairs. It felt a lot less weird once we'd each picked up some vodka.

"Fuck him," I said.

He slumped in midair like on a barstool. "That's what got me mixed up with those weird... young, hot old-timers. They give me the heeb-jeebs."

It wasn't just me, then. "It's like they've been dead so long, they've forgotten their manners."

"That's not all," he admitted. "You seen how they fight? You'd think they've had all the time in the world to sort their shit out. It's like they snap right back to how they were in the first place, over and over."

"Maybe they're just bored."

"I sure fucking hope so," he said, shuddering. "I'd hate for that to happen to me, when I get up there in age."

I held up a play at a toast. "Here's to being forever young."

We pretended to clink glasses, before getting up for a real drink.

I hadn't noticed before that there were plastic jack-o-lanterns sitting on the counter, fake cobwebs on the napkin holder, rubber bats and tissue ghosts hanging above the bar. So we were coming up on Halloween. Nobody looked dressed up, so we hadn't missed it yet. Not that there was much I could still do on this side. But I hadn't made any effort to celebrate the last few years. It would be a shame to miss out again, especially as a ghost.

Ren hadn't mentioned it. He must not have had any plans.

"Where've you been?" asked Carlos. "Even if you don't like the company, they still know how to throw down."

I made a face. His mouth had already parted in protest, so I rushed to slide my point in first. "Whatever happened to your appreciation for science?"

His eyebrows shot up. He looked away, like he could hide his guilty grimace. "We got all our data down. It's done. Or my part's done, the talking bit, not so much the brains. So, party time."

"It's been over a week since you've talked to her, you know that?"

He turned back to me, searching my face like I could be joking. "For real? You been keeping track?"

"I haven't," I said. "But your lab partner has."

His face brightened, but quickly dimmed again. "I'm always inviting her, but every time, she blows me off, says she's busy. I'm not sure she even wants me around anymore."

Something between a laugh and a scoff escaped me. "Seriously?" I gestured around us as drinkers living and dead hooted and caroused. "This *really* isn't her scene."

His mouth curled up in a thoughtful pout. "Right."

"You'd better find some middle ground if you want to keep her close."

He pulled himself up from his slouch with a look of determination. But rather than spirit off, he just stepped right into the path of a drinker.

I threw up my hands. "Bruh."

He gave a sheepish shrug. "I think better when I drink."

Was this how it felt to deal with me, back in my heyday? I crossed my arms, arching my eyebrows.

Carlos sighed. That must've been a blow to his buzz. "I know. I'm not the best friend. But... better than no friends, right?"

I'd never thought of it that way. Usually, once I couldn't keep up the good behavior, I got gone. Never stuck around to find out if I'd be forgiven.

He clapped my shoulder, meeting my eyes with his best sober face, only slurring a tad. "I *will* make it up to her."

I had a feeling the overwhelmingly warm fondness in his chest wasn't meant for me. Well, not entirely.

He spirited off, leaving me alone and tipsy for no good reason. I probably should've waited to sober up before heading back. But I didn't.

TWENTY-FIVE

✱»» ««✱

I found Ren alone at a twenty-four-hour laundromat with lights so blue and eerie they hurt my non-existent eyes. They made us both look dead. A couple of cheap paper ghosts hung by the wide windows, cobwebs drawn with chalk markers on the glass.

He barely looked up from the clothes he was unloading from the dryer as I hopped up onto the machine next to him.

"So, what's up with you and that handsome ghost?" he asked.

I bit my tongue to keep from answering too quickly and giving myself away. "He's just a local nuisance." I counted a few beats in my head, trying to make the change of subject natural. "You have any plans on Halloween?"

He averted his eyes, concentrating on folding his clothes. "I've never been big on it, to be honest. I get enough thrills and chills every day."

That broke my heart. It was my favorite holiday. My mother had forbidden it in our home, so, of course, I always had to sneak out, do my best to dress up with whatever I had in my closet. In college, I'd go all out, slutting it up like I had much to flaunt. I'd never missed out, up until the last two years.

"Well, it used to be every day," said Ren, glancing up with a grateful smile. "You wanna stay in and laugh over some bad ghost movies?"

That sounded fucking adorable. Too much.

I swallowed around a lump in my throat. "I can't."

He gave me a rapid blink. "What, have you got, like… otherworldly business?"

"Well…"

It would be an especially wild night at the Haunt. Not that I'd join. But it would be a good time to check on Evie.

"So there's like a whole party out there somewhere?" he said, like he'd been thinking about this all day. "All kinds of spirits you could've been hanging out with this whole time, instead of me?" My dead heart skipped a beat under his searching gaze. "I can't help but wonder what you're even doing here."

I stole one of his shirts out of his basket, trying to steady my hands by making myself useful, though I wasn't very good at folding. "You looked like you needed the company."

He didn't take it like I'd intended, beaming as he grabbed his shirt from me, shook it out, and folded it again. Only for me to snatch it back and lightly whip him over the head with it.

"I mean you need to get out more. If you died now, would your sendoff put the 'fun' in funeral, or would your turnout be as sad as mine?"

He gave up on the shirt, tossing it unfolded in the basket. "You make a depressing point."

"Damn right," I said. "Have some fun while I'm gone. You'll have your place to yourself, if you want to have company over. Get dressed up, get drunk… get some."

Just as I'd hoped, he blushed. The scowl kind of ruined it. "Is that the kind of night you'll be having? Is the handsome ghost invited?"

I probably mirrored his expression, my face flushing. "He's an insufferable ass." But I didn't have to defend myself. "Not that it's any of your business."

"You're right. It's not." He moved to plant himself in front of me, looking up into my face. "As long as we're still pretending we never kissed?"

"Well…" I gulped. "We didn't. Not really." I unfolded my legs, dropping through the dryer and stepping out from the other side. "If you wanna make out for real, you've got to look elsewhere."

He gripped the basket tight. "I guess I could go for a drink."

"So…" I followed him to the exit. "What are you gonna wear?"

Ren came home early from work the next day with a fairly vanilla skeleton costume. I liked the way it clung to his lanky body. The makeup I dabbed on his face brought out his cheekbones and jawline.

"How do I look?" he asked.

I couldn't answer, at first, like I'd had the breath I didn't need knocked out of me. He wore death better than I could've dreamed.

"You look like you're getting lucky tonight."

I walked him to a bar that wouldn't be too overwhelming for a homebody. Just a cozy hole in the wall, every inch covered in band stickers and graffiti, obscuring most of the tables and counters, scratched through wax and wood. They'd hung yellowing paper skeletons and witches and cats that might have been brought out every year since they'd opened decades back, though the orange lights and fog machine were new, as was the playlist they didn't blare too loudly.

I should've known tonight would be more crowded than most. We had to weave around the milling bodies in their gaudy colors and cheap fabric—or lack thereof. So much thigh and cleavage. I couldn't help but stare, flushing with lust and self-consciousness, before looking down at my own same old fucking clothes as always.

Some of the costumed girls were looking at us. At him. I couldn't blame them. I'd done a damn good makeup job. He looked haunting, with those good bones of his brought to the surface. The tight skeleton suit didn't hurt, either.

I tensed with a sudden shock of nerves that weren't my own. Ren had probably meant for that to be a comforting brush of his hand through mine, but he only pooled our anxiety.

He held his phone to his ear. "We're really doing this?"

His painted brow creased in worry. That gave me the backbone I needed to grin up at him. It didn't hurt that somebody had stumbled slightly through me, wobbling with what felt like a sugary cocktail, grown-up candy.

"Don't worry, I'll warm you up first."

He gulped. I couldn't help but slip into a smoky drawl, standing on tiptoe to murmur in his ear. "What would you say to me if you saw me in this bar in life?"

He yanked his hand away all of a sudden, not soon enough to hide a hot burst of shame. "I wouldn't be here."

That shut down my newfound boldness. He found an opening at the counter and took it, looking as if he were frantically phoning a late friend for some company, annoyed to be alone.

"It's a good thing you've got me, then," I said, as I took a seat in midair beside him. "I feel right at home."

He turned to me with a thorough up-and-down look, as if he were imagining what I would be wearing. "I wish you were here."

I didn't know what to say.

The bartender spared us any silence. Ren fumbled with his order, not expecting to have to specify a brand, like he'd never been in a bar. I suggested a mild beer, which he repeated gratefully. As he sat there waiting for it, I looked around. We needed to hurry up and find somebody he could touch.

At last, one of the noisy groups in the corner vacated their table, and behind them, I spotted her. She was perfect, dressed like a ragdoll, about his age. Not the prettiest, but mostly symmetrical, with mousy brown hair in pigtails and real freckles under the painted ones, plenty of handfuls to grab under her frilly frock. Her green witch's brew cocktail looked near finished as she sat there alone in a booth, like she'd been waiting for a while. Maybe for a date, but maybe not.

"She looks nice," I said. "I bet she'd appreciate some company."

He stared at her, then at me. I put my hand through his, until the bats in his stomach turned to butterflies.

"You've got this," I said.

His smile looked too wistful. But he made sure to down the rest of his beer, with unexpected grace, before heading her way.

She looked up as he approached, then glanced down shyly and nervously drained the last of her cocktail. In that costume, with the innocent circle of blush on her cheeks, she looked like she'd gotten lost on her way from hosting a kids' party, or had a rough day supervising holiday fun after school. The kind of girl he could take home to mom. He wasn't the type to leave in the morning, either. This could be the start of something.

He slid smoothly into the booth across from her, slipping into his laid-back, never-seen-a-ghost customer service voice. It made me shiver and flush at once. "Mind if I sit here?"

Her pigtails waggled as she shook her head, her soft voice swollen with a smile. "Not at all."

As I watched them from across the bar, the cobwebs and paper skeletons trembled as if from a draft. Nearby, some costumed girls tried to cover their bare skin, shivering.

Time for me to bow out.

TWENTY-SIX

✳»» ««✳

E vie wasn't alone. I'd thought it would end up being just the two of us keeping each other company, the rest of the ghosts busy on Halloween. But the wallflowers had found each other after all. Carlos might not have counted, but Evie and Danny sure did. They were huddled together in a quiet suburban street, hiding in someone's well-manicured bushes as if someone might see them.

"Trick-or-treating?" I asked.

They all cried out, loud enough to nearly scare me right back. Evie clutched her chest, like she'd really been spooked. "Mal!"

"You're here," said Danny, with a shy smile.

Carlos waved me over. "Come join us!"

I crept closer, like I also had to hide. "What are you doing?"

"It's a Halloween tradition," said Carlos.

"At least, on this side, according to some of the other ghosts," Danny added.

"We go to see our folks," said Evie. She had her hair piled gorgeously high with her scarf knotted in a bow, though no one aside from us would see her for the occasion. "All together, so we stay safe."

"And we ring the doorbell, so it's not intruding, either," Danny added.

"Hold up," I said. "You're ding-dong ditching your own families?"

"If we make a game of it, it's less sad," said Carlos.

Evie gave an uncharacteristically mischievous smile. "Sometimes they see you."

I shook my head. "No way."

"I don't believe that bit," said Danny.

Carlos practically bounced on his heels. "We'll have to find out."

"So whose place is this?" I asked.

"Mine," said Danny. "I grew up here."

Her eyes were wide and glinting, despite her nervous smile. So that's why we were hiding.

She must've had a suburban childhood, like mine. Unlike me, she must've gotten along with her folks. She probably came home every holiday for dinner with all the relatives, surrounded by love. That only made it harder to lose them.

Carlos put his hand on her shoulder. "Second thoughts?"

"I already said goodbye, sort of," she admitted, between taps to her lips. "That's not so usual, at our age. But I had some time to prepare, come to terms."

"Uh, how?" asked Evie.

"I got diagnosed," said Danny, her voice swelling, still having trouble conveying the words even afterwards. "Big C."

"For real?" I asked. "You look good."

"Well, that's not how I died." Her hands shook as she waved them in agitated flaps. "I supposedly had six months to a year. Then I dropped some notes crossing the street to class, and I needed those, so I stopped, but the shuttle didn't. Everybody always jokes they'll pay your tuition if that happens, so you want to get hit, but, well… you have to live through it." She'd talked fast, even faster than usual, as if she wasn't sure she could tell the whole story without breaking down. "So I died a couple months before my prognosis. But before that, I still had more time for goodbyes than most."

"Not enough," I said.

She nodded.

Carlos took her hand and swung it, back and forth. "Let's go see them."

We went slowly, like little kids approaching a house with a whole yard full of zombies and skeletons and grown-ups dressed to terrorize, rather than a tame porch with nothing but uncarved pumpkins and a scarecrow.

Danny rang the doorbell with a shaking finger, before bringing it to her mouth to nibble the fingernail.

The door swung open. "Hello?" called a well-fed, middle-aged white lady, with a kind red face and comforting Midwestern accent, holding a bowl of treats at the ready.

"Hi, Mom," said Danny. For once, she was worryingly still.

"Hello?" her mother said again. "Anyone there?"

"Come on, hon," called a man from inside, most likely her dad. "It's probably just some pranksters who ran out of eggs already."

But Danny's mom looked wistful, staring through us and blinking mist from her eyes, before she turned and shut the door.

Danny burst into motion, flapping her hands as she tried to breathe, faster and faster until she began to sob, unable to take in any air but still going through the motions as she cried.

"You did it," said Carlos.

He pulled her close, not minding the way she fluttered her hands against his chest. Not hard enough to push him away, just bouncing her anxiety off him. She went quiet soon enough. Maybe it had been worth it, filling her more with relief than regret.

"Are you ready?" she asked.

Carlos spirited us to another house. From the wild, weedy grass, and bikes covered in stickers on the porch, not to mention all the empty beer cans scattered all over the place, I guessed we weren't here to see his parents.

"Is this where your folks live?" asked Evie, rather doubtfully.

"Fuck my folks," he said. "They left me to rot in the street. Or, well, couch to couch, but still. I got my own family, and my own house. At least I died real comfy at home."

"How'd you go?" I asked.

He answered fairly easily. "I mixed the wrong meds."

"Were you trying to get high, or get better?"

"Same difference, am I right?" he said, with a grin.

This time, we strode up through the yard faster, older and ready for mischief. The only decorations outside were pumpkins, carved with grown-up fears: STUDENT LOANS, GLOBAL WARMING, and GHOSTING, illustrated with a message bubble containing HEY, above a checkmark, and in smaller letters, READ AT 2:07 AM.

Inside, they were blasting "Thriller" on repeat. Through the thin curtains of the window, I could barely make out the music video on the TV. Closer to the door, as if to protect it above the others from any smashers, one last pumpkin rested, white and spectral, carved with DEAD FRIENDS, and, below, RIP CARLOS MIRANDA, along with his birth and death dates. Taped in between was a candid Polaroid portrait.

Carlos hit the doorbell with his fist.

Inside, someone yelled, "Kiddos!"

"Chil'ens!" another responded, in a funny voice.

"Fuck, where's the candy?"

"Don't say 'fuck' in front of the babies!"

Several guys scrabbled for the door at once, all young and

uncostumed, one with a short blue mohawk, the rest plainly dressed, band tees and jeans, one carrying a huge bowl of mostly wrappers. They looked around, their excitement fizzling into confusion.

"You scared them off," said one of them.

"Shouldn't have said 'fuck,'" added another.

We had to dodge as the one with the mohawk barreled down the yard to look out into the street.

"There's nobody out here," he said. "We got ditched."

"Who still does that?"

"At least kids still go outside?"

They headed back in. We all turned to Carlos.

He grinned real wide, even as he wiped his moist eyes. "They're still the best boys."

Evie hesitated before taking our hands to spirit us off.

"My sister might not be home," she said.

"We could still visit," said Danny.

"We'll just throw a rock or something," said Carlos.

She shoved him. As they were laughing, and we joined hands, I wondered why she didn't want to see her parents.

We blinked in the fluorescent light of a meeting room, possibly a church, all the tables plastic and chairs fold-up. There were verses on the wall alongside generic, inoffensive motivational posters. I recognized the crowd, a mix of old and young, tatted and pierced opposite starched and plain. It couldn't be anything but a support group of some kind.

I recognized Leah from Evie's memory. She looked like an older, worn-out version of her little sister, big eyes low-lidded, mouth frownier. She wore a red dress with some quick and cheap horns sticking out of her straightened hair.

"This feels so silly sober," she said. "Must be why everyone out there's getting fucked up."

Her companion, a tatted Black guy around her age, rolled his shoulders at her. "You've got to loosen up, use your own courage, instead of the liquid kind."

"I don't have any of that," she said.

"You've got enough to be here, instead of out there."

Evie reached for my hand. I didn't want her to see my own memories of this kind of place, the few times I'd bothered attending. I pretended not to notice, turning to the wall to read the posters instead.

LIVE AND LET LIVE.
ONE DAY AT A TIME.
YOU ARE NOT ALONE.

Carlos went to her instead, not shy about hugging. Danny hung back, but still rubbed a hand up and down her shoulder.

"I got in a crash under the influence," Evie explained. "So we both went sober."

She cried for a while. But the longer she did, the longer it would be until we got to my turn. After giving her the cold shoulder, I didn't want to make it even worse by taking off, skipping my turn, even if that had definitely occurred to me.

When we all joined hands again, it made my head hurt, trying so hard to board up my walls.

We were in a bar. For a moment, I thought I'd spirited way too far of a courtesy distance. Cris could've been passing by in her car or something. Then, through the kaleidoscope of colorful costumes, she emerged, wearing a matching white button-down and pencil skirt to go with a pathetic little set of wings she'd had since childhood. We hadn't been allowed to celebrate Halloween, or even Día de los Muertos, so those were

Christmas pageant wings she'd appropriated for the occasion.

"I can't do this," I said.

I didn't want them to see what I'd done to my sister. And I especially didn't want to open up about how I'd died.

Evie surprised me with her answer. "You want to go?"

She reached for me, but I dodged her hand, again.

"It's been fun," I said, and meant it, even if it had also been sad. "But I really need to be alone right now."

"Are you sure?" asked Danny.

"We're not supposed to be," said Carlos.

"This is why we're here," said Evie.

"Seriously, guys," I said. "I'm not kidding."

But they weren't going to leave me alone. Because they weren't bad friends. So I had to do—or say—something drastic. Something I almost didn't mean.

"Please, just fuck off, would you?"

That did the trick. They were taken aback, and, after what we'd been through together tonight, vulnerable.

Danny began to flap, not in a good way.

"Let's go," Carlos muttered, taking one of her hands.

Evie stayed the longest, as if to give me the chance to change my mind. I just turned and went to grab a drink. When I got back, she'd gone, too.

TWENTY-SEVEN

✦》》 《《✦

Cris had found a corner to sit by herself, nursing a champagne flute. No surprise she didn't often get approached by guys, in spite of her looks. She looked so out of place in the sea of skin, scanty costumes all around her.

"Did it hurt?"

I smiled at the familiar sultry voice. As usual, when I turned around, I saw my ex's cleavage first, popping out of a corset she didn't need a holiday as an excuse to wear. I couldn't tell what she was supposed to be, aside from sexy.

"Huh?" asked Cris. I would've thought, given all the Catholic schoolboys she used to date, she must've heard the pick-up line about falling from heaven.

Vicki rolled her eyes. "Never mind."

While my ex struggled to slide into the booth in her tight leather skirt, my sister shotgunned the last of her champagne.

"Thanks for meeting me," said Cris.

My eyebrows shot up. I figured it had been the other way around. Did she know who exactly she'd invited for drinks? I'd joked occasionally, tested her tolerance, but I'd never come out to her.

"I'd never dare turn you down," replied Vicki, with a wink.

Judging from her stammering, my sister suspected now, at least.

"What'll you have?" asked Vicki. "It's on me."

I'd never seen Cris drink anything aside from champagne, only one or two in a row, and after that, she'd have a full glass of water. But she put on her mask, raising her chin.

"Mal's usual."

Vicki raised her thin eyebrows. "Sure you can handle that?"

"What does it matter?" Cris smiled. For some reason, it made me shiver.

"All righty then," said Vicki.

She wriggled back out of the booth. I followed her, looking for a good drink myself. As if I had much of a choice amongst all the skin and paint and plastic masks. At the first accidental sip, I couldn't help but laugh, having a good time whether I liked it or not.

As soon as we got back into the booth, Cris tossed back my straight whiskey. She didn't gag, or even grimace, though she couldn't blink back the tears. They spilled over, beginning to run her mascara. Vicki acted quickly, taking the edge of a napkin and wiping away the inky trails. That salvaged her makeup before it could get any worse.

"Not bad," said Vicki.

I had to agree.

Once she'd drunk for courage, my sister didn't bother with any more niceties. "Tell me about her."

That ought to have been my cue to leave.

"Diving right into it, huh?" said Vicki. "What do you wanna know?"

"Everything."

Vicki sighed. "Buckle up."

She started at the beginning, when we met as roommates in college. "The first time I saw her, she was wearing this horrid denim overall dress that went all the way down to her ankles, just completely covered up while she brought in her boxes, and her mom hung an actual crucifix on the wall. I got so scared and excited, like this is either gonna be my chance to corrupt a Catholic schoolgirl, or I'm gonna get hate-crimed. But she beat me to the corrupting. By the end of the week, she was borrowing my clothes, and the crucifix was gone."

Cris finished her whiskey and started borrowing sips of rum and Coke. I'd already told her about my first band, the all-girl punk group, when I came home for vacation, lending her secrets to keep in lieu of having her own.

I'd wanted to brag. Besides, it distracted her from the divorce. Gave her a glimpse of what life could be like with no more house rules.

"It didn't take long before she got noticed by some real talent in the making, stolen out of our garage for a popular new local band. Then she dropped out to go on tour. She and I didn't last long after that. I almost dropped out myself to follow her on the road, but—"

I gulped, watching a fleeting wince of pain cross her face. So it still hurt, even after all these years. My limbs tensed, wondering how she'd explain it.

But she just smiled, like she didn't care all that much anymore. "Well, she'd already moved on to the next lead singer."

Maybe she considered herself lucky, losing me sooner than anyone else did.

"I don't know what happened during the tour," said Vicki. "I mean, straight from her. I heard they kicked her out for drinking too much, missing recordings, jerking around with everyone's feelings. She wouldn't answer my calls, so I don't know for sure."

"We got back in touch after that," said Cris. "I mean, she didn't tell me much about it, either. She tried to call before, but Mom wouldn't let me answer."

Vicki straightened up. "What do you mean, wouldn't let you?"

Cris flushed, her drunkenness starting to show in the slur of her words and gestures. I cringed on her behalf.

"Mom said—I thought—she'd gone to the devil."

"What the fuck does that mean?" asked Vicki.

My sister's eyes glazed over. "I couldn't save her. She'd strayed too far, and, like, wanted to take me with her."

Vicki's hand shook, clutching her empty glass. "I swear, the shit your mother put in your heads."

"Well, it didn't stay put," said Cris. "I started talking to her again when I moved out. Only she went radio silent again, for too long. I tried not to think anything of it, but then—" Under the table, she balled her hands into fists. "She texted me goodbye."

I didn't remember that. I'd been blackout drunk. When I got my phone back in the hospital, she'd blown it up with messages, and I'd felt too guilty not to answer.

Vicki's red lips hung open. "Wait, what?"

"She drank herself into a coma," said Cris, her voice flat. "Had to get her stomach pumped. It looked like an accidental binge, but... well, then why the goodbye?"

"Fucking hell," said Vicki. "Did she go to rehab, or counseling, or... no, wait, I know the answer to that."

"She did go to a few AA meetings," said Cris. "But they were too churchy for her. She tried going to a psychiatrist, too, but she had spotty insurance, job-hopping too much. So that didn't work out, either."

"Well, I underestimated her." Vicki stabbed at the ice at the bottom of her empty glass with her straw. "And how hard it is to get help in this shithole country, on top of having to stomach asking for it."

I braced myself for an impassioned rant, looking forward to the tangent that would distract from all the talk about me. But Vicki got up to get more drinks instead. I followed suit.

Once they'd gotten a couple of gulps into their candy cocktails, they switched turns.

"Tell me about her," said Vicki. "I mean, whoever the fuck you were burying."

"She crashed with me for a while," said Cris. "Then she got a job and moved out."

"Didn't she make any royalties?"

"Not enough to pay the record company back for breaking contract."

They'd sued me, actually. Hospital bills took care of the rest.

"What job?" asked Vicki.

The alcohol probably didn't help my sister recall the list. "Uh, something in finance, I think administrative, but that one didn't last so she slung coffee for a while, then worked at a couple of call centers."

Vicki blew out a puff of air, flapping her lips. "Ugh, boring."

Cris stared, eyes glazing. "She knew if she didn't change, she'd die young."

"So, to keep living, she stopped living? What the hell? It didn't even work. Why didn't she just join another band? She played so many instruments. Or she could've stayed behind the scenes if she wanted, just writing."

"Whenever I asked, she got snappy and stopped talking for days. Whatever went down with the band, it made her miserable. I thought she'd be better off moving on."

"No way," said Vicki. "She couldn't have been happy without music."

Cris sobbed. It made me tense, so sudden and short. "I wish I'd known," she said. "Do you think it was an accident?"

The light above their table dimmed, then flickered even brighter.

Vicki didn't even answer. She just groaned as she squeezed back out of her side of the booth and went over to my sister's, putting her arms around her, like I wished I could.

I wondered what would happen if I tried touching her. Whether I'd pick up on her thoughts. Perhaps there'd be comfort in my touch. But I didn't dare, in case I couldn't handle what she felt.

"This is fucking sad," said Vicki. "Come on, she'd gag to see us crying over her in the club. Let's drink to her memory, and then just drink."

Cris recovered surprisingly quickly, like she'd gotten used to crying lately, able to sprint through the stages. "I can't stay too much longer. I've got a makeup exam tomorrow."

Vicki sighed. "At least you're pretty."

She replied with the sulky shrug of the perpetually single. It must've gotten hard to date and still keep her virginity pledge at her age, unless she'd secretly given up, too embarrassed to tell me.

"Don't get a lot of attention?" asked Vicki. "Not a surprise, you project that halo of yours pretty far."

"Really?"

"Keep drinking, let's see if it falls off."

Cris's laugh unsettled me. Not her usual soft, restrained giggle under her breath. She always hid her outbursts as if she were still sitting on my bed at midnight, trying not to wake our parents. This one grated, harsh and gravelly. More like mine.

"I think it already did," said Cris. "I mean... I don't believe anymore."

For years, I'd been trying to poke holes in her faith. But just enough to let in some air. I hadn't thought it would give me so little joy to watch it collapse. Believing might've given her some comfort right about now.

"So you think she's just gone?" asked Cris. "Nowhere, nothing?"

Vicki pursed her lips, like she didn't like the reminder, but she couldn't deny it. "There's the fucking rub."

"Never mind," said Cris. "Let's drink. I might as well catch up, while I'm still here."

"That's the spirit," said Vicki.

Their glasses were empty, but they clinked them anyway.

I couldn't tell who made me more jealous: my sister, for getting cozy with my ex, or my ex, for getting to take my sister on her first drunken adventure. At least she'd finally loosened up, even if it was too late for me to enjoy it with her.

Alastair had been right. I shouldn't watch her grow up without me.

TWENTY-EIGHT

✸»» ««✸

I'd forgotten not to spirit to Ren. He might've gotten lucky tonight, and I'd be in for a sight I'd never forget. Instead, I flinched in surprise to find him sitting on his kitchen floor, his face hidden in his folded arms.

I dropped to my knees. "Ren?"

He lifted his head. He'd tried his best to take off his skull makeup, though gray smudges still smeared deeper shadows than usual around his eyes, which were hazy, a touch drunk. Even so, he looked unsurprised by my arrival, like he'd felt me coming.

My hands were reaching with a mind of their own for his face. Then I remembered myself, pulling back. "What's wrong?"

"Nothing," he said with a giggle, as if he were lying, playing innocent. Then he closed his eyes, leaning his head back with a sound that pitched too low for a laugh, his mouth curled the wrong direction. "Nothing at all."

I ought to have felt disappointed. My chest eased, unburdened.

I wanted to trace his jawline, have a sip of whatever he'd been having. But if he couldn't hold it, then I wouldn't, either. I got up and grabbed him some water.

"Did you strike out?" I asked, sinking beside him again. "It's happened to the best of us. And, you know, me."

He shook his head, or tried at least, like moving too much made him dizzy. "I didn't."

"What do you mean?"

"We could've, but—I just—"

I couldn't tell if he was too drunk to articulate, or overwhelmed by something else.

"Why not?" I asked.

After downing the whole cup, he sounded more focused, trying to sharpen the tipsy haze on his tongue. "I just had this moment, washing off the paint in her bathroom sink, then looking up in the mirror, and realizing—"

He bit off whatever he'd been about to say.

"What?"

I shouldn't have asked, because he straightened up, looking at me with sudden resolve. It made me shiver, like the chill before a storm. I dug my nails into my palm, in lieu of anything else to hold, clutch for life.

"Don't be mad," he said. "But I did fall for you, after all."

I let my head fall back, wishing I could bang it good and hard against the cabinets. My voice trembled. "I told you not to get sappy."

He moved to kneel over me. "Look, I don't care if we can't get physical. Tell me you don't still feel something whenever we touch."

"It's not that," I said, hugging my legs.

"Then what is it? Why can't we give this a try?"

I covered my face. "Don't make me say it."

"Mal—"

"I've thought a lot about us, all right?" I got on my knees, so I could meet his eyes. His mouth kept rising and falling between a smile and a frown as I went on. "I can't even sleep, but I'm constantly dreaming about you. Not just about getting into your pants, either. I'm fucking haunted by the possibility that if we'd met in life, we could've gotten somewhere. Maybe not white picket fence stuff, but like… sharing a place, for real, with lights and plants and real furniture. Being the kind of people who throw dinner parties for their friends and family. I'm not painting a very good picture, but it doesn't matter, anyway." I sank back down on the floor. "We're too late."

He stared at me, blinking like he didn't know where to start. At last, he said, "We did meet."

I shrugged helplessly at him. "What in the hell…?"

"You used to have blue hair, right?"

I'd never told him that. "Why do you ask?"

"I didn't get a good look at your face, at the time, but I remember your hair. The same as all your pictures when I looked you up. I'm sure it was you."

Now I knew where he'd seen me, why he'd hesitated to bring it up. That must've been how he'd managed to get through to me, back when I went geist. Why he'd looked younger in my mind, strapped to a bed at first, before aging up into his usual self. It had started as a memory. It choked me with a wave of nausea, sick with sympathy and surprise.

"You were on the ward with me?"

We'd each had our own breakdowns keeping us from getting a good, lucid look at each other.

"I think you can figure how I ended up in there," he said.

"Same."

"But you didn't get committed with me to psych, unless you went someplace else?"

"I played dumb, talked them into thinking it was an accident, like I didn't know my alcohol limit. So I detoxed, went to a couple meetings, never mentioned all the symptoms that might've gotten me a more accurate diagnosis."

His mouth fell in disbelief. "You got off lucky."

"I don't know about that."

It hadn't exactly been the best time and place. In fact, it might've been the actual worst time and place. But we'd both been alive.

My voice rasped low, barely above a whisper, like I could tiptoe around it, say it without saying it. "What if I'd transferred with you, gotten some help?"

His jaw went tight. "As if."

"I know they didn't help you—"

"They don't help *anyone*, locking them up like animals."

"That's not what I mean—"

"Mal, I'm sorry, but if you knew the things they do to you in there—they did to *me*—"

All the locks and chains in his place began to rattle. We looked around, but there were no geists.

It was too late to hit the brakes on this conversation. I watched as the crash turned into a pile-up.

I growled. "Fine! Not transferred, not *committed*. But if—if I did get help somehow… what if I could've gotten better?"

He bit his lip, shaking his head, eyes glistening.

"I might still be here with you, but… not like this."

I showed him my palms, like they were see-through, or decomposing. He reached for them.

"You are still here," he said.

I could hardly take the tenderness in his gaze, let alone his hands, if he tried and failed to touch me. I shied away. My throat closed, as if to keep me from saying it. "It's all my fault." I tasted salt, wiped at my face. Through the tears, I looked up, and flashed my coin-trick smile. "I lied."

Not just to him, or to Cris. Mostly to myself. Every time I came close to letting the truth break the surface of my mind, the lights would flicker, or the walls would crack, or the radio would blare. So I buried it, again and again.

Now the kitchen light flashed, the faucet poured open, the stove glowed red.

"I did kind of kill myself."

Up on the roof's ledge, looking down at the void below, I'd danced. Just a joking little two-step, playing ding-dong ditch at death's door. When I slipped, it might as well have been a jump.

Ren didn't flinch at all. Not even when the lightbulb popped and the cabinet doors splintered open and the coffee pot burst into pieces. He kept his eyes on me, like if he looked away, I'd disappear.

"You're here," he said. "It's not the best time, but we met, we're here."

His hands through mine weren't tangible, but they filled me with warmth. Or they would have, if I weren't so cold, like lighting a match in the rain. What he felt for me couldn't hold a candle to my darkness.

Then I couldn't feel anything at all, aside from the chafing on my wrists and ankles.

Those might've been my tears on his cheeks. "Please don't go."

If I didn't, I'd go geist. I could barely talk for the tube crawling down my throat.

"I'm already gone."

Stage Six:
Anger Sex

TWENTY-NINE

❋》》》 《《《❋

I found myself in a haunted house—the fake kind, with strobing lights and plastic cobwebs, blaring spooky organ music punctuated by pre-recorded screams. I latched onto every detail, clinging to the darkness to keep it from turning into the white of a hospital.

Weren't you going to wait till you're twenty-seven?

An actual scream startled me lucid.

"That wasn't funny!" said a feminine voice.

The masculine answer sounded confused. "I didn't do anything."

"Don't touch me!"

"I didn't!"

I barely stepped aside in time as the couple stormed past me.

"Boo," said a familiar voice.

I didn't flinch. My annoyance must've grounded me somewhat. I could talk without the tube down my throat. "Shut up."

Alastair drew closer, getting sharper in my vision. Like he was coming out of a fog, and not one made by a machine. "I thought I'd have to drag you out tonight."

I wanted to retort that I'd expected better from a real ghost than coming to haunt this place, but combined with the hospital fading in and out of my vision, the scares weren't so cheap.

As he peered down into my face, his grin overturned. He gripped my shoulders, hard enough to hurt, but it steadied me.

"What's wrong?" he asked. "Didn't I warn you off lingering among the living? Your guilt and regret are as good as hellfire."

I tried to growl as usual, but my voice came out strangled. "Really, must you?"

"I'm sorry." He gave a slight sigh. "Truly, I am."

His hands slid down my arms, circling my wrists, as if he were trying to replace the restraints. It worked. My skin went from cold and chafed to warm and throbbing. Just as I'd hoped. That's why I'd come to him, my last resort. I needed something to feel.

"Go on, then." I stared up at him through my lashes. "Make it up to me."

He stepped back, heaving an exasperated breath. "Not *now*."

I thrashed my arms, his hands moving with them. "Haven't we danced around long enough?"

"We literally haven't."

"What, you need some wining and dining first? I didn't take you for a romantic."

I tried to lean in, our noses brushing. But he still pulled back.

As he gazed down at me, brow furrowed, the glint in his eyes might've been pity. "Your tears aren't dry yet."

Of course, he had to pick the worst time to be a gentleman. "They're just late."

When he released me, my stomach dropped, as if I were about to fall. I clutched at his chest, digging my fingers into his shirt. He compromised, putting his hands over mine, too gently. I needed it harder.

"Please, I'm ready." I tried calling to him through our touch, the same as on the dance floor, sharing through my blood exactly what I wanted him to do to me. "Show me a good time. Give me a warm welcome. Make me feel like I'm better off dead."

He shook his head with a woeful smile. "I'd hoped you'd be feeling better by now."

Now that I'd finally admitted to myself what I'd done—what I'd cost the ones I loved—there was no hope for "better."

I brought his fingers to my lips in a murmur of a kiss. "Just help me forget."

His walls were still up, if only by a couple of loose boards. But his blood answered, hot and tempted. "I suppose we all grieve in strange ways."

At last, he leaned in, letting his eyes drift shut, lips unguarded. I took them, moaning with the rush of tasting again. Not to be outdone, he clutched me by the nape of the neck, until he had me bent back and clinging onto him. Thunder and howling crescendoed over the stereo.

He wasted no time undoing my buttons, shocking my nerves back to life as he teased his mouth down my neck and chest. Before long, he'd sunk to his knees, lifting my skirt and peeling down my underwear. I clutched his hair, joining the taped chorus of screams. Even if it weren't really his own tricks of the tongue my body remembered, he played the part so well.

When he rose back up, he took me with him, doing his best to pin me against the wall. He gripped my wrists again, though the hospital bed had been replaced with much better restraints in my memory. Just for fun this time. I wrapped my legs around his waist. When he buried himself in me at last, it felt like the other way around.

By round two, he'd pushed us through the wall, into a room with a graveyard scene. After being bent over a fake headstone, my phantom knees were shaking, ready to collapse. Once we finished, I did. He followed me down, lying beside me like he thought I might want to cuddle.

But he never did like wasting nightfall. After I stayed put, making it clear I wouldn't draw any closer, he sprang up, like I hadn't tired him at all.

"Get decent," he said, pulling his pants up, but leaving his vest and shirt open. "Or don't, I suppose there's no need anymore, is there?"

I sat up, my skirt still bunched around my waist where he'd ridden it up, along with my tank top, though my blouse and underwear weren't coming back anytime soon.

"Why?" I asked.

"Did you think I'd let you off so easy?" he said. "Come on, the night's still young."

He held out his hand. I took it.

We swung by Clementine's for a drink, blowing out the lights to the delighted shrieks of the costumed crowd. As we drank, we brushed shoulders on purpose as we passed, and perhaps some of those strangers turned to strike up conversations, thinking they'd bumped into each other.

Once we'd gotten good and tipsy, we hit the streets. Bigger kids stealing candy got their bags ripped open, spilling their stolen loot. Smaller kids afraid to visit scarier houses found the jump-scare decorations didn't work until after they'd grabbed their candy, so they could run for it. At a tween sleepover, all the Ouija board questions were answered with encouragement about their crushes and final grades.

After the kids went to bed, we stayed up for the afterparty. We went to a costume ball, though none of the living danced as well as the dead. It did help to accidentally pick up somebody's acid trip. All the costumes looked real, dancing ghouls like me.

By the time daybreak glowed blue between the buildings, mingled with the orange of the last streetlights, I didn't want it to end. We were walking side by side down the street, candy wrappers whirling in the wind along with the dead leaves around our feet.

"You know what day it is?" he asked.

I'd nearly forgotten. My accent tasted rusty in my mouth. "Día de los Muertos."

Gloria never even mentioned it. She'd thought it too pagan. I ended up learning about it in school. While all the other kids made tiny shoebox ofrendas to Frida or Elvis or Kurt Cobain, I'd done one for my dad. I kept doing it on my own, every year, until I got old enough to start bringing them to his grave, leaving him more realistic offerings of booze and cigarettes. Up till I'd started touring, at least. I hadn't picked up the tradition again afterwards.

"Come with us," said Alastair.

I couldn't help but side-eye him. "Why are you celebrating?"

"You think I'd pass up a party in our honor?"

Funny how I felt so protective of a holiday that didn't even feel rightfully mine, like if I didn't feel entitled to it, he shouldn't, either. "I don't think you're the dead my people are expecting to come home tonight."

He answered in Spanish, this time slowly enough for me to follow, even if it took me a moment to contextualize the words. "You don't think I've been invited? Your ancestors were happy to have me, down in Mexico."

I turned my head to hide how far my eyebrows had ridden up and refused to come down. Not only did he have better pronunciation than me, but for once, he'd acknowledged his age. I'd known from the start that I'd decided to fuck a much older man, but I didn't particularly want to do the math. No wonder he'd had time to practice his accent.

"It's different in your time," he admitted. "Have you ever heard of the danse macabre? Back during the rule of kings, they used it to comfort the poor, these etchings of skeletons dancing together free of flesh, no crowns or rags, equals in death. Everyone gets theirs, no matter their birth."

I'd wondered why I'd seen so many ghosts of different colors getting along, despite their different eras. Even so, he sounded a little idealistic. "Are you saying we don't have bigots on this side?"

He smirked. "You know which direction they go."

I laughed, wanting to believe him now. "Good riddance."

His hand found mine. Our touch was easier than ever, my walls more like a fence, low enough for the neighbor boy to perch on.

"So," he said. "Will you be joining us?"

He swung our hands, whirling me slowly and gently around, relying on me to go along with it. I did, even if it still made my heart skip a beat, thinking of dancing at last.

But what else could I do? Now that we'd slowed down enough for me to finally recall what had happened last night before I fled, the streetlight above us buzzed like a dying insect.

"Hey," said Alastair.

He pulled me in for some more kissing. I hadn't really expected we'd still be going at it. I'd thought he only needed to get me out of his system, and afterwards, he might not even care about getting me in the band anymore, satisfied with a win of another kind.

"Think about it," he said. His hands wandered over and then under the clothes I'd barely gotten back.

"Again?" I asked. "So soon?"

"I'm sorry," he said, with a mocking pout. "Did I tucker you out already?"

As much as I expected to be tired, when I thought about it, my aches had already eased, all the bruises and bites gone too soon.

"No way."

I went to my knees, my turn for some taste. He grabbed my shoulder, spiriting us somewhere I didn't even care to look. I would've had him right there on the street, for all the world to not see.

He trailed his hands through my hair. "So much for being a killjoy."

THIRTY

✹⟫⟫ ⟨⟨✹

It had been a long time since I'd slept with the same person two nights in a row. It felt different the second round, without so much buildup and fanfare, and on a bed for a change. This time, I couldn't help but try and peek behind the patchwork curtain of memories that lined up with his every touch. My skin may as well have been a map, every part his hands and mouth pinched and nipped already long charted. I found myself wondering whose skilled tongue I really felt, not to mention whose shape and size he slipped, which my mind must've judged to be a good fit. It made it harder, this time around, not to think of someone else I'd never really get to touch.

This time, once we'd finished, he got bolder. Rather than roll over, he stayed put, draped over me, like he knew well enough how quick I'd spring up to leave otherwise. I couldn't help it. All the morning sunlight spilling in through the broken windows told me I ought to be dust already.

I finally thought to take a look at his room. I hadn't even noticed most of his furniture was actually stacks of records, decades' worth of music, thick enough to hold up an ancient Victrola and antique boombox and a relatively new flatscreen TV to go along with his smaller, less stable collections of cassettes, CDs and DVDs. I was admittedly impressed with his music collection, but it disappointed me to learn that he watched TV like the rest of us. Probably to keep up with modern slang.

My chest tightened as he stirred. He stood straight through the bed as he got up. His clothes came back, like he knew how to do it on purpose, complete with the tailcoat.

Evie's coat. My heart knocked painfully in my chest. I nearly cursed out loud.

I'd forgotten about her crush. Rather, I'd ignored it, because I hadn't cared enough. Otherwise, I might've had to think twice about my actions, and, of course, I couldn't do that.

Alastair went to pick through one of the record stacks. "What do you want to play tonight?"

My body tensed, ready to flee.

"I've got to put together the setlist," he said, as he thumbed through album after album. "But I'll give you first pick. I know we're pretty retro around here, but that's why I'd love to hear something new."

"I don't remember signing a contract."

One of the records fell straight through his hands. I cringed as the vinyl slipped out of its sleeve, clattering to the floor. He didn't move to fetch it, taking his time turning to me, his mask in place.

I knew I should've left.

"What do you think of this home I've built?" he asked.

I curled myself up, like bringing my knees to my chest might shield me from his stare. "I'm here, aren't I?"

"You're not about to leave again?"

"I don't plan on it."

He let his mask fall with a sigh, tilting his head down at me, his eyes filled with pity. I bristled, but didn't move.

"Why do you keep forsaking this gift?" he asked.

I didn't know how I could possibly explain to him. So I made something up. "It's not as if I could ever measure up to the greats here."

His pity gave way to laughter. It made my stomach drop.

"What greats?"

So that's why I hadn't been able to name any band members. I'd figured it had been my failing, not theirs.

"Have you seen anyone famous here?" he asked. "They're all in hell, most likely. None of the band here were truly great in life. They didn't get their shot until afterward."

"So I still wouldn't fit. I already took my shot." I pointed him some finger guns, briefly, before letting them break apart in my palms, backfiring. "I missed."

"I'm giving you a second chance."

"I don't want it."

He stared at me, and kept staring. For once, he had nothing to say. At last, he made his way back through the bed, brushing his thumb over my chin. "Right when I thought we'd gotten somewhere."

He didn't have to let down his walls for me to feel the blow to his pride.

"What, just because I let you hit? You're hot, and I hate myself anyway."

"Are you telling me playing wouldn't help you with that at all?"

I played dumb, going for the laugh. "How would it make you less hot?"

Not even a smile.

"I'll see you tonight," he said. "No earlier, don't look for me in the daytime."

"Why not?"

He let out a slight sigh under his breath, worse than any of his usual dramatic affectation. "You're not my first foundling. You won't be my last. You have no reason to think you're so dear, out of all the generations of souls I've comforted."

"You could just say you want to see other people."

"That's not what I'm saying," he said. "Anyway, I know the torch you're carrying isn't for me."

For once I had to watch the other person leave, literally disappearing, like I always wished I could.

While I lay in bed, waiting for my clothes, I wondered what to do about scaring off the wallflowers the night before. I considered not bringing it up. It even occurred to me that if I was careful, I wouldn't necessarily have to see them, ever again. But if I was going to stay here from now on, I couldn't avoid them for what might be literal eternity. Surely, they'd have to forgive me in a couple of years, or decades.

And I wouldn't mention any of this to Evie.

Just as I began to debate whether most of the ghosts here would care if I walked around naked, and if I should care so much myself, somebody spirited right in. Turned out I didn't care much, since I didn't even move to try covering myself up. Not until I realized who'd come in.

Evie covered her blushing face, muffling a high-pitched noise like a hiccup, somewhere between a gasp and a sob. She hadn't done her hair yet, wrapped up in her satin scarf like a turban.

"Shit," I said.

Whatever happened to courtesy distance?

She turned to hide, rushing right out through the wall. I gathered the unnecessary sheets around me and moved to follow her.

At least she couldn't concentrate enough to spirit away as she rushed down the hall. The back of her gown had ties to keep the slit closed, but without Alastair's coat, she clutched the two sides shut anyway.

I nearly dropped the sheets as I reached out to try slowing her by the shoulder. She turned to me with no resistance, letting me see what I'd already felt from her touch, her face damp and darkened. I hadn't thought she'd take it this hard. He fucked around with so many other people.

"My bad," I said. Then I thought better of it. Maybe I could still salvage this. "I mean, about what I said last night. Back there, though, that wasn't what it looked like—"

Her eyes went unexpectedly cold. "I'm not a fucking child," she said. "I know whose room you were in—whose bed."

My mouth dried up.

"So, you found something better to do," she said. "Or should I say somebody?"

It had been stupid, thinking I could pull the wool over her eyes. I knew she never should've trusted me. That I'd let her down somehow.

"Don't let me ruin your fun." She spoke so softly, her tone mild, I nearly thought she meant it in earnest. "There's no call for you to sit on the sidelines with me."

She must've really liked him. So much, she wouldn't even give anyone else a shot.

"No wonder you're always missing out around here," I said.

That sure as hell didn't come out right.

She whipped her head around, though I could still see her hands wiping at her face.

Somehow, she managed to spirit off. I didn't try to follow her. She couldn't stand the sight of me, still naked, wrapped in his sheets.

It might not be the worst idea to avoid her for a while, after all.

THIRTY-ONE

✸》》 《《✸

Once my clothes came back, I spirited off. Light and shadow rippled over me, tumbling down through tree branches. Dying grass and dead leaves lifted beneath my feet, whispering together in the wind. I rubbed my arms, shivering with the memory of a breeze. I'd really begun to feel at home in graveyards. I'd always found them pretty welcoming, my dad's plot in particular. I used to visit as if it were court mandated.

I tried to brush off his headstone, even if I had nothing to clean it with, like I usually brought, along with the offerings. I pretended to prop myself up against it, as usual.

Funny how I'd never stopped missing him—rather, stopped regretting his absence from my life—even if he'd left me on purpose. I hoped Cris would one day feel the same.

Movement on the edge of my vision made me tense up, wary of geists. When I turned to look, it appeared to be a big family gathering, their voices clear and alive. Some kids ran weaving around the headstones, not heeding the shouts from grownups telling them to slow down, be respectful. They looked like they'd just come from a festival, their faces painted up like skulls, still munching on candy. Following them through the cemetery, the adults hauled coolers, tubs of food, and a stereo.

Soon enough they were settling into what must've been their family plot, like they were at a tailgate, blasting Tejano music while the grownups cleaned up the graves, draped them in marigolds, set up the pictures and saints and personal belongings. Even the kids had settled down, looking more somber now with the photos out, reminding them of family they might've met, or at least heard about. After making their sweet bread and tequila offerings, the grownups settled in fold-up chairs with beer and tamales, leaning back to shoot the shit for the dead who hadn't gotten to hear it. After their inevitable sugar crash, the kids listened quietly, hardly understanding why their parents and aunts and uncles were laughing one moment and crying the next. They would get it in a couple of years, when they looked back.

I could imagine it would make it easier—whether lying on a hospital bed, or in the street after a crash, or however many other ways there are to die—knowing your grave would host a party.

It would be too early for my own ofrenda. They weren't traditionally put up until after the first year. But Cris wouldn't know, from the one and only time I'd brought her along. I'd wound up babysitting that day, but I didn't want to miss my yearly visit. She'd tagged along for the chance to see a cemetery, making up for another missed Halloween.

I'd filled her in on what we were doing, but I'd had a hell of a time explaining to her how a ghost could come back, if he was supposed to be in heaven. I'd ended up admitting that I didn't really believe any of them came back. I hadn't mentioned I'd begun to doubt heaven, as well. She moved on to the next line of questioning: how I'd scored smokes and booze. I told her they were purely ceremonial, like wine during the sacrament.

Sure enough, when I spirited there, I found Cris kneeling at my grave, still marked with a temporary sign rather than a headstone.

She hadn't changed, her clothes from last night rumpled, though she'd taken off the wings. The grass hadn't yet grown back after my burial, dirt staining her white pantyhose and shoes. Streaks of mascara had dried on her face, bags under her eyes.

I nearly panicked and disappeared again, but I didn't know where to go. Not in the daytime. The party wouldn't start for hours. And suddenly, I didn't know if I still had it in me to dance. Above us, the dying leaves still clinging to branches rustled violently, some falling to tangle in her hair. The sunlight brightened so suddenly, I raised my hands to shade my eyes—until I realized the bright white came from the hospital walls closing in.

Then I caught the whiskey and cigarettes nestled on the grass. She'd remembered. The walls melted away.

A sudden hand on my shoulder nearly scared me to death, again. Alastair, of course. I huffed at him.

"Don't start," I said. "We're supposed to be visiting family today."

For once, he wasn't stern, his glance and voice both soft. "Not alone—and certainly not sober."

I couldn't believe that got me to smile. His hand slid down my arm to twine with my fingers.

Cris still kneeled there in silence. I wished, for once, she would try talking to me. She probably didn't believe I could still be around to hear it. These offerings were more for herself than for me, just like the ones I used to leave on my dad's grave, for my own sake.

"Did you ever give her that message?" Alastair asked.

His touch steadied me. "We tried."

"What did you want to tell her?"

I closed my eyes, trying to raise my walls. But it didn't really matter. He'd likely seen flashes of the rooftop in my memory. Or he'd suspected from the moment he read my obit.

"Lies," I said.

He squeezed my hand. "There's no need. Trust me, she's already lying to herself, whatever she needs to believe about you."

Maybe it would be better if she never got answers. Just like I would never know for sure whether my dad had truly meant to leave me behind. I still came to visit him anyway.

And even if she did suspect the worst, she couldn't be that mad at me. After all, she'd brought along some of my favorite vices.

Alastair tugged at my hand. "I think that's long enough for a visit, don't you?"

It made my skin flush with shame to be sniffling in front of him again, as if that were worse than everything I'd already shared through our touch.

"I told you there's a natural cycle," he said. "Listen to all that laughter out there. In another year, she'll be joining in. She doesn't need you interfering with the normal, healthy stages of grief. In fact, it goes both ways."

"What do you mean?"

"We have to cope differently on this side," he said. "Our own preternatural cycle, abnormal stages."

My throat closed around the words. "How could I leave her again? Wouldn't it make me a monster?"

He tilted his head at me, mouth agape for a moment. Then he cupped his hands to my face.

"My dear…" His brow furrowed with melancholy, even as he smiled. "We're ghosts."

I choked on a strangled laugh, or a sob.

"Besides—" He gestured down at the booze and smokes. "It seems to me she's given you her blessing."

I couldn't drink and smoke her offerings, but it felt like permission to indulge myself.

This time, only a few tears escaped. Not the flood I'd once dreaded. It might have done me some good, letting it out last night.

I turned to her for one last look. "Thanks, sis."

I rested my brow on his chest, closing my eyes and letting him spirit us away.

When night fell, for once, we didn't stay in the Haunt.

As I came back together from mist, the pulse slipped into my veins, all the way down to my marrow. Around us glowed an orange haze, cast by flame. Candles, dozens of them, floating amidst marigolds and bowed heads and crosses of stone. They lit the cemetery, more crowded with people than I'd ever seen. More tailgaters, most of them made up like sugar skulls, though some of the painted grins were wearing off from eating and drinking and crying. I picked up on a shot of tequila from someone's raucously laughing tío.

For a moment, I thought we'd spirited someplace I'd never been, the country where my great-great-somebody-or-others came from, so long ago and so far away I'd never considered it home. But there were a few faces unlike the others in the crowd. Like some families with no Latine heritage had come to pay respects and were invited to stay for the food. I couldn't be far from where I'd started.

But where did the pulse come from?

Alastair led me by the hand, following it. My feet fell in time with the beat. Somewhere nearby a mariachi band played, but the pulse drowned them out in my ears. All around me the living played at being dead, laughing and drinking beer and kissing each other. Little did they know the afterlife they acted out wasn't far from the truth. And now, I wanted to live up to it—so to speak.

Amongst the oldest of the graves on the edge of the yard, the ones with no family and no names, we found the band. They'd conjured their ghostly instruments like gossamer in their hands. Around them the dancers circled, like the shadows the living once feared on their cave walls. They whirled further and further out amongst the stones as more and more dancers swept in, like fog blown by the wind.

Goosebumps prickled my skin, seeing everyone close enough to be together, living and dead, celebrating the afterlife. Could any of them feel our presence? Would they be scared, or comforted?

"Ready to shuffle off your mortal coil?" asked Alastair.

I shrugged, as if I wasn't trembling. "No matter what I did, I would've ended up here, wouldn't I?"

"It's time to let go." He didn't gloat, no smirk, just a serene smile. "Look around—does anyone here look sorrowful to you?"

I couldn't agree with him. All around, I saw sorrow along with joy. But I'd had enough of the former, blaming myself for being here, not permitting myself to enjoy it. Time to let loose like the calaveras around me, laughing in the face of la muerte.

He offered his hand. "Come and dance."

As the band crept into another song, I recognized the voice starting to sing. Evie's usually sweet voice suddenly dove low and raw, in a growl that grabbed me roughly and wouldn't let go. Even she was extending an invitation to join.

I didn't take Alastair's hand—not just yet.

He knew why. Pulling back, he rolled his shoulders, tapped his feet, waiting. In my own limbs rippled an echo of his movement. I let my waist loosen. Our bodies whispered to each other, carried along by the pulse. His arms told mine to snake up, let palms meet without touching. We each swung to the side, away from each other, rolling briefly away in our own dances before circling back to meet again. My skirt whirled around my legs, fanning out.

We tumbled through the gravestones as we circled around and around. I couldn't tell who chased who as we wove together and apart. Our hands finally met. He swung me into a bonfire, and we danced black and red in the white light, like we were going down in flames.

Suddenly, he pulled me close, and the music died. I cried out loud to have the pulse ripped from me. Around us bloomed the empty ballroom of the Haunt.

"Shh," he told me, face close in the dark. He held his fingers to my lips. "Shh. Listen."

He stroked my hair. I closed my eyes.

My ears pounded, as if with an echo. It grew, like over the years the pulse had been embedded in the very walls. Or it carried all the way from the cemetery, our souls in tune with it no matter where we were on earth, a beacon calling us home.

"You hear it?" he asked.

His love for this place, down to every dead leaf and cobweb, flooded my chest with warmth. Evie's voice flowed in my veins, pounded in my head, drummed in my bones. My own heartbeat had never thundered so hard.

"I hear it."

I opened my eyes, tapping my feet. He grinned, shuffling backward, beckoning.

"Welcome home."

He vanished, and I followed.

We danced through shafts of moonlight. He kept spiriting out of reach, all over the mansion. I followed, shimmying forward, spiriting. At the stairs he mock-grabbed the rail and swung, and I did the same. He spirited higher, and higher, over the stairs, until our feet forgot the ground. I couldn't deny the roller-coaster thrill in my stomach and drumroll in my chest—the same I'd felt looking down from the roof in my last moments—as he and I did a two-step in the air. He looked as good to me as the oblivion that had waited below.

This time, I fell on purpose.

THIRTY-TWO

)》》 《《

Night after night, I started to forget that I'd died. We were all so alive while dancing, so many lifetimes at my fingertips as I swung from partner to partner. My body opened to theirs, my legs and arms and hands moving to the memories of dances long dead, not long enough to linger on anything else. It shook awake my every numb limb until they began to ache, and even then, I couldn't stop. It hurt too good. The pulse beat harder through my blood than my own heart ever had.

Once the sun rose, I couldn't help but hit the bed with some of my dance partners. We couldn't keep up that rhythm without the pulse, touching too long to keep memories from spilling. I saw too many wives and husbands and sweethearts, some of them long dead, others lingering on, sometimes fresh in their memories, other times gray and wrinkled, like they'd gone back to visit. It gave a bitter aftertaste to every brush of skin and lips. But my mouth got so sick of its own taste. I had nothing else to put in it. So I kept taking in strangers, until I'd long passed the number of partners I'd had in life, no risk of catching anything aside from melancholy.

I'd never had so many nonverbal, usually drunk encounters when I was alive. Most of my old one-night stands had been much more romantic. I liked to banter, from the bar to the bed. It smoothed over the awkwardness of clothes catching on limbs, nakedness failing expectations, sneaking off into the sunrise with no intention of spoiling the near-perfect little love affair with an unnecessary lifespan. Even if I didn't remember many names, I'd never forget those nights.

I rarely ever learned names at the Haunt. I hardly even noticed what era their clothes revealed before they came off. If my walls slipped, as I waved my hands looking for sheets to clutch, their memories often spanned so many generations they didn't seem real, worn and blurry as old photographs, like I'd fallen asleep to a documentary. Even without reaching old age, it got harder and harder for them to get their lives straight. *What dress did I wear that night? Did she have brown eyes? What year was it, before the fire? After the march, or the shooting, or the war? Was I really there, or had I only seen it on TV?*

My memories were probably much sharper, unbearably so. More often than not, they had to ask for me to try harder shutting them out. Though they weren't all memories. Just wistful fantasies I couldn't help but indulge. It felt even more embarrassing than calling out the wrong name.

Though I did that too, sometimes. Thankfully, nobody cared enough to bother asking, "Who is Ren?"

After we'd finished, I usually tried my best to sleep in on a threadbare velvet loveseat in one of the parlors, even if I didn't need sleep, just to pass the afternoon. I never did anything until five o'clock, when they opened the doors at Clementine's. We didn't need to get tipsy to dance, but it gave us something to do, woke us up, like coffee and a cigarette at the start of the day.

As slow as they were going, all my days were blurring together. I had nothing to distinguish them. No particularly good breakfast or lunch or dinner. No classes or work or any other responsibility. It felt like a weekend that would never end, losing the meaning of a weekend in the first place when I didn't look forward to it, or dread its coming to an end. Not unlike my last few weeks of life, wallowing in unemployment, and haunting my apartment afterwards. At least this time instead of lying around at home, I'd been getting laid. This place definitely beat my last.

One night at Clementine's, I found myself getting closer to all my predecessors when I saw a head I didn't recognize, modern enough to be living if she hadn't just passed through a table. I almost jumped right on her, eager to take in a new face, chew on some new conversation, maybe explore a new body. Then I recognized her. It had been a hot minute.

Danny looked lost, like she hadn't meant to spirit in. Not to mention, I could've sworn she wouldn't be caught dead here, literally.

I hadn't seen any of the wallflowers since I'd come to stay, aside from Carlos. But he hadn't talked to me. We glided coolly past each other on the dance floor, and I didn't see him often at Clementine's. He must've really taken me seriously when I'd told them to fuck off.

"What are you doing here?" I asked.

Before she could answer, someone passed through her. I reached out, but couldn't find the words to warn her in time. She blinked wildly, wobbling.

Suddenly, she gave a whoop, not just flapping but throwing her arms fully up and down. I burst out laughing.

"That's tequila!" she said.

Remembering I didn't need to catch my breath, I wheezed. "You drink?"

"Wait!" Her shoulders drooped. "Aww, no, I hate tequila."

"Why—"

She cut me off, like she'd registered my last question a little late, shuffling around in a full body wiggle. "I used to, with my friends. Just not to—to—what's it called? Bach—back in—oh, you know, the god, like the one they have at Mardi Gras."

"Bacchanalian?"

"Right, we didn't go that far." She attempted to sit, falling through the bar stool. I caught her elbow, hoping I wouldn't add too much to her drunkenness. Judging from my own near loss of balance, she was a lightweight.

"Oh, right," she said, staying put in midair. "Thanks! So my friends, we'd make some tasty cocktails—stuff like berry wine or approx—approx—what we think ancient beer would taste like, y'know anthropology grads—pair it with dinner and cuddle up with a good—or really not very good—movie. Then we'd all go to bed."

That sounded nice. I couldn't help but picture the scene in my apartment—or the apartment in my head, with the lights and plants and pictures.

"But isn't it fun to go out and get trashed every once in a while?"

"Going out, sure, sometimes, but why getting trashed?" she asked. "Do you have to go so hard? That's why I hate tequila. Don't you want to have a good time you'll actually remember?"

I could barely get my lips to lift. "I don't have time to reminisce if I never stop."

She peered at me, pressing her fingers to her lips. "So that's why you haven't you been around?"

Evie must not have mentioned anything. Of course she wouldn't, if she wanted to keep her secret.

I lied. "Why would I want to hang around and do nothing when

I could be out living it up?"

She didn't seem too offended by my implication that she did nothing all day, just a square compared to me. I wondered if she agreed. Maybe she only needed a nudge to give my lifestyle a try.

I put my hand on her knee, nearing her thigh.

"Care to dance?" I asked.

Her eyes widened as she tried to put her walls up, but I could feel her repulsion.

"Um," she said.

I withdrew immediately. "Sorry, I must be rusty," I said. "I could've sworn you're not straight."

"I'm not," she said. "But I'm ace. My sexuality is… no thanks."

"Oh."

No wonder she didn't dance—on this side, it must've been way too sensual for her, all that writhing and throbbing and unspoken beckoning in the blood. Though at least she had one less hunger to try and fail sating on this side.

"That must be nice," I said, completely serious. "But how do you even keep busy? If not *that* kind of busy."

"I've got my work, mostly," she said. "And friends—"

"Who's your friend?" asked Wilhelmina, the corseted lady.

Flo, the flapper girl, looked up and down at Danny. "Well, we can't all kick the bucket on our way to a party, dressed to the nines." She smiled, fingers creeping along in the air. "But we could get you out of those pajamas."

I swatted her away. "Hands off."

Danny surely wouldn't appreciate her lack of walls.

"Oh, we're respecting prior claims now?" asked Wilhelmina.

I pinched my brow. "Not this again."

She'd pestered me every other night since I'd started sleeping with Alastair. If she hadn't played the harp for the band, I had to wonder whether he'd put up with her at all, or if she'd be the one ghost he wouldn't mind kicking out on her own to go geist.

"That's fine by me." Flo flashed her starlet grin. "I'll keep you company, and your little friend. The more the merrier."

At least I knew what to expect when she draped an arm over my shoulder. She had a fun catalogue of memories in bed, even if they'd begun to fade and blur together.

Danny raised her eyebrows, her wide eyes glazing. "Right, that's my cue."

I shrugged in apology, before she spirited off.

"How rude," said Flo. Before withdrawing her arm, I caught her disappointment sinking in my own stomach. I hadn't thought she'd get so bored of me already. Just another blurry face in her memory.

They fluttered back to a newer arrival, leaving me alone again.

I hadn't completely abandoned Ren. Once or twice, at night while he was out driving, I'd spirited to his place to check for geists. There weren't many new ones, but I didn't know how long it took for them to accumulate. I would circle the apartment a couple of times to be sure. It hadn't changed at all, aside from a new coffeemaker. He hadn't put any locks back on.

I always spirited onto his fire escape, in case he turned out to be home. This time, I had good reason. There were voices coming through the window. At first, I thought he must've been watching something, staying in for a weekend I hadn't noticed coming and going. It sounded like porn, judging from the heavy breathing and soft moans. I covered my laugh.

Then it got louder, too loud to be his laptop speakers. And the voices were familiar, one of them really familiar, even if I'd never gotten to hear it like this, draw those kinds of noises from his lips.

He had someone over.

I ought to have gotten the fuck out of there. Instead, my knees buckled. I slid down with my back to the wall, my hand still over my mouth. My limbs seemed to think they couldn't move, let alone disappear, no matter how badly I wanted to. I didn't expect it to ache this much. And, even worse, in the wrong places. Even as my chest caved, and my stomach turned, I had to cross my legs.

Through the wall came a crash. For a moment, I'd thought they'd just gotten more intense in there, as if he had a bedframe to bang against the wall, hanging pictures to knock down. But they went quiet.

His partner sounded scared. "What's that?"

"It's a ghost," said Ren.

So that had been me.

"That's not funny."

Her curled-up little voice reminded me of the ragdoll from Halloween. If he'd gotten a second chance with her, I ought to be happy for them. After all, I'd set them up.

This didn't change anything. He'd already been unavailable, off the menu, out of the question.

"I'm not joking," said Ren. "That's my old roommate—she died."

I nearly gasped out loud. If he could tell my presence apart from any other visitor, I really shouldn't have come. Yet I still couldn't move. I couldn't think of anywhere else I really wanted to be, aside from that mattress.

"You really believe that?" she asked. "Are you, like, self-aware about your hallucinations, or are you having some kind of not-so-lucid moment right now?"

"Take your pick."

He did sound mad, but not at her.

"Look," she snapped. "Just because you're sick, that doesn't give you an excuse to be an asshole."

His voice softened, more like himself. "I'm sorry. I really am having a moment. Next time I'll say so. I mean—if there even is a next time?"

She gave the kind of slightly exasperated sigh that made my heart sink. I'd kind of figured, or maybe hoped, that it might be only a hookup. Even if it should make no difference to me.

The affectionate groan escaping her mouth hinted otherwise. "I don't scare easy."

At that, my feet remembered their skittishness, always ready for an exit. I spirited still sitting down, sprawled on the floor of the upstairs saloon at Clementine's, as if I were already beyond shitfaced.

"Mal?" said Alastair.

He shrugged off the arms wrapped around him, rushing to kneel before me.

Wilhelmina gave an indignant scoff. "Beg pardon? How dare you pipe off—"

"Not *now*."

For once, his chilly tone shut her up.

Alastair swept me onto my feet. I barely got my walls up in time, brick by brick, but by now he knew not to peek over. He pushed me into the bathroom, then spun me around to grip my wrists, so much harder and hotter than the hospital restraints.

"She's going to be sulking for ages," said Alastair. "You wouldn't happen to play the harp?"

I leaned up to catch his lip in my teeth, too hard. He pulled my hands over my head, even if he couldn't actually pin me against the wall. As hard as he tried, he couldn't fully anchor me with no earth to ground us. Wrapping my legs around his waist came close enough.

"How do you do it?" I asked, as his mouth trailed down my neck. "How come you're different from the other ghosts, not stuck repeating yourself?"

His laugh tickled my collarbone. "Sweetling, the number of times you've forced me to repeat myself—"

He pinned both my wrists in one hand, freeing the other to snake under my skirt.

I writhed against him, although I enjoyed being trapped, the simmer of annoyance yet more heat under my skin. "You know what I mean."

"Since you insist on wandering where you shouldn't, anyway—" His fingers distracted me from the gravity of his words, but not entirely. "I might not be a part of the world anymore, but I keep up with it—read, watch, travel—and it brings me down sometimes, which is why I caution against it—"

My voice ran ragged. "That's why you don't wanna be followed in the day."

Wherever he went, whatever he witnessed, he didn't want to share. And then, when he came back in the evenings, he kept acting like he didn't have a care in the world, boozing and fucking and dancing it all off.

"That's right," he said, even as a flick of his wrist sent me over the edge. I buried my gasp in his shoulder for a moment of blissful forgetfulness. But only a moment.

He pressed a kiss in my hair. "I whet my memory on the sharp edges of the world, at risk of dashing myself against the rocks."

As I tried on instinct to catch my breath, I laughed. "I've been bashing my head and I'm still here, aren't I?"

"Just don't get cocky."

Still one-handed, he unbuttoned his pants, barely getting started. He sighed as I tightened my thighs around him.

His lips brushed my ear. "Who's the girl?"

My nails dug into my palms. He'd peeked through the cracks in my walls, after all. Even if I hadn't seen it, I couldn't stop thinking about the ragdoll, lying on the mattress I used to share, her hair spilling over the pillows like mine never could. Meat on her bones, blood under her skin, breath in her lungs.

"Forget it."

THIRTY-THREE

❋》》》 《《❋

Liam and I were still avoiding each other. It felt like the breakup all over again. We were casually aloof, taking conversation elsewhere if our clusters collided at Clementine's, brushing hands like a formal handshake if we swung toward each other in the ballroom. Though I'd felt relief through his fingers the first time he saw me there, he must've backed off thanks to the guilt over our last conversation I returned in exchange. He might've been waiting for me to call off my demand for space.

So, every chance touch after that, he tucked an unspoken question into my hand: *How about now?*

But I always replied, *Not yet.* Until one night, I didn't. Rather than let go, I held onto his hand. It might've been the heat of the dancers around us, or just the fact that neither of us had made a bad decision for a hot minute. I couldn't tell who thought of it first. As we held each other's gaze, circling, we leaned in close.

Then I thought better of it. At least, I hoped it had been me. I let go. Neither of us went far, still dancing together. He'd never moved this well in life, no longer inhibited by his size, unafraid of toppling anyone over as he weaved and bobbed weightlessly. Everyone nearby sensed to give us a wide berth, and I could feel when to lean away and close back in, matching his waving hands and swinging feet.

We were so in tune, we didn't want to part. Usually, that meant I'd found my partner for the night, and we'd get a room. Instead he asked, "Wanna grab a drink?"

I spirited us straight to Clementine's. We didn't stop dancing through the crowd, getting real smashed so fast, already stumbling and laughing like we were approaching the end of a long day and even longer night, years ago.

I considered apologizing for our last talk. But nothing I'd said had been untrue. I also didn't exactly want to remind him and bring the mood down. Just showing up at all might've been enough of a concession for him.

"Nice of you to finally join us," he said. "I missed the old you."

"Right back at ya."

I'd nearly forgotten he'd gone off and gotten married, not to mention had a kid. It felt like no time had passed at all. As if we'd never stopped partying, or even playing.

I didn't mind pretending that our last conversation had never happened. Let alone the last few years.

"Let's go back," I said, grabbing his hands.

He must've felt what I meant, through my touch, but still needed to ask. "Uh, where?"

Back in time to the band house, shotgunning beer in the backyard, or crowding around the slightly lopsided pool table in the basement of our favorite dive bar, or wandering around shouting and laughing on the streets of a strange city as we searched in vain for someplace to eat in the wee hours of the morning. Those places felt the closest I'd ever come to finding a home. Even the strange streets, as long as I walked them with my family.

Though the floor-bound mattress of a certain nearly empty little apartment came pretty close. Just like the rest, I couldn't go back there.

"We're good right here," said Liam.

"It's not the same."

As much fun as I'd been having, I meant it. Drinking didn't feel the same without tasting the burn of alcohol, waking up with no consequence the next morning. Fucking didn't have the same thrill, knowing the other person's thoughts, love bites and bruises disappearing all too soon. And I couldn't call any of the other partygoers family.

"You're right," he said, like he meant it. "It's even better."

I did my best to hide a shudder. "You sure?"

"This is what we've always wanted," he said, with a light in his eyes that I recognized from the old days. I'd always thought of it as the reflection of our stars rising. "We've got no attachments, no responsibilities, and no more hangovers." He took my hands and swung us around. "It's a party that never ends."

As much as I wanted to go along for the ride, something still weighed me down. "What about your folks?"

Siblings always grew up and went their own way, even if they were supposed to come back together in times of joy and grief. But he'd started his own family, baby and everything. They'd depended on him.

His shrug made my stomach twist in unease. "What about 'em?"

"You haven't been checking in?"

He gave an incredulous shake of the head. "Why would I do that?"

I had to swallow down a wave of nausea, my guts writhing. "Don't you care how they're holding up?"

He didn't look so carefree anymore. There was tension along his jaw, darkness in his eyes overtaking the light. "What could I do about it? They might as well be the ones who died, not me. Isn't moving on what I'm supposed to do?"

He had a point. I'd been trying to do the same.

We stood helplessly for a moment, all but wringing our hands for want of a drink to hide behind. As if possessed, we both sought immediate distraction—which happened to be each other's lips.

That sated some of my longing for old times, as well. He tasted the same as ever. But no matter how hard he fronted, he still cradled the memory of his wife in the back of his mind. I could almost taste her myself.

We broke apart again.

"This isn't working," I said.

He shook his head at me sadly. "I keep forgetting we're so much better with some space between us."

"We never should've dated."

"I wouldn't say that." That took me aback. "Just because we didn't stay together, that doesn't mean it didn't matter. You weren't the one, but who's counting?"

He probably meant for that to be comforting. I didn't expect how his words landed, like they'd knocked something loose in my chest. It choked me, until I had to cough it up.

"I never met the one."

At least, not while I lived.

"There is no 'the one,'" he said. "You had lots of ones."

Except I hadn't stayed with any of them for the rest of my life.

"What about your wife?" I asked. "Isn't she the one?"

"She could've left me, or died first, and maybe I would've been too depressed to try and date again, especially as a single dad, but then what if I bumped into somebody at the grocery store? Or if my baby's kindergarten teacher turned out to be hot? Even if I remarried, it's not like I would've been happy about my first wife being out of the picture. Or that I'd wish we'd never even gotten together, especially since our baby wouldn't exist. And I never would've met my second wife if all that hadn't happened. Or I wouldn't have been ready to love her, if I hadn't learned from all my other ones—especially you."

He'd clearly put a lot of thought into all that.

"But you're the one who died," I said.

"Why do you think I've been beating myself up over this? I might not have been the one for her. And that's fine. Like I said: Who's counting?"

"I can't help it," I said. "It must be easy for you to ignore the numbers when you did settle down with just one person. I didn't."

He looked at me with what might've been envy. "You were considerate enough to die alone."

Ouch. After our last conversation, I'd deserved that. But it killed my buzz stone-dead.

It must've been winter by then. I couldn't feel it, but I could see it. Frost rimed the dead leaves on the walls. Snow found its way inside, gathering like dust under windows and through cracks and holes in the ceiling, and in the cold of the dark, it didn't leave. At Clementine's, drinkers came in heavily padded, and struggled to find a home for their coats if they wanted to dance. They were playing all the usual seasonal songs on the jukebox.

None of the other ghosts acknowledged the time of year, except in their disdain for the music. I think it took them back, in a bad way. Whenever I ended up half naked in the upstairs bathroom again, trying to distract myself with someone I couldn't call a stranger anymore even if I still didn't know their name, their memories weren't exactly a turn-on. It felt like flipping through a photo album I'd found, decades of living rooms full of families around the tree, except I could hear the same songs playing on their old radios and record players and stereos through the walls. We gave up trying to change the jukebox. We weren't the only spirits trying to command the music.

More of us had family still living than I would've thought, some not far from joining us, and others they'd never gotten to meet—children grown up, grandchildren who would hear stories about them. We were drinking more than usual, dancing harder and fucking faster, trying like hell to forget.

I didn't care much for the holidays. My mother had never gotten me anything I wanted, and no matter how much I tried, how long I crafted or how much I saved up, she'd never been impressed with any of my gifts, either. I did miss celebrating on the road with my bandmates, trying to crack each other up with the worst gift-shop kitsch we had time to find, wrapped in the same brown paper bags we got from the liquor store.

Cris and I had a no-gift rule. I'd been broke when we reconnected, and too prideful not to reciprocate any presents. Instead, last Christmas Eve, she bought the takeout, I brought the booze, then we watched *It's a Wonderful Life*. After that, I'd told her to give Mom my loathing, and she'd steeled herself for dinner without me while I polished off the rest of the champagne.

If she wasn't doing so well, there wasn't much I'd be able to do for her, unless I could find another medium who I hadn't strung along then promptly abandoned, and figure out just the right words to say to keep her from floundering. Besides, I'd just gotten to a stage of grief that I rather enjoyed. It wouldn't do to backtrack. I tried to ignore the urge to cheat, check in on her just the once, natural cycle be damned.

But one night, I spirited in to find it empty at Clementine's. Rather, there were no breathers, the bar closed. The piano still rattled away upstairs, laughter the living wouldn't be able to hear echoing in the rare silence. It had to be Christmas Eve.

I'd have no shortage of company tonight, even if we'd be having a dry evening. As I lingered in the relative quiet of the empty first floor, I couldn't help but wonder if it was just as silent for Cris. Whether she'd be on her own tonight, unable to go home.

I half-expected to find her drinking alone in her apartment, keeping the bottle all to herself without me. But when I spirited to her, she wasn't home. I found myself at another party.

Somebody had decked out a sleek, minimalist condo with miniature white and gold trees and big silver ornaments hanging like disco balls from the ceiling. All the milling and laughing and dancing guests broke the monochrome color scheme wearing their holiday best, plenty of flamboyant red and green, a good bit of white trim fringing bared skin. I wished the host luck with the post-party cleaning bill, watching a girl spill her cocktail on a white couch as she climbed up to dance.

I almost didn't recognize Cris. She'd made up for her Halloween costume by going all out with Santa-inspired crimson velvet, complete with a hat. I'd never seen her wear a dress so short, even with the striped tights underneath.

And I'd rarely seen her so cozy with a guy, either. The blandly handsome white guy with an arm stretched behind her on the couch was dressed more modestly in a regular black suit, boring in comparison to everyone else. Their knees were touching. She didn't do that even with established boyfriends, always leaving room for Jesus.

Vicki approached in a matching dress, though on her the neckline plunged way further out. A giggling, green-haired girl trailed behind her, hand in hand.

"I'm outta here," said Vicki. "Don't forget to text me."

Cris all but rolled her eyes. "Sure, Mom."

Vicki pointed a finger at the guy. "Treat her right and make her come at least twice, or I will find you."

He burst out laughing. If he hadn't taken it well, I would've been suspicious. That was probably why she'd said it in the first place.

Cris hid behind her hand, going red. Vicki blew a kiss and waggled her fingers before sashaying away with her friend in tow.

"Friend of yours?" asked the suit.

"She's my roommate," said Cris, still red-faced.

So she'd moved out, after all. She could do worse than living with my ex. Even before we'd gotten together, she'd looked out for me. Always checking in to make sure no one had roofied my drink, holding my hair back whenever I curled up sick around the toilet, fetching me water and aspirin in the morning.

Maybe if I'd stayed with her, she might've slowed my spiraling better than my bandmates had. More likely, I wouldn't have listened to her, either. But my sister wasn't as much of a handful as me.

"Looks like she won't be home, then," said the suit.

Cris sounded breathy with nerves. "Guess not."

He reached to brush a strand of hair out of her face. She let him. He leaned in, and she permitted that, too, closing her eyes. I turned away as they locked lips, not wanting to see any more.

She wasn't doing too bad, after all. Apparently, we were in the same surprisingly enjoyable stage of grief. We just weren't meant to share it.

Stage Seven:
Hope

THIRTY-FOUR

❋》》 《《❋

I'd begun to dread the daytime the same as sleepless nights in life. At sundown, my afterlife always began again, keeping me distracted through the night. If I finished early with any partner at sunrise, I'd be left alone while everyone rested as best they could through the late morning, hours to wait until we could start again.

At first, I thought I must be daydreaming. I heard that voice in my head all the time. But I didn't suspect it could be coming through the walls. I ducked into the library, trying to listen in, over my heart drumming in my ears.

"Don't linger," said Alastair.

"Why not?" asked the voice that sure as hell sounded like Ren.

I sank down on an armchair like it could catch me if I collapsed.

"You really need me to explain?" said Alastair. "It's not natural for the living to mingle with the dead. It begs for some sort of universal comeuppance."

"What, like, bad luck?" said Ren, for sure. "You went through so much trouble to get me here, and now, you're trying to scare me off?"

"I just wanted to say hi," said Evie. As if she'd been there the whole time, quietly waiting for her turn.

Alastair must've been rolling his eyes. "Don't waste too much breath—he's only got so much of that."

That sounded like a sign-off, before spiriting away.

"Where were we?" said Ren. "Oh, right, hi."

From the warmth in his voice, he had to be smiling. I'd forgotten they'd known each other in life.

"Thank you for bringing all of this," said Evie.

Ren shrugged it off. "Don't mention it."

"It's not too much trouble? I hope you didn't have to pay for everything."

I wondered what he'd brought. This must've been how we'd gotten all the newer furniture, not to mention the books, old VHS tapes, DVDs and CDs, the TVs and computers we played them on, plus old games and consoles. All from a former medium. I wondered what had happened to them.

"It's on the company card," said Ren.

"Is that stolen?" She sounded impressed.

"Just borrowed. Somebody around here hasn't had their relatives cancel it yet. I get to use it for myself, that's part of the deal. So I'll take the trouble."

Something about her giggle made my stomach drop. My chest sank, like I'd gotten the air knocked out of my nonexistent lungs, as I recalled the way she'd talked about him on our first introduction. Lab partners in chemistry. Didn't she say something about him bringing her ramune? And, later, flowers at the hospital.

She must've been the high school crush he never asked out. In the following quiet, I wondered if they'd ever touched in life.

"How've you been?" Evie asked.

"I'm surviving," he said. "Uh—no offense."

"Oh, none taken! We slip up all the time, ourselves."

"I'm so sorry about before, when I told you to fuck off," he said. "I thought you were a figment of my horrible imagination. And I can't believe I missed your funeral. I didn't even know you'd—"

"It's all right." Her voice curled up, embarrassed. "I'm here now."

"Well, it is good to see you again."

Something unsaid hung in the air, faintly bittersweet. Evie rallied on in spite of it, her voice light. "You look so different!"

"I do?"

"You're smiling! You used to just be like—"

I would've killed to see her imitation of his high school self.

"Shut up!" He gave a startled laugh. "Fuck, how did you put up with me?"

"You weren't that bad, once we…"

For a moment, they quieted, and I worried their natural shyness had caught up with them, choking off any more conversation. Next would be excuses to leave, and I could come out of hiding. But I wouldn't have minded staying put a little longer, enjoying that voice while I could.

I nearly got up—whether to leave, or to join them, I didn't know—but I sprang to my feet when the silence broke.

"Hi there," said Carlos.

"Uh, welcome," added Danny.

Evie made an awkward murmur.

"He looks like he knows how to have a good time," said Carlos. His tone made me shiver, too close to that of the elder ghosts—not ravenous, but bored. "How about it, you ready to party?"

"Or not," said Danny. "If that's not your scene, you're in good company."

"Should I tell them?" asked Evie.

"I'm not dead," said Ren.

He gave them a minute, in which I could only imagine they were staring. I wondered if he would find it funny or not.

"Say what?"

"You see us?"

Ren laughed, more sweet than bitter for a change. "I see you."

He sounded so sure, it didn't feel like he was talking about his second sight. Like they were friends, and he was jokingly calling them out on some kind of mischief. *I see what you're doing there.*

"Don't worry, I won't tell anybody," he went on. "I'm just here to bring stuff, and, like, get a sneak peek of the afterlife, I guess."

"Are you seriously… not dead?" said Danny.

You'd think we were the living and he was the ghost.

"May I?" asked Carlos.

"Go ahead."

He must've tried to touch Ren. Of course, his hand would simply disappear through him.

"That's so wild!"

Ren owned it. "Right?"

"Who are you?" Danny's voice went low with awe. "How is this possible?"

"If you figure it out, let me know," said Ren.

"Do you mind if I ask you a few questions?"

"Not at all."

"Make yourself at home," said Carlos.

"So, you've been able to see us for a long time?" asked Danny.

Ren laughed. "It's a long story."

I tried to think of where else to be. I couldn't risk staying while he lingered under the same roof. He could appear around any corner, so out of place amongst the vines and crumbling walls, breathing in all that dust and fuck knows what else. This place couldn't be any better for his lungs than I'd been for his heart.

I spirited to his apartment. As long as I knew he wouldn't be there, I might as well check for any new geists.

It didn't take long. Not nearly long enough. I circled twice. While I waited, giving him some more time, I lay down on the bed. As if I could rub my cheek on the pillow, take in his scent. I could only imagine it, lying there, remembering how his face looked so close to mine.

All too soon, I had to get up, because I felt a little creepy. Then again, as a fucking ghost, I couldn't exactly help it.

I didn't really want to be at Clementine's. But I couldn't go back and eavesdrop anymore. Or join the wallflowers and Ren, still talking even after they'd surveyed him.

So I just got drunk by myself, ignoring all the other ghosts. Nobody had anything new to say, as usual. And I didn't feel like eating leftovers.

"Long time no see," said Carlos.

I flinched in surprise, not expecting that he'd ever speak to me again, after so long giving me the cold shoulder. Had I done something to piss him off again? He might not ask me to step outside, but he wouldn't be shy about telling me off, either. I braced for it.

"You'll never believe who showed up at the Haunt."

If my surprise showed on my face, he must've thought I hadn't heard anything. I played along like I hadn't eavesdropped. "Who died?"

"Nobody, that's what's so wild! It's your old roomie."

"Ren?" I asked, pretty convincingly. I still hardly believed it. He must've given them the full story.

Carlos told me all about their hangout, from the parts that

I'd heard up to everything I'd missed. After the survey, he'd stuck around to shoot the shit while playing some games. It sounded like a good time.

"It's too bad he's alive," said Carlos. "He's so cute."

I really wanted a drink to hide behind.

"You should hang out with us next time." He must've really meant it, forgiving me at last, because he leaned in to clap me on the shoulder.

I barely had enough time to get my walls up, trying to keep from cringing, stiff to the touch. "I don't know if I'd be welcome."

He let go, gesturing widely. "Are you kidding? We miss you. It got weird for a minute there… but just a minute. We've got forever, so let's make like all these dusty old fuckers and forget."

Maybe I shouldn't have asked. "Does *everybody* miss me?"

"Ren talked about you a lot," he said, with a wingman's smile that chilled me to the bone.

"What about Evie?"

That killed the grin. He let out a sympathetic whistle. "Just talk to her."

I gave a decisive shake of the head. "I hurt her too bad."

"She's more hurt that you didn't even say anything."

"You sure?"

"I mean, she and I had to have the same talk." Judging from his wince, it hadn't been fun. "But you can't be the best friend all the time, remember? You have to work at it, not just give up and then have no friends left."

I had given up in life, died friendless. No wonder my wake had such a shitty turnout. Meanwhile, his own must've been an absolute rager.

Somehow, despite all the twisting guilt in my guts, I managed to smile. "Thanks for giving me another shot."

"Someone's gotta pull you out of the gutter." He winked.

"You really want me around?" I asked. "No takebacks. From here on out, I'll be ride or die. Or... you know."

"No choice," he said, with a laugh. "Just ride."

It made my stomach bounce to think of facing Ren, after Evie. But I didn't want to miss out anymore. I got to my feet.

"Wish me luck," I said.

He gave me a hug for courage.

THIRTY-FIVE

✹》》 《《✹

Evie must've been feeling nostalgic. We were in a sports field, full of school kids shouting over the blaring music from the bleachers. Probably a spirit rally, because rather than tossing a ball around, all the athletes were doing dance routines, or something like it. Back in the day, I'd always skipped this shit to go smoke.

I found her sitting off by herself in midair before the front row, near the teachers. Her hair peeked in two thick braids from under her loosely tied headscarf.

My breath caught sharp in my throat. All the second thoughts I'd worried might catch up with me simply turned back and left, because something told me she shouldn't be left alone.

I sank down beside her. It made her recoil, hands flying to her chest.

"My bad," I said. "I didn't mean to spook you."

Her eyes were hard again. It made me writhe in place, as if I could shift in such a way to make that piercing glance hurt less as it dug into me.

"What do you want?" she asked, quiet and resigned, like I'd only come because I needed information, as usual, not companionship.

It came out violent and a touch resentful, but I coughed it up, all the same. "I'm so fucking sorry."

She closed her eyes, bowing over halfway to her knees. When she pulled back up, her eyes were soft, if still wary. As relieved as she looked, she tensed too, for her turn.

"You shouldn't have to be," she said, thick and throaty, more like her singing than speaking voice.

"I had a feeling," I said. "I just ignored it."

"It's not like I've got dibs."

"But I should've thought about you."

"It's never going to happen between us," she said. "So you may as well have your fun with him. I can't."

"You sure about that?" I asked. "He can't see you as a kid forever."

"Why not, if I never get to do any of the things you're supposed to do when you grow up?"

There were so many milestones she'd missed. Of course she felt confused.

After the last team wrapped up their barely coordinated routines, and some theatre kids were generously given thirty seconds to announce the spring musical, the principal stepped up on the field with a microphone in hand. He started with some standard call-and-response about how the night was going so far, whether the kids were excited for the rally, and if the seniors were looking forward to graduating. I started tuning his speech out on instinct.

Suddenly I realized how quiet some of the kids had gotten. On the field floated a white screen, revealed by a sudden projection of light, like they were about to show a movie.

"Now, not to be a downer," said the principal. "But imagine, for a moment, that it's the first day of summer after your graduation. You're about to start the rest of your life. How would you feel if your life stopped right there?"

He allowed for a moment of comparative silence, considering his audience.

"What I've just described to you happened to four students on graduation night, three years ago."

On the screen appeared their young, awkward, beaming faces. Evie hadn't changed much. In most of the pictures, she had braces, like she'd barely gotten them off before it happened. There were mostly group photos, like the four of them had been inseparable, at least one of them always caught with their eyes closed or looking away, laughing and clutching each other and pulling silly faces, all dressed up for every school event and dance, no dates but each other. I wondered what it must've been like having friends like that, not spending those years alone. No wonder she'd attached herself to me, casting out a lifesaver, looking for anyone to help weather the storm.

"They do this every year," she said.

The principal went on to name each of them, praise their good grades, list all their clubs and activities, reveal the colleges where they'd been accepted, everything short of naming the churches they'd attended with their parents every weekend as he extolled their virtues. Then he turned on them, because they'd touched alcohol, just once. Their karma had been instant. They were the perfect cautionary tale, putting a face on all those statistics about underage drinking and drunk driving. Sign this pledge: If not for yourself, for them.

None of the kids on the bleachers were about to stop drinking, if they had started already, or wait until they were of age. You couldn't tell them these were the best years of their lives and then expect them to behave, especially if they'd been having some shitty years so far. They hadn't even started living yet. But from the way the principal talked about graduation, their lives would be coming to a literal end after high school.

"I can't wake up," she said.

I put my hand over hers, partly to check if she was on the verge of going geist. She shrugged me off and shot up.

She didn't make it far under the bleachers before I caught up. This spot gave me much more nostalgia. It felt like I ought to pass her a cigarette, or dare her to kiss me; it didn't count if we were only practicing for boys.

But then she peered up at me just long enough to betray the glint of tears.

"It's not fair," I said, on the verge of choking up myself. "I can't lie to you and say you didn't miss much. You barely even got to start your life before it ended."

"It didn't."

I didn't even register what she said next, convincing myself I'd misheard. She sounded so flat, almost nonchalant.

"What's that?"

"I'm not dead."

She looked up in time to see me staring like an idiot, unable to form a response. Above us, the kids broke the silence with screams, music flaring up again. There must've been some sports or something starting.

"I'm still in a coma," she said. "My soul is here, but my body is alive."

"No way," I said. I couldn't conceive that she'd lie to me, but even that seemed more likely. "That's not how it works. You were trapped. I felt it, in your memory. You were trying so hard to wake up, but you couldn't."

"I got help," she said.

I shook my head, still in shock. If she was telling the truth, then it hurt. It stung and ached and I didn't know why, when it should have been good news, light at the end of the tunnel. At least, for her.

"You weren't supposed to tell anyone," Alastair said.

Evie and I both balked at the intrusion.

"What are you doing here?" she asked.

"Sorry I'm late," he said, showing his teeth, lashing out in his hurt. "Did you really think I'd miss the rally?"

She looked down at her sock-covered feet. Apparently, she thought the better of her guilt, because she put her chin back up. "It's not like I could talk to you about it. Besides, don't you trust her?"

He looked at me. "It's not about trust."

What did he think I'd do with this information? I still didn't understand.

I gave up and asked, "What's going on?"

Evie took my hand and spirited us away.

Evie's body had been moved from the hospital to her home. Her room looked like it hadn't been disturbed since the accident, preserving her late adolescence. All the bright colors were muted by the darkness, band posters and photos of her friends and old stuffed animals that looked as if they should be covered with dust, overgrown with vines, like the towering chamber of a sleeping princess. Machines blinked and whirred around her bed, an oxygen tube under her nose, keeping her body alive without her in it.

She didn't look alive. That body looked more like the ghost, an eerie echo. Her hair hidden beneath a plain black bonnet, soft curves starved away to nothing.

"What the fuck?" I asked.

"I know, right?"

She didn't have time to explain further. Alastair spirited before us. "I'm sorry—why exactly can't you talk to me?"

He tempered the harsh words with gentle fingers reaching

under her chin. She closed her eyes, leaning into his warmth, before smacking his hand away. He and I both gaped at her as she raised her voice, like the way she sang.

Except now, she screamed.

"You always tell me the same thing, that death is so much fun, I'm lucky to be here, life sucks, who needs it? But you won't deliver and do with me what you do to every other foundling you give that speech. You just leave me to rot while you go fuck everyone but me."

She'd begun to cry, but neither of us moved to comfort her. She might not be done with the screaming and swiping. Then she looked at our faces, and suddenly seemed to shrink back down again, embarrassed.

"I'm sorry," he said. "I know you've grown, but you're still so young."

Her tone curled up quiet again. "I know."

That's when he pounced, nearly growling. "If you're going to be so careless, why should we even keep this thing around? I might as well finish the job."

"Please don't."

He still turned and reached out, as if to play with the cords and wires twining like vines around her doppelganger. "You're not in a hospital anymore. They won't have time to bring you back."

She tried to shove him away. "You couldn't!"

Something about their words and gestures felt practiced. Like they'd had this conversation already, going through the motions to see if anything had changed.

"Why not?" he asked. "If you cross, you'd just go to heaven."

"But there's so much I've never done."

"So what? There's plenty I've never—"

Alastair's voice caught in his throat. Not soon enough. He swallowed hard, but he couldn't take back that start of a confession.

It rooted heavy in my phantom heart. He always made such a big show of reveling in his afterlife, it had never occurred to me—he secretly envied the living.

Evie still had a chance to come back. That's why he'd never pushed her to dance, or drink, or anything else. If she had too much fun on this side, she wouldn't want to wake up.

I put myself between them, facing him. "If you want her to live again, why don't you just say so?"

He slipped into his mask and said nothing. As she gaped up at him, he gulped.

"I thought you were in love with death," she said.

Rather than reply to her, he glared at me instead. "As if you're not lusting for the life in that body, lying there for the taking. You can't tell me it's not tempting. All the things we could never do again, close enough to touch."

If I had her life, I'd have parents who loved me, another shot at my career, even a chance at love. It wouldn't even matter how different I'd look. Not to mention, if I filled out that body again, I'd have some curves at last.

"But it's not possible to get in," I said. "Is it?"

"Sure it is!" said Alastair. "That's why we shouldn't go around telling everyone."

Evie balled up her fists, shaking. "You think I didn't try like hell to wake up? Of course I did. I couldn't. It's not possible. There's no coming up for air when you're drowning in the dark."

"It's still worth a try," he said, turning to me. "Isn't it?"

Evie watched me, more curious than concerned.

"What's it going to be?" asked Alastair.

I shook my head, trying to laugh it off. "As if," I said. "You really think I'd take someone else's life?"

He didn't look surprised. "Even if it'll go to waste?"

"It's hers. She can do whatever she wants with it."

Even if that was nothing. I believed her, that she'd been trapped, with no way out. But I couldn't help but wonder if after all she'd seen and learned, and with friends to give her a hand, whether it might be worth another try. If it didn't work, we could pull her out again.

And if it did work, then I'd miss her. We all would. It would be worth it.

Maybe she had to want it enough. I didn't mention it, because she'd started to cry.

"I can't wake up," she said.

He went and pulled her in close, pressing a kiss to her brow. She buried herself in his chest.

"I'm sorry for being so hard on you," he said, murmuring low into her curls. "You know it's because I love you, right, little one?"

Her sobs came out muffled.

I could wait. They needed a moment. And, after everything, so did I.

THIRTY-SIX

❋⟫⟫ ⟪⟪❋

After a few drinks at Clementine's, waiting in the upstairs lounge, I got antsy, deciding to check on Alastair. When I spirited to him, it startled me to find myself surrounded by open sky, dawn blushing pink on the edge of the blue night. We were on the roof of the Haunt.

Alastair sat with his knees folded up. I sank down beside him. It felt like we ought to be drinking a six-pack up here, though this roof loomed much higher than the one-story band house. But not as high as my apartment building.

"Did you tuck Evie in?" I asked.

He tilted his head at me in weary incomprehension.

"Don't you see her as a daughter?" I asked.

His eyes blew wider than I'd ever seen them, in absolute horror. "I'm not old enough."

I burst out laughing. "You could be her grandfather, probably great-great-something-grandfather."

"I died young," he said. "I may have seen a lot, but I haven't done much. I don't feel a day over twenty-seven."

"You're my age?"

He simply stared at me, not even having to say it.

"Look what I've done with my time," he said, gesturing at

nothing, which represented his afterlife pretty well, the way he told it. "You see me gaining years of wisdom through decades of hard work, supporting a family across generations? I've just been dancing."

"But you're the head of the Haunt."

He scoffed. "I've got no real authority."

"So why does everyone answer to you?"

"It's because I act like I've got all the answers. And to some extent, that's true. I've gained knowledge, if not wisdom. It's better than nothing, for all the souls who arrive on this side with questions. I play the psychopomp, and they follow along, not minding at all that we're only going in circles."

I exhaled. "That's why you pretend to still be in love with death. It's for the kids."

"There are times when I'm not pretending," he said. "But they're getting fewer and farther between, with every passing decade, and each time is more fleeting."

"Would you really want to live in my time?"

"I don't envy a good deal of it, with so many of the problems I thought had been solved popping back up, robber barons and lynching, so many things that have no right coming back from the dead when I can't. At the same time, you've got sushi, and water parks, and not only did you shrink down telephones until you could fit them in your pocket, but on such a tiny and breakable device, you have access to a greater wealth of knowledge than I had my entire life as an educated white man of my time, and I went to Oxford."

"You went to Oxford?"

"Shit, no, I didn't," he said. "Or did I?"

"Take it easy," I said, with a laugh. "That doesn't tell me anything about your age."

He leaned his chin on his hand, staring wistfully. "On that internet of yours, I've found the very same books I used to study at school, free to read. I've uncovered records of the lives and deaths of my old friends. I've even tracked the places we used to frequent, whether or not the buildings still stand, or if there's a sushi restaurant in their place now."

"You seem really preoccupied with sushi."

"I'd kill to know how in the world it tastes. It looks so strange and fantastic!"

I didn't have the heart to tell him that I didn't really like it, myself—or what, in my opinion, he'd really missed out on, depending on when and where pizza and pho and ice cream had been invented. If only I'd had a phone on me, I could've looked it up.

"Have I mentioned how much I love planes?" he said. His grin had never looked farther from cool, practically nerdy.

"You've flown?"

"Of course! We have to travel like the living, if we want to get someplace we've never been. And you ungrateful little shits complain about the food and the waiting. Try haunting a ship full of retching, starving, scared families for ten weeks. Now you can cross the Atlantic, flying through the fucking firmament itself, in just eight hours."

He sank back, no longer smiling. "I've seen the future," he said. "But I'm stuck in the past."

His eyes were glistening. It made me start, like his mask had made a sound when it shattered.

"All this time, I didn't want you to mourn too hard," he said. "Because if you did, I didn't know if I could bear to be around you long enough to try pulling you back. I've been mourning for years and doing my damnedest not to show it. But… it's catching up to me."

I wondered if I'd see into his memory for a change, if he were to go geist. We couldn't have that. He pulled himself together, righting his fall before having to catch himself.

I could put my hand over his with no risk. Our walls had lowered to fences, less about keeping each other out and more for leaning on while we talked.

He tilted his face down toward mine. I turned my head, letting him catch my cheek.

"So, this is it?" he asked, and for once, rather than put on his affected pout, his mouth curled up, trying to hide it. "That's what I get for opening up?"

"Come on," I said, ignoring the ache in my chest. "Don't get sappy on me."

"I jest," he said. "I'd rather not keep hurting her, either, especially when you and I aren't serious. It's hard to be, on this side. There's nothing tethering us together—we can't share a house, dreams, children."

My skin flushed in surprise. "Uh, whoa."

He gave me my favorite pout after all. "Don't be so horrified."

"That's a lot coming from someone who won't even tell me his real name."

That answered an unconscious question I'd had for myself before I'd even dared to let it form words in my head—let alone out loud. I'd been wondering why this hadn't gone further. It couldn't, as long as he stayed too cool and mysterious to even tell me the basics about himself.

"I will," he said.

"For real?"

He put his hand to his dead heart. "I swear on my grave. In fact, why don't I show it to you? So you'll know it's true."

I gaped at him as he stood and held out his palm.

We spirited to a cemetery older than any I'd ever seen. All the grass overgrown, moss overtaking the stones, these long-dead souls truly given back to nature, some even pushing up small white wildflowers. No visitors here. We were the only ones at his grave, standing there hand in hand.

"This is it," he said. As if I couldn't tell from the goosebumps, which weren't mine.

Those dates, birth and death, were a lot later than I would've guessed. But I didn't mention it. I could feel through his fingers that he wanted me to focus on something else.

"Is that really your name?"

I could see why he'd changed it in death. It hadn't aged well. Not particularly suited for screaming in bed.

I fought a smirk, mustering as much sincerity as I could. "I'll keep your secret."

He flashed me a playful sneer. "You fucking *will*."

What a shame that he'd opened up to me so late. Though it might've been for the best. I couldn't go falling in love with him now. Even if I might've had room in my heart for more than one love at once.

I gazed up at him. "Do you think it would've worked between us in life?"

He answered way too quickly. "No."

We both cracked up.

He must've felt my slight affront, because he took my other hand, like we were about to dance. "I'm sorry I didn't get to be your ex-husband."

It might've already happened in another life. Maybe that's why he'd annoyed me since we'd met. And it could happen again, another time around.

I squeezed his hands. "Now how do you like me, out of all the foundlings you've brought here?"

"You might not be the most dear," he said, smiling. "But you've certainly been the most difficult."

He said it like a compliment, his voice as warm as his hands. Through his fingers, he slipped me a feeling, like a note under a door. After so many years of being fawned and fought over, it had come as a real shock for me to turn him down, over and over. Like downing a shot, or descending the drop of a roller coaster, that shock had turned to a thrill.

"Thanks for the ride," he said.

I winked. "Till next time."

Evie didn't sleep, of course. She simply lay in bed, staring up at the ceiling, not unlike the empty body she'd left behind. Through the walls the pulse thumped, and yet, somehow, she resisted its pull, lying there perfectly still. Even when I went to sit on the edge of the bed, she didn't stir. I wondered how she managed, if she did this every night that she didn't sing.

No need to mince words. "We broke up."

She winced, shutting her eyes tight. "You didn't have to do that."

"It's no big deal. We were hardly even dating," I said. "But I'm not here to talk about boys."

Her eyes fluttered open. She sat up, hugging her knees as she faced me.

I spoke as gently as I could. "Why not give it another go?"

At first, her face went blank. I worried she'd pull from my bag of tricks and spirit right the fuck off.

"I already tried." She pulled off her scarf and began to unbraid her hair, her fingers trembling as she combed them through her coils. "After the crash, I found myself outside the car, and my body, so I climbed back in. It worked. I think it kept me from dying. But I couldn't finish the job. I couldn't wake up."

"We could always pull you back out again, if you can't."

She shook her head, hair fanning out. "Ally didn't just pull the plug. He couldn't, not in a hospital. They'd have caught it even faster with all those alarms and such and just plugged me back in. So… he had to use a pillow." Her hands twisted in the scarf on her lap.

"That gave us time to leave before they resuscitated me."

I remembered, now, the pounding dark of empty lungs. But it didn't seem like she was scared to face it again. It was whether he had it in him to do it, now that he knew her.

"You know he'd do whatever you asked."

She smiled, almost involuntarily; then she winced again, like a spark failing to become a flame.

"Now my body is back home," she said. "I don't think there'd be time to save me again, keep my body running. I'd probably just die for good and cross over."

"Would that be so bad?"

Her face finally calmed, as she looked away for a moment to think. Then, she glanced back up slightly, enough to bare her bashful self-consciousness. "I know if there is a heaven, it's supposed to be eternal paradise and all, but, well… do you think they have sex up there?"

I couldn't help but smirk. "Believe me, I've sure wondered myself."

Her voice strummed on the edge of a sob. "There's so much else I've never done that I might not get a chance to do, up there. At least down here, I could still try."

Trying might be all she could do. She lacked the memories needed to feel certain sensations. There weren't any firsts to be had on this side.

Instead of pointing that out, I said, "You could do it all if you were alive again."

That only made her shake her head, too tired to keep protesting. As much as I hated to push, she needed it. She looked uncomfortably like my sister, with the brave face she tried to put on, as I struck. "Didn't you want to go to school?"

"I don't think they're still saving that scholarship for me," she said. "Not to mention, my folks have gone broke paying to keep me alive."

"What about your music, getting to perform for a live audience?"

"It's a tough business. I'd probably never get in. I don't know if I'd ever even get dexterity back in my fingers, when it would take years learning to walk again."

"How about dating?" I asked.

"I haven't had the chance. I'd be so behind, I don't know if I'd ever catch up—and that's without being an invalid living with her parents."

I hadn't thought about all her counterpoints. They were hard to ignore. And yet.

"Who cares?" I asked. "I'd do anything to live again."

She squeezed her eyes shut against the tears. "Me, too," she said, voice trembling, like the last breath before a sob. "But I'm so scared."

Nothing I could say would compare to how it felt. I put my arms around her. It made her cry out even louder, but she needed it. She had to feel it. I buried my head hard in her shoulder as I let it all pour out: everything I'd begun to want for myself, now that I could never have it. I'd never get to hug my sister, get breakfast with friends drunk at three in the morning, wake up to the same beloved face every day.

I didn't even mind the crying, but I could hardly stand her guilt coiling in my stomach.

"We don't have to try yet," I said, choking up myself. "You could take your time, say all your goodbyes. I'll be right there with you once you're ready."

At last, I had to pull away, aching too much for my touch to soothe. I stayed with her while she finished up her cry, ready in case it hurt hard enough to go geist. Finally, her sobs turned to deep breaths, and her tears began to dry on her face.

"What about you?" she asked.

"I'm dead, for real." I wanted to shrug, smile, shoot finger guns—anything to show it didn't matter, no big deal—but instead, I said it with a straight face. "I'm never, ever coming back."

"You're still here," she said. "That's not nothing. If I try to live again, you have to promise me you'll do the same."

"I'll try," I promised.

I stood up and out of the bed, holding out my palm. "Come and dance."

She stared at my hand, slightly wary.

"It's about time," I said.

I wondered if this was how it felt for Alastair. She looked away, second thoughts fleeting across her downturned eyes, even as her hands trembled in restraint against the pull of the pulse.

"I've been putting it off so long," she said.

"If you wait any longer, it's only going to make it harder."

"What if I'm not good at it?"

I leaned in closer. "You'll get better with practice."

At last, she took my hand. Her stomach gave a little roller-coaster thrill as I swept her up onto her feet. We practiced right there in her room first. My fingers told her how to move, our hands twined for a silly push and pull, warming up our feet.

But she ached to move faster and wider than she could in my arms. I let her go, watching her whirl away on quick feet, her arms flourishing and hips rolling. She'd caught on fast, eyes hazy with my memories. I had some moves, and so did everyone I'd danced with here. We shimmied around each other, our laughter literally breathless.

I caught her hand again. Her heart drummed nearly as hard as the pulse thundering around us as we spirited into the midst of the dancers. Their surprise to see her rippled through the crowd. She rode along too fast for me to keep up as I swung through other arms.

When I finally caught up with her, she'd stilled, standing motionless in the crowd across from Alastair.

I tensed, worrying as they stared that he might refuse her. Up until he held out his arms. Her shyness fell away as she took his hands.

At first, he held her at arm's length, but as she whirled with ease every way he twisted and turned her, he let her closer. They looked good together. She beckoned with her curves as he teased with his lithe limbs, never too close. But they didn't match the heat of the other dancers. They gave off a softer warmth. It didn't pull, or invite, tugging at the limbs. It simply ached with a bittersweet twinge, like a goodbye embrace.

It might not have been what she wanted from him, but she smiled anyway, and so did he, as he dipped his head to touch his forehead to hers. Then he let her go, and she danced away.

THIRTY-SEVEN

❋⟩⟩⟩ ⟨⟨⟨❋

Ren would usually be working around this time, in the wee hours of the morning, around three or four o'clock. I half-expected to find myself on the side of a busy road, ready to wait on the sidewalk for hours until he headed home, if that's what I had to do.

Maybe he wouldn't even want to talk to me. Not that I'd blame him, after the way I'd taken off. I only had one way to find out.

Rather than the glare of streetlamps and headlights and distant roar of cars, I found myself wrapped in the quiet blue of a cemetery at night. Around me, dark like ink stains against the white snow, familiar headstones rose. One of them especially familiar.

My grave had a visitor kneeling on the pale ground. That had to be cold, even with a new jacket over his old hoodie. My heart perked up so hard and fast, it hurt. I took a play at breath and pretended to lean on the headstone, like my limbs weren't trembling.

"Hey, boo."

For once, he jumped. His face shook me right back, though I knew it already—all but woke up to it every day, not so long ago. But as he gazed up at me, I still took him in as if for the first time, or the last. His hair had grown longer, falling right back into place despite his slightly frantic efforts to push it back.

"Mal," he said, with a gulp.

"In the flesh," I said. "Or, well, not."

He wanted to see me, after all. Otherwise, he wouldn't be here.

"Come here often?" I asked.

He blinked hard, not enough to hide the glimmer in his eyes. That's when I finally noticed what he gripped in his hands, glowing bright and gold as candles. Sunflowers.

My eyes pricked with tears.

His voice wavered, rough at the edges. "Well, up till today, I had no way of knowing if you were as dead to me as the rest of the world. You couldn't have at least checked in? Not even a call? Or a fucking text from an unknown number or something, like in a dumb horror movie? Anything to let me know you weren't gone for good?"

I bit my lip, but I didn't look away. The words came up easier than I would've thought, despite the lump in my throat. "I shouldn't have disappeared on you."

He didn't say anything. He'd been ready to stay mad, not expecting an actual apology. I gave him a moment. His face lit briefly as he sparked up a cigarette. I wanted to ask if we could share, though I might have lost that privilege.

"Just don't do it again," he said. "At least, not without leaving a forwarding address."

"You know where to find me now."

I settled across from him on the snow, my bare feet chilly as usual, but nowhere near as freezing as they should be. His breath showed in the air between drags. I envied it.

"How's the weather?" I asked.

"It sucks." He shrugged. "You're probably better off."

I didn't answer that.

He took a swig from a bottle, my brand of whiskey. After all this time, it might not have been the same bottle. Still, I had to ask.

"Is that mine?"

At last, he cracked a hint of a smile. "You owe me."

He reached and rested his hand over mine. I sighed, my limbs going warm and loose from the nicotine and alcohol. We both leaned back against my headstone.

"So, I took your advice," he said, like an admission of guilt. "I tried to see other people."

"Same here," I said. "How's that going for you?"

He laughed, holding up the bottle in a toast. "Nowhere fast."

My head swam as he took a big swig. I found myself sinking into his shoulder. He tried his best to curl his arm around me.

"I could've gotten somewhere," I admitted.

My skin simmered with secondhand jealousy.

"You mean with that handsome ghost?"

"Don't worry," I said. "We called it off. Nobody is looking to get married and have kids here, or, you know, just live together. We don't have lives to share."

I kept my voice steady and my face still, yet he stared at me as if I'd wavered, let something slip.

"Is that something you wanted?" His voice went soft, trying to deliver the blow as gently as he could. "I didn't think you were the type to settle down."

"Me neither. But I didn't get the chance to find out for sure." I blinked hard, but I couldn't keep the tears from falling. "Maybe you would have been the exception."

At least this time, there weren't any coffee pots to shatter, though the whiskey bottle might've been in peril. For once, my wrists didn't chafe. Perhaps his shared drunkenness softened the blow. Or his touch anchored me more firmly than usual, more tangible, like the veil between worlds had thinned around us.

Through our touch, I felt his chest cave in, aching on my behalf. As if it wasn't obvious enough from the way he looked at me.

"It feels like it's not enough to say I'm sorry," he said. "Or that it's not fair, and I hate this, it sucks so fucking bad."

My little laugh sounded wet, sniffly and gross. "You're telling me."

"I want to do so much more than bring you flowers and pour one out for you."

"Don't you ever pour one out for me," I said. "Just give me a toast and enjoy."

"What else?" he asked. "Is there anything else I could do to make it better?"

I shouldn't have looked down at his lips. He noticed.

"Well, it might take a while for me to forgive you," he said. "Not to mention, we both just got out of relationships. And we've been drinking. This would be absolutely terrible timing, but if I wait any longer, you might just fucking disappear again."

"I mean, the ideal timing would've been before I died. At this point, it's so hopeless, it doesn't make much difference."

"Fuck it," he said. The warmth of his words bloomed inside me, even before leaving his mouth. "I love you."

I bit my lip, unable to resist. "You shouldn't."

He laughed. "You told me to live a little, and this is how I want to do it. If it's a mistake, I'll learn. And if not, I'll never know unless I take the risk."

Maybe we'd never get over each other unless we found out just how far we could go. If it turned out to be awkward and sad, then we could hopefully laugh it off and stay friends. Or it could be a night we'd never forget. He could tell future drinking buddies about the time he fucked a ghost.

"All right, don't say I didn't warn you."

We both leaned in, our lips wisping together. I thought we'd go faster, harder, making up for lost time. But he pressed in so soft and slow it ached, deep in my chest, like thumbing a bruise. It must've been his longing for me, sharp as hunger pangs. His mouth pulsed against mine as if with his heartbeat.

He pulled back just enough to press our brows together. My head went light, not only from the whiskey. The warmth filling me all the way down to my toes radiated straight from him.

"Come home," he said.

Since he'd been drinking, we had to take the bus. I made a game of having to wait that much longer, nipping at his ears and neck, making his breath catch and his hands clench.

He kept my flowers in his lap.

When we got to the apartment, I gaped, too surprised to make a sound. Our mattress no longer sprawled on the floor, but lay elevated on a proper bed frame. It even had a nightstand next to it, somewhat flimsy and scratched up, but still real furniture. In the corner of the kitchen stood a small table with sides that folded over for space. None of it matched, like it had been thrifted, or brought in from a curb, same as all my stuff in life. But not a bad start.

"What do you think?" asked Ren.

It embarrassed the hell out of me to be tearing up again already.

"You just need some lights," I said. "And some pictures to put on the wall, and a plant or two, and then it'll be perfect."

"I'm almost there," he said, pointing me toward the window. The new curtains had been pulled back to reveal a tiny cactus. I had to cover my face.

"Thanks for the geist control, by the way," he said, because of course he'd figured it out. "I couldn't have done any of this if it weren't for you."

I didn't expect to blush. "Don't mention it."

He put on the last show we'd been watching together, the very next episode, like he'd been waiting for me rather than watch it on his own. Then he went to the bathroom.

I sat down on the tall new bed, which felt off somehow. It was too high. I'd been missing him the wrong way, still picturing us on the floor.

"This is weird," I said, when he came back.

He leaned down, brushing his thumbs on either side of my face. "You'll get used to it."

I leaned up to meet his lips. He pressed closer, his legs going through my knees, until I opened them.

At first, we went slow, like nervous teens, getting used to the strange new feel of each other. His hands were tentative, afraid of pushing boundaries—not the personal kind. Soon enough, that tingling in the vague shape of gentle and curious fingers made me quiver and writhe, like being grabbed in the dark. It felt as if he were the ghost, like I was being rubbed up on by shadows, getting bumped in the night. Or that was how I made him feel, reflected back at me.

But we both ached for actual friction. Trying to grind my hips as I straddled him felt more like teasing than relief.

I didn't have the patience to taunt him button by button, so I whipped my shirt over my head. He did the same. We laughed as we each got trapped in my skirt and his jeans, respectively, and had to do an undignified little dance to get them off, falling over each other. I could only pull myself up so far up for a good look at him, not wanting any more distance.

"So, how are we going to do this?" he asked.

His trembling ran through me, nervous and elated, shared shivers hot and cold down my spine.

"We've got our own hands," I said.

He gulped. My stomach jumped with his apprehension. "I've thought about that. But what if it's less sexy and more… fucking mortifying?"

"No way." I bent down for a kiss. "I've got you."

His smile spread warm through my chest. I leaned back again, for a better view.

"Put your fingers right here."

I brushed my fingers over my lips. He did the same, tracing his mouth for me.

"Now both hands."

I ran my hands through my hair. He did the same. I couldn't help reaching out, his hair moving under my touch, as if I were a breeze. He closed his eyes, leaning into it. Then he reached for me in turn, running his hands over my chest. I used my own to try giving him a show, even though I didn't have much to work with, but from the heat coursing through us, he didn't mind at all.

"All right, are you ready?" I braced one hand by his head, through the pillow. I let the other slip between my legs. He followed suit, maybe picking up on my own shamelessness at last as our bodies overlapped.

Our eyes met, and suddenly, we were laughing in relief. His blush bloomed over my cheeks and down my shoulders.

"How do I feel?" I asked.

He needed a moment, staring up at me in a daze, answering the same. "It's just like a dream." I tried my best to pinch him with my free hand, and it must've worked, because he protested with a laugh. "I don't need any more convincing."

He looked so alive, now, his skin no longer pale, but flushed and glowing, lips red and swollen from biting, breath coming hard and fast. His other hand reached up, fingers splayed along my jaw and under my ear, keeping our gaze steady through our rocking and pitching.

I couldn't tell which of us finished first, but it sent us both over the edge. We stared at each other in disbelief for a moment, before laughing again, a bit embarrassed after all. We'd been friends longer than lovers, and after all the fanfare, we weren't used to seeing each other naked.

We curled up together, with the laptop still playing in the background, and it felt exactly like old times, aside from the lack of clothes. I laid my head as close as I could to his chest, and he tried to run his fingers through my hair, though it didn't work so well the other way around. At least I could hear his heartbeat.

Suddenly, my stomach cinched up with anxiety, not mine.

"What's wrong?" I asked.

He tried to laugh it off. "You plan to leave your number?"

"I can't." I did my best to nuzzle his neck. "But I'll stay to watch you make breakfast."

Something squeezed in his chest, as if he were doing in his soul what he couldn't do with his arms, trying to hold me closer.

THIRTY-EIGHT

❋》》 《《❋

Ren must've had some sweet dreams, because the hazy broadcast helped me float the closest to sleep I'd been since I died. His alarm blared earlier than usual, judging from the thin bright slice of light on either side of the curtains. He snoozed it the same as ever, groaning and reaching through my waist, because apparently trying to hold me needed conscious effort. It hurt to have to get up, untangle our bodies.

I'd really gotten out of practice in the kitchen. It might've been the burned smell of my first pancake attempt that woke him. He jolted right up, looking around. His shoulders eased as soon as his eyes fell on me.

"You're still here," he said.

So he'd leaped to a certain conclusion when he woke up to an empty bed. I couldn't really blame him. Even if my feet were calm, my tongue still fumbled with promises. I couldn't tell what I wanted to say, let alone let it out. He beamed anyway, making his way toward me, trying and failing to subtly fix his bedhead. I had to stare down at the stove, trying to remember I didn't even have to breathe.

He leaned on the counter. "I'd say you shouldn't have…"

"But it's the least I could do."

None of the flour stuck to my hands while making the batter, but I ran a finger along the dusted counter, trying to focus on being sticky. It came away coated. I powdered his nose. He laughed, and tried to retaliate, picking up some powder and blowing it in my direction, though it just went through me.

I tried again, dusting my hands, putting one on his chest. It left a print. We both went quiet, looking at it.

"So…" He cleared his throat. "Carlos invited everybody to a show tonight. His old roommates are all in a band."

I hadn't been to a show in so long. At least, not the living kind.

He caught the corner of his mouth in a bite before breaking into a smile. "Are you busy?"

I wouldn't know how to act around him with other people around. In fact, I'd suddenly forgotten how to act around him at all. It had been easier in the dark last night, when we were both tipsy.

"I'll check my schedule."

He left me alone to shower and get dressed while I finished up. I curled my toes, trying to quiet my restless feet.

When he came back, with wet hair and an unfloured shirt, I had a plate ready for him. It felt nice to sit with him at a table, for a change. He even put my grave flowers out in a cup.

But he finally had to go and say what we were both thinking. What we must've been wondering all along, since the first time he looked twice at me.

"Remember what you said about wishing we could've met back when you were still alive?"

I got up. It made him start, but I only went to go put his brand-new coffeemaker in one of the kitchen cabinets, just in case.

"You mean, if I hadn't bullshitted my way out of the hospital, and gotten committed with you instead?"

I couldn't let myself picture it, the two of us meeting there, wearing those pajamas, complaining about our shrinks over checkers, one of us getting out sooner but coming back to visit, waiting for the day we could finally check out and start the rest of our lives together. Even if neither of us would have been in the best mental place to fall in love, it might've been a start.

As I sat back down across from him, I had to ruin my fantasy for myself. "You'd still be convinced of the wrong diagnosis."

"So what?" he said. "I still question my sanity, anyway."

"I thought you hated—you know—the institution."

"But I didn't need help," he said. "Maybe it wouldn't have been much, and it might've given you other kinds of damage, but… you needed it."

My wrists didn't chafe, not yet, but I rubbed them instinctively. "There's no cure for wanting to die, except death."

"Are you sure about that?" he asked, leaning in with curiosity and concern. "How do you feel now?"

He had me there. My death wish hadn't been sated by dying. As much as I'd gotten better, deep down, sometimes I still craved oblivion. Maybe I always would.

"There's no medication on this side," I said. "And I don't know any dead psychiatrists."

His eyes glistened, even as he smiled. "You could always try yoga."

We laughed. His eyes dropped to my mouth, waiting for me to close the small distance, but I let it gape between us, staring at him as if from across space and time, rather than only a kitchen table.

"I fucked up."

He did his best to put his hand over mine. "You don't have to keep punishing yourself forever."

"That's why I came back," I said. "I'm just trying to appreciate what I have. It's a bit late, but better here than nowhere."

His mouth twitched up hopefully. "You mean here with me?"

This still wasn't a good idea. Just like drinking, I might not be healthy for him in the long run, but for a short while, I could make his existence a little livelier.

"I'm in no hurry to leave just yet."

I sated my restless feet by reaching them under the table and bumping his. He didn't say anything, but he smiled, and bumped me back.

"Don't let your breakfast get cold."

Ren drove us to the show, all the way out to the suburbs where there weren't any venues, as far as I knew.

"You didn't tell me it would be a house show."

"Is that bad?" he asked.

I laughed, shaking my head. "Well, it might not be good." I'd gotten my start in garages and basements. Before the thought of fame even whispered in the back of my mind. "That's not the point."

Come to think of it, I might've been happier as a nobody, playing free gigs on weekends. It wouldn't have paid the bills, but I could've figured out something to keep me afloat the rest of the week. No stage, no persona—just me and the music.

The crowd milling around the house looked nearly the same as the one I'd known years ago, all piercings and rainbow hair, patched jackets and band tees. We followed them down to the basement, where an audience of about fifty or so crammed around a tiny makeshift stage. While they gathered, the opening band did sound checks.

"You made it!" said Carlos.

He threw an arm around each of us. Or tried to, in Ren's case.

"Wouldn't miss it," said Ren. In the din, it went unheard.

Danny waved. "Hey, guys."

"I'm so glad you're here," said Evie. I took her outstretched hands and went along with her excited little shake.

We didn't have a lot of room, but everyone who bumped through me was in high enough spirits, some buoyed with beer, that it didn't feel too invasive. No more than usual for shows.

The band began to play. They weren't great, the guitar solos too long, and the horn section somewhat rusty, but the beat got everybody moving. That's what mattered.

Danny moved awkwardly but enthusiastically, doing all the usual jokey moves. Carlos put aside his natural rhythm and joined her, embracing the bad. Evie mostly jumped up and down, loose hair bouncing, trying to keep up with the frantic energy.

I'd forgotten how to dance on my own, without the pull of any partners in the ballroom, anticipating their next move and timing mine just right, both of us intertwined with the pulse. Now I had to guess what to do next, hoping I didn't look stupid. At first, I followed everyone else with the bobbing and skanking. Then, like I used to do in life, I went my own way, letting my hips and shoulders guide me, reinterpreting the aggressive beat by channeling some gentler grace.

Soon enough, a good handful of fans in the audience—friends and girlfriends and even family—all began to sing along, screaming back the call and response. Others in the audience tried as well, picking up on the chorus.

My friends were all singing, even if no one could hear them. I wondered how they'd look to me from up on stage, if we weren't dead. At least at shitty venues, you could still see faces.

When the chorus came around, more and more people picking up on the bitterly hopeful refrain, I tried opening my mouth, pushing my voice past the drought in my throat. It came out small and cracked. I could barely hear it as I tripped over some of the words. But on the last line, I shoved enough force through my lungs to shout, and somehow, I hit it just right with that smoky old growl of mine. I'd always been embarrassed by it, so deep and rough. Back in the day, my bandmates had to beg me to do any backing vocals. Hearing it again, it didn't sound so bad. I'd missed my own voice.

Soon enough, all the wallflowers were pointing and singing to each other, crooning like dorks. I closed my eyes as if getting really into it; actually, my eyes were filling.

As one song ended, everyone went quiet as the band took a moment to explain the next.

"This song goes out to Carlos," said the lead singer. He picked up a beer from behind an amp, just to pour a sip onto the floor. "I hope you're listening, wherever you are."

Carlos laughed, wet and nasally, then drew his sleeve over his face. "I'm right here, buddy."

Danny and Evie and I all put our arms around him. Ren did his best not to look like he was patting the empty air, though nobody around seemed to notice.

The band took a risk playing this slower tempo after having built up so much energy. Some people were still trying to show their approval by bouncing and bobbing their heads, but most of the crowd went still. I wondered if they appreciated the potent lyrics, or if they were disappointed they couldn't keep dancing.

The band wrapped the song up and rushed into the next, whipping up their previous frenzy again in a hurry.

Carlos showed Danny how to skank, kicking up one foot in front of the other and letting the weight follow through with a lanky rhythm. Evie mirrored my dancing and let herself slow down, laughing as she shimmied her shoulders and snaked her arms. Ren began with bouncing and bobbing his head at first, but then, I turned to him, and somehow, we ended up circling each other, in our own tiny pit. My hair waved back and forth in front of my face as I peered up at him, while we danced closer and closer. That made it easier to bear the way he beamed at me.

For a moment, I forgot. Like I'd stepped for a moment into another universe, where we were alive and well and together. I could've been at one of my own early shows, getting in some dancing before having to go on with some friends who'd come to see me. Maybe I'd spotted this cute boy at other shows, getting my chance to dance with him at last. I'd have to decide whether to make my move now, or after, once he'd heard me play.

Someone passed through me, cutting between us. A pink-haired girl danced closer to him, her intentions unmistakable. I'd felt them.

I turned away, ducking into the crowd, bumping through far too many people. Their enthusiasm barely rubbed off on me. If the broadcast went both ways, I'd brought them down.

There were people upstairs, milling with beer in the kitchen, so I kept going, through the wall and into the backyard. Patchy grass poked up through the melting snow, scattered beer cans all around, but they'd crisscrossed some fairy lights between the tree and garage. The music still blared loud enough that it probably bothered the neighbors.

"Mal."

Of course he'd followed me.

Ren held out his hand. "Come dance."

I couldn't help but laugh. But I didn't take his hand. Instead, I shimmied my shoulders, slowly, in a coy shuffle. Soon, we were moving together, his hips and shoulders echoing mine. At first, we were both looking down at ourselves. Once again, I forgot how to do this like I had in life. He might've been close, but he felt so far away, without the pulse to pull our veins like marionette strings.

Instead, I had to move freely, with nothing but rhythm and instinct telling me what to do. I could only hope to think and move fast enough for us to look good together. *Feel* good together.

We drew closer, staring bashfully at our feet, stumbling through each other's toes. We had to compensate for a lack of push and pull, but at least with our fingers twined, I could pick up his intention, where he wanted us to move, when to let go and then come together again. Even without holding each other, when he lifted his arm, I spun around in a twirl and found his hand again. He threw out his arm and I knew to spin the other way, before curling back into him with a laugh, my back to his chest, his arms around me.

He spun me back around so we could face each other. It happened without thinking, as the tempo slowed down, my arms around his neck and my feet resting on top of his own, the two of us rocking gently together. As I looked up at him, into those soft eyes, I came close to forgetting again.

I wondered how our other selves were doing, in other lives, in other universes, whether we'd found each other at a better time and stayed together for the rest of our lives, or if I'd fucked it up as usual. Or maybe we'd missed each other completely, whether by death, or bad luck, or stupid carelessness.

His brow furrowed. "What's wrong?"

I dipped my head down against his collarbone, hiding my face. "You're not going to be young forever. If I weren't here, you'd be dancing with some other girl. Someone who could help with the rent, meet your mom, maybe pop out a kid or two."

His startled laugh echoed in my own chest. "I'm getting by, rent-wise. I love my mom, but you don't want to meet her. And, uh, my biological clock isn't ticking yet."

I wanted to tell him I couldn't be the one—just one of many. But that felt presumptuous, not to mention dramatic. Better to wait and see where this went. We had time to figure it out. It couldn't hurt to keep him just a little longer.

"Good," I said. "I'm not ready to give you up."

And hopefully by the time I was, he'd have learned from me, ready for the next love to come along.

My chest overflowed with warmth as he pressed his smile to my lips. It felt like we'd done this before, like we'd already been doing this for a lifetime. Maybe in another universe. He laughed, the sound rising out of my own lungs as well, and I didn't give a fuck anymore how my alternate selves were doing, whether or not they had it better than me. We were here, still here, together.

After the show, we were too pumped to turn in, not that most of us could rest anyway. We waited until the basement had emptied so we could talk freely.

"What should we do now?" asked Evie.

Carlos sounded wistful. "We used to order pizza, drink some more, watch cartoons."

My band and I used to do the same, along with all our friends and girlfriends and couch crashers, shitfaced and starving.

Danny gnawed her nails. "I'd die again for some pizza."

"Don't even say it," said Evie. "You're making my belly rumble."

"We could still watch cartoons," Ren added.

We all piled into his car to ride home with him. He let us pick the music to blast on his old sterco, passing a case of CDs to the backseat.

Carlos commented knowledgeably on everything. Evie weighed in here and there, with the slight hesitation of someone doubting her own taste. Danny proclaimed unabashed ignorance.

"Oh, shit!" said Carlos.

I got shivers, like a premonition of doom. It must've been the panicked look from Ren.

"I forgot about Goodbye Courage," Carlos continued.

"Who's that?" asked Danny.

Evie remained quiet. I wondered if she knew or not. I'd never told her the band's name, but she could have gleaned it from my memory, or looked me up, given us a listen.

Carlos leaned way forward into the front seat and slipped the disc right in. He hit the skip button twice. He might as well have slapped me in the face.

"I like the first two tracks," Ren said.

"We could go back," said Carlos. "But this one's my favorite. Let me see if I can remember the words."

And then the first few piano notes I'd written began to plink. After all this time, I'd half-forgotten them. I went rigid with stage fright, as if I weren't sitting surrounded by friends.

Ren reached over to me, his hand warm on mine. I wasn't alone, and there wasn't any stage.

Danny snapped her fingers. "Oh, I do know this song!"

"Me, too," said Evie.

Carlos murmured the opening lines. I wondered why I'd hated them so much, back when we were writing them, then repeating them in the studio, take after take. They weren't so bad. In fact, they were almost good.

Danny joined in. Together, their voices strengthened, like they were no longer self-conscious, or doubtful about the lyrics. Evie echoed them, every other word and then every other line, like she didn't know the words as well. I wondered if she'd only listened because of me.

Ren did his best to grab my hand, and then—looking at me for as long as driving would allow—he sang. All the lights from surrounding cars, and traffic lights, and passing buildings, blurred with my tears. I shut my eyes, trying to keep my sob quiet.

It turned out to be much easier to just scream along instead, letting the tears stream down my face. Everyone who didn't know must've thought I'd gotten really into it.

It seemed to end too soon. I kind of wished we'd written one more verse, or at least repeated the chorus again.

"You've got a killer voice," said Carlos. "It reminds me of someone, I can't remember."

Ren grinned at me. Evie giggled in the backseat.

On the next track, I had more backing vocals.

"Keep listening."

THIRTY-NINE

✳»» ««✳

Ren and I spent days holed up together. I couldn't really tell how many, since we didn't change it up much, aside from a trip to a sex shop to try some stuff out. He didn't go to work, and I didn't have to be anywhere at all. So we mostly stayed in bed. It felt good, having a bed again. I liked pretending to wake up to his face.

On what I suspected might've been the third day, I had to ask.

"I hate to bring it up, but… don't you need to make rent?"

He groaned, stretching lazily under the sheets, as if about to get up. But he just rolled over and threw an arm around me. "I'll do a few rides later, and I'll get groceries with the dead guy's credit card."

The doorbell rang. He sprang right up, jumping into some boxers and jeans before throwing the door open. I forgot myself, going to cover up with his sheets, before remembering. There wasn't anyone outside, anyway—just packages. Huge ones.

"What are those?" I asked.

"Furniture," he said, dragging one of them inside, then the other. "One for me, another for the Haunt."

There'd be no better way to tell the wallflowers about us than to show up for a delivery together.

On the drive there, I put my feet up on his dashboard, imagining I could feel the wind from the rolled-down windows whipping my hair. We sang together to one of his ancient CDs. I'd memorized the lyrics from listening backstage.

"I can't believe you opened for these guys," he said.

I winked. For once, the recollection didn't hurt.

At first, it looked like lots of traffic jamming the street in front of the Haunt. I figured the big yellow excavator must've been passing through. But there were lots of crewmen running around, and they weren't going anywhere. The excavator left the street, making its way slowly and laboriously over our front lawn.

In my panic, I forgot to concentrate on staying in the car. It drove right through me, leaving me collapsed in the street, open-mouthed and staring. Only for a moment. I didn't have to feel my knees to use them, forcing myself upright.

Ren wrenched into park, tires screeching, and got out. I spirited straight to him, grabbing his sleeve.

"What are you doing?" I asked.

He'd gone pale, as rattled as if it were his own home about to be torn apart. "I could talk to them."

"And say what? 'My friends are in there—and by the way, they're dead'?"

"I've got to do something."

He hadn't even known the wallflowers for long. But he'd probably never had so many friends.

I tightened my grip as he tried to shake me off. He just slipped out of his hoodie, not caring how it would look floating in my hands. I dropped it and spirited again, right in front of him.

Before he could barrel past me, or right through me, I reached for his face. That surprised him into staying put.

I didn't put it gently. "You'll look crazy."

"I don't care."

He didn't sound all that convincing, his voice low. I leaned up for a kiss, like I could pass some sense to him that way, borrow a bit of courage in return. We jolted apart as the excavator gave a roaring whine of life.

I let go of him. "Wait here."

He tried one last time. "Let me help."

"You're not one of us," I said. "We'll be fine in the rubble. You won't."

With that, I risked leaving him alone out on the street as I spirited away.

Alastair lounged outside, pretending to sit at a café table, flipping through an abandoned newspaper like the pages were being turned by the wind. For a moment, I forgot the cause of my shaky limbs and leaden stomach, as if I were just nervous about bothering him in the daytime.

It must've shown on my face, because as soon as he looked up, he sprang to his feet. "What's wrong?"

My voice echoed strangely in my ears. "They're tearing us down."

He didn't bother hiding the alarm in his eyes. That bared emotion scared me more than anything, until his brow eased, mouth set in a line.

"It's happening at last."

His resignation scared me even more.

He disappeared. When I followed, I squinted up through the sunlight at the huge yellow excavator. It dipped its great claw down toward the west corner of the entrance, which already lay broken open. It went for the first floor, starting at the foundation. Once that went, the rest would soon fall.

I spirited inside. All the walls were shaking. Leaves dropped off the dried vines, and crumbling plaster fell like snow from the ceiling. I could feel all the other ghosts as if we were dancing together in the ballroom, but with no pulse. Instead, they gave off waves of surprise and despair.

Danny and Carlos stood right in the thick of it. Ever the scientists, they had to come and investigate. My instincts told me to grab them and yank them back, their bodies so soft and vulnerable against the size and noise of the great metal beast devouring our home. But they'd be fine. As part of the ceiling began to collapse, the spray of plaster and brick went right through them.

"We can't let them do this," said Danny. Her hands jutted and stuttered. "My research, it's all on paper and hard drive."

"Could we hide it somewhere safe?" asked Carlos. "Or upload it somewhere?"

I hated to bring it up, but they needed to hear it. "What if someone finds it?"

That might earn some smiting. I wondered if the powers that be had sent the excavator like an old-fashioned plague.

The crane went still. And it stayed still, long enough that it might've stopped. The building ceased to shake and crack and powder down.

Somehow, we all knew to meet in the ballroom. I'd never seen it so full in the daytime. Now, rather than moving in unison, everyone stood apart. Wanderers from so many times and places, stark in their differences without music to wind them together.

Evie found me in the crowd. I didn't even flinch when she reached for me, each of us clutching the other by the arm in a tense embrace.

"Where's Ally?" she asked.

I held out my palms helplessly, because as much as I wanted to tell her he'd take care of everything, I didn't know for sure. He might've slipped straight into the machine, but I didn't know if he had enough working knowledge of modern mechanics to do anything. Or whether we could get away with interfering with the living so openly without consequences.

It made me cringe with guilt not to be there with him. But— for all the fuss I'd made about not wanting to be here anymore—at that moment, it didn't seem so tempting to try and cross over. I'd just warmed up to the idea of sticking around a while longer. And I'd thought a good deal of that time would be spent here in this ballroom, dancing the years away. If anything, I'd figured I'd be the one to go first, long before this roof came down.

I let go of Evie. As much as I wanted to hold her through this, I couldn't keep my walls up. She didn't need to feel my existential dread.

"Come on, we're ghosts," said Carlos. He paced restlessly, eager to spring to action. "We could just scare them off."

Danny's voice was worryingly deadpan, despite her constant motion. "It's not like we can file a complaint."

Some of the other ghosts took up the rallying cry. They weren't as practical.

"Could we put blood on the walls?" a foundling suggested.

"You know how to do that?" asked Flo.

"They're not going to be spooked by a bunch of stacked-up chairs," said the mall rat. "We've got to bring on the chills."

"Don't even think about it," said Alastair.

There were murmurs and shouts and even clapping as he appeared. He looked wrecked, trying to heave in unneeded breath, as if he'd somehow found a way to overexert himself on this side.

"You stopped them?" asked Flo.

His look was dark. "For now."

Wilhelmina crossed her arms. "What's that supposed to mean?"

"They're not going to let an odd equipment failure ruin this job and send them back to their contractor offering a refund. Somebody wants this place razed. They'll reschedule and return."

I nearly laughed. Like anybody here would grasp modern business jargon, let alone care about the mundane motivations behind the destruction.

"So stop them again," Danny said.

Alastair's mask held, but his voice ran ragged. "I can't."

"Why not?" asked Carlos.

"I've interfered enough," he said, raising his voice, then dropping it just as quickly. "If I do any more, I might cross. So would all of you, if you tried anything cute."

That garnered him a moment of silence to catch his breath. I looked around at all the expectant faces.

"What are we going to do?" I asked.

"We'll have to move on."

His words dropped heavy on the crowd, sending ripples of shouts and whispers. He silenced the waves with an upheld palm.

"Don't forget: We're dead. We don't need shelter over our heads, or ground under our feet. As long as we stay together, we'll always find someplace to dance."

After a respectful silence of acknowledgment, all the ghosts got to talking again, steadier and lighter now, in agreement.

"Not all of us dance," I said.

If he heard me, he pretended otherwise.

FORTY

❋))) (((❋

Ren had waited like I'd asked. He sat with an arm dangling a cigarette out of the car window, watching the dead excavator get towed from our yard. The crew didn't seem to have a backup. I wondered how long it would take for them to fix it or get a replacement, if there'd be issues rescheduling, any red tape to help hold us up.

He got out of the car as soon as he laid eyes on me. We both reached out, wrapping our arms around each other, not caring how it might look to anyone watching. But the longer he tried to hold me, the more noticeable it would be to any onlookers how strangely he was posed with his empty arms. I had to let go.

"Are you all right?" he asked.

Not exactly. I played dumb, gesturing at my phantom self. "What could they do to me? I'm dead."

He saw right through it. "This is your home."

I wasn't ready to process this. For once, instead of snapping, thinking of the worst thing to say to get him to back off, I came up with the opposite. "I've got another one of those."

At least, I did for now. I'd see him move out of the apartment and into a house of his own long before I'd ever leave the Haunt.

His gaze went soft, even as he let out an exasperated breath. "What about everyone else? They'll be back. Some asshole is paying them to do this job. So they can build a fucking... parking lot, probably."

"We can't keep interfering, or we'll expose ourselves."

"I could try cuffing myself to the doors."

My stomach dropped. "That's crazy."

That word choked me. I wished I'd swallowed it back down, regretting it as soon as it left my mouth. But Ren didn't even flinch.

"I'd do it for you."

I flung my hands up in exasperation. "Is that supposed to be romantic?"

He gave a single, resolute shake of his head. "I mean for all of you."

I followed his glance to find the wallflowers heading toward us, eyes downcast, shoulders slumped. I shoved down the urge to raise my voice, since I didn't particularly want to argue in front of them. Maybe he'd think twice about this plan later, after we'd all calmed down.

"I don't know about you guys," I said. "But I could use a drink."

Clementine's had a weird energy that night. All the ghosts, dancers and wallflowers alike, headed there to blow off steam. But our mood must've afflicted the drinkers we passed through, bringing them down. So many breathers left that soon enough, there were more of us than them, for a change.

"Did something happen?" one of the servers whispered to another. "Who died?"

It wasn't a good first introduction to the place for Ren.

"This is your favorite spot?" he asked, phone to his ear. At least in the emptiness he was able to claim a table for himself, surrounded by unseen friends.

"It's not usually so… well, dead."

If only it would be this easy to scare off the demolition crew. That would take a lot more than a sudden sense of dread hitting them unexpectedly on a night out.

Danny and Carlos started up a game of "Never Have I Ever," though we quickly figured out that most of our company had more "nevers" than "evers" under their belts. We had to play the reverse, drinking if we'd also never.

Then we encountered another challenge.

"Oh, no," said Evie, when everyone turned to her expectantly. She waved her hand bashfully. "I'm just watching."

"She's straight edge," I said.

She flashed me a grateful smile.

"You could do something other than drink," said Ren. "The whole point is how embarrassing it is getting shitfaced in front of your friends, so…"

Danny piped up. "Spin around until you fall over?"

"How about a dance?" asked Carlos. He folded his arms, tucking his hands to his chest and flapping his elbows.

Evie covered her face with a squeak, so he must've been onto something.

Ren used ketchup packets to keep a tally for the number of steps she'd have to do of the chicken dance at the end of the game.

But something distracted me, made me zone out instead of laughing with my friends. I found myself searching all the faces nearby whenever I went to take a sip. I excused myself so I could search upstairs.

Liam wasn't here. And I hadn't seen him at all back at the Haunt.

I headed back down to our table. "Have any of you guys seen Liam?"

"I haven't," said Evie, who knew him from the band.

Carlos gestured with his hands. "Big guy, right? I don't think so."

"Did you ever survey him?" I asked Danny.

"I did," she said. "But me neither."

Ren didn't know him, of course. He just reached for my hand. "Don't be long?"

I rolled my eyes. "You'll live without me."

Even so, I bent to kiss him. My nerves eased from his half-drunk old-fashioned and I spirited off.

I found myself in another bar, bigger and slicker, with way less character. It had a built-in stage, where a gorgeous tan woman with short blonde hair crooned to an acoustic guitar. I tried to ignore my pang of envy. I wondered if any of her friends and family were in the crowd standing in front of the stage. Over a man's shoulder bounced a baby with tiny noise-cancelling headphones.

Liam hunched at a table near the back, with something spilled on it, so he wouldn't be disturbed until the busy staff were able to make the rounds.

"What's up?" I said, sitting over a chair, and putting my feet up on the table, since nobody could stop me.

"Where've you been?" he asked, barely short of slurring. "You haven't been dancing."

"Uh…" I had no idea where to begin. I'd never been the settling down type. That might've been stranger to him than dating on the other side.

The crowd cheered at the end of a song, and the singer greeted the audience, her voice strangely familiar.

"Are y'all having a good time tonight?"

Another burst of cheers.

"Well, that sucks, 'cause I'm about to bring you down," she said. That got a few laughs. "So, not to be a bummer, but this is the first time I'm playing solo without my husband."

My jaw dropped. I hadn't recognized her with the new haircut and bleach job, not to mention bigger hips. And I wouldn't have thought he'd be stupid enough to come.

"Are you kidding me?" I asked.

He didn't react, his eyes fixed on her.

Haley went on. "I wasn't gonna bring it up till later, after making you like me, but it's just too weird that he's not up here. So before we start, I wanted to say he was a good man, a great father, and the best guitarist I've ever met. I'm doing my best, but—you should've heard him."

Liam drew a breath, like a dry sob, before I even realized he'd been crying. On instinct, I reached out to him, barely remembering to raise my walls as I rested my hand over his fist.

"All right," said Haley. "I promise the rest of the night will be bummer-free from here on out."

That got some relieved laughter and supportive clapping. She quickly gave the name for their next song and launched right into it. I could hardly hear her.

"We should leave," I said, tugging at Liam's hand.

He tore out of my grasp. "I should be here."

"It'll make you go geist."

Right on cue, the table wobbled, the glasses on it trembling, making the spill ripple and spread farther.

"I'm tired of being a deadbeat dad," he said.

"It's only self-preservation."

His laugh made me shiver. "You'd know all about that, wouldn't you?"

He didn't usually get like this when he drank. Made sense that he'd been repressing so hard, if this was what happened when the dam broke.

I didn't know how to make him budge. But he shouldn't have to face this alone.

I felt bad making this all about me, but I didn't know how else to distract him. I went ahead and admitted why his words stung so much.

"You're right," I said. "I decided to stop checking on my sister, rather than risk going geist. It's just that every time I see her, all I can think about is how I left. Maybe not on purpose, but... I did want it."

It worked. He leaned forward, trying to get a better look at me through the tipsy haze. "What do you mean?"

"I didn't just fall off a roof."

He barely even blinked. "I kind of thought as much, but, you know, how do you go about asking that? So I left you to it. I'm sorry."

"Don't be," I said. "I wouldn't have answered. I wasn't ready to admit it to myself. In fact, I got so deep in denial, I tried to—"

It might not be such a good idea to tell him I'd found an actual medium. It hadn't done me much good trying to pierce the veil.

Or maybe I owed it to him.

"What would you say to your wife?" I asked. "If you could talk to her, somehow?"

He didn't take long answering. "Just that I love her."

"...That's it?"

"What am I supposed to tell her—she should stop seeing her second, because it's only an open marriage if I'm still in it? If he wasn't around, she'd be so miserable, I couldn't deal."

"What about your kid?" I asked. I wondered if she was the baby with the noise-cancelling headphones.

"Same thing, tell her Daddy loves her."

Once again, I almost protested. It seemed like such a given. Greeting-card shit. Then I wondered how I'd feel if somehow— whether scrawled in a yellowed old letter in an attic, or passed to me through some kind of psychic—my father could tell me, in spite of leaving so soon, he still loved me.

My mouth fell open. "I'm such an idiot."

Cris and I had never exchanged those exact words. I didn't know why. Perhaps because our mother never taught us.

She didn't really want to know if I'd taken my own life. All she wanted to hear was whether or not I'd been thinking of her, up on the ledge. And, truthfully, I hadn't. But that didn't mean I didn't love her.

Thankfully, that should be a much simpler message to pass along.

"I can't argue with that," said Liam.

I'd all but forgotten what I'd said before, rolling my eyes as I remembered. "Thanks."

His grin didn't last long, falling again when he laid eyes on his wife, taking in her wistful voice.

No point holding back. "What if I told you that you can still talk to them? I, uh… know a guy."

He didn't betray the surprise I'd expected. "Oh, you mean the medium?"

So he knew about the deliveries to the Haunt.

"Yeah, no," he said, laughing as he shook his head. I didn't expect the sudden warmth in his eyes. "That would never work."

"Why not?"

"Haley thinks we're bullshit. You think I haven't tried getting her attention before? She just replaced the carbon monoxide detector, called an electrician, and put the dog on anxiety meds."

Funny how he sounded kind of proud of her for it. They might've been married, but she'd found a way to play hard to get, even after his death.

It must've been a short set, because the audience gave what sounded like a final round of applause, and the band began packing up. I let out a breath like I'd been holding it in. We'd made it.

He got up from his seat in midair. I stumbled up onto my feet, as well.

"Where are you going?" I asked.

"We always have an afterparty."

It looked like everybody from the show had made it, crammed into the living room, the couch full and everyone else milling, spilling over into the kitchen. Most of them were laughing, but some of them sniffled into their pizza and beer, like an informal wake.

"This is my house," said Liam.

It looked nice. Not at all like the one we'd shared years ago. Modern and clean, modestly furnished but well arranged, with all the band posters and original art in frames. There were lots of toys stored in bins. That would no doubt change when the baby began to walk.

An Alaskan Malamute barreled toward us. For a second, I forgot why that was so weird.

"Daisy," said Liam. She might not have been able to feel his hands, but he managed to ruffle her fur all the same. She tried and failed to lick his face, finding nothing but air. It made her whine in distress, then bark. I'd always been more of a cat person, but as far as I could tell, she didn't sound aggressive—more as if she were trying to alert her humans that something was very, very wrong.

I tried to pat her side, not that it helped. "I feel you. We don't understand what's going on, either."

"What's up with you?" asked Haley. "She used to be so good at parties. Come on, girl."

She coaxed the dog away, letting her out in the backyard. When she got back, she allowed herself a much-needed beer, dried mascara tear marks tracking down her face. In the meantime, a good-looking, bearded guy about our age fussed over the baby.

"That's her second," said Liam.

I would've tried dragging him away again if he hadn't looked so calm, even with another man holding his child. The baby began to fuss, trying out a huff or two before launching right into a wail. She had her dad's lungs.

Haley popped right up from her seat. She looked embarrassed, though all the guests kept on talking and laughing, trying their damnedest not to mind. But it did feel weird to hear a baby in the midst of this party, reminding everyone they weren't so young anymore.

"I've got her," said her second. He got up to go change her.

I nudged Liam. "Are you going to introduce me?"

That got a smile. In life, aside from the last few years, I'd never needed to wait before jumping into conversation with strangers. Here, I could only listen, introduced at a distance. He told me about all his friends as they talked about him in turn, how he'd touched their lives, all the ways he would be missed. I wondered if they would've been my friends, as well. If I could have filled my apartment with this much laughter.

Haley didn't seem to be doing so bad. She had a good support system. Only her eyes didn't look the same. She'd been death-touched. Her gaze cradled the people around her, fraught with their fragility, how tenuous this moment in time, and their place in her life. Who would be next, gone in a blink? If she tried hard enough, she could keep them alive forever, if only in the memory of this moment.

Through the walls, the baby wailed again.

"I tried everything," said the second. "Bottle, diaper, goodnight song, she's not having it."

Haley went to go check, only to come back and give her diagnosis with a weary wave of her wrist. "She's overtired. She'll stop crying and fall asleep any minute."

"She needs her daddy," Liam said.

My stomach dropped with dread. But I didn't say anything. Maybe he needed this. It might do more good than the bad that I feared. I'd be right here.

I followed him into what turned out not to be a nursery, just the master bedroom. I recognized some of the framed posters and dumb little gifts on the dresser. He'd kept all the band stuff.

As the baby screamed from the crib beside the bed, I tried not to cringe. He leaned over her, cooing and fussing, singing. She couldn't hear him.

Under his breath, as if to himself, he asked, "Where's my guitar?"

"You can't."

"No one will even notice."

I ended up chasing him all over the house as he looked for it, put someplace he wouldn't have wanted it after his death. He found it in the living room, like it had been recently borrowed.

"You're gonna get caught!"

"So be my lookout," he said, already lifting the damn thing.

There were way too many people. A whole bunch of people, skeptics and believers alike—if they could all confirm what they'd seen—

Somehow, without quite knowing how I did it, or even thinking twice, I blew out the lights. Better they couldn't see anything.

As usual, everyone seemed more excited than annoyed, all whooping and rationalizing, several people leaping to action, volunteering to look for flashlights and candles, go check the circuit breakers.

Someone offered another distraction. "Let's play seven minutes in heaven."

All the rest laughed and shuffled around in excitement, like this was another party game.

With all the commotion, at first, I didn't hear the muffled guitar through the wall. It twanged with the gentle lilt of a lullaby. Once it came to my ears, it wouldn't leave. I'd killed the music along with the power, making the house quiet.

The baby had stopped crying. Haley noticed—and she froze.

"Am I the only one hearing that?" she asked.

"It's just the music," said another guest.

"There's nothing playing, power's out."

"Is it the neighbors?"

All the volunteers came back with the flashlights and a couple of wavering candles, like they were going to a vigil. Anyone thinking they'd gone off for a secret jam session stood corrected.

"Where's that coming from?" one of them asked.

"It sounds exactly like—"

"I know that guitar—"

Haley rushed to her feet. "It's the goodnight song."

No need to hear any more. I beat them to the bedroom, spiriting straight there. Right on time to see the guitar fall to the floor, beside the crib.

"Liam?"

The baby cooed happily in her sleep. Haley passed through me, throwing her hand over her mouth, muffling her own cry on motherly instinct. Her daughter had finally drifted off.

She bent down, hands shaking as she picked up the guitar. Through the walls, the dog howled as if in pain.

I tried spiriting to Liam. But it only brought me to his grave. He was gone.

Stage Eight:
Depression

FORTY-ONE

》》》 《《《

Alastair looked annoyed. I'd ignored the courtesy distance, appearing right on top of him. But as soon as he saw the look on my face, his hands were on me, steadying me. Around us, the other ghosts at Clementine's were whispering, watching for a scene to unfold. I gave them one.

"He's gone."

"What happened?" he asked.

"Liam." I braced my hands on his chest. "I can't find him— he's gone."

He tried spiriting us. We only ended up back at the grave again.

"I'm so sorry," said Alastair.

Through his fingers, for the first time, something spilled over. An ache too old to be mine. He'd felt this before, enough to get sick of it: the abandonment and guilt of watching friends disappear.

"Where did he go?" I asked.

He pulled me close, softening my fall as I sank to the earth. "I don't know."

My eyes were dry. As much as I hated to cry, this felt worse.

"Is this how it feels?" I asked. "When someone you love dies?"

"It's close," he said, with reassuring authority once again, like I wanted to hear from him. I shut my still dry eyes, letting myself sink into his chest.

"What am I supposed to do with myself?"

He spoke soft and lilting, delivering the bad news as tenderly as a lullaby. "There's nothing you can do, aside from sit for a while in shock, feeling numb. Then feel bad for feeling numb, and then feel stupid for trying to feel one way or another, as if it's a performance. You go from the top and back again, over and over—because the reality of their absence from the world is too much to wrap your head around, when it's easier to argue with yourself about how you should be feeling."

I raised my head enough to peer up at his face. "How do you know?"

His face lay unmasked. "I've loved and lost, in life and in death."

He sat with me as I did exactly as he said, wondering how I should be feeling, and for how long. It felt selfish, but I couldn't help it. Right after the enormity of his absence, it scared me most to wonder how long this would hurt.

It helped to imagine how this would have gone if we were alive. If I'd heard about his death back when it first happened, flown in for the funeral.

I wouldn't be the only person to hurt so badly. I'd see the state of his wife, and, whether she was bravely stoic or wailing and gnashing her teeth, in a weird way, it would make me feel better. Seeing someone hurting so much would make me compose myself, get a grip. You can't outdo the widow at a funeral, any more than the bride at a wedding. But it might make her feel better, as well, like every tear held back and sob swallowed was one less she had to perform herself.

Even seeing all the guests that were less affected than me would help. We'd all be miserable, drinking bad coffee and sitting in fold-up chairs, making awkward small talk with strangers and avoiding former friends, watching the family take out their grief on each other.

Once we'd said our goodbyes, hopefully there'd be booze, and if everything went just right—if he'd lived the right kind of life— there'd be laughter as well as tears. And then I'd give myself something else to worry about by going to bed with somebody I shouldn't have before flying home.

I didn't have any of that. I'd gotten to hold onto him for longer than any of his family and friends, but not by much. And now, I had to face losing him alone, with no life to get on with afterwards.

Well, not alone.

Alastair must've felt that I wanted to extricate myself, because he let go. He'd been holding me for a long time. Much longer than I'd ever let him when we were sleeping together.

"Thanks," I said, as I got up.

He shadowed me. "Where do you think you're going?"

I curbed the urge to roll my eyes. After all, he meant well.

"I've got somebody waiting for me."

His mouth curled to the side. "And who might that be?"

"It's exactly who you think it is."

I didn't know if I still needed to spirit a courtesy distance from Ren. But I didn't trust myself to burst right into the middle of the apartment right now, in case I started going geist. So I waited out on the fire escape, though the already cracked glass of the window made me nervous as I peered in, ready to knock.

There were voices inside. The wallflowers must've invited themselves over. I laughed when I recognized what they were doing, sitting on the floor surrounded by bits and bobs of particle wood.

"It's wrong," said Ren.

"What's the chance you bought a factory dud?" said Danny. "We're probably not looking at the right piece."

Evie piled her hair up high and tied it with her scarf up to keep it out of her face. "It's supposed to have holes, isn't it?"

"That's cool," Ren said. "You can still change your hair?"

"Well, I try." Evie smoothed her hands over the satin. "It's not very neat."

"It looks nice."

Danny pointed to the box propped against the wall. "Did we leave any pieces in there?"

"It's empty," said Carlos, tossing the package to demonstrate. "Ow."

"Sorry, I forgot you're corporeal."

"But we found it," said Evie, retrieving a board from under the bed.

Ren took it, flipping it over for a look. "Never mind, there's no holes."

"Do you have a drill?" she asked.

"I don't even have a screwdriver."

I'd fallen back into my old eavesdropping habit, watching from the outside, looking in. It felt safer that way. I didn't want to bring the party down if I couldn't hold it together. Nobody wanted shattered glass for confetti, bursting faucets for noisemakers.

But I shouldn't be alone. So, with a sigh, I lifted my hand and gently rapped my knuckles on the glass, so gingerly I didn't even make a sound at first.

Ren blinked at me on the other side as he approached.

"Why are you knocking?" he asked, after he opened the window. "Just come in."

Despite the invitation, and the welcome sight of his face, I couldn't move. They came to me instead, crowding around the window.

"You scared us," said Evie.

"I thought you were one of his geists," said Danny.

Carlos laughed, shaking his head. "We're the worst ghosts."

I felt guilty for wincing. They were my friends, after all.

"What's wrong?" asked Ren.

He climbed out through the window and onto the fire escape for a closer look at me. I uncrossed my arms and tried to uncurl my spine, too late. His hands were on me, but as sweet as his concern ached in my chest, he couldn't ground me like I wanted.

Evie's hand flew to her chest. "The Haunt?"

"Did they come back?"

"Is she still standing?"

I waved them all off. "No, no, yes."

Evie stepped straight through the window onto the fire escape, reaching out to anchor me with hands I could truly feel. "What is it, then? You can tell us anything."

All that touch broke me down with too much tenderness to bear. I flushed with embarrassment, choking on weird half-formed sobs, as my eyes stung and face ached with overdue tears.

"Liam."

I didn't want to be the one to break the news, even if they wouldn't take it as hard as me. It put them in such a weird position. If I were them, and I knew him so little, I'd have a hard time knowing how to react.

It felt so weird to say it. As if I'd given up, accepted it, by putting it into words.

"He crossed."

After finally getting it out, my throat seemed to give. I couldn't reply to their condolences, all the *I'm-so-sorry*s and *it's-*

*going-to-be-OK*s and *we're-here-for-you*s. I could hardly even process whose hands were on me, surrounding me. I must've been prickly to the touch, so much wounded pride, my own embarrassment mirrored back at me through their touch. Yet they didn't let go. They hadn't even known him, but they were willing to take my pain and share it. It made me cry harder, even as I began to feel better.

It ended sooner than I would've thought. I stopped right in the middle of a sob to catch my breath, but didn't feel the need to finish, going quiet. It felt hollow in a good way, my chest opened up and emptied out, freshly exhumed. We parted, leaving me alone in my own skin again. I knew they weren't far, though.

"You must've been close," said Ren.

Out of everyone, only he hadn't met Liam. That didn't lessen how drawn his face was with concern, just from seeing me this way.

"He was my ex," I said. That got some raised eyebrows. But it didn't quite cover it. "And my friend, and… my old bandmate."

"No kidding," said Carlos.

"I can't imagine," added Danny.

Evie went quiet, like she had to process herself. He'd been her bandmate too, if much more briefly.

"Let's get inside," said Ren.

He tried to coax me, but I pulled back.

"Could you put the coffee pot in the cupboard?" I asked. "And the lamp and the plants in the closet, just in case."

"On it," he said, before going inside to geist-proof the place.

"Is there anything else we could do?" asked Carlos.

"Tell us what you need," said Evie.

I couldn't meet their eyes, unaccustomed to this kind of attention. "Just don't mind that I'm going to be a bummer for a while."

They all chimed in that they couldn't possibly, no way, my feelings were valid, and I had to feel them, however long it would take. As soon as we got inside, I gave in to the urge to sink to the floor. They all joined me.

"Let's get this put together," I said, picking up one of the particle board slabs they'd been working on, some kind of shelf.

"What are we going to do without tools?" asked Danny.

"I could help with that," said Alastair.

We all jumped. Definitely not the best ghosts.

Evie beat me to the question. "What are you doing here?"

"Just checking in," he replied, looking at me. I had to wonder if he was worried I'd gone off on my own, or if that made a convenient cover for coming to spy on who exactly I had waiting for me.

"Where are the screws?" he asked.

Ren didn't look all too rattled by the intrusion, coming back from the kitchen with a bottle in hand. "Boo, you want some beer, or do you think that's too unhealthy a coping mechanism?"

Alastair raised his eyebrows, silently mouthing "Boo?"

I shrugged at him, going for shameless, but my blush ruined it.

"I've had enough for tonight," I admitted to Ren. "You mind not having one?"

"I'd rather get to cuddle."

He put it down and came to make good on his words, sinking down behind me and doing his best to coax me back onto his chest.

Carlos located the small bag of screws and passed them over. Alastair used his hands to drive them into the cheap boards. We gave a round of applause.

Danny picked the instructions back up.

"We don't need those," said Alastair.

Several protests spilled from all sides.

"Trust me," Carlos insisted. "It's not as simple as it looks."

"You might think it's pure logic," said Danny. "But really, there's no logic to it at all."

"You don't know what you're dealing with here, old man," I chimed in.

Ren let go of me so he could grab the instructions, as well as the next piece. Alastair relented, no longer a host, but a guest.

All of a sudden, I noticed the silence. I was about to ask what kind of music to put on—but I got a better idea. As everyone compared and traded parts, like some kind of random board game with big and small and possibly missing pieces, I scooched back out of the circle for some space, and so it wouldn't be too loud and intrusive when I began. I needed some room to be rusty.

It felt silly at first, like playing air guitar. Suddenly, my fingers grazed strings. My first guitar rippled like smoke in my hands.

They all looked up at the twang of my first faltering chord. Then they looked at each other, and with an unspoken understanding, did their best to pretend not to notice. They went back to what they were doing, letting me get back into practice with no pressure.

My next chords didn't stutter. I played just as smoothly and boldly as I used to do in dreams, like I'd never had the chance to forget. My memory came alive in my hands. Or maybe it was an extension of my soul, once poured into the instrument, and brought back when I needed it. Bared for all my friends to hear.

Wherever he'd gone, I hoped Liam would be listening.

FORTY-TWO

❋»» «‹❋

Ren and I curled up in bed once everyone had gone home, long past dawn. Fully clothed, like old times. I liked that I could literally bury myself in his chest, hide from the world inside him. But not forever.

"How are you feeling?" he asked.

I pulled back to meet his eyes. He tried to rub circles on my back.

"You know," I said.

He placed his lips over each of my tired eyes.

I'd almost forgotten the revelation I'd had earlier—the decision I'd made. "I'm ready to try again with Cris."

He blinked at me. "I thought you'd given up."

I couldn't quite shrug lying down against him. "I did. It's not like I want to tell her she was right about my sort-of suicide."

My limbs clenched instinctively, waiting for lights to flicker, chains to rattle. But there weren't any lights on, and the locks and chains were long gone. The coffee pot stayed safely in its cupboard, the curtains didn't rustle, the stove didn't burn.

The guilt remained, but it didn't bleed anymore, beginning to scar over.

"That's not what she really needed to hear from me," I said.

"And what's that?"

The echo tasted bittersweet in my mouth. "Just that I love her."

I didn't feel his smile against my hair so much as sense its warmth in my stomach. "That sounds easy enough to say."

"Not as easy as you'd think."

He did his best to wrap his arms tighter around me. "We need to come up with a better plan than last time."

"I'm working on it."

We'd been in too much of a hurry before, for no good reason. He'd been a stranger. They needed to bond for real if he was going to communicate just as intimately as a sister—even a distant, emotionally stunted one. She needed new family to make up for the one she'd lost.

This time, we wouldn't go in so unprepared. And I had an idea of where they could meet again.

"What's the date?"

Cris and I were supposed to have a new tradition. Last year, on her birthday, we'd spent the whole day together. Brunch, shopping, then a small dinner party with her church and college friends, who I'd managed to charm into thinking I was one of them, sparing her the embarrassment of the truth. We'd agreed to keep it up every year, making up for all her birthdays I'd missed in college and on the road, back when she lived with our mother, who sucked the joy out of parties.

I'd broken that promise. But I didn't think she would.

Vicki's new place looked a lot like her old one, the same vintage burlesque posters hanging on the wall, and the big shipyard-looking trunk she'd thrifted for a coffee table. She'd traded in all her other starter furniture for stuff that must've cost way more and actually matched. But she still hung all the same art, made by friends of varying talent, and the band posters she used to collect—including ours—just framed and arranged better. I kind of wanted to snoop in her bedroom to see if she'd kept any of our old toys.

Vicki came out of the kitchen in a red silk robe, her hair in rubber curlers, clutching a novelty coffee mug shaped like tits, right as keys jingled in the doorway and the person I'd meant to check on arrived.

Cris rolled in wearing a messy updo, smeared mascara, and a tiny, clinging silver dress. It took me a second to notice.

"What have you done to your hair?" I asked.

She'd gone and dyed it blue. It looked much better on her than it had on me.

Vicki didn't whistle. She used to whistle whenever I completed a walk of shame in our dorm, before we started dating. And she'd done the same for a crash-couching friend of ours once, so she didn't reserve it just for her crushes, doling it out as a general compliment.

"You should've come," said Cris.

Vicki settled heavily into a leather armchair. "Well, don't shoot me. I'm not old enough to put out to pasture just yet."

I never thought I'd see the day she finally slowed her roll.

Cris pointed, on her way to the kitchen. "Did you make me any?"

"I thought you had work today."

So she had to pay her own rent now. I wondered if she could still afford school.

"I got my shift covered," said Cris over her shoulder, as she went about making her own coffee. She banged the cabinet loudly. "I'll pick up an extra next week, it's fine."

Vicki turned around in her chair to peer at her. "When are you going to find time for class?"

"I dropped one."

"Again?" asked Vicki. "Uh, how many do you have left? Don't you have a limit to meet for your loan?"

I'd been foolish to think she'd be fine, neatly compartmentalizing her party time the same as she'd always balanced school and church and volunteering.

My sister's shoulders went stiff. "Can the cross-examination wait till after I've caffeinated, Mother?"

Vicki mumbled into her mug, "You could use one."

That didn't go unheard, judging by the sigh from the kitchen, bordering on a growl.

"Are you even having fun?" asked Vicki.

Cris whirled with a glare. "Really—coming from you?"

"I know what's good for me," said Vicki. "At first, I figured you were still hung up about sinning or whatever, and once you got over it, you'd enjoy yourself, but…"

Rather than finish, she took a bracing swig, as if her coffee were a stiff drink.

Cris looked dull, in spite of the blue hair and glittery dress, paler than usual and skinnier, with bags under her eyes. So that's why she hadn't earned a whistle. I used to come home messy, but grinning.

I'd wanted to believe the partying was a good sign, last time I checked on her. But this wasn't my little sister. She hadn't loosened up so much as unraveled.

"I don't need any preaching." Cris gave up on the coffee, marching across the kitchen and living room. "I've had enough of that for a lifetime."

For a moment, I thought she'd straight up leave. Apparently, she wanted a shower first. She stormed into the bathroom and slammed the door.

The kitchen light flickered. I wriggled my wrists, fighting off the ache.

I never thought, between the two of us, I'd be the sister who staged an intervention.

Cris's birthday arrived not long after. Ren and I sat parked at my cemetery all morning, after stopping to pick up another sunflower bouquet. But he could've slept in longer instead of nursing a second coffee in a thermos. She probably wasn't an early riser anymore.

"Are you sure she'll show?" he asked.

"She wouldn't miss it," I said, only to second-guess myself.

If she had work today, some kind of service job with weekend shifts, we might be fucked. Or maybe she wasn't keeping track of the date anymore, either.

Out of the window, I spotted a streak of blue amongst the melting snow and emerging green. "That's her."

I could still hardly believe the length of her skirt. Another walk of shame.

"Now what?" asked Ren.

"It's cool," I said. "Just go on and pay me a visit, like you're not bothered she's there."

"I would be bothered, though. I'd wait until she left."

"Let's say some of my devil-may-care attitude rubbed off on you, when we were supposedly dating."

He smiled. "At least that part's not a lie anymore."

And he'd gotten a lot better at making friends lately, though I didn't mention that.

We got out of the car and made our way down the rows, all the lingering ice aglow in the sunlight. It must've felt good, at least on the skin. But the bright glare couldn't be good for a hangover.

Cris had a solution for that. She kept drinking, my brand of whiskey, as she curled up on the newly grown grass of my grave. It might not be the best time to talk, but there'd probably never be a best time. We'd waited long enough.

Ren sidled up to her, casting a shadow. She looked up, but he didn't acknowledge her as he tucked the sunflowers under his arm and lit a cigarette.

She sat in silence for a while longer, before she finally asked, "Who the fuck are you?"

I flinched, still not used to hearing her curse.

He just smiled. "You don't remember me from the wake?"

She did a double take. "Wait—her special friend?"

At least she didn't look mad. Well, not any madder than she'd been already.

He squatted down beside her, laying the flowers at my headstone before offering her a drag. She took it, then coughed, like she wasn't used to smoking. She washed it down with my whiskey, which she offered in return. He only took a small sip.

"So you're the one who's been leaving the sunflowers," she said.

"Thanks for the booze."

She gave a toast, and then began to pour one out. But he grabbed the bottle before she could tip it over. Their hands brushed.

"What gives?" she asked. She must've gotten that phrase from Vicki.

"Mal wouldn't have wanted you to waste it."

Cris laughed, surprised. It didn't sound like her laugh, delicate and restrained—more like mine, witchy and irreverent.

Ren must've noticed. "If I didn't know better, I'd think she'd come back to possess you."

"As if she'd ever come back."

He couldn't resist raising his eyebrows at me. "I don't know about that."

She pointed her bottle at him in challenge. "Where do you think she went? What happens after we die?"

It had been a long time since I'd seen him rein his expressions in, keeping his face as stony as when we'd first met, bent on ignoring my existence. "That's not a fair question."

"No shit."

"I mean for me, specifically." He'd begun to blush. I'd forgotten he'd never shared the truth with another breather. At least, not with anyone who'd believed him. "It'd be easy for me to believe if I could trust myself. That's the problem, though. Sometimes, I can't."

That got her to make the effort of lifting her head. "Trust yourself about what? Have you ever…" She hesitated, embarrassed to even entertain the idea. "…Seen anything?"

"You could say that. But the thing is—I'm not about to tell just anybody."

She rolled her eyes and took another swig. "Well, I'm not just anybody, if you were really that close with her."

He drew himself up, brushing the grass off his jeans. "You want to go find something better to sit on, and something non-alcoholic to drink?"

She dropped her glare, putting her whiskey in her purse. "What the hell."

My stomach sank unexpectedly when he offered her a hand, and she took it. I couldn't tell which of them I envied more.

It hit me. I hadn't coached a single thing he'd said. They'd been bonding all on their own, exactly like I'd hoped. They hadn't met normally, brought together by my otherworldly intervention, but if I took a step back, their connection would develop naturally. Part of the cycle.

Cris started walking ahead. Ren looked back, waiting.

I waved him off. "Go on without me."

He shook his head, silently questioning.

"This is how it's supposed to be," I said. My eyes stung, but I smiled. "I'm already gone, remember? But you're still here."

He bit his lip, but he couldn't exactly argue, not out loud.

"I'll drop by later, so you can tell her the words and I can hear them. Till then, you don't need me haunting you."

Cris paused a few paces ahead. "You coming?"

He sighed, eyes heavy with melancholy. But he turned away, running to catch up with her.

I watched them leave. It felt right, in spite of the tears. Where they were going, I couldn't follow.

FORTY-THREE

))) ※ **(((**

Alastair loomed like a shadow in the white of a hospital room. On the bed below him wheezed an old woman who was visibly fading away, so small and gray in her bed, surrounded by machines on one side and family on the other. No wonder, at first sight, I'd mistaken him for a psychopomp. He looked so out of place as he intruded on this private moment, he could've come from another world entirely.

As bad as she looked—perhaps in pain—I rankled with envy.

"Waiting to ask her to dance?" I asked.

He laughed, but with no mirth. "I don't think she'll stick around."

"What does it look like when a soul crosses over?" I asked. "Any light, or tunnels, or fire and brimstone?"

"Nothing," he said. "They just disappear. At least, every one that I've witnessed so far. It could be different this time."

Probably not. That might've been why he took me aside, out to the waiting room. Or he'd decided to put me first, no longer bothered by my intrusion.

"How are you holding up?" he asked.

I took a pretend seat, grateful not to feel the stiff, square hospital furniture haunted by anxiety and impatience and bad news—the worst news anyone could get. He followed suit, letting his legs sprawl wide, supporting his elbows as he leaned toward me with his chin on his hands.

"It's strange not having him around," I said. "Not being able to go see him. Knowing he won't be there."

He stared through the coffee table covered in magazines, as if he knew any of those faces. "Being left behind."

It hurt to know now exactly what I'd done to Cris.

"I don't think he went to hell," I said. "Though I can't really picture him in heaven, either." I'd been meaning to ask this for a while now. "What do you think it's like?"

I braced myself for theatrics. But his voice hummed low, contemplative, as he stared into space. "I'm so used to having a body—even on this side—and talking, going places, having company. What if heaven is nothing like this? If we just become light, or one with the universe, or love? All disembodied and…" He finally looked at me. "Dull as fuck?"

I couldn't help but laugh. "Even hell might be more interesting."

"If it's the opposite, then it will be darkness: being nothing, apart from anyone and everyone."

For a moment, I felt an instinctive tug. I'd once wanted exactly that—oblivion. But it didn't tempt me so much anymore. Just a little, the lingering echo of self-hatred whispering that I'd be better off going before everyone else left me first. Now, I had so many more people who I knew weren't as ready to abandon me as that voice claimed.

"I don't like either of those options."

"Me neither." He gave a wistful smile. "I don't know if there are any others, but I hope I'll come back. Live again and die again. Over and over, and hang out here for a while in between, check in and see how you're running things around here."

"Hold up," I said, startled onto my feet.

His smile trembled a bit. "I'm not truly going to be around for all eternity."

Some crying came from inside the hospital room with the old woman. We must've missed her.

"Don't you have a better contender?" I asked, trying to soothe my urge to flee by pacing through the coffee table. "Somebody older and wiser?"

"Around here, age doesn't necessarily correspond with wisdom."

I slowed down, turning to look at him. "How about… more cool and mysterious?"

He tilted his head up at me. "You think you're not?"

I did keep to myself. You could call that mysterious. But I had to gesture at the outfit I'd died in.

"It's not that bad," he said.

"Are you kidding me?" I asked, holding out my skirt. "I could be a librarian, or a secretary back when they were called secretaries, or a fucking missionary."

He gave a generous shrug. "I'd call that kind of temporal ambiguity rather mysterious. What really matters is that you got three new souls to join us. You've already recruited."

My instinctive start of a rebuttal withered in my mouth unsaid. He had a point.

My biggest objection made my guts churn. "What if I don't last here as long as you?"

"I know you will," he said. "You've already proven me wrong so many times. And you know what else? You've grown. I've often fretted that we can't, on this side. But we can change, after all." He laughed, almost to himself at first, then louder, triumphant, getting up to rove around in excitement, spreading his hands wide. "Perhaps that's why we're here, in this limbo between heaven and hell. Even if most of us don't take the opportunity to learn, at least we still get the chance!"

I covered my mouth, blinking to ward off yet more tears. He sounded too eager, asking questions like he expected answers sooner rather than later. "Why are we even talking about this? It's not like you're going anywhere."

His lips pursed guiltily, like he knew something I didn't, and for once, he felt bad about it. "You never know."

"You can't leave."

"We all go, sooner or later," he said, getting up and taking my hands. "I take it you're going to miss me?"

I had to smile to keep from pulling an ugly crying face. "Fat chance."

Cris and Ren were laughing together. She sounded more herself. I hung back, wondering if I should give them more time. They were leaving a coffee house he'd no doubt suggested to sober her up. In place of whiskey, she now nursed an expensive-looking bottle of water. He trailed cigarette smoke.

I followed them to the corner where he'd parked. They hovered, no doubt dancing around whether they were going to stick together, or split.

She looked so much like me with her blue hair and paler than usual skin that I couldn't help it. I had to pretend for a second she was me, on a real date with my boyfriend, like I was watching outside of myself. That made it more bearable when she leaned up and kissed him.

He hesitated before pulling away—just for a second. I almost couldn't blame him. She looked like me, maybe even smelled like me, tasted like me after all that drinking and smoking.

"Um," said Ren. "I hate to make this weird—but remember how I literally just told you I'm still in love with Mal?"

He and I both flinched back as she suddenly and immediately sobbed. I shut my eyes, letting out a slow sigh. He glanced up at the passersby weaving around them on the sidewalk, knowing exactly how it looked. So he led her down a nearby alley for privacy.

Through her hands, she managed, "I don't even know what I'm doing anymore."

He had to light another cigarette. "I think I do. You're trying to be just like big sis, right? Take up her place?"

By now, all remnants of her makeup had been wiped and worn and cried away. She must've meditated on her next words long enough that they seemed to come unbidden, fighting up past her swollen throat as if she were possessed.

"It's like there's this empty spot, this void in the world. Nobody else sees it, but I feel it. It's nothing—literal nothingness—and there's lots of nothing in the world, but *this* nothing feels so wrong. There's not supposed to be nothing there. Everyone's going about their lives like there isn't something missing. She might as well have never existed. I can't let her not exist. It's up to me; I've got to fill up the void. But it's so hard. It keeps closing up, and for little bits at a time… I forget. I actually *forget*. I can't do that. I've got to save her space in the universe, or else—what if it closes up? What if there's really nothing left?"

As her shoulders caved, overtaken by sobs, he went ahead and put both arms around her. This time, I envied him more. At least she finally got a good fucking hug, even if it wasn't from me.

"If you're right—" He gulped, staring over her head. "If she's really gone—"

Even after all this time, perhaps he still struggled to fend off a shadow of doubt.

He sniffed, eyes glassy. "You don't have to worry about holding her shape in the world. She's doing that herself. I'm not the same, now that I've known her." He pulled back enough to look into her eyes, hands still steadying her shoulders. "There's so many people she's touched and molded you don't even know about, all her fingerprints you can't see."

Cris's tears weren't even dramatic anymore. Simply there, gliding quietly down her face. "I just want her here."

He finally glanced up to meet my stare, fighting a smile. "Maybe she is. But I'm pretty sure she wouldn't want to see you cramping her style."

As his hands slid off her shoulders, he grabbed her purse strap. She didn't seem to notice until he started rummaging through the bag.

"Hey!"

He handed the purse right back, after confiscating her bottle of whiskey.

She growled. "How am I supposed to sleep tonight?"

"You won't."

Despite her glare, she made no move to try and snatch the bottle back.

"Call me if you feel tempted," he said. "No matter how late it is. I'll do my best to talk you out of it. Just don't try anything sexy."

That got an old-fashioned scoff out of her, like I used to rile her up to hear. So for all her posturing, she still had some of that old prudery left. I welcomed it back.

They traded phones to put their numbers in, and began the dance again, staying or splitting.

"Wait," said Ren.

She went still. My phantom heart thundered in anticipation.

"Just so you know—" He gulped, voice hoarse. "Mal loves you."

Her lips twitched, eyes glinting again already. "When did she say that?"

"She didn't," said Ren. At least, I hadn't until recently. But he had to go off the sister she knew, not the person I'd grown into after death. "Not in so many words. I used to hear it in her voice."

"What did she tell you?"

Good thing we'd spent the last few days preparing.

"Everything," he said. "She was so proud of you, every time you nailed an exam, or met your goal for a canned food drive. And she worried for you, about your mother's influence, whether you'd ever meet a guy who's not too scary religious. She regretted missing so much of your life. But she thought you guys would have time to make it up."

I didn't expect what burst up out of her mouth to be a laugh. "You do think she's still around, though, don't you?"

He shook his head, a little panicked.

"You said she loves me—present tense."

Ren breathed a ragged sigh. "You got me."

She smiled—her own smile that I hadn't seen in a long time, faint and slightly mysterious, like the Virgin. "Even if she isn't here—if she's gone for good—I still love her."

My lungs seemed to fill impossibly, as if I'd opened my ribs like shutters, letting in some fresh air.

Ren smiled back. "See you around?"

Her soft gaze withered. "You'll be hearing from me when I can't fucking sleep."

She turned to go at last, her blue hair bouncing over her shoulders, curling again at the ends.

Once she'd left, he remained in the alley, finishing up his cigarette. I waited for him to get the obvious out of the way.

"I'm so sorry," he said. "She made the first move—you saw that, right? It surprised me, but you know I'd never. I mean—not that she's gross or anything, far from it—but she's not you."

He stopped and stared, wide-eyed and gulping in the face of my silence. I just laughed.

"Don't be sorry," I said, and nearly meant it. "I'm kind of glad you got a real smooch."

His eyes hardened. "What do you mean real?"

"Come on, you know what I mean." I waved it off, because I didn't want to talk about it, not yet. "Aside from that, it seems like you had a nice time."

His slight shrug was defeated. "As much as I could with another breather."

I tensed at that word choice. "What?"

His skin flushed. "I just wish I could've told her the truth about you and me, and the afterlife. I forgot how it feels to have to hide."

My guilt roiled in my guts. "You might be getting too comfortable rubbing elbows with the dead."

He pulled in closer, reaching for me. "I like you better than the living."

I tried not to make it too obvious as I leaned away from his touch. "Right, that's the problem."

"What do you mean?"

My words tasted bitter, like medicine, coming up rough. But they'd do him good, even if it felt more like harm. "Does it really count as a social life if all your friends are dead?"

Now he glared, his eyes glistening. "How about my love life?" His voice shook, though I couldn't tell if it was with anger, or anguish. "Don't you count?"

I could hardly keep my own voice together. "I didn't think this through. Do we really have to talk about the long term, here? I mean, we met past our expiration date."

He refused to look away, not fighting the tears. "I thought you'd changed. You said you wouldn't disappear again."

"This isn't about that! I'd stay with you if I could, for the rest of my life, even—" My voice pitched, and then cracked. "Except I don't fucking have one."

I didn't mean to yell at him. Only at myself. I'd carry this regret for the rest of my existence, however long that lasted.

We stared at each other, a couple of inches away, but worlds apart. The gulf between life and death. Like the void between a high rooftop and the earth below.

Then we both reeled back from the figure appearing between us.

Evie looked apologetic for spiriting with no courtesy distance. But she had good reason.

"They're back."

Ren turned to me. "Go on," he said. "I'll catch up."

He didn't wait for me to reply, sprinting down the street to his car. It might be a while until we got to finish this conversation.

FORTY-FOUR

❀»» «« ❀

The demolition crew were already setting up a perimeter, orange posts and yellow tape surrounding the lot, keeping the spectators on lawn chairs from getting too close. So there'd be an audience, as if the impending destruction were some kind of show.

I went to say goodbye. Even if I couldn't feel any of it, I let my hands trail along the pocked walls, practically held together by the vines. My feet trod harmlessly over all the broken glass and fallen plaster and dead leaves. I blinked in the afternoon sun glinting off the marble, straight through the glassless windows. There must've been a breeze, judging from the gentle dance of the leaves, green and new.

The wallflowers were watching the crew set up from the front lawn.

Danny moved her hands so fast they blurred. "What are we going to do?"

Evie's voice pitched with mounting panic. "Where's Ally?"

Carlos chanced kicking a discarded beer can. Luckily, it didn't make any sound on the grass, resting like a breeze had tried and failed to lift it farther. "You heard him—he's not going to do anything."

It wouldn't make any difference. But that wouldn't be comforting. Instead, I said, "Ren is coming."

"Does he have a plan?" asked Evie.

"I'm sure he does."

I only hoped it wouldn't be too compromising.

Once he pulled the car as close as he could to the perimeter and got out, I tossed some plaster from the last attempted demolition to distract some of the crewmen. He hopped over the barrier while they weren't looking.

Evie raised her arms like she meant to embrace him. "You're here!"

"We knew you would be!" Carlos clapped his shoulder.

Danny hung back, her hands too busy. "What's the plan?"

Ren looked from them to all the spectators, pointing as subtly as he could without looking like he was gesturing to the seemingly empty air. If he kept on like this, he'd get noticed sooner or later, and escorted out of here before he could try anything.

I tugged on his shirt, beckoning him up the stairs and through the front doors, which we shut quickly behind us.

"Could we have some space real quick?" Ren asked.

Once the gang went back outside, we didn't even have to say anything after all. Maybe something had slipped through our touch, because without a word we were in each other's arms. He pressed his brow down to mine, before trying his luck and leaning down. I kissed him back.

"You don't have to do this," I said.

"I didn't even tell you what I'm going to do."

I made for his bulging back pocket, pulling out a chain and lock. The same ones that used to rattle on his cabinets. I'd hoped he'd thrown them all away.

He reached for the chain defensively, like I might hold it back. I let go.

"You'll look crazy."

"It'll be worth it," he said. "I promised my friends."

We went back outside. I helped him bind his left wrist to the door knocker, which forced him to keep his arm raised above his head as if in victory.

It shouldn't have gotten me a little hot. But since it did, I let him know with a quick kiss, swallowing his anxiety and putting my laugh in his mouth. A sudden roar of noise made us jolt back, pulling apart.

Some of the bystanders were pointing and cheering, getting the attention of the crewmen. Now there'd be a real show.

Carlos darted his eyes back and forth, squinting. "This is the plan?"

"It could work," said Danny. "I mean, until we come up with something more, right?"

"Is this safe?" asked Evie.

They weren't the only ghosts to gawk. More spectators began to crowd around, enough dead to match the living on the other side of the tape.

"Wait, you're a breather?" asked the hippie girl.

"I thought you were one of ours," said the man in the bowler hat.

Ren grinned. It made me shiver. "I might as well be."

I'd have to add this to the words we were going to have later. Right now, he needed my support.

He stood tall, surrounded on all sides by friends old and new, as a foreman in an orange helmet approached.

"I've got bad news," the foreman said. "Or good news, if you were hoping for attention."

"I'm thrilled," said Ren. "This is exactly the kind of attention I've always wanted."

Some of the other ghosts laughed, but I only gulped down my nausea, watching the rushing blood show through his skin.

"Why this place?" asked the foreman.

Ren couldn't help but look around at us, by his side. "I've got friends that love this place."

"Well, where are they?"

Another crewman approached with a sledgehammer.

"You've got to be fucking kidding me," said Ren.

"We have to do something," Carlos hissed.

I choked on the words, not wanting to let them out. "We can't."

Ren flinched instinctively, though the crewman only aimed for the door hinges. It ripped through the wood like paper. As the remains of the door tipped over, I spirited straight through to the other side and caught it. If I hadn't, the door would've fallen flat, breaking more than just the hinges.

I had to let go as the crewmen took each side of it, so they wouldn't feel my resistance.

"Can't we do anything?" asked Evie.

Ren looked back at me, as they dragged him along. "Stay there," he said, heedless of the living in earshot. "Don't give up."

"What the hell are you talking about?" asked one of the crewmen.

The other one laughed. "Obviously we've got a crazy here."

"I'm not," said Ren.

"Where are your friends?" asked the foreman. "They're up here, huh?"

He knocked on his helmet.

"I'm not crazy," said Ren. His voice rose, louder and louder, until he began to scream. Just what he shouldn't have done if he wanted to look sane. "I'm not fucking crazy!"

I covered my face, trying to hide the tears.

"I'm so sorry," I said, even as they'd dragged him too far to hear me. I ignored what he'd said and spirited to his side.

"What are you doing?" said Ren. The crewmen dropped the door on the ground not far from the living spectators in their chairs, forcing him to his knees. "Leave me."

I would've argued, if I hadn't noticed the dark figure appear in front of the rolling machine, looming over it with a roar.

Alastair grinned like Death himself coming to collect, as if the machine before us had a soul for him to take.

"Don't even think about it," I said.

Standing beneath the excavator made me tremble, still aware of how small and delicate my body used to be in the face of such a beast.

He turned his smile on me. "There's no call to fret."

"But you taught me not to trespass any boundaries," I said. "What are we supposed to do if you cross?"

His eyes were gentle, despite his smirk, like I'd missed the punchline. "You'll take care of everyone."

My tears were already flowing again, the dam broken. "I'm not cool and mysterious enough yet."

"That'll come with time."

I threw my hands out helplessly. Being exasperated by him felt so old and familiar—almost welcome—I couldn't help but laugh, soft and shaky. "You're really not scared?"

He gave a gleeful shrug. "I didn't say that."

His mouth trembled as he smiled. He leaned in, and I let him. It would be his last kiss—at least on this side.

"Catch you next time around," he said.

At long last, he finally showed me why all the other spirits revered him.

Alastair swaggered straight up to the excavator, climbing up into the body of the machine. His elbows and feet stuck out as he moved inside it, and it froze in place, the shovel hanging stiff in midair.

"Shit," said the driver, pressing buttons, pulling levers. But he couldn't see the oil beginning to leak onto the pavement. He went still as smoke began to rise. "Shit!"

He hopped right out, stumbling as he hit the ground, hard. Another crew member ran up and pulled him to his feet, both fleeing as the engine caught fire. Only a small one, nothing catastrophic, but enough to really fuck their whole day.

"What the fuck?" one of the spectators said, leaning forward in his lawn chair. The onlookers tittered amongst themselves, pulling out phones.

Alastair held up a hand, and like a sudden gust of hurricane winds, all the lawn chairs toppled right over, the spectators crying out as they hit the pavement.

It wasn't until they'd pulled themselves up, looking at each other, asking "What was that?" and "Did you see that?" that he glanced up at me with one last smirk and a wink.

I blinked. When I opened my eyes again, he'd gone.

I couldn't stop to mourn. Someone screamed. I knew that voice.

"Evie?"

When I spirited back to the wallflowers on the front lawn, they were frantic.

"What's happening?" asked Danny.

"Don't touch her," said Carlos.

He held her back from reaching Evie. Her eyes were glazed over, staring through us. Alastair's coat had disappeared from her shoulders.

My first instinct told me to grab her, as well. Try and anchor her. She must've been watching the whole time as the man she loved crossed over. I should've thought about that before letting him go. Had he even said goodbye?

Unlike any other geists I'd encountered, she'd gone silent. That scared me more than if she were gibbering nonsense. At least it would've given her some semblance of life. She went still, rather than wandering. I'd never even seen that before.

"Come back," I said, like that would do anything.

"What can we do?" asked Danny.

"Is it too late?" said Carlos.

They were clutching each other, tearful and scared.

"It's not," I said. I'd have to go in. She'd done the same for me. "If I don't come back, take care of Ren."

Before they could protest, try and pull me back, I closed my eyes, stole a play at breath, and laid my hands on Evie.

It all went dark. No memories unfolded before my eyes. Nothing but darkness. I couldn't move. I wasn't sure how long I'd been trapped there, minutes or hours.

I drifted in and out, like sleeping, except I never got to wake up. It might've been days, even weeks, and as badly as I wanted to freak out—flail my hands, or at least tense my muscles, open my mouth and cry out—I couldn't. Even tears wouldn't come. I could only lie there in the dark, helpless. And this time, nobody came to lift us up and tell us we weren't dreaming.

Colors swirled, folding into shapes. I could see through my own eyes again.

Evie's eyes were still staring through me.

"Are you back?" asked Danny.

"Did it work?" said Carlos.

It hadn't. I couldn't bring her with me.

But I had one other option.

"Stay here with her," I said. "I'm going to try something."

Her body still didn't look like her, so thin and bony. All those machines maintaining its life looked more like they were taking it away. Aside from pulling the oxygen tube out from under her nose, I didn't want to mess with any other instruments. She might still need those after I'd finished.

Alastair had been right the first time around. It would be easier to use a pillow.

I took one from under her head and pressed it over her face. At first, nothing happened. I had to push it down harder, sealing off all air. Her heart rate monitor pitched from steady beeping to a siren wail. But her body remained still.

My hands shook, but I had to keep pushing, as her heart beat faster and faster. At least she couldn't feel it. Or so I hoped. It took so long, strangely still and quiet, since she couldn't fight back, only lie there and take it. Her monitor began to wail.

Through the walls rattled the slam of a door, feet thundering down the hallways.

"Evie!" called a frantic maternal voice.

At last, she flatlined. I threw the pillow aside and spirited straight back.

"Did it work?" I asked.

Danny and Carlos were in tears. Evie's ghost had disappeared.

"Don't panic," I said. "I'll explain, but I've got to hurry."

Mrs. Green bent over the bed, face shining with tears as she pumped her hands over her daughter's chest.

"Come on, baby," she said. "Stay with me, it's not your time yet, please, please…"

My own eyes spilled over, warm and stinging. For a moment, I could only stand there and stare at them, helpless.

I wiped my face and leaned over the side of the bed, down to Evie's ear.

"Wake up."

I pressed my lips to her brow. Something sparked, the same as when I touched Ren—almost electric.

Her heart rate blipped.

"Yes, that's it!" said Mrs. Green. "Come back, sweetheart, come back."

"Are you in there?" I asked.

She didn't answer. But she had to be, back from wherever she might've briefly crossed. I wondered if she would remember it. Or remember us, after she woke up. She had to wake up.

"What in the hell?" asked Carlos.

"Did you do this?" said Danny.

I didn't know where to begin explaining.

FORTY-FIVE

✳»» «««✳

Ren had gone from being chained to the broken door to being tied to a hospital bed. I should've known this would happen. I rushed to his side.

"You're going to be OK," I said.

He turned to me sluggishly, his eyes bloodshot and glazed. They'd doped him up. His left wrist had been put in a cast. I wondered if he'd broken it while struggling, or if the cops hadn't been gentle when they brought him in.

"Fucking pigs," I said. "Are you under arrest?"

No response. I couldn't tell if he was too drugged up, or just mad at me. At least he'd ended up here in the psych ward, rather than jail. It could've been worse, not that he needed to hear that.

I noticed the way he flexed the fingers of his right hand, as much as he could in his restraints. As if he was waving at me. Once he got my attention, he strained to point a single finger. He couldn't aim straight at the camera on the ceiling, but I found it all the same. I stepped up into the air and tipped it up to point at the wall, away from his face.

With that out of the way, he spoke, still staring over the edge of the bed. "I'm fucked."

I kneeled into his line of sight. "Why's that?"

He wouldn't look at me. "I'm going to get committed again."

"You don't know that."

"I've got a record," he said. "It'll follow me the rest of my life."

Slowly, I reached out. He had room to flinch back if he didn't want to be touched, but he let me brush his hair out of his face. "I'll be here with you."

"Don't be."

I barely hid my wince.

"I don't want you distracting me while they're watching," he said. "Besides, you should be with the gang."

He must've been pissed at me. I took a guess why.

"I'm sorry about the kiss," I said.

His face and tone remained literally sedate. "Did it feel real?"

I managed not to roll my eyes. "If it makes you feel any better, he's out of the picture."

"I don't scare easy," he said. "We're even now."

If that wasn't what had pissed him off, then we hadn't made up as well as I'd thought before shit went down. We still had to address the question of what would happen now between us.

The Haunt still stood, for now. The demolition crew had hauled away their second failed machine. From the pandemonium inside, you'd think the roof was falling.

"Where's Alastair?"

I hadn't realized, with all the change the older ghosts had seen—the world spinning on without them—this place and its host had been the one constant they could rely upon. Nobody had expected he would one day disappear. He seemed beyond it—beyond any of us.

"Where did he go?"

So many ghosts were blinking in and out, trying to spirit to him. They'd only end up at his grave. I wondered how many of them would stop to read his name.

"This ain't funny," said Flo. "He should be here."

"He's gone," said the mall rat.

"You're lying," Wilhelmina sobbed, tears streaming down her face.

"I saw it happen," mall rat insisted. "He just disappeared."

After that came the weeping. They weren't stoic about it, either. Old-fashioned mourners, not quite gnashing their teeth, but definitely wailing. I had half a mind to join them. It hadn't quite hit me until then just how many years on this earth I'd have to spend without him. We'd all thought he'd be here for the decades ahead, even centuries.

He would've been the one to comfort us in times like these. Now, it fell to me. My own cry would have to wait. For now, I had to suck it up.

I tried on Alastair's grin for size. "Come on, he wouldn't want us to mope around."

"What else are we supposed to do?" said Wilhelmina.

"We ought to celebrate his afterlife," I said. "We're going to throw him a wake."

It would have to be a dry wake, unfortunately. Clementine's wasn't open yet. But that might've been for the best. I didn't think any of us wanted to leave. We might not have much time left in this place. We had to make it count.

I had to get everyone's attention, over the noise and rushing around. It happened with barely a thought. My empty hand suddenly closed around the shadow of my old drumstick. I crashed it against a phantom cymbal, nothing more than a memory, but the sound thundered loud enough for everyone to hear and look up at me.

"Listen up."

They did. I took a step up in midair, onto the imagined stage where the band played every night.

"Alastair isn't gone," I said.

Several ghosts piped up in protest, all talking at once, but I shut them up with another cymbal crash. I hadn't earned their trust yet, but I could get their attention my way, by being louder and more annoying.

"He might not be with us anymore," I admitted. "But he brought us all together. And now that we've known him, we're not the same. We've all learned something from him. He showed me how to make the best of my lot, so that's what I'm doing. As long as I'm here, I'm going to have a good time. And I want to make sure the rest of you do, too. That's how he would have wanted us to honor him. It's a bit of his soul that's rubbed off on the rest of us, and as long as we keep it alive, he's still here."

I took a seat in midair. That stage in my head became real, after all. But all the waiting faces were bathed not in darkness, but light. I only regretted the one I didn't see.

Under my breath, through the tears, I said, "Sorry it took me so long."

Hopefully he'd be listening, somewhere. Backstage, waiting in the wings.

In my opposite hand my other stick appeared, chafing my old callouses. Around me, barely tangible in the sunlight, formed the shadow of my favorite drum set. I tapped the cymbals, soft as a whisper on the wind, before hitting it.

For a moment, everyone went silent, simply watching. Then came the lilt of a piano. We were off to a somber start. Soon we picked up the tempo, and along with it rang the bombast of horns. I'd never had the privilege of attending a jazz funeral myself—and, sadly, I hadn't thought to request one—but some of my fellow bandmates had played their friends out, and others returned the favor. Their memory guided our fingers, the same as the rest of them picked up the chords and words from me. They played as if it were an ancient anthem they knew in their bones.

All the ghosts began to dance. Even as machinery roared outside—the demolition crew had brought a backup for a third and final round. We didn't stop as the walls shook, leaves shaking down from the dried vines, crumbling plaster falling like snow, and then like hail. At last, the ceiling came crashing down on us, walls toppling soon after that. The rubble went through our heads. Once it crashed to the ground, it looked like we were rising from the dust. And still, even with tears on our faces, trembling in our bones, we kept dancing and playing as the house came down.

It had never been ours, anyway. We only borrowed it for a time. And we'd find another, just the same. At least we were still together. We could always find someplace to dance.

FORTY-SIX

※》》《《※

Most of the ghosts were still dancing by nightfall, like always. I might not have been able to pull myself out—taken by the feverish heights of the pulse as we staved off our grief—were it not for the sudden dread drenching me like ice water. My drum set disappeared in the moonlight. The usual drummer stopped dancing and took my spot immediately, eager to play himself. That gave me my chance to slip away.

Something had called me, not unlike the pulse. Much fainter, and more frantic, but just as rhythmic, like a heartbeat. Only this one thundered in distress.

Evie still slept in her coma, but she'd been moved, from her old room at home to a hospital. I wondered if there had been aftereffects of some kind. Even some promising signs, like twitching, or a kick.

Ren's bed, on the other hand, lay empty. I would've thought he'd been taken to the bathroom, if not for his monitor screeching in the absence of his pulse. It made some of the other patients join in wailing. There were nurses running. I beat them there.

We were up on the roof. He stood on the ledge, taking in the lack of a view. Nothing but neighboring rooftops, the little sky beyond the clouds too hazy for stars. I could almost smell the rain, just like on my last night alive.

My dead heart seemed to stop beating.

"Don't you dare."

"I thought you'd understand," he said. It must've been what he'd told himself on his way through the hospital and up the stairwell. That I would welcome him with open arms.

He still faced the void rather than me. I wondered if it felt good. If there was a nice cool breeze on his face; whether he felt the same roller-coaster thrill in his stomach as I had.

"I understand," I said, as softly as I could, worried raising my voice might startle him another step farther. "That's why I'm telling you—don't."

"Why not?" he asked. "You did."

"I wish I hadn't."

He finally turned to me, searching my face, like he didn't believe what he'd heard. "But you're so much better off."

I shook my head. Somehow, through the stinging tears, I managed a wry smile. "Believe me, I've got some serious hindsight going here. I'm better than I used to be, but that just goes to show I could've gotten somewhere, if I'd stayed. There's so much I want to do now that I can't."

He looked dead already. So pale, his eyes barely open, like they didn't care to take in any more of the world.

"Same here," he said, flat and unconvinced. "It's not like I would ever get to do those things, anyway."

"We all know life isn't fair. You think death is any better? We've found ways to survive here, but that doesn't change how hard it is to exist apart from the world. At least, on that side, you're still a part of something greater, even if it isn't so great most of the time. You still have a chance to make it better."

His eyes widened. He turned toward me slightly, still called to the edge. "I thought you'd understand."

"Of course I understand!"

I got up with him on the ledge so that he had to look at me, not the void. So that I had to look at him, and not the void.

"I'm still sick," I said. "In fact, sometimes I still want to die. Just a taste of oblivion. It would be so much easier than all of this. No matter how much I love you, and all our friends. That voice, or impulse, whatever, it's still in here. I've just gotten better at telling it to shut up. And you know what? Maybe I could've done that in life. I could've bought myself another year, or more, even a decent lifetime. If only I'd tried."

I made to grab for his hand, like I could share with him the same as another ghost. My fingers didn't pass straight through. My hand met his.

Just like that, the whole world flipped. As if we'd traded sides of a looking glass. My head swam with the wrongness of it. Never in all my countless daydreams did I ever think getting to touch him would turn my stomach.

In my surprise, I pulled away. "You didn't."

His gaze faltered.

It would have been so easy to shatter. Just let go. I already had so much grief I'd shoved down just to make it through the day. This ought to have finally broken me. I wanted to fall to my knees and tear out my hair and scream like a widow.

Aside from the risk of going geist, there wasn't time for that. I wasn't good at denial for no reason.

"It's not too late."

I looked down over the ledge, his body pale as a sheet in that papery gown against the green of the lawn. He'd fallen several stories. But he'd landed on soft earth—in front of a hospital.

That sparked a fire inside me, springing up bright and fierce in my stomach. I put my hands on his chest, trying to kindle my hope in him. "You could still go back."

Evie had done it.

He opened his mouth, but I could feel his doubt without him having to voice it.

"We're at a hospital," I said. "There are paramedics seconds away. They'll try to resuscitate you. As long as you're in there, there's still a chance."

He stared, wide-eyed now, my hope blooming in his chest even as his fear ran cold down my spine.

"Won't it hurt?"

I nearly laughed. "No shit."

That nearly extinguished the glimmer of possibility stirring in his limbs. But I lifted my hands, stroking up his chest and neck, reaching to cup his face. As I did, under all our hope and fear, I showed him we weren't dead yet. We warmed each other, both new and familiar, somewhere between puppy love and old and settled.

"It'll be worth getting to feel again at all," I said.

He nearly closed his eyes, leaning into my touch. "But I couldn't feel you."

It stung to have to pull back, cold in the absence of his warmth. I had to lean away to keep him from yanking me back.

"That's all you could do around here," I said. "There's so much more to love than that. We couldn't build a life together on this side."

I gave in and pulled him close again, as he shut his eyes, his sobs catching in my throat.

"You forget how hard it is, just to stay alive," he said.

"But you're no better off dead."

Over his shoulder, down on the lawn, there were paramedics beginning to surround his body.

His resolve steadied me, even as his regret burned in my chest. "What about you?"

Though he couldn't see it, he surely felt it, as I tried my best to flash my coin-trick smile. "At least I exist."

His lips felt as familiar as if I'd been kissing him for a lifetime. But we only had a moment, and even that might've been too long. So I pushed him. He let himself fall back to his body.

I couldn't bear to look down. I stepped off the edge and dropped to my knees, staring up at the clouds.

"Please," I prayed. It surprised me, but I didn't stop. "Please, please."

Stage Nine:
Adapting

FORTY-SEVEN

❋»» «« ❋

Evie opened her eyes. But as the doctor explained to her parents and sister, it didn't mean she'd woken up. It might've been a promising sign, especially for a patient who'd been under for as long as she had, but they shouldn't get their hopes up. Not until she began to move.

And she did, about a week or two later. During a pain stimulus test, when a nurse dug a thumb into her shoulder, she flinched. That merited some medically approved excitement.

Over what must've been weeks, she inched her way toward measurable consciousness. Opening and closing her eyes, sometimes on request, gradually beginning to flex her fingers and toes.

Danny and Carlos helped keep watch for me, since I couldn't be everywhere at once. I had a new Haunt to find and then run, plus keeping the ghosts occupied in the meantime. And she wasn't our only coma patient to watch over.

At last, she started to talk. Or at least tried. It started off as whines and groans. They weren't so pleasant to the ear as her usual voice. She hadn't spoken for so long, she almost had to start over completely, as if she were a newborn.

That made me the most nervous. Aside from the possibility she'd never wake up at all, merely move to a minimally conscious state. Being able to sit upright again, blinking for yes or no, even swallowing food on her own, might've been the most her parents could dare dream.

I could only hope I hadn't made a mistake—that she hadn't been better off dead.

Ren hadn't woken up yet, either. Rather, he hadn't regained consciousness. His eyes opened, and his arms and unbroken leg flailed, and his moans were loud enough to be screams. Once again, they had to tie him down to his hospital bed, so he wouldn't yank out any more tubes, or worse, try to scratch at his head. His skull had been opened up for surgery, leaving jagged movie-monster stitches zigzagging down his shaved head, under the bandages and netting keeping his scalp on.

Then his moans got more coherent.

"Mal."

"What did he say?" asked his mother, who had even more gray in her hair now.

His sister shook her head, not looking up from the textbook in her lap. Her homework couldn't wait until after this family emergency, especially when it had already gone on for weeks. Her other brother had gone back to work already.

"It didn't sound like anything to me," she said.

He opened his eyes. It almost looked as if he could see me.

Just in case, I did a sweep of every floor, from the basement morgue to the upper wards, clearing out more geists than usual. No wonder I'd never liked hospitals.

Ren's family didn't know it, but we all took turns looking after him. They talked to him during the day and put on movies and music they knew he loved. And most nights, when I wasn't blowing off steam playing at Clementine's, I did the same. I'd lie beside him in the hospital bed, sometimes whispering, and other times singing.

Most of the time, I chatted to him about nothing much, like the doctor had advised his folks they should do. I told him about the ghosts, how we were managing, where we were looking for a new Haunt. Or I reminisced, taking us back to our first date, or when we tried to be roommates, and especially our precious little time of being properly together.

Sometimes, I couldn't help it.

"Come on, Ren," I said. "Remember what I told you. You deserve to live. I promise it's worth it."

When he opened his eyes, some tears fell.

"You're here," he said.

He slipped away again. Too bad I couldn't wake up his mom and tell her the good news.

She heard it herself the next morning. He said her name, asked for the date, then conked out. Next time he woke up, he said exactly the same thing, calling for his mom, and then asking her the date. According to the doctor, that would happen often enough to get annoying. His short-term memory would be one of the last things to come back.

"What's Mal?" asked his mom.

The doctor shook his head. "Who? What?"

"He keeps asking for it."

"I don't know what that is," admitted the doctor.

Ren winked at me. I held my finger to my lips.

It got really crowded upstairs at Clementine's while we were in the market for another abandoned building. We didn't want to settle for just any foreclosed house or old barn. Our new home needed some character, old enough to have history, big enough for us to sprawl out.

Alastair must've taken forever finding the first Haunt, no doubt wandering on foot, visiting places he'd known while alive, looking for something still standing but no longer occupied. But I didn't have to follow his footsteps exactly. I searched online at a nearby library in the dead of night. There were websites that listed locations of abandoned places, filled with pictures taken by urban explorers. I wouldn't mind having to scare those kinds of people off, once we settled in somewhere.

Danny or Carlos would keep me company as we explored each abandoned hospital and boarding school and military fort, defunct subway stations and crumbling theater houses. We'd make as if we were a heterosexual couple house-hunting in the suburbs.

"Look at this bathtub, honey," said Carlos, peering over a claw-footed tub so full of rainwater, it had become a self-contained swamp. "Spa night!"

"How about this for a man cave?" I asked, when we got to the surgical theater.

We even checked out a theme park. Even though we obviously weren't about to move in, we needed to blow off steam. We took turns pushing each other on the defunct Tunnel of Love and House of Haunts and the rickety old Ferris wheel that would've fallen apart anyway in a squeaking heap of rust if we hadn't touched it.

When we got to the hotel, we couldn't even joke around. We were silent with awe, looking up at the chipped art deco ceiling, stepping over the jeweled remnants of a fallen chandelier. After that, we followed the dingy red carpet twisting and tangling down endless hallways, up so many floors with room after room, enough for every ghost to have one to call their own. The views of the city skyline from the broken windows and sometimes missing walls were lovely, so much sunlight splashing inside that plants grew from the dusty floors. And most importantly, it had a ballroom. Not as grand as our last—the gilding long faded from the columns, walls marred by graffiti, but we could fix that. We started by tearing down the boards from the tall windows, letting in some light.

Danny flapped triumphantly. "What do you think?"

It felt like a silly question. But she looked to me all the same.

I said the same thing I soon told the rest of our sprawling family, crowded around the boarded doors, watching as I spread my arms with pride.

"Welcome to the new Haunt."

Ren and I were as alone as we could be, with his mother asleep in a chair in the dead of night. He could sit up well enough, free of his restraints and bandages. His hair had started to grow back, short and awkward. It made him look so young—everywhere but his eyes.

"You're still here," he said, again.

"Where else would I be?"

He tried shaking his head, but couldn't quite manage it, wincing in pain instead. "Didn't we break up?"

So that memory hadn't been forever lost to brain damage. After all, he'd been outside of his body for it. I'd been prepared to act as if it hadn't happened and stay with him for as long as he still needed me. I hadn't planned as far as having to break up with him again. I'd done it for a reason.

"Second thoughts?" he asked, but he sounded doubtful, not getting his hopes up.

I shook my head to try and knock the tears back in. "Well, you literally killed yourself. I couldn't leave you alone. But…"

His voice went rough. "You don't have to say it again."

Thank fuck. "Do you want me to leave?"

"Stay," he said, quickly. "Just a while longer."

I couldn't help it. I did my best to throw my arms around him. My eyes spilled over, after all, but the tears weren't just mine.

"I'm sorry I got you mixed up in this," I said.

"Don't be. I probably would've tried at some point, anyway. If I hadn't met you, who would've talked me down?"

I pulled back to look into his face. "So you don't regret coming back?"

He tried for a laugh. "Not after the grief everyone's giving me. I would've been in the same mess as you when we first met." His smile looked pained. "I'm an idiot."

I grinned back. "But you're alive."

His face went grave. "It better be fucking worth it."

"You won't be alone," I promised. "My sister could use a friend."

"How's she doing?"

I didn't have a lot of time to check on her, with two patients and a hotel to run. I'd found her in class, and at a café where she apparently worked, but that wasn't much to go on. "We're going to find out."

Ren got his phone back in the morning. At first, the brightness made him wince with an audible gasp. He dropped the phone, clutching his temples.

His mom and I both spoke at once. "Migraine?"

The doctors had said those might be a problem. They'd been keeping the lights off in his room. His sister reached over to dim the phone brightness while his mom supplied some ibuprofen.

Once he'd recovered somewhat, I leaned over to see as he checked his phone again. He'd missed eight texts and three calls from Cris. With her pride, it might as well have been double.

"Do you mind if I make a call?" he asked.

His mom stayed put. "Go ahead."

"I mean, in private."

After bitching him out in Japanese, she relented, since his sister pointed out in English that it could be about a girl.

"Sort of," said Ren.

Once we were alone, he said, "I hope she didn't start drinking again."

"Let me go see."

I spirited straight to her. She was sleeping in, not in her own bed. At first, her phone didn't wake her. By the time it did, and she managed to find it in her purse, it had stopped ringing.

"Try her again," I said to Ren.

He did, putting the phone to his ear.

"You asshole," said Cris. "I could call anytime, you said, and you'd talk me through it."

"I'm in the hospital."

He let that sink in, before smiling and saying, "Sorry, who's the asshole?"

She apparently forgave him. "What's wrong? Are you all right?"

"It's a long story," he said. "But I can't wait to get to the punchline. So, I died. Only for a couple minutes, but long enough. You'll never believe who I saw."

I went to check if she was still on the line, since she'd gone so quiet, not even breathing. She covered her mouth, but her tearful eyes were smiling.

Ren's voice crackled on the line. I didn't need to see his face to hear his grin. "It's crazy."

FORTY-EIGHT

✳》》 《《✳

E vie took months to finally sit up and talk. Her voice croaked with disuse, almost infantile. It got stronger as her requests deepened in complexity: water, fresh air, knowledge. Every time, she had to ask the year. Her parents, worn but kind-faced older Black folks who would hold hands and pray out loud over her bed, began to gently remind her every time she woke up.

Soon, once she could articulate enough through her raspy throat, she started asking tougher questions.

"Hey there," she said, looking right at me.

I froze. At least we had the rare opportunity of both of her parents being gone. Her dad had gone out to get them lunch, and her mother had stepped out, probably to the bathroom.

"Have we met?" she asked. "I've been forgetting a lot lately."

She could see me. And she must've remembered at least some of the afterlife, if my face was familiar.

She'd find out sooner or later—but I couldn't decide which would be kinder. She'd been through a lot lately.

Then again, if a geist came walking through the walls, she'd no doubt point it out to her folks. They wouldn't see it, and they'd think she had even more brain damage than the doctors had charted. Better for me to be her first ghost. Well, maybe not ghost. Something more comforting.

"I'm your guardian angel."

"… Huh?"

But she did need a slight scare, for starters. Just so she'd take me seriously. So I waved my hand through her IV. She gave a yelp. For good measure, I went through the chairs, and the end of her bed, so there'd be no doubt in her mind what she'd witnessed.

"Fear not," I said.

Her eyes were huge. "Too late."

"There's no easy way to break it," I said. "You came back from the afterlife, which causes some side effects."

"More side effects?" she asked.

"Not physical, more… well, metaphysical."

Right at the worst time, her mom came back from the bathroom.

"You're awake," said her mom, and then she told her the date for good measure, and asked if she needed any water.

"She can't see me," I said.

"Uh huh," said Evie—to me, not her mom. She took the offered water anyway.

"I'll tell you more later," I promised. "For now, try your best to go back to your life."

Later that night, while her parents slept, I came back. I felt bad waking her, but not too bad. She'd had plenty of sleep the last few years.

"It's me."

"You're no angel," she said. "The Haunt… it wasn't a dream?"

"I wish," I admitted.

Her face fell suddenly. "What about Ally?"

My throat closed up, trying to prevent me from breaking it to her, after all she'd been through already. I couldn't lie anymore.

I shook my head. "You don't remember?"

Her eyes spilled over. "I hoped it wasn't real. But… you saved me?"

I tried to wave it off. "Don't mention it."

That made her laugh through the tears. "I've got to! How—how can I pay you back?"

"Just live."

She did her best to hold her arms open, beckoning me closer. It didn't feel the same anymore, now that she had her own body. The warmth of her gratitude didn't flood me anymore, but it still bled through.

She couldn't hide the quiver of a sob in my ear. "I'm still scared."

"You're not alone," I said. "You know who else is going to be here in rehab?"

"Wait, who?"

This time, it wouldn't be a missed connection.

Ren got transferred to the same brain injury rehabilitation center as Evie. As soon as he could leave his room unsupervised, he didn't ask permission to go visit. While he rolled his wheelchair down the hallway, I reached up and dimmed the fluorescent lights for him until he reached her room.

Through the walls, Mrs. Green asked, "What's wrong with the lights?"

Leah answered the door, sharing a double take with her mom. "Ren, right?"

Evie gave a tiny shriek. "Your hair!"

Her family raised their eyebrows. She shouldn't have been up to date about anybody's hair.

He covered for her. "I've had it pretty long since high school."

Mrs. Green's eyes lit up. "Oh, that's right! I remember—you brought flowers."

"We'll let you two catch up," said Leah, with a conspiratorial smile that her mom didn't seem to catch. But I did.

Ren pulled up by the bedside once they left.

"What happened to you?" asked Evie.

"I might've taken a tumble over the side of a building."

She couldn't keep from glancing at me, understanding what he really meant. "I'm sorry."

"I made it, at least," he said. His eyes glinted as he grinned at her. "*We* made it."

I shivered. The two of them now shared an experience that very few—if any—others could ever claim. And they were both alive.

Gingerly, he reached out, watching her face for any sign of protest. Her eyes were soft. He touched his fingers to hers. A slight gasp escaped her, and she smiled. So he went ahead and squeezed her hand.

It hurt more than I'd thought it would.

FORTY-NINE

✳》》 《《✳

When the doctor knocked, I assumed she was another in a series of specialists that were monitoring Ren, a physical therapist, or another neurosurgeon. She introduced herself with a long, unfamiliar name I didn't catch, shaking hands with his mom and his brother, before asking them politely to leave the room.

Ren and I exchanged worried looks, before he tore his gaze away, not wanting to be caught staring meaningfully at nothing.

"Blink once if you want me to stay," I said. "Twice if you want me to leave."

He blinked once, and then again, not looking at me. As much as I would've liked to stay, he didn't need me distracting him.

I hated having to eavesdrop, listening through the walls. It felt like a step back. Soon enough, I might have no other choice if I wanted to know how he was doing. I couldn't stay in his life forever.

"Mr. Takahashi," said the doctor, perfectly warm and casual. "Should I leave the light off?"

"Please," said Ren.

Chair legs scraped on the tile floor. "How are you doing?"

Ren hesitated, just as I would've done. It felt like a trick question. "I'm not dead."

Not the answer I would've chosen. At least, not while talking to a mental health professional. But I'd never intended to answer truthfully. Maybe he did.

She didn't hesitate to take that opening. "Why did you jump?"

"It seemed like a good idea at the time," he said. "I thought I'd get committed, and I really, really didn't want to go back there."

For a moment, she spoke almost too low to hear. "I… I understand." Louder, she went on. "I see here you were involuntarily hospitalized for a… violent schizophrenic episode."

"Not violent." His voice trembled. "I scared some people, but I didn't hurt anyone."

"I believe you."

He went silent. I wished I could see his face, so I could tell whether he believed her back.

She continued questioning him about the history of his diagnosis. He owned up to it, or at least didn't bother trying to change anything already on record. Then she asked if he'd ever made any previous attempts, and if this one had been planned. He hadn't, and it had been spontaneous.

"Have you ever had suicidal thoughts?"

"Sure," he said, so casual, as if it were easy to admit. "Doesn't everyone?"

"I can't speak for everyone."

"Do you?"

I covered my mouth, laughing in disbelief. My eyes welled up, suddenly pained, like I'd popped a stitch. I still bled with love.

The doctor's reply sounded light, possibly leavened with a wry smile. "Once you study for eight years and show me your certification of psychiatry, you can ask me that question."

"Maybe I will," he said. Not flippant—thoughtful.

It took her a moment to put on her professional voice again. "Did anything—excuse me—have you experienced any major life changes lately?"

"Not really."

That might've been his first lie. But he couldn't go into detail about any of his recent life changes.

"Have you been experiencing any feelings of hopelessness or despair?"

He actually laughed. "Um, no shit."

"Could you tell me more?"

"I've been kind of depressed lately, about my job, and, uh— relationship—and the future in general."

That gave her pause. Some papers were rustled. She might've been checking notes, or taking them down. She asked for some further details about said job and relationship and the future in general. He answered truthfully, up to a point.

And then she asked more about the relationship.

"It's wonderful," he said. "Or, you know, it used to be, up until she died."

She sounded for real. "I'm sorry to hear it."

"Thanks."

"That's a major life change," she said, as coolly as she could, slightly miffed he hadn't brought it up sooner, rather than throwing her a curveball.

"It happened about a year ago."

"It's very common for bereavement to cause major depression. You must miss her terribly."

"I wanted to join her. That's how she went. She killed herself, jumping off a building."

It still hurt to hear.

"How did you feel, when you found out?"

He might be getting in over his head with this version of the truth. But he gave it his all. "So fucking mad."

"Why's that?"

"She could've been the one."

"Is that why you were depressed?" she asked. "About the future, in general?"

"Well, plus—you know—global warming and all."

"We're all feeling that." She betrayed a small sigh before clearing her throat. "So you felt alone, after your partner passed."

"… Right."

"And deprived of the future you'd envisioned."

He must've nodded, perhaps overwhelmed.

"How do you think your mother and siblings would feel, if you had succeeded?"

"I get it," he said. "I didn't think about them. And she didn't think about anybody else, either. We were wrong."

"Do you regret making the attempt?"

"Well, it would've saved me a lot of brain, and, like, being able to walk, if I'd just come to my senses earlier. So, fuck yes."

She couldn't stifle a laugh. Then she cleared her throat, trying to stay professional. "So, now that you're awake, and very much lucid, we only need to keep you around for another seventy-two hours for observation. After that, I'm going to recommend outpatient therapy."

He didn't hold back his sigh of relief.

"I hear you've already made some friends here?" she asked.

"You must have all the hot gossip."

"Keep in touch," she said. "They'll go over this in therapy, but it's important you build a strong support system of family and friends. Think of them as a safety net to catch you if you start to feel like you're falling." It took her a second. "I'm sorry, that's not a good one-size-fits-all metaphor for some patients, is it?"

I could practically hear his wry smile as he quipped, "None taken."

Her papers shuffled again, and a chair scuffed across the floor. "It's been good to meet you."

"I'm glad to be here for it," he said.

She went to go speak with his family. I went back into the room.

Ren beamed at me. "Outpatient."

I rushed to him. "You're going home?"

He could safely shrug again. "I mean, with my folks."

"That's going to be rough."

"Well, if I'm not paying rent... maybe I could afford to give school a shot."

As soon as he said it, I knew. We didn't have a lot of time left together. About seventy-two hours, in fact. After that, he'd be starting a new life—one I couldn't share.

It had been about sixty hours.

"You think it's time?" I asked, sitting on his bed.

He didn't try to hide the tremble around his mouth. "If you think so, there's nothing I could say to convince you otherwise, is there?"

I smiled. "That's not true."

He grinned back, even as his eyes filled. "I can't think what to say, though. So this must be it."

I didn't bother wiping my own eyes. I had to swallow hard to manage any words. "We had a better goodbye last time."

"Sorry for ruining it."

"Well, you can't live trying to plan perfect lasts. This isn't goodbye forever. Maybe, after you've had a long and full life, and you're tired, and happy to go, I'll see you again. Don't worry about your future partner, whoever that might be. Or any of my next lovers. They can join us. You think they'll allow orgies in heaven?"

He cracked up through the tears. That's when I snuck him a quick kiss on the cheek. Because if I gave him the chance to kiss me back, I wouldn't be able to stop. We'd have to come up with another goodbye, and I didn't know if I could top my last joke. So I just spirited away.

Evie awoke, as if she could sense my presence.

I didn't mince my words. "I can't stay."

She gaped at me. "Why not?"

"Ren's got to move on with his life. I don't think either of us will be able to do that if I linger."

Her eyes welled up. "You can still see me—can't you?"

"I'd rather not risk it," I said, sitting down on the bed. "You guys will be together a lot."

"Really?"

"You'd better be. I need you to take care of each other."

Since she still had to work on her motor movements, I leaned in and wiped away her tears.

"Are you sure you can't just… drop in? Say hi?" she asked.

"I'll still grab geists, but if you see me, you'd better pretend you didn't, all right? Don't make this hard on me."

She sniffed. "I already miss you."

I tried my best to squeeze her hand. "You, too."

FIFTY

✳》》 《《✳

I didn't mind hospitals so much anymore. Maybe I'd just gotten
used to them. Most morgues are at the bottom of one, and there's
no better place to meet people than the morgue.

But I made sure the welcome committee would feel like one this
time. There'd be no surveying until the foundling had acclimated.

It took about a month or two of making the rounds to finally
find our first.

I didn't expect to see a third figure standing at the autopsy
table, not dressed for it, in a dark hoodie and jeans to match. Under
the hood, the young Black man looked just as surprised to meet
my eyes, if way calmer than I would've expected. Especially because
the body being opened up on the table looked about the right size
and shape and skin color to be his own.

"Can you see us?" I asked.

Danny and Carlos hung back so they wouldn't have to look at
the autopsy. I did my best to ignore all the red in my peripheral,
not to mention the nudity. At second glance, the corpse didn't
quite look like him.

The new ghost took his hoodie strings out of his mouth, looking
embarrassed. Maybe he didn't indulge that habit if he thought
anybody could see him.

"Um, hi," he said. "Are you guys, like—are you—this is going to sound stupid, but—"

"We're not with management, if that's what you're wondering," said Danny.

"Not angels, or reapers, or anything," added Carlos.

"Just ghosts like you," I said. "They call me Mal."

Danny and Carlos introduced themselves in kind.

"Terence," said the new ghost. He gestured at himself and us. "So this is what's up? It's ghosts?"

"There's probably more," I said. "We'll get to that."

Carlos couldn't contain himself. "You're not watching your own autopsy, are you?"

"That's not me."

"We all have different ways of coping," I said, trying to exude non-judgmental understanding.

"I'm a mortuary science major," he said. "Or, you know… I was. I didn't even get to this part. I used to be kind of scared I'd get here and want to change my major again, but… well, I feel nothing. I guess we're just meat, in the end."

"Well, not exactly," I said.

"Oh, right," he said, looking at us—and himself—in renewed disbelief. "I didn't expect this."

"Neither did I," said Danny. I'd never seen her eyes shine like that, her cheeks pink. "I'm a fellow scholar of the dead."

The new ghost's face lit up. "Oh, for real?"

"Well, not the fresh kind—the opposite, actually. Anthropology."

"Ah," he said, nodding. "Maybe I should've picked—"

His face fell. He wouldn't be changing his major ever again. But that didn't mean he'd have to stop learning.

The new ghost spread his hands. "So what's going on here?"

"Do you drink?" I asked.

He quirked his brows.

"It's fine if you don't," added Danny. "There's still lots of fun to be had on this side."

"Er—we can—what?"

I offered my palm. "Come with us."

He stared at my hand suspiciously. "Where we going?"

"It's just a bar."

"Why would we go there?"

"So we can grab a drink, if you like. Or shoot some pool, play pinball."

He scrunched his face at me. I didn't need to be so cryptic, but it was kind of fun.

"Look, I know you must be feeling pretty overwhelmed," I said. "Or you're not feeling as much as you think you should be. It's different for everyone. Whatever the case, I want you to know you shouldn't feel guilty for seeking distraction and comfort. It's not an easy transition. But you've got a whole afterlife ahead of you, and you've got to start somewhere."

Slowly, carefully, he extended a sleeve-covered hand. I took it, walls well-fortified. Even if we couldn't feel skin, he must've picked up on my warmth, his mouth parting in a surprised smile.

I grinned. "And you're not alone."

The Haunt kept me busy, enough that I hardly noticed the years passing, except that the leaves in the hotel windows were either green and glowing, or withered and dying, the rooms carpeted with moss one moment, snow the next.

It must've felt like forever for Evie. I could only imagine how slow and painful and even boring it felt as she struggled in physical rehab. For once, I didn't envy her possession of a body. It could be a vessel of pain as well as pleasure, though I'd take the former just to feel the latter again. It would be worth it, in the end. Especially with her family there to hold her hands.

Ren came to cheer her on as often as he could. He had his own struggles with migraines and fatigue, but he still showed up for emotional and sometimes physical support. I couldn't linger too close, occasionally peeking through the windows, but mostly listening through the walls.

Once, when her sister had work and her mother had a doctor's appointment, he was the one to hold her when she broke down in tears.

"I'll give you guys a minute," said her physical therapist.

Evie's breath pitched. "I can't—I can't—"

Ren's voice was warm. "I'll carry you."

She gave a hiccupping little laugh. "I'm not that light, you know."

After she'd gotten out of the hospital, she'd begun putting her weight back on, looking more like her old self. She didn't seem to know how good those curves looked, how much healthier she'd become.

"I'll work out," he said. "Until you're so light, I can carry you whenever you need it. And we can dance. I'll hold you up and spin you around."

She laughed again, fuller this time. "Just don't get dizzy. You'll drop me!"

"Slowly, then."

They quieted. I wondered if their mouths might be otherwise occupied. But from the way I'd overheard Leah and Mr. and Mrs. Green tease Evie, and Mrs. Takahashi interrogate Ren, they weren't together. Not yet.

Evie nearly whispered. "You really mean it?"

"Cross my heart," said Ren.

"But not hope to die."

"Right—not that."

Evie worked for years to regain enough dexterity in her fingers to play the piano again. Once she did, though, it didn't go unnoticed that she'd only had a few lessons in life—certainly not enough to play like a virtuoso. It didn't take long before the girl who woke up from a coma as a "musical prodigy" began to make headlines. Soon she sold out bookings for private lessons on weekdays and shows at a local jazz club on weekends.

I snuck in to see her, of course, watching from the crowd. It made my dead heart skip a beat to see her in an emerald satin dress, her hair piled high and woven with tiny white flowers. And yet, as far as she'd come, as her fingers thundered on the piano, her voice was wracked with all-too-familiar yearning.

I'd hoped we were all done pretending we didn't want what we wanted. That wasn't any way to live.

After the show, I waited for her in the green room. She struggled to get the door open from her wheelchair, so I went to prop it open for her.

"Oh!" she said. "Thank—"

Her eyes widened as she took in my face.

"Mal!"

"Actually, I'm the ghost of unspoken longing."

I went to the wall where a dry bouquet of blue anemones hung upside down by the vanity mirror, gingerly cradling them as I turned them over to read the attached card aloud.

"Evie, you did it! I won't say I told you so... but I'm writing it down, winky face. *Seriously, though, I'm so grateful to have you in my*

life. I couldn't imagine coming back from where we've been without you." My voice caught, unexpectedly, but I managed to carry on. "*Love, Ren.*"

When I finally looked up, tears filled her eyes. I hadn't exactly warmed her up. She noticed, giving a sniffly laugh.

"I'm doing wonderfully, thanks," she said. "And how are you?"

I shrugged. "Still dead."

She rolled her eyes. "How about this? I'll be honest if you are."

I hung the flowers back up and pretended to sit on the vanity table, haloed by the lightbulbs lining the mirror. "I'm not so bad." Funnily enough, I found I meant it. "We've got a new Haunt."

Her hand went to her heart. "Really?"

"It's a hotel, lots of space, absolutely horrific and cozy."

She wheeled closer, laughing. "I wish I could see it."

"Well, hopefully not anytime soon."

"Please tell me you're in the band now, though."

I grinned so wide, I must've looked like a sap, but I didn't care. "Yeah, yeah."

We talked for a while about the new Haunt. Danny and Carlos made a proper welcoming party now. I even hoped that Danny might get together with our first new foundling, Terence. That made a natural opportunity to circle back.

"So, uh—" I resisted digging my nails into my palms. "What's the holdup with Ren?"

Her face shuttered up. "It's nothing," she said, too quickly. "I don't see him that way."

"Look, I get it. But you've got a real tiny dating pool."

"You mean being disabled?"

"Well, there's that, but I meant more like… as a medium. As far as we know, you're the only ones. Or at least, the only two who talk to each other. You share something maybe nobody else on earth does."

She blinked, going quiet for a moment, like she'd never considered that. She still stuttered in protest, "That's not all it takes."

"Then it's a good thing you're both hard to kill, and still kind in spite of all the knocks you've taken. Not to mention really hot."

Her cheeks darkened, but she smiled, not looking away. "You think so?"

Since she'd gotten older, and owned all her years now, I went ahead and bit my lip. "I mean, if I had a body…"

I meant to joke, keep it light, but she saw right through it. Her smile didn't last long, trembling on the edge of a frown. "It's not fair to you."

"You saw him first. Besides, I'm dead. Who cares about me?"

"I do," she said. "And so does Ren."

That ached more than I would've thought. I nearly gave it away on my face.

"We still talk about you all the time," she said.

"What a mood killer."

She gave a slight sigh of admission. "A bit."

"I've heard the way he talks to you, not to mention *about* you," I said. "You're his next love."

Her voice faltered as she looked away. "I couldn't."

I got up, looming over her. "Come on, I didn't save your lives for you to waste them."

She looked warily up at me. "You really wouldn't mind?"

"Do you think I haven't been messing around myself?"

"That's not an answer."

Now I had to look away. If I were going to convince her, then I had to hide how much I did mind. But my love for them outweighed how much it would hurt.

"It will be worth it," I said, turning back to her, trying to smile away the tears in my eyes. "Seeing you both alive, and sharing your lives. You might even make some more."

Her eyes blew wide. "Good grief."

I couldn't help but rub it in. "Promise you'll name one after me."

She laughed. "Only if you promise to shut up about it."

Her laughter went quiet, but her shoulders still shook. I leaned down and tried my best to put my arms around her.

"I wish you were here," she said.

It hurt to let go. And yet, it felt like I'd lingered too long already. As I pulled away, I pressed my lips to her brow, looking into her face and doing my best to smile.

"I'll always be here."

Stage Ten:
Acceptance

CODA

❋»» ««❋

Cris stayed in school, thankfully. From the look of it, she wasn't keen on repeating any more of my mistakes. Or slinging coffee part-time had reinforced her interest in sociology, after all.

At some point, she got back in touch with our mother. Gloria must've humbled herself, inviting her home, like she ought to have done with me. From the sound of the one-sided phone conversations I sometimes overheard, and the awkward vibe over holidays, she had to submit to new boundaries if she wanted to keep the only child she had left. Cris walked out once at Thanksgiving dinner, all the way to her car. Gloria had to chase her out in the snow in her slippers and no coat, her undignified pleading carrying across the street.

It did sting, seeing her change, too late. But I couldn't begrudge my sister for holding onto what was left of her original family, even if I much preferred the new one she'd found.

Cris cut back the drinking to one or two glasses of wine at a time, usually at the dinner parties she threw with Vicki. They weren't exactly the ragers my ex used to host, but the warm yellow light and peals of laughter spilling out of the window made me feel like a street urchin spying on a family opening Christmas gifts.

I had no choice but to watch from afar, often through windows, since she still hung out with Ren. They went to a bereavement group together; later on, they'd meet up to study, since he'd started taking night classes. From the snippets of conversation I overheard through the walls, he'd begun working toward a degree in psychiatry.

Eventually, I'd see all of them through Vicki's kitchen window, framed by her hanging ferns and herb planter as they came to grab drinks, serve food, help with the dishes. Since they were together so often, and it got harder and harder to eavesdrop unnoticed, I finally began visiting less. I could trust my old friends to take care of my little sister, like they'd once done for me. Someone had finally convinced her to stop straightening her hair, those old curls I'd missed bouncing freely on her shoulders.

But no matter how many new friends and lovers I made on the other side, I never stopped missing them. Judging from all the sunflowers and bottles of whiskey and packs of cigarettes forever crowding my grave, they felt the same.

Every Día de los Muertos, in addition to my dad and Liam, I visited Alastair. Not that I could leave any offerings, but at the very least, I caught him up on how we were all doing while I brushed the moss off his gravestone. Sometimes I swung by to talk to him year-round. There were some things I couldn't confide to anyone else, given the image I had to maintain. Only my predecessor would understand, if he was listening.

"Hey there, old man."

It must've been spring, judging by the blooming daisies. I plopped down in the grass and picked a few.

"We're doing really good at the new Haunt," I said. "Remember Terence, the mortuary science guy? He got together with Danny. They're so sweet, it's nauseating. Carlos and I are still breaking hearts, of course. Oh, and I finally had a new harpist land in my lap! It's been, what, years?" Wilhelmina had crossed not long after Alastair, as if she'd had some say in it, not wanting to linger without him. "This new girl is shy, but no offense, way less of a problem. I could do with less drama from the rest of the band, but I'm handling it. You made it look so easy."

I finished my daisy bouquet and laid it across the headstone.

"So here's something funny. For one night only, there's gonna be a tribute band for Goodbye Courage."

Cris had the flyer on her fridge one morning when I found her staying in and making breakfast instead of going to her new church.

"I'll probably regret going, right?" I asked. "So, of course, I have to do it. I just won't go alone. If you're not busy, do me a favor and look down, or press an ear up."

I kissed my fingers and pressed them to his name—the real one I'd never tell a soul.

"Hurry up and be reborn," I said. "Don't make me wait too long."

When I got up, the wind tossed the tree branches above me, stirring big enough gaps to let a little sunlight through. I could almost feel my face warm.

I waved it off. "Quit being such a sap."

The tribute show gathered more of a crowd than I would've thought. I nearly had to dance to get around touching all the living cramped together in the subterranean dive bar. Cris and Vicki barely got through, even with bodies to part the way.

"You never told me you were so popular," said Danny.

Carlos put an arm around her. "Well, you missed the heyday."

"I must've gotten rediscovered post-mortem by all the hipsters," I said. "Either that, or they've got some kind of drink deal going on."

"Check it out," said Carlos, pointing up at the stage beneath the low ceiling.

I started at the sight of my face. They had pictures of me projected on a white sheet thrown over the red brick, alternating with pictures of Liam. Each had a big, cheeky "RIP" in a red Halloween font.

Cris gave it a good, stoic stare. Vicki laughed.

"Are they honoring my life?" I asked. "Or glorifying my death?"

"Why not both?" said Carlos.

Danny grabbed both of us and wordlessly began inching back. I looked up to see Ren and Evie bobbing amidst the crowd.

I'd wondered if it would feel the same as reuniting with Liam. If I'd look at them and only feel scar tissue, like an old lady aching whenever it rains. But the sight of them still pulled me in, like the tide to the moon.

As soon as the hipsters and old-school punks noticed, they started pushing and tripping over themselves to let them through. Evie had decorated her plain metal canes with ribbons, matching the ones woven into her braids. Ren hovered, but let her walk on her own. He wore pink-tinted glasses and small black earplugs.

Carlos let out a low whistle. "They look so good."

"Older," said Danny. "I mean, in a good way, but it's weird. I forgot—forgot they *could*, you know? Get older."

I couldn't reply with my heart in my throat.

Ren and Evie were given enough space to get a standing spot toward the front. Once they'd gotten there, he steadied her with an arm around her waist, like he couldn't help himself.

"Are you all right?" asked Danny.

She reached for me, but I recoiled on instinct. I didn't want her catching any of my mixed feelings.

I tried to focus on the good parts. Mostly relief, and a hint of smugness, since I'd set them up. I even managed to get a bit turned on. That didn't necessarily feel good, paired with the envy I did my best to repress, but it spoke to my resilience.

Carlos waved a hand in my face. "Color?"

I coughed. "Green."

He raised his eyebrows. I huffed.

"Greenish-yellow."

That meant I wanted to stay, but they should keep an eye on me, just in case.

Cris and Vicki finally made their way to the front with Evie and Ren. They didn't have enough room for full hugs.

The audience quieted at the whine of a microphone as the lead guitar began to speak. It didn't take him long to acknowledge the pictures being projected behind him.

"As I'm sure you all know, we lost the brains behind the brilliant music. Over seven years ago, lead guitarist Liam Marston had a heart attack at only thirty. Six months later, Mal Caldera, the consummate crazy drummer, took her own life and joined the twenty-seven club."

He allowed for a brief moment of silence.

"But we're not here to mourn—we're here to celebrate. Tonight, we party in their memory. I want them to hear us in hell!"

The crowd practically rattled the glasses at the bar with their cheers. I couldn't help but join in. Somehow, I found myself laughing.

Ren's head whipped right around, and he made eye contact with me.

Danny and Carlos stared, like they thought they'd have to follow if I spirited away. They both put a hand on my arm for that purpose.

I didn't move. Neither did Ren. We didn't have to touch to know what the other must be thinking.

"Green," I said.

There wasn't much room to dance, but the crowd undulated anyway, feet bouncing, heads bobbing. Cris's dark, curly hair swung gorgeously over her shoulders as she twirled, swinging with Vicki. Evie passed her canes to a good Samaritan who propped them by the wall, so Ren could pick her up, letting her stand on his feet. They swayed in place, arms wrapped around each other.

Carlos gave me a playful shove. Danny joined, and we stomped and skanked, laughing in our own tiny pit until we were panting, as if we had any breath to lose.

After the set, some of the crowd went to mill outside and smoke until the next band went on, while the rest drank inside. Cris, Vicki, and Evie went out for air. Danny and Carlos left early to go get our own band warmed up back at the hotel.

I cocked my head toward the emergency back door. Ren nodded.

Sure enough, when I got to the alley out back, I turned around to find him standing there. His hair had grown to its old length, except for the shaved sides. It was hard to see the raised scar on his scalp curving over his ear, mostly hidden under the buzzed hair. How often did he get asked about it? Did he share as readily as the dead bragged about our demises, but as a story of survival?

"You look good," I said.

He took off his glasses to return my sweeping gaze, eyes glistening. "You, too."

Of course, I hadn't changed at all.

I shuffled my feet, playing coy, like that could disguise my suddenly real shyness. "You wouldn't happen to have a smoke?"

"Nah, sorry." His lips twitched, bittersweet. "I heard they'll kill ya."

"Right, so they say."

I couldn't find it in me to smile all the way. "You know, we're ruining our goodbye again."

"I thought you told me counting lasts is no way to live," he said. "I'd rather have another hello with you, even if it means another goodbye."

"How are we going to make this one memorable?"

"Well, I never did thank you—for everything."

"Please don't." I'd thought giving thanks had been hard, once. That was nothing compared to receiving. "I'm just glad to see you alive and well."

His eyes were as tender as ever. "How are you holding up?"

My lips tugged with an echo of my old coin-trick smile. "I exist."

He grinned, blinking back tears.

Suddenly, he turned, as if he could feel her before she even showed up. He pulled the door open for Evie.

She made her way slowly over to me with a smile. "I'd say 'long time no see,' but you're not as sneaky as you think."

"Please, no more thanking me, I'm rolling in my grave."

Her eyes widened with the kind of innocence she had to fake now. "How is everyone?"

"They're happy at home."

I told her about the way I'd split the party into two. Before sunset we'd hold a jam session so all the wallflowers new and old could mingle for some low-key, sometimes silly dancing. Once it got dark, it would heat up like usual when the rest of the ghosts showed up for the afterparty.

"Oh, that's so thoughtful," said Evie. "I wish I'd come up with it."

I didn't mention that I'd gotten the idea from eavesdropping through Vicki's window.

Evie's little smile was almost sly. "You know… you don't have to stay away."

"I do, though." My lungs bloomed with a swallowed sigh. "You've both got your lives to live."

"We're doing that already."

Ren shook his head at me. "Same old excuse, huh?"

"Aww, come on." Hopefully, they couldn't see well enough in the dark to make out the blush burning my cheeks. "Don't tempt me."

It would never work.

"Thanks for keeping an eye on my sister," I said. "Speaking of which, are you keeping an eye out for my sister?"

They got the hint, looking around, like she might arrive any moment searching for them. Then they turned back to me, staring, as if I were that picture projected on the wall. They were already making a memory of me, in case I didn't come back. But even if I ended up reconsidering one day, I decided to make this one a funny memory, and shot them some finger guns.

"See you on the other side."

RESOURCES

I know all too well how hard it can be to open up about mental illness and suicide ideation, especially when not all institutions can be trusted to help more than hurt. If you're struggling, or worried about someone, I've created a list of charities and hotlines on my website that could be the start of a safety net: nadireedperez.com/resources.

I've done my best to vet services that do not work with police in the US, but please be aware that many organizations in the UK and elsewhere are required to report to emergency services if they believe your life or someone else's is in immediate danger. Otherwise, these charities all provide confidential services. For more specific information, you can consult the confidentiality policy of the organization in question.

Please stay safe, and most importantly, stay here.

ACKNOWLEDGEMENTS

My eternal love to Mom, for always believing in me, no matter how lofty my dreams, and to my brother, for keeping a roof over my head while I finished this book. Kurt, you kept my writing skills sharp distracting me with our other projects—here's to many more!

Boundless gratitude to my incredible agent Larissa. From our earliest interactions your warmth and sincerity shone through every exchange. The first draft I sent you was pretty rough, but you saw its potential before anyone else, and I'll never forget it. Thank you for sifting through its flaws and helping me cut and polish the heart of this story, then finding it a home. You are a kind soul and fierce advocate, and I couldn't have achieved this dream without you.

Endless thanks to my wonderful editor Katie Dent. Your enthusiasm for this story was so infectious, it renewed my love for this book and powered me through the last of the many, many edits. Your finishing touches truly grounded my afterlife and balanced out the despair with hope. Thank you for sheperding this story out into the world with the kind and thoughtful touch it needs.

Thank you to everyone at Titan Books for making me feel so at home, even across the pond. Props to Natasha MacKenzie for designing my dream cover, literally—I used to daydream about seeing the title on a headstone, and you must've read my mind!

Thank you to my mentor Roma Panganiban for all your insight and inspiration. You helped make Mal better—by making her worse. I will forever cherish every comment you left that had me screaming with laughter.

Thank you to Brenda Drake and the team behind Pitch Wars for the life-changing opportunity. You all worked so hard for so many years to uplift writers like me. Pitch Wars was such a special program, and I hope we'll see its like again someday.

Thank you to my dear friend Isi for all your encouragement and wisdom. You are a beautiful badass, like Buffy Summers.

Shout out to Jordan Link, Emily Abdow, the Cephalosquad, and my Avengers of Color friends who adopted me in spite of not making it into that program. Thank you for beta reading, weathering the query trenches together, and all the laughter.

Thank you to Mrs. Hendry and Mr. Larson, my high school Creative Writing and English teachers, for being gentle and encouraging cultivators in the garden of young minds. I wrote the first words of this book in your class, Mrs. Hendry! (Needless to say they did not end up in the final version, but eventually, that nameless narrator and "Ainsley" evolved into Mal and Evie.)

Much love to Cole for letting me ramble on.

Finally, no thanks to the former residents of Casa Basura, no thanks to my college Creative Writing professors who tried to steer me away from the fantasy genre, and no thanks to my old coworker who tried to mansplain publishing to me. I made it in spite of you all, though I made good use of your ghosts. Have a nice life!

But to end on a sweeter note—thank you, dear reader. I hope this story brought you as much catharsis as it did for me. Remember: you deserve to live.

ABOUT THE AUTHOR

Nadi Reed Perez is an author and writer for *The Call of the Flame*, a fantasy fiction podcast. They live near Denver with a growing menagerie of cats and a few probable ghosts. *The Afterlife of Mal Caldera* is their debut book. You can find them on Instagram, YouTube, and (for better or worse) on Tumblr @nadireedperez.

For more fantastic fiction, author events,
exclusive excerpts, competitions, limited editions and more

VISIT OUR WEBSITE
titanbooks.com

LIKE US ON FACEBOOK
facebook.com/titanbooks

FOLLOW US ON TWITTER AND INSTAGRAM
@TitanBooks

EMAIL US
readerfeedback@titanemail.com